A THOUSAND SOULS
SPEAK AS ONE . . .

A night in October 1970, several dinner guests gather around a Ouija board. Their casual conversation turns to anxious awe as they become witnesses to an incredible event: *communication with a voice from beyond . . .*

Taking the name of Michael, the voice is the essence of a thousand souls, speaking as one. They have known love and terror, trust and treachery, and now offer their benevolent celestial philosophy for us to contemplate and consider.

This volume, compiled over the course of more than twelve years, continues the enlightened lessons that started with *Messages From Michael* and *More Messages From Michael.*

   . . . how to recognize and use knowledge attained in earlier lives.

   . . . the balance of love and sexuality in our lives.

   . . . time in the physical plane and how it relates to our karmic development.

   . . . and much more!

MICHAEL'S PEOPLE

Berkley Books by Chelsea Quinn Yarbro

A BAROQUE FABLE

MESSAGES FROM MICHAEL
MORE MESSAGES FROM MICHAEL
MICHAEL'S PEOPLE

CHELSEA QUINN YARBRO

Continuing the Michael Teaching

MICHAEL'S PEOPLE

BERKLEY BOOKS, NEW YORK

MICHAEL'S PEOPLE

A Berkley Book / published by arrangement with
the author

PRINTING HISTORY
Berkley edition / July 1988

ISBN: 0-425-10932-1

A BERKLEY BOOK ® TM 757,375
Berkley Books are published by The Berkley Publishing Group,
200 Madison Avenue, New York, NY 10016.
The name "BERKLEY" and the "B" logo
are trademarks belonging to Berkley Publishing Corporation.

PRINTED IN THE UNITED STATES OF AMERICA

10 9 8 7 6 5 4 3 2 1

The material in this book, as in *Messages From Michael* and *More Messages From Michael,* is taken from the transcripts of mediumistic sessions. Michael's opinions do not necessarily reflect the opinion of any members of the group or of the mediums who channel the information.

*This book is dedicated to
the good people who produce*
THE MICHAEL MESSENGER

Introduction

This is not a guide to instant enlightenment. Michael will not make you younger, thinner, more aerobic, richer, or happier. This teaching offers answers to questions much in the way that a library does, without any demands on those who seek information. How, or if, you choose to use it is entirely up to you—it is your application or lack of it that will make the difference, if any, in your life.

For the members of the Michael group, the teaching has had various influences on their lives, and in this book they will share some of their experiences with you. Not all of those experiences have been pleasant, and not all have had lasting impact on them, yet each member of the Michael group has found something of worth in the teaching.

As in *More Messages From Michael*, every other chapter is Michael's entirely. All information is compiled from material gathered over more than a dozen years. The only editing I have done is in the organization of the material and in changing names of the people concerned; other than that, Michael's teaching is precisely as dictated through the mediums of the group.

It is not my intention to try to persuade anyone to agree with Michael. As before, the material is being offered for study, and no one—least of all Michael—requires that you accept what is said. There is no correct response to this teaching. If you are interested in the material, I hope you will do what most of the group members have done over the years: Test the information, question it, evaluate it so that you can determine if it is useful to you. You may wish to gauge the applicability of this teaching in relation to what the group members have done in that regard over the years.

In terms of the group members, I have, as before, disguised them in order to insure their privacy. Due to the particular nature of this book, I have made fewer conglomerate or combined personalities than in the two previous works, since that would make it difficult for each member to discuss his or her own experiences. The mediums are treated as they have been in *Messages* and *More Messages*, as themselves but with names and occupations changed.

The Michael group continues to meet twice a month, as it has for about fifteen years. It is a closed group; no outside questions are answered. Any other group claiming to channel Michael or any other teacher is not associated with this group: such channels are neither endorsed nor impugned. It is not the intention of the Michael group to become involved in an enlighteneder-than-thou debate.

Because of the volume of mail received, because it is not possible to answer it, and because of the proliferation of various channeling groups, we have started a quarterly newsletter for those interested in additional information from Michael. It is produced by an outside newsletter firm from session transcripts and is under the supervision of the mediums, two group members, and me.

If you are interested in subscribing, please write for information to: *The Michael Messenger,* 511 Sir Francis Drake Boulevard, Suite C-141, Greenbrae, California 94909. We request that you do not include questions for Michael, as the newsletter firm that produces *The Michael Messenger* will not be able to obtain answers from the group.

Chapter 1

MICHAEL: ON THE HAZARDS OF THE PHYSICAL PLANE

THERE ARE LESSONS THAT ARE POSSIBLE ONLY ON THE PHYSICAL PLANE; TO SEEK AND AVOID THEM DENIES THE NATURE OF LIFE AS AN ENSOULED FRAGMENT. EACH OF YOU HAS CHOSEN TO BE PRESENT AT THIS TIME, IN THIS LIFE IN ORDER TO CONTINUE THE EVOLUTION NOT ONLY OF YOURSELF AS AN INDIVIDUAL FRAGMENT, BUT AS PART OF YOUR CONTINUALLY EVOLVING ENTITY AND CADRE. THERE ARE EXPERIENCES THAT CAN ONLY OCCUR WHEN THE FRAGMENT IS IN A BODY; FOR EXAMPLE, AND MOST BASICALLY, BIRTH AND DEATH.

FROM THE TIME ESSENCE ENTERS THE BODY, WHICH IN ALMOST ALL INSTANCES IS WHEN THE NEWBORN INFANT TAKES ITS FIRST BREATH, THE FOCUS OF THE WORK OF THE FRAGMENT IS IN LARGE PART TO DEAL WITH THE HAZARDS OF THE PHYSICAL PLANE. WHILE THIS MAY APPEAR OBVIOUS, TO SOME IT IS A CONSTANT STRUGGLE TO ACCEPT THE REALITY OF BEING INCARNATE IN PHYSICAL FORM. THERE ARE THOSE OF YOU WHO SEEK THIS OR ANY "SPIRITUAL" TEACHING IN ORDER TO AVOID THE JOB OF "LOOKING AFTER" THE BODY. THIS DOES NOT SIMPLY MEAN THE PROBLEM OF FEEDING, CLOTHING, HOUSING AND KEEPING CLEAN THE BODY YOU ARE INHABITING, BUT REACHING THE STATE OF PERCEPTION THAT TRULY OWNS THE BODY WHILE AT THE SAME TIME BEING AWARE THAT ESSENCE TRANSCENDS IT EVEN WHILE IT OCCUPIES IT.

BECAUSE OF THE OBDURACY OF MATTER, THE PHYSICAL PLANE OFFERS HAZARDS THAT ARE PRESENT NOWHERE ELSE. LEARNING THE NATURE OF THESE HAZARDS AND EXPERIENCING THEM FOR YOURSELF ARE REAL AND VALUABLE LESSONS FOR ALL FRAGMENTS EXTANT ON THE PHYSICAL PLANE THROUGHOUT WHAT YOU CALL THE KNOWN UNIVERSE. OFTEN THOSE WHO CHOOSE SERIOUSLY IMPAIRED BODIES FOR A LIFETIME DO SO IN ORDER TO DEAL WITH EXPERIENCING THAT PHYSICAL REALITY. THERE MAY ALSO BE MONADAL AGREEMENTS OR KARMA INVOLVED IN SUCH CHOICES.

THAT IS NOT TO SAY THAT THINGS CANNOT GO WRONG. BODIES ARE SUBJECT TO WEAR AND TEAR, AS IS ALL MATTER. DAMAGE OF THE BODY IS REAL. DAMAGE TO THE PSYCHE IS REAL. SUCH DAMAGE NEED NOT BE CHOSEN IN ADVANCE: PLEASE NOTE THAT WE SAY "IN ADVANCE." HOW A FRAGMENT *CHOOSES* TO REACT TO DAMAGE, BE IT AS MINOR AS A CUT FINGER OR AS SIGNIFICANT AS A NONLETHAL STROKE, IS WHERE THE CRUX OF CHOICE IS FOUND. THOSE WHO HAVE SUFFERED PHYSICAL DAMAGE MAY CHOOSE TO INGNORE IT, TO ACCEPT IT, TO RESIST IT, TO BE OVERWHELMED BY IT, TO BE "PHILOSOPHICAL" ABOUT IT, TO BE ANGRY ABOUT IT, TO BE RESIGNED TO IT, TO DENY IT, TO TREAT IT AS A LEARNING EXPERIENCE, TO FEEL GUILTY ABOUT IT, OR ANY NUMBER OF OTHER RESPONSES. THE MORE LONG-LASTING THE PROBLEM, THE GREATER THE NUMBER OF RESPONSES AND CHOICES THE FRAGMENT INVOLVED IS APT TO MAKE. LET US STRESS THAT THERE IS NO "CORRECT" WAY TO CHOOSE. CHOICE AND THE RAMIFICATIONS OF CHOICE PROVIDE THE ESSENTIAL LESSONS OF LIFE. IN A VERY REAL SENSE, YOU CHOOSE TO BE HERE SO THAT YOU CAN MAKE CHOICES.

SUCH THINGS AS HURRICANES, EARTHQUAKES, VOLCANOES, TSUNAMIS, FLOODS, FAMINE, AND SIMILAR PLANET-ORIGINATING DISASTERS ARE PART OF THE RISKS OF LIVING ON A PLANET. AN ATMOSPHERE ALMOST ALWAYS MEANS THE POSSIBILITY OF STORMS. "SOLID" GROUND, BY THE VERY NATURE OF PLANETARY CON-

STRUCTION, HAS BEEN KNOWN TO SHIFT UNDER THE STRESSES OF CONTINENTAL DRIFT. WEATHER PATTERNS HAVE DIRECT IMPACT ON CROPS AND LIVESTOCK, WHICH IS CLOSELY LINKED TO FOOD SUPPLY. THESE ARE LEGITIMATE CONCERNS OF THOSE EXTANT ON THE PHYSICAL PLANE, NO MATTER WHAT PLANET THEY LIVE ON. THERE IS NOTHING SPIRITUALLY "WRONG" ABOUT BEING AWARE OF THESE POSSIBILITIES AND IN TAKING REASONABLE CARE TO MINIMIZE THE IMPACT, IF PRACTICAL, WHEN THEY ARISE.

WE WOULD NOT, HOWEVER, ADVISE ANY FRAGMENT TO LIVE IN CONSTANT ANTICIPATION OF DISASTER. THIS IS NOT ONLY COUNTERPRODUCTIVE TO REASONABLE CHOICES ON PERSONAL ISSUES, IT TENDS TO INCREASE THE FEAR IN THE LIFE. THAT IS NOT TO SAY YOU ARE NOT FREE TO CHOOSE DREAD AS A WAY OF LIFE, BUT IF YOU MAKE SUCH A CHOICE, IT IS LIKELY TO DISTORT YOUR PERCEPTIONS MORE RADICALLY THAN MOST CHOICES DO.

THERE ARE, OF COURSE, MAN-RELATED DISASTERS, SUCH AS WAR, PLAGUE, MARKET-DETERMINED FAMINE, TOXIC WASTES, NUCLEAR WASTES, ATMOSPHERIC AND OCEANIC POLLUTION, POPULATION-DENSITY STRESS, AND A NUMBER OF OTHER PROBLEMS THAT YOU CAN ENCOUNTER IN THE NEWSPAPER. THESE, WHILE MORE "ARRESTING", OFTEN HAVE THE SAME EFFECT THAT THE STANDARD PLANETARY ONES DO, WITH THE ADDITIONAL WEIGHT OF THE POSSIBILITY OF CONTRIBUTORY RESPONSIBILITY, SUCH AS THE FRAGMENTS WHO ARE DISTRAUGHT ABOUT SMOG, WHILE THEY DRIVE THEIR AUTOMOBILES FORTY MILES TO WORK EVERY DAY. IF SUCH A SENSE OF RESPONSIBILITY BECOMES UNBEARABLE, THE FRAGMENT MAY EVENTUALLY CHOOSE TO CHANGE JOBS, MOVE CLOSER, TAKE LESS HAZARDOUS TRANSPORTATION, OR HAVE A HEALTH BREAKDOWN IN ORDER TO AVOID THE WHOLE ISSUE.

LET US POINT OUT TO ALL HERE PRESENT THAT ONE OF THE RAMIFICATIONS OF CHOOSING TO INCARNATE ON THE PHYSICAL PLANE IS GARBAGE. THE PHYSICAL PLANE, BY ITS VERY NATURE, CREATES GARBAGE. THERE IS

NOTHING "WRONG" IN THIS; IT IS WHAT YOU WOULD DE-
FINE AS "NATURAL", WHICH IN THIS INSTANCE IS NOT
INCORRECT. CERTAINLY SOME FRAGMENTS CREATE
MORE GARBAGE, SOME CREATE LESS, BUT TO A GREATER
OR LESSER DEGREE, IT WILL INEVITABLY HAPPEN.

WHILE MANY FRAGMENTS CHOOSE TO BE PASSIVE
ABOUT THIS, OTHERS PREFER TO CHOOSE TO MINIMIZE
THE IMPACT. BOTH CHOICES, AND ANY OTHER CHOICES,
ARE VALID. HOWEVER, AS LONG AS THIS PLANET IS VIA-
BLE TO YOUR SPECIES, YOU WILL RETURN TO IT, INCARNA-
TION AFTER INCARNATION, AND FOR THAT REASON IF NO
OTHER, YOU MIGHT CONSIDER HOW MESSY YOU CAN
STAND IT TO BE.

WE HAVE SAID BEFORE AND WE WILL STATE AGAIN,
THAT IN OUR VIEW THE SINGLE GREATEST THREAT TO
YOUR PLANET AT THIS TIME IN TERMS OF MAN-RELATED
DISASTERS IS OVERPOPULATION. ALL OTHER MAN-RE-
LATED POTENTIALS FOR DISASTER ARE DIRECTLY OR INDI-
RECTLY RELATED TO THAT SINGLE FACT. MANY SPECIES
ON MANY PLANETS HAVE FACED, FACE, AND WILL FACE
SIMILAR PROBLEMS. WE WOULD WISH TO POINT OUT, IN-
CIDENTALLY, THAT IN GENERAL IT IS NOT THE FITTEST
THAT SURVIVE, IT IS THE MOST ADAPTABLE OR VER-
SATILE.

VERY FEW FRAGMENTS GET THROUGH AN ENTIRE LIFE,
EVEN A BRIEF LIFE, WITHOUT A DEGREE OF PHYSICAL
DAMAGE. THAT DAMAGE MAY BE SHORT- OR LONG-TERM;
IT MIGHT HAVE MINIMAL INFLUENCE ON THE LIFE CHOICE
OR MAJOR ONES. WHEN MASSIVE DAMAGE OCCURS THAT
WAS NOT PART OF THE LIFEPLAN—AND OF COURSE SUCH
THINGS CAN AND DO HAPPEN—THE ELEMENT OF CHOICE
BECOMES SIGNIFICANTLY MORE CRUCIAL TO GROWTH
AND EVOLUTION OF THE FRAGMENT THAN WHEN THE
DAMAGE IS CHOSEN AS PART OF THE LIFEPLAN. THAT
DOES NOT MEAN THAT THERE IS THEREFORE A "CORRECT"
CHOICE IN RESPONSE TO SUCH AN EVENTUALITY. CHOICE
AND ITS RAMIFICATIONS ARE THE LESSONS HERE, NO MAT-
TER WHAT THE CHOICES AND RESULTANT RAMIFICATIONS
MAY BE.

LET US POINT OUT THAT CHOICES AND RAMIFICATIONS AS RELATED TO PHYSICAL DAMAGE ARE SOME OF THE VERY FIRST LEARNED BY THE FRAGMENT IN INFANCY. THE WAY IN WHICH DAMAGE IS DEALT WITH IS EXTREMELY IMPORTANT IN TERMS OF HOW THE FRAGMENT LEARNS TO CHOOSE AND TO REACT TO DAMAGE. WHILE COMFORT IN PAIN, NO MATTER HOW BRIEF OR MINOR, IS POSITIVE FOR ALMOST ALL INFANTS, FUSSING AND TREPIDATION ARE NOT, NOR IS IGNORING OR BELITTLING PAIN, FOR SUCH RESPONSES CONFUSE THE EXPERIENCE SO THAT IT IS DIFFICULT FOR THE INFANT, LET ALONE AN OLDER CHILD, TO COMPREHEND WHAT IS ACTUALLY GOING ON, AND THEREFORE CHOICES ARE NOT DEFINED AND THE RAMIFICATIONS ARE NOT UNDERSTOOD.

OF COURSE, RESPONSE TO PAIN AND THREAT ARE IN LARGE PART CONDITIONED BY FAMILY AND CULTURE. A YEAR-OLD INFANT ALREADY KNOWS WHAT IS THE "APPROPRIATE" RESPONSE TO PAIN AND THREAT, AND WILL BEHAVE IN THE WAY THAT HAS ALREADY BEEN FOUND ACCEPTABLE, AND THE RESPONSE PATTERN FOR THE FAMILY AND CULTURE WILL LARGELY DICTATE THE WAY IN WHICH THE YOUNG CHILD REACTS RATHER THAN THE EXPERIENCE ITSELF.

THAT IS NOT TO SAY THAT CULTURE AND FAMILY ARE "WRONG". ONE OF THE EXPERIENCES THAT CAN ONLY BE HAD ON THE PHYSICAL PLANE IS THE EXPERIENCE OF FAMILY AND CULTURE. WHILE THERE ARE FAMILIAL ELEMENTS IN THE CADRE, ENTITY, AND CADENCE TIES, AS WELL AS IN THE ESSENCE TWIN AND TASK COMPANION BONDS, THE DIVERSE ASSOCIATION POSSIBLE IN FAMILIES HAPPENS NOWHERE ELSE. BY EXTENSION, CULTURE IS LIMITED TO THE PHYSICAL PLANE AS WELL, AND IS OF SIGNIFICANT IMPACT ON THE COURSE OF THE LIFE.

THERE IS NOTHING "INCORRECT" IN BEING PART OF A CULTURE; IT IS PART OF THE MOST POWERFUL LESSONS OF THE PHYSICAL PLANE. IT IS TREMENDOUS IN ITS IMPACT, AND THE EXPERIENCES GAINED ARE OF LASTING BENEFIT FROM LIFE TO LIFE. IN ANY LIFE WHERE MORE THAN ONE CULTURE IS DEALT WITH CLOSELY, THE

GROWTH IS SIGNIFICANTLY GREATER THAN WHEN ONLY
ONE IS ADDRESSED. FOR EXAMPLE, THOSE FRAGMENTS
WHO COME FROM MIXED CULTURAL BACKGROUNDS, WHO
LIVE FOR LARGE PARTS OF THEIR LIVES IN OTHER CUL-
TURES, OR WHO DELIBERATELY SET OUT TO IMMERSE
THEMSELVES IN THE VALIDITY OF ANOTHER CULTURE
TEND TO ACCOMPLISH MORE IN TERMS OF THEIR OWN
EVOLUTION THAN THOSE WHO DO NOT.

THAT IS NOT TO SAY THAT THEREFORE A FRAGMENT
"MUST" AT ONCE UNDERTAKE TO LEARN ANOTHER CUL-
TURE. WE DID NOT SAY THAT NOR DID WE IMPLY THAT.
WE ARE SAYING THAT WHERE GROWTH AND PERCEPTION
OF THE LESSON OF CULTURE IS CHOSEN, MORE IS AC-
COMPLISHED BY THE "COMPARE AND CONTRAST"
METHOD THAN MOST OTHERS.

WE WOULD URGE FRAGMENTS WHO ARE CURIOUS
ABOUT SUCH MATTERS TO TAKE THE TIME TO DISCOVER
THE CHANGING PATTERNS IN CULTURE. THE PRESENT
PERIOD OF THE CURRENT CENTURY IS SHOWING MORE
CULTURAL EVOLUTION OCCURRING AT A MORE RAPID
RATE THROUGH MORE OF THE STRATA OF SOCIETY THAN
HAS BEEN APPARENT IN THE PAST DURING ANY OTHER
TIME THAN EXTREME EMERGENCIES. THAT THIS EVOLU-
TION IS NOT THE DIRECT RESULT OF CONTINUING
EMERGENCIES IS QUITE REMARKABLE, AND HAS LED TO
SOME VERY INTERESTING PROBLEMS IN TERMS OF ASSESS-
ING THE ROLE THAT THE CULTURAL EVOLUTION PLAYS
IN THE LIVES OF THE FRAGMENTS CURRENTLY EXTANT
ON YOUR PLANET AND LIVING IN THE TECHNOLOGICALLY
ADVANCED CULTURES.

CONSIDER COMMUNICATION: THE MASSIVE AMOUNTS
OF INFORMATION CURRENTLY AVAILABLE TO THE AVER-
AGE CITIZEN FAR EXCEEDS ANYTHING POSSIBLE BEFORE
IN THE HISTORY OF YOUR WORLD. KNOWLEDGE AND ALL
RELATED AREAS OF INFORMATIONAL RECORDS HAVE UN-
DERGONE AN EXPLOSION OF SORTS. IT WAS NOT LONG
AGO—NO MORE THAN FIVE HUNDRED YEARS—THAT A
LONG-LIVED AND WELL-EDUCATED MAN COULD IN THE
COURSE OF A LIFE LEARN IN THE ACADEMIC SENSE ALL

THAT THERE WAS TO KNOW. A SINGLE FRAGMENT COULD CHOOSE TO AMASS ALL FORMALIZED KNOWLEDGE BEFORE THE FIFTH INTERNAL MONAD [that is what Michael calls the senior-citizen monad, when what has been accomplished in a life is compared to what the fragment set out to accomplish] BROUGHT RETROSPECTIVE PERCEPTIONS TO BEAR IN THE LIFE.

AS MOST OF THOSE HERE GATHERED ARE AWARE, SUCH AN ACCOMPLISHMENT IS NO LONGER POSSIBLE OR EVEN DESIRABLE. FRAGMENTS MUST CHOOSE EARLY IN LIFE— OFTEN AS THE RESULT OF THE EXPECTATIONS OF OTHERS RATHER THAN THE GENUINE INSIGHT OF ESSENCE—THE COURSE THE EDUCATIONAL ASPECT OF THE LIFE IS TO TAKE, WHICH IN TURN DIRECTLY INFLUENCES WHAT KNOWLEDGE AND INFORMATION WILL BE ACCESSIBLE TO THE FRAGMENT AS THE LIFE GOES ON. IN GENERAL WE WOULD HAVE TO SAY THAT WHAT YOU CALL THE EDUCATIONAL SYSTEM SERVES MORE TO ENFORCE PARENTAL AND CULTURAL EXPECTATIONS OF YOUNG CHILDREN THAN TO OFFER THEM GENUINE OPPORTUNITIES TO GAIN ACCESS TO EDUCATIONAL POSSIBILITIES. WITH THE ENORMOUS ADVANCES IN INFORMATIONAL TECHNOLOGY, THIS CULTURAL ATTITUDE WOULD APPEAR TO HAVE BECOME INAPPROPRIATE, BUT IT IS MADE MORE INFLEXIBLE RATHER THAN LESS, AS ITS FUNCTION CONTINUES TO DETERMINE ITS EFFECTIVENESS.

WE WOULD WISH AT THIS TIME TO REMARK ON WHAT MIGHT BE CALLED THE COMMUNICATION GLUT. THERE IS SO MUCH INFORMATION FLOODING THE TECHNOLOGICALLY ADVANCED SOCIETIES AT THIS TIME THAT IT MIGHT BE SEEN AS OVERWHELMING AND WHOLLY UNWIELDY. THIS IS NOT ENTIRELY INACCURATE. WHILE WE WOULD AGREE THAT ENHANCED COMMUNICATION IS DEFINITELY A "FORCE FOR GOOD IN THE WORLD", LEARNING TO ADJUST THE COMMUNICATION DIET IS A TECHNIQUE THAT HAS NOT YET BEEN DISCERNED OR ADDRESSED BY SCIENCE OR ART. IN THAT AREA THAT IS OFTEN TERMED "ENTERTAINMENT", OFTEN PERJORATIVELY, THE GLUT IS MORE EASILY DEFINED. WE WOULD LIKE TO OBSERVE IN

RELATION TO THE ENTERTAINING ARTS—AND WE DO NOT USE THE WORD *ENTERTAINMENT* IN A PERJORATIVE SENSE—THAT FOR ALL BUT A VERY, VERY FEW LIVING IN "FORTUNATE" AREAS, ONE HUNDRED YEARS AGO A PERSON ACTUALLY ATTENDING A SYMPHONY ORCHESTRA PERFORMANCE BY A QUALIFIED SYMPHONY ORCHESTRA FIVE OR MORE TIMES IN A LIFE WAS CONSIDERED A CULTURED PERSON. NOW, OF COURSE, IF YOU CANNOT ATTEND A CONCERT, THERE ARE RECORDINGS, VIDEOTAPES, BROADCASTS, AND SIMILAR METHODS OF APPROACHING THE EXPERIENCE AT *ALMOST* THE SAME LEVEL OF INTENSITY AS THE PERFORMANCE ITSELF. THERE ARE ALSO MANY OTHER MUSICAL ENTERTAINMENTS, TO LIMIT THE REMARKS TO ONE PERFORMING ART, COVERING AN ENORMOUS AUDIENCE, REACHING FRAGMENTS WHO ONE HUNDRED YEARS AGO MIGHT HEAR ONE OR TWO SUCH ENTERTAINMENTS IN A LIFETIME. IT HAS ONLY BEEN IN THE LAST CENTURY THAT A PERFORMANCE COULD BE "CAPTURED" IN RECORDING AND EXPERIENCED MANY TIMES BY TREMENDOUS NUMBERS OF PEOPLE. THE VERY EXISTENCE OF SUCH VARIOUS RECORDINGS AND THEIR PROLIFERATION CONFERS AN ASPECT OF "IMMORTALITY" ON THE PERFORMERS THAT WAS NOT POSSIBLE UNTIL RECENTLY.

WHEN THE OBSERVATION APPLIED HERE TO PERFORMING MUSICIANS IS EXTENDED TO ALL AREAS OF FORMAL KNOWLEDGE, THE COMPLEXITY OF THE AVAILABILITY OF INFORMATION TAKES ON PROPORTIONS FEW IF ANY OF YOU CAN ACCURATELY ASSESS. THE SELECTION AND ASSESSMENT OF INFORMATION IS ONLY ONE ASPECT OF THE LIFE, BUT IT HAS BECOME SO CENTRAL TO THOSE FRAGMENTS LIVING IN THE TECHNOLOGICALLY ADVANCED SOCIETIES THAT THE MECHANISMS OF THE SOCIETY ARE NOT ADEQUATE TO ACCOMMODATE THE DEMANDS CURRENTLY OPERATIVE.

THOSE FRAGMENTS LIVING IN SUCH SOCIETIES AS WE HAVE BEEN DISCUSSING OFTEN SUFFER FROM WHAT HAS BEEN CALLED "FUTURE SHOCK" OR "CULTURE SHOCK" BECAUSE THE MECHANISMS OF THE CULTURE TEND TO

LAG AT LEAST TWO GENERATIONS BEHIND THE ACTUAL-
ITY OF THE CULTURE ITSELF. DURING EMERGENCIES,
SUCH CULTURAL PATTERNS ARE OFTEN ABANDONED "FOR
THE DURATION" WITH THE UNDERSTANDING THAT EVEN-
TUALLY FRAGMENTS LIVING IN THAT CULTURE WILL RE-
TURN TO THE WAY OF LIFE THAT EXISTED BEFORE THE
EMERGENCY. THIS, OF COURSE, IS NOT ACTUALLY POSSI-
BLE. HOWEVER, FOR A CULTURAL FLUX OF THE NATURE
CURRENTLY EVOLVING WITHIN THE SOCIETY OF THE
TECHNOLOGICAL COUNTRIES TO BE WITHOUT THE
"BOUNDARIES" OF AN EMERGENCY GIVES RISE TO MANY
CONFLICTING AND COMPLEX REACTIONS ON THE PART OF
THE FRAGMENTS ATTEMPTING TO DEAL WITH THE REAL-
ITY OF THIS CHANGE.

THE IMPACT OF THE CHANGE IS NOT LIMITED TO THE
AREAS OF THE PLANET HOUSING TECHNOLOGICAL
SOCIETIES. THERE ARE THOSE COUNTRIES AND AREAS
WHICH ARE OFTEN CALLED "THIRD WORLD", OR THOSE
SOCIETIES THAT ARE NOT HIGHLY TECHNOLOGICAL IN
FOCUS. IN FORMER PERIODS OF HISTORY, THESE COUN-
TRIES HAVE BEEN REGARDED FIRST WITH SUSPICION AND
THEN PROPRIETARILY, AND MOST RECENTLY IN THE MAN-
NER WE MIGHT DESCRIBE AS BEING LIKE STEPCHILDREN
WITH EMBARRASING PROBLEMS. THE SOCIETAL GAP IS
WIDENING STEADILY, AS IT IS WIDENING WITHIN THE CUL-
TURES OF THE TECHNOLOGICAL SOCIETIES BETWEEN
THOSE WITH TECHNOLOGICAL KNOWLEDGE AND THOSE
WITHOUT.

THAT DOES NOT MEAN THAT THE PROBLEM IS WITHOUT
SOLUTION, NOR DO WE MEAN TO IMPLY THAT BECAUSE
OF THE GEOMETRIC INCREASE IN INFORMATION AND
TECHNOLOGICAL ADVANCES THAT ALL FRAGMENTS
"MUST" EVENTUALLY AND INEVITABLY BE "OVERCOME".
CERTAINLY THERE ARE FRAGMENTS WHO WILL CHOOSE
TO AVOID THE INFORMATIONAL AND TECHNOLOGICAL
"HOTHOUSE" IN FAVOR OF LESS RIGOROUS TASKS. THE
PRESSURES OF GRAPPLING WITH THE TECHNOLOGICAL
EDGE IS FOR THE MOST PART THE PROVINCE OF YOUNG
CYCLE SOULS WITH A FEW BABY, MATURE, AND OLD

SOULS CONTRIBUTING THEIR OWN SORT OF BALLAST TO THE OTHERS.

OF COURSE, NOT ALL FRAGMENTS WHO CHOOSE TO LIVE WITH FEWER "MODERN MIRACLES" ARE BABY, MATURE, OR OLD SOULS. CERTAINLY THERE ARE YOUNG SOULS WHO CHOOSE, FOR ANY NUMBER OF REASONS, TO DO WORK IN AREAS OTHER THAN AT THE HEART OF THE TECHNOLOGICAL PROJECTS OF THE SOCIETY. EVERY FRAGMENT LIVING IN A SOCIETY AND SHAPED BY A CULTURE WILL AT ONE TIME OR ANOTHER "HAVE" TO DEFINE FOR ITSELF WHERE THE PARAMETERS OF "SELF" AND "SOCIETY" LIE, A PROCESS THAT IS MOST OFTEN PART OF THE FOURTH INTERNAL MONAD [Michael defines the Fourth Internal Monad as the transition from the personality a person was raised to be to the manifestation of the personality that the fragment chose as the means to accomplish the life task, the Overleaves] OR WHAT IS SOMETIMES IDENTIFIED AS THE MID-LIFE CRISIS. THOSE FRAGMENTS WHO CHOOSE TO AVOID OR ABDICATE THE FOURTH INTERNAL MONAD ARE SHAPED ENTIRELY BY THE CULTURAL AND SOCIETAL PROGRAM THROUGH THE ENTIRE COURSE OF THAT LIFE.

WE DO NOT WISH OR INTEND TO ENCOURAGE OR DISCOURAGE ANY FRAGMENT FROM PARTICIPATING IN ANY PART OF SOCIETY, FOR THAT WOULD INTERFERE WITH CHOICE. THOSE WHO CHOOSE TO ACTIVELY PURSUE THE GREAT TECHNOLOGICAL PROMISE HAVE AS MUCH OPPORTUNITY FOR GROWTH AND EVOLUTION AS THOSE WHO DO NOT, ASSUMING THAT SUCH ACTIVITY ACCOMMODATES THE ACTIVITIES OF THE LIFE TASK.

IT IS NOT INAPPROPRIATE FOR THOSE FRAGMENTS WHO CHOOSE TO REJECT THE PURSUIT OF THE EXPANDING TECHNOLOGY TO REVIEW THE RAMIFICATIONS OF THEIR CHOICES, JUST AS IT IS NOT INAPPROPRIATE FOR THOSE WHO CHOOSE TO PARTICIPATE IN THE TECHNOLOGICAL EXPANSION TO MAKE A SIMILAR REVIEW, FOR WE WISH TO EMPHASIZE THAT EACH AND EVERY FRAGMENT IS RESPONSIBLE FOR THE CHOICES HE OR SHE MAKES, AND THAT NO MATTER WHAT THOSE CHOICES ARE, ESSENCE— THAT IS, THE INDIVIDUAL SOUL OF THE INDIVIDUAL FRAG-

MENT—WILL ASSESS AND PERCEIVE EVERY CHOICE WITH TRUE IMPARTIALITY AND RESPONSIBILITY.

OFTEN IT IS DIFFICULT FOR FRAGMENTS TO DISCERN WHERE THEIR "BEST EFFORTS" MIGHT LIE, AND, OF COURSE, THERE IS NO SIMPLE OR OBVIOUS SOLUTION. EACH FRAGMENT HAS CHOSEN A TASK FOR A LIFE, ONE THAT CAN BE ACCOMPLISHED IN MANY WAYS. IN ADDITION TO THAT, THERE ARE OFTEN AGREEMENTS, MONADS, AND KARMA IMPINGING ON THE STRUCTURE OF A PARTICULAR LIFE, AS WELL AS CONTACT WITH FRAGMENTS WITH WHOM THERE ARE CLOSE TIES OF ONE SORT OR ANOTHER. IT IS FOR THE INDIVIDUAL FRAGMENT TO ESTABLISH THE PRIORITIES HE OR SHE CHOOSES FOR HIM OR HERSELF. EVERY FRAGMENT IS FREE TO CHOOSE AND TO CHANGE THAT CHOICE AT ANY TIME.

FOR EXAMPLE, A FRAGMENT MAY BE DEEPLY CONCERNED ABOUT THE PRECARIOUS CONDITION OF THE OZONE LAYER—AND WE WOULD AGREE THAT FOR THOSE FRAGMENTS EXTANT ON THIS PLANET AT THIS TIME THERE IS REASON FOR CONCERN—AND, BECAUSE OF THAT CONCERN, ABANDON USEFUL WORK IN THE AREA OF AGRICULTURAL CHEMISTRY, WHERE, IN FACT, HIS OR HER EFFORTS MIGHT OFFER "REAL" ADVANCES; INSTEAD, THE FRAGMENT OFFERS PETITIONS AND DOES RESEARCH THAT IS NOT LIKELY TO HAVE ANY DIRECT IMPACT EITHER ON THOSE PRODUCING THE CHEMICAL SUBSTANCES THAT ARE CONTRIBUTING TO, BUT ARE NOT THE SOLE FACTOR IN, THE DETERIORATING CONDITION OF THE OZONE LAYER, ESPECIALLY AT WHAT IS CALLED THE SOUTH POLE. THE CHOICE IS WHAT IS SIGNIFICANT, AND THE RAMIFICATIONS OF CHOICE, WHICH, IN THIS CASE WE WOULD THINK MIGHT BE ULTIMATELY FRUSTRATING TO THE FRAGMENT, ALTHOUGH, OF COURSE, "MORALLY" SATISFYING.

TO EXAMINE THE ISSUE AT HAND IN ANOTHER WAY: A FRAGMENT MAY DECIDE WHILE QUITE YOUNG TO STUDY MEDICINE AND WORK AT ONE OF THE TRUE TECHNOLOGICAL EPICENTERS OF THIS SOCIETY. THE FRAGMENT, AWARE OF THE PROBLEM OF MISSING CHILDREN, MIGHT

POSSIBLY CHOOSE TO GIVE HIS OR HER TIME TO EFFORTS
TO IDENTIFY AND TRACE THOSE MISSING CHILDREN.
AGAIN, GIVEN THE MASSIVE NATURE OF THE PROBLEM
AND THE ENORMOUS EMOTIONAL STRESS THAT IS PART
OF THIS ISSUE, THE FRAGMENT CHOOSING TO WORK IN
SUCH AN AREA MIGHT FIND IT FRUSTRATING AND DRAIN-
ING, BUT AS "MORALLY" SATISFYING AS WORKING TO-
WARD AN UNDERSTANDING OF THE RISKS RELATED TO
THE OZONE LAYER.

NEITHER CHOICE—THE OZONE LAYER OR MISSING
CHILDREN—HAS ANY "ADVANTAGE" OVER ANY OTHER.
THERE ARE FRAGMENTS WHO CHOOSE TO DAMAGE THE
ATMOSPHERE, WHO CHOOSE TO ABDUCT CHILDREN, WHO
CHOOSE TO DO ANY AND EVERYTHING THAT YOUR
SPECIES IS CAPABLE OF DOING. FOR THE MOST PART,
FRAGMENTS CHOOSING TO WORK ON THE LIFE TASK WILL
EXPERIENCE GREATER EVOLUTIONARY GROWTH IN A
LIFETIME THAN THOSE WHO CHOOSE TO ABDICATE OR
AVOID THE LIFE TASK.

OFTEN THE ASSESSMENTS OF PLANETARY HAZARDS—
SUCH AS VOLCANOES OR THE OZONE LAYER—ARE OF
NECESSITY LARGELY PREDICATED ON GUESSWORK. THIS
IS NOT AN "ERROR"; MERELY THE NATURE OF THE PHYS-
ICAL PLANE ITSELF. A VOLCANO WILL NOT ERUPT AT THE
CONVENIENCE OF YOUR SPECIES; THE OZONE LAYER WILL
NOT IMPROVE BECAUSE IT IS "TOLD" TO. WHAT A FRAG-
MENT DECIDES TO DO ABOUT THIS, IF ANYTHING, IS UP
TO THE FRAGMENT. OF COURSE, THOSE FRAGMENTS
LIVING NEAR VOLCANOES ARE MORE APT TO CONCERN
THEMSELVES WITH OBSERVING THE "BEHAVIOR" OF VOL-
CANOES THAN THOSE WHO DO NOT HAVE TO CONTEND
WITH SUCH PLANETARY HAZARDS.

RELATED TO THAT IS THE TENDENCY OF FRAGMENTS
TO CONCERN THEMSELVES WITH WHAT IS MOST "PRES-
ENT" AROUND THEM; MOST ESKIMO LANGUAGES HAVE
MANY WORDS FOR SNOW AND ICE, EACH DEPICTING CER-
TAIN ASPECTS OR CONDITIONS OF SNOW AND ICE. HOW-
EVER, UNTIL RECENT TIMES, THE LANGUAGE OF THE ES-
KIMOS HAD NO WORD FOR *BANANA* BECAUSE TO ALL IN-

TENTS AND PURPOSES THE BANANA DID NOT EXIST. BY THE SAME TOKEN, THE MAYAN PEOPLE HAD MANY WORDS FOR THE GROWING PATTERNS OF VINES, BUT ONLY A VAGUE CONCEPT OF SNOW.

WITH THE CURRENTLY EXPANDING POSSIBILITIES OF INFORMATION, THESE LIMITATIONS ARE BEING BLURRED AND EXTINGUISHED RAPIDLY. IN MANY INSTANCES THE RESULTS ARE BENEFICIAL FOR THE FRAGMENTS WITHIN THE SOCIETY, BUT THE NOTION OF CULTURAL IDENTITY IS BECOMING INCREASINGLY UNCERTAIN, WHICH HAD ADDED A SUBTLE STRESS TO MANY FRAGMENTS.

FOR ALL FRAGMENTS, BECAUSE YOU ARE FRAGMENTS, THE SENSE OF IDENTITY, NO MATTER HOW THAT IS CULTURALLY DEFINED, IS OF TREMENDOUS IMPORTANCE. TO HAVE THAT IDENTITY COMPROMISED CANNOT ONLY ERODE SELF-ESTEEM, IT CAN CAUSE TREMENDOUS DISORIENTATION AND DAMAGE, WHICH IS OFTEN DEFINED AND PERCEIVED AS MENTAL OR EMOTIONAL DISORDER. SHIFTS IN SOCIETAL AND CULTURAL PATTERNS TEND TO CREATE A HIGHER LEVEL OF SUCH DISORDERS THAN OCCUR DURING LESS "ACTIVE" TIMES, WITH OR WITHOUT EMERGENCIES TO "SPUR THEM ON". TO MANY FRAGMENTS, QUESTIONING WHAT THE NATURE OF THE INDIVIDUAL IDENTITY IS, IN CULTURAL AND SOCIETY TERMS, IS SUFFICIENTLY DISRUPTIVE AS TO BRING ABOUT SERIOUS CONFLICTS AND PERSONAL TURMOIL.

WHILE IT IS TRUE THAT EACH OF YOU HAS ESSENCE [one of seven Roles: Slave, Artisan, Warrior, Scholar, Sage, Priest, and King] AND OVERLEAVES [cycle, level, mode, goal, attitude, centering, and chief feature], YOU ARE ALSO INCARNATE IN A MAMMALIAN SPECIES. YOU WILL EXPERIENCE ESSENCE THROUGH MANY PLANES OF EXISTENCE, BUT YOU WILL NOT BE MAMMALS ANYWHERE BUT ON THE PHYSICAL PLANE, WHICH IS ONE OF THE MOST IMPORTANT LESSONS THAT CAN BE BROUGHT TO BEAR IN ANY INCARNATION. ESSENCE AND OVERLEAVES FUNCTION THROUGH THE EXPERIENCE OF BEING A HUMAN MAMMAL. TO DENY THE HUMAN MAMMAL IS TO DENY THE BASIC NATURE OF INCARNATION. TO PERCEIVE THE NECESSARY

UNITY-IN-DICHOTOMY OF ESSENCE AND MAMMAL IS TO VALIDATE THE LESSONS OF A LIFE IN A COGENT AND WORTHWHILE WAY.

WE WERE ONCE AS "HUMAN" AS YOU. WE HAVE BEEN MAMMALS ON YOUR PLANET, JUST AS YOU ARE. THAT WE NO LONGER INCARNATE, HAVING ALL COMPLETED ALL OUR LIFE CYCLES, DOES NOT MEAN THAT WE DO NOT UNDERSTAND THE HAZARDS OF "HUMANITY". WE COULD NOT AND WOULD NOT BE TEACHERS IF THAT WERE THE CASE. ALL OF US HAVE UNDERGONE THE SAME HAZARDS YOU EXPERIENCE—PLANETARY AND MAN-RELATED—OCCASIONALLY IN DIFFERENT EXPRESSION, BUT WITH THE SAME REPERCUSSIONS. TO SAY THAT WE DO NOT COMPREHEND YOUR CURRENT SITUATION BECAUSE WE NO LONGER INCARNATE IS MUCH LIKE A FIRST-GRADER OBJECTING TO A TEACHER THAT THE TEACHER DOES NOT KNOW HOW HARD IT IS TO LEARN TO READ BECAUSE THE TEACHER LEARNED TO READ SO LONG AGO. WE KNOW—NOT UNLIKE THAT FIRST-GRADE TEACHER—THAT NOT ONLY IS LEARNING TO READ DIFFICULT, IT IS ONLY THE BEGINNING.

Chapter 2

"BENEDICT AND ABIGAIL HORNE"

Their names are in quotes because these are not the real names of the couple in question, and although they do own a business together, it is not the chain of kitchen-supply stores I have made it for the purpose of this book.

"Ben" and "Abby" have been in the Michael group for over four years. They were introduced to the group and the teaching by the female half of "Leslie Adams". They met in college, have been married for eighteen years, have no children.

When asked what good the Michael teaching was, in terms of applicability in real-life terms, Abby answered first. "It's a little hard to say, just off the top of my head. I know it's useful. If it wasn't, Ben and I wouldn't keep coming to sessions."

"It started out being intriguing," Ben says, not quite ready to be more emphatic. "I didn't know what to expect, or what sort of person was going to be there. I'd heard enough about these channeling groups that I was pretty skeptical at first. If it hadn't been Leslie who asked us, I doubt we would have gotten involved."

"That's the way I felt, too," Abby agrees. "I figured at the time we'd give it the benefit of the doubt, as much because of Leslie as . . . well, I was feeling a pinch then that Ben didn't feel to the same degree. I knew that what I had been doing so far wasn't working anymore, and what I'd tried to sort it out wasn't working either. It seemed sensible to give it a try." She is self-effacing when she speaks, though there is no lack of certainty or authority; Abby is a woman who has learned to be cautious.

Ben consults one of the three large ring binders on the coffee table in their living room. "I think what started to convince me was some of the information we had on our employees. I started asking for Overleaves as a matter of course. I won't say it ever kept me from hiring someone, but it often determined how much responsibility and . . . well, slack, I'd give a new employee. And I will say that the Overleaves have never steered us wrong about someone. The Overleaves have always been accurate and useful.'' He pulls out one of the sheets. "This one, for example: a second-level Mature Slave in the caution mode with a goal of acceptance, a pragmatist in the moving part of emotional center with a chief feature of stubbornness. Well, one of the things I doubted this man would want to do is work with the public—he told me a year after we hired him that he hated to do sales or work with customers—and so I put him in charge of inventory control when we opened our second store. He's done a marvelous job for us; in fact, he put us in touch with a company that deals in high-quality dried herbs; and we've started to carry that line. He's thorough and dependable to a fault.''

"The person in charge of sales at the store is a Young Sage, and if there's such a thing as the enthusiasm mode, she's in it,'' Abby says. "She's wonderful with customers.''

"And if she had to handle inventory control, she'd go bananas and quit in a week,'' Ben finishes.

What about good sense and evalutation? What about the interviews both these employees had? Didn't that suggest where they'd be most effective?

"Sure,'' says Ben, "but during the interview all prospective employees are on good behavior, and so are we. They also have to make some reasonable guesses about the nature of the work required in the job that there is no direct way to tell them because like all jobs, a degree of it is learned by 'feel', not by questions or even demonstrations.'' He looks at the Overleaves again. "Frankly, the Young Sage was being demure for the interview and I don't think I would have been able to see how much sales ability she actually had if I'd gone on her behavior then. She was only twenty-five and this was her second job; the first was in insurance after going to one of the better community colleges in the area. Doing insurance work had taught her to keep a lid on her very bubbly nature. As it was, when she started out working as the assistant sales manager in our first store, she didn't really start to shine until about three months went by.''

"I remember talking to her boss,'' says Abby, "the sales manager in our first store, and she said she wasn't sure that Kit would work out because she was so quiet. But as that wore off, Sandra admitted that Kit was an excellent choice, though she hadn't thought so at first.'' She pauses. "Is that mundane enough for you?''

Does the mix of mundane and spiritual ever bother the Hornes?

"God, no,'' says Abby, searching through her transcripts. "Here. This applies.''

IN REGARD TO WHAT ARE PERCEIVED AS MUNDANE MATTERS, WE WOULD HAVE TO SAY THAT SUCH APPLICATION SERVES MANY PURPOSES. THE FIRST IS DEALING WITH REAL-WORLD PHYSICAL PLANE PROBLEMS, WHICH ARE, OF COURSE, PART OF THE LESSONS OF THE LIFE. IN ANOTHER SENSE, CHOOSING TO ADDRESS SUCH MATTERS AIDS IN VERIFICATION FOR THE FRAGMENTS, SHOWING THE VALIDITY OF THE TEACHING IN VERY DIRECT AND "TESTABLE" WAYS. IF DISCOVERING WHAT THE CAUSE OF A SORE BACK IS, OR FINDING A WAY TO SELECT A MORE USEFUL AUTOMOBILE, CAN BRING WIDER VALIDATION TO THE EXPERIENCES OF A LIFE, WE WOULD PERCEIVE SUCH ANSWERS AS POSSESSING SPIRITUAL VALIDITY. WE ARE AWARE THAT THERE ARE THOSE FRAGMENTS WHO PREFER THEIR SPIRITUALITY "UNTAINTED" BY PHYSICAL PLANE REALITIES, BUT WE WOULD THINK THAT THIS OFTEN SERVES TO DEFEAT THE VERY PURPOSE OF INQUIRY. MOST TEACHING IS GAUGED BY THE RESULTS IT PROVIDES. IF THERE IS NO WAY TO TEST THE RESULTS, THEN FOR MOST FRAGMENTS THE IN-

STRUCTION, WHATEVER IT IS, IS PERCEIVED AS USELESS. OF COURSE, WE DO NOT SHARE THIS PERCEPTION. NOTHING IN YOUR LIVES OR IN THE PLANES OF EXISTENCE BEYOND THE PHYSICAL PLANE IS EVER WASTED. THOSE WHO CHOOSE TO USE THIS OR ANY OTHER TEACHING IN A BASIC, DAY-TO-DAY MANNER ARE OFTEN MAKING MORE DIRECT PROGRESS THAN THOSE WHO RELEGATE THEIR SPIRITUAL STUDY TO AREAS SO ESOTERIC THAT NOTHING CAN BE "CHECKED OUT" IN WHAT MIGHT BE CALLED REAL LIFE. THAT IS NOT TO SAY THAT ALL TEACHING REQUIRES IMMEDIATE OR CONCRETE RESULTS. MOST RESEARCH WOULD NOT BE POSSIBLE IF THAT WERE THE CASE. OFTEN THE MARKS OF PROGRESS IN AREAS OF RESEARCH AND ADVANCED ACADEMIC STUDY ARE SEEN IN DEGREES AND GRANTS AS WELL AS PRESTIGE. PRESTIGE AND SYMBOLS OF ACCOMPLISHMENT ARE AS MUCH REAL-WORLD VALIDATION AS AN AUTOMOBILE THAT STARTS RELIABLY IN MID-WINTER IN THE CANADIAN ROCKIES.

How do those remarks influence what Ben or Abby ask at sessions?

"It's hard to say," Ben allows. "I certainly don't feel any constraints on what I ask. I don't feel that there are questions I mustn't bring up, though every now and then, when I want to know about something that troubles me or is painful, I'll hesitate, but that's because of me, not Michael."

"When we started out, I was a great deal more cautious about what I asked, largely because I was worried about what the others in the group might think, or what sort of answer I might get. I knew the kinds of things Michael could come up with, and I didn't want to have them say anything like that to me." Abby pats the largest of the ring binders. "Transcripts."

How many pages of transcripts are in the ring binders?

"Of regular sessions for the last four-plus years?" Abby asks and looks at the binder. "Well, there are twenty-five to twenty-six sessions in a year. We average five to six pages of transcripts, single-spaced, per session. You figure it out."

"It's about four hundred-fifty pages," Ben says. "Plus a couple of hundred Overleaf charts, and then occasional private sessions with Milly. There are about a hundred-fifty single-spaced pages of those."

"I help type the transcripts," says Abby. "Louise Fisher and I split the session; one of us takes the first round, the other the second. That way neither of us gets stuck with too much work. Occasionally, when one or the other of us isn't at a session, Bill Dutton fills in for us."

Is it much of a chore?

"You mean, does it take time?" Abby asks. "Sure. And there are times that deciphering handwriting, even my own, gets pretty difficult. If Michael is going fast, we all tend to scrawl."

"Except for Alison. She takes shorthand," Ben interjects.

"No help; I don't know shorthand," Abby counters at once. "But I have called Alison from time to time when I really can't figure out what a line of squiggles means." She holds up a notebook, the same kind used in school. "This one's almost filled. It has about another session's worth of pages left and then I'll get a new one."

"I find I can get most of the material down pretty clearly for about an hour. After that it's chancy," says Ben.

"The thing about typing the transcripts is that I often get more out of what Michael has said while I'm doing it than during the session itself. I have more of a chance to think about what is being asked and what the answer means. Not just for myself. There are times when Michael answers a question for someone else, oh, maybe for Lizzy, and when I read it over, I find out that it has application to my questions as well."

"There are times Michael seems to have a theme to harp on," Ben says. "They say they don't harp, but we know better."

IT IS NEVER OUR INTENTION TO SELECT A TOPIC FOR ANY OF YOU. WE DO DIGRESS WHEN DIGRESSION IS NECESSARY IN ORDER TO PROVIDE A COMPLETE ANSWER TO A QUESTION. OFTENTIMES MEMBERS OF OUR LITTLE

GROUP ARE ENCOUNTERING SIMILAR PROBLEMS OR IN-
SIGHTS AT MORE OR LESS THE SAME TIME, AND FOR THAT
REASON, MANY OF OUR ANSWERS WILL HAVE AREAS OF
MULTIPLE APPLICATION. THAT DOES NOT MEAN THAT WE
HAVE CHOSEN TO ADDRESS A SINGLE ISSUE, BUT THAT
OUR STUDENTS ARE CURIOUS ABOUT ISSUES WITHIN CER-
TAIN PARAMETERS THAT LEND THEMSELVES TO "FILLING
IN THE GAPS".

"It always makes me wonder how many gaps we have
left to fill in," says Abby with a hint of a sigh.

"More than we'll ever get to in one lifetime," Ben says.
"I think that's part of what Michael means when they say
that nothing is wasted. It's strange to think of how much is
really accessible to us, and most of the time we not only
don't make the effort, we don't know it's there to be made."

WHAT IS CHOSEN AS THE COURSE OF A LIFETIME IS
SIMPLY THAT: CHOICE. ALL PREVIOUS PLANS CAN BE AB-
DICATED OR ABANDONED, EVERY TASK AND INSIGHT IG-
NORED, AND STILL THE LIFE WILL NOT BE WASTED. THERE
IS NO WAY ANY FRAGMENT CAN WASTE A LIFE. AS SOON
AS YOU TAKE YOUR FIRST BREATH AND ENSOUL THE
BODY, THERE IS EXPERIENCE AND ALL EXPERIENCE—AND
WE EMPHASIZE *ALL*—IS TRUE AND VALID. YOU MAY
WASTE RESOURCES AND OPPORTUNITIES, BUT YOU CAN-
NOT WASTE A LIFE, FOR YOU CANNOT AVOID CHOICE AND
THE RAMIFICATION OF CHOICE. AS WE HAVE SAID MANY
TIMES BEFORE AND WE REPEAT YET AGAIN, ALL IS CHO-
SEN. TO DO NOTHING IS A CHOICE. THERE IS NO WAY YOU
CANNOT CHOOSE.

"That's choice lecture number eighty-two, subparagraph
four," says Abby. "Typing the transcripts has really brought
home to me how much of the Michael teaching is tied up
with choice."

"Though there are times when Michael says 'Should you
choose to do so' that I feel as if they were adding, 'And
you're a bloody fool if you don't.' " Ben pauses and con-

siders. "Or if they don't feel that way, I sure do."

"According to Milly and the Leslies, Michael really doesn't feel that. Milly sometimes says that she senses a kind exasperation in the answers, but nothing more than that." Abby opens her notebook and is searching for a particular page. "There was one session we did a couple of weeks ago, on the subject of what Michael does or does not feel. I'll have to unscramble my handwriting for you."

TO SAY FEEL IN REGARD TO OUR PERCEPTIONS IS TO LIMIT THE PERCEPTIONS IN TERMS OF THE PHYSICAL PLANE, WHICH, OF COURSE, IS NOT VALID FOR THOSE OF US EXTANT ON THE MID-CAUSAL PLANE. OUR CONTACT IS COMPLETE, AND SO FEELING, AS YOU UNDERSTAND IT, IS NOT AN ACCURATE DESCRIPTION. NOTHING IN HUMAN SPEECH—OR THE COMMUNICATIONS OF ANY OTHER EN-SOULED SPECIES ON THE PHYSICAL PLANE, FOR THAT MATTER—IS CAPABLE OF EXPRESSING WHAT THE EXPERI-ENCE OF ENTITY UNITY IS. LET US OBSERVE THAT WHERE THERE IS TOTAL INTIMACY—THAT IS, ESSENCE CON-TACT—THERE IS TRUE AGAPE. BEYOND THIS PLANE THERE ARE OTHER PLANES OF GREATER UNITY, WHERE THE CONSCIOUSNESS OF MULTIPLICITY WITHIN AN ENTITY VANISHES AND IS SUPERSEDED BY A HIGHER COMPREHEN-SION THAT IS AS INCOMPREHENSIBLE TO US AS WE ARE TO YOU.

"Not that they've made it much clearer," says Abby, "but it does give an idea of what is going on."

"Who asked that?" Ben asks, moving nearer to look over her shoulder.

"Rod."

"The mad chemist strikes again," Ben says, chuckling. "Rod's one of the most tenacious questioners in the group."

"We Warriors are like that," says Abby almost primly. "It's part of the wiring."

What is the makeup of the group like?

"As usual, we're top-heavy on Scholars," says Abby. "Scholars may be only fourteen percent of the population, but we can be forty to fifty percent Scholars at sessions. Artisans are twenty-two percent of the population, but Ben's the only one in the group. We don't have any Priests or Slaves in the regular group at present, though there are about four Priests who have been part of the group in the past, and three Slaves. That's out of proportion too. Priests are eight percent of the population and Slaves are twenty-five percent of the population. Kings are four percent of the population, and we have one of them: Alison. The rest of us are Warriors, and out of the regular group, there are four of us. Warriors are seventeen percent of the population.''

"Michael has said that their teaching tends to appeal most to Scholars and Warriors, and that over the long haul, more of those Essences will tend to stick with the group than other roles in Essence. That has been the pattern so far.'' Ben shrugs. "So here I am, the lone Artisan in the group. Luckily Milly, who's a Sage, is not only on the Expression polarity with me, we're in the same entity, and that tends to help both of us.''

"For a while we had another Old Sage, but he's not living in the area anymore, so we don't see him very often. He's been able to get to a session once or twice a year.'' Abby looks over her notebook again. "The last time Geoff was in town was in August. That's almost six months ago.''

"Then we're about due for another visit,'' Ben says, adding, "We do get occasional call-ins from Geoff. There are a couple dozen group members who don't live near enough to attend sessions and—''

"New York, Texas, Phoenix, London, Winnipeg,'' Abby fills in, ticking off names on her fingers. "Los Angeles, Seattle—''

"And all the rest of it,'' Ben finishes for her.

"Milly and the Leslies all say they dread the day everyone in the group shows up for a session at once.'' Abby indicates the living room. "We don't have room for a mob like that. Neither do the Leslies or Milly.''

"We could shoe-horn them into Alison's and Rod's place, maybe,'' Ben suggests, selecting the couple in the group with the largest living room.

"Nice of us to ask them, isn't it?" Abbys says, then returns to some of the subject at hand. "The trouble with trying to talk about the difference Michael has made is that it's an uncontrolled experiment. I don't know what I would have done if I hadn't been able to ask Michael questions. I know that I'd reached a point in my life where something different had to happen because I no longer felt I could fit in anywhere. When I was a kid, I fit in very well. Then, when I couldn't do it"—she makes quotation signals with her fingers—"'right' anymore, I thought that I was to blame. Something had gone wrong. One of the most valuable things I've gotten out of Michael's teaching is that I don't think that anything really went wrong. I needed to redefine myself in relation to the world. Otherwise known as the Infamous Fourth Internal Monad." The tone of her voice supplies the capitals. "I'm a mid-cycle Mature Warrior in the observation mode with a goal of growth, a pragmatist— oh, boy, am I a pragmatist!—in the emotional part of intellectual center with a chief feature of stubbornness and a secondary chief feature of greed fixated on service. Coming to understand the workings of the primary and secondary chief features has made a very big difference to me. It shows me the self-undermining I've been doing and helps me to stop it. The trouble with both chief features is that they have a way of making themselves seem very positive. I'm coming to see that this isn't the case."

"I'd say the same thing about the chief features," agrees Ben. "But for me the big difference, if there is one, is that I am more willing to accept others as they are. It's helped me to be more genuinely tolerant of what others do. I still have trouble from time to time understanding that no matter what I do, I can't necessarily bring someone else around to understanding things the same way I do. Five years ago I thought that meant some kind of failure on my part. Now it doesn't bother me." He reconsiders this. "As much. In terms of Overleaves, I'm a fifth-level Mature Artisan in the observation mode with a goal of dominance, a realist in the moving part of intellectual center with a chief feature of impatience and a secondary of self-deprecation."

Has knowing that made any difference for you?

"Well, yes and no. It didn't surprise me, if that's what you mean. Instead, it was an amplification of something I knew deep down but never had words for. Having the definitions helped to broaden my understanding." Ben pauses. "In terms of the past-life information, it is useful in one of those hard-to-define ways. It takes the pressure off. I don't have to do it all right now, totally."

"That's dominance/impatience speaking, in case you don't recognize it," Abby interjects.

"It sure is," Ben agrees. "On the other hand, I also feel that I'm better able to take advantage of current opportunities, of recognizing them when they come along. Decisions are easier to make now, because I don't feel as much stress as I used to."

"Another thing that helped me," says Abby, "was finding that there were other people who were interested in material like this who weren't completely nuts. I didn't have to sit around for days at a time chanting, or go to an ashram in Kashmir in order to develop a sense of inner awareness. That was very freeing for me. I didn't want to have to trade in one set of rigid rules for another set of rigid rules."

THERE ARE NO RULES TO ATTAINING SELF-KNOWL-EDGE. THE KNOWLEDGE ITSELF TENDS TO BRING ABOUT AN END TO INTERNAL RULES AND SUBSTITUTES THE REALITY OF THE REAL PERSONALITY, THE VERIFICATION OF THE OVERLEAVES. WE HAVE NO INTENTION OF REQUIRING ANY FRAGMENT TO FOLLOW OUR TEACHING; WE OFFER WHAT WE TEACH TO THOSE WHO CHOOSE TO LISTEN; TO THOSE WHO CHOOSE TO HEAR THE WORD, WE GIVE ANSWERS FREELY AND IMPARTIALLY. THOSE WHO TAKE SOME ACTION ON WHAT IS LEARNED, WE RECOGNIZE AS OUR STUDENTS. NO ONE IS REQUIRED TO LISTEN, OR TO HEAR THE WORDS, OR TO BE STUDENTS. NO ONE IS REQUIRED TO AGREE WITH US, OR TO ACCEPT WHAT WE SAY. THERE ARE MANY GOALS AND MANY PATHS TO THESE GOALS. IN THE COURSE OF MANY LIFETIMES, ALL AVAILABLE PATHS WILL BE TROD. THOSE FRAGMENTS IN

OUR LITTLE GROUP HAVE, FOR THE TIME BEING, CHOSEN
TO LISTEN TO US, TO HEAR THE WORDS, AND MOST HAVE
TAKEN THE STEPS TOWARD BEING STUDENTS. THIS IS
NEITHER "RIGHT" NOR "WRONG"; IT IS A MATTER OF
CHOICE AND THE RESULTS OF CHOICE.

"Michael does not believe in the hard sell," say Ben.
"About the only thing they hard-sell is the issue of choice,
and that is a-whole-nother ball game."

"Another thing that Michael has discussed at length that
is turning out to be a real help to me is the balance of life
task, true rest, true play, and true study." Abby opens the
largest of the ring binders again. "That's been an issue for
the last two or three years."

"Most of the people in the group have been interested in
the rest/play/study/life-task question. We tend to resist it,
but that's changing." Ben indicates some sketches on the
wall. They are very good, done in charcoal over pastel
washes. "Part of my true rest. If nothing else, Michael's
rekindled my interest in art, and whether that does me any
spiritual good in the long run, it sure helps me unwind right
now."

"True rest is supposed to do that," Abby reminds him,
and they both grin. "Remember that time Michael told me
to go fly a kite—if I chose to?"

What happened?

"I went and flew a kite," says Abby merrily. "It was
great fun. Kite flying turns out to be part of my true play,
and all I can say is that I came back with my head clear
and I felt so refreshed that I wanted to take on another three
hours of work before dinner."

"I said no," Ben adds. "Abby is one of those nose-to-the-
grindstone workers, and I had a hunch that if she started
doing a couple hours of work, we wouldn't get around to
eating until midnight, and I was hungry."

"I'm not quite that bad," Abby protests.

"If you say so," Ben tells her, clearly not believing it.

"Not everyone has sketching as true rest or kite flying as
true play," Abby adds. "There are some wonderful things

in here. Rod's got noncompetitive outdoor entertainments as part of his true play.''

"Sounds like picnic time to me," Ben agrees. "And Ginny Watson has wine tasting as part of her true play, also impromptu equestrian games and gardening.''

"Lucky thing Ginny has horses." Abby regards me. "You two still ride together?''

"When we can," I answer. "We board our horses in the same place. My schedule is a little more flexible than hers.''

"Horses are true play for you, too, aren't they, Quinn?'' Ben asks.

"No; true rest.''

"Seems like strenuous rest to me," Ben remarks.

"Well, one of the Scholars has painting the interior walls of buildings as true rest, and that's right there in the league with horses. And one of the others has touch football or touch field hockey as true rest.'' Abby has been checking the transcripts in her binder.

RESTFUL IS NOT THE SAME AS SLEEPFUL. OFTEN MEMBERS OF YOUR SOCIETY AND SIMILAR TECHNOLOGICALLY ORIENTED SOCIETIES CONFUSE THESE TWO FUNCTIONS. JUST AS NOT ALL PLAY IS ESCAPIST OR CHILDISH, ALTHOUGH OFTEN IT APPEARS THAT WAY SINCE THIS SOCIETY TENDS TO RELEGATE THINGS DESIGNED AS PLAY TO THE ACTIVITIES OF CHILDREN AND NOT OF ADULTS, EXCEPT UNDER CAREFULLY STRUCTURED RULES, SUCH AS COMPANY PICNICS WHERE PART OF THE OBJECT OF THE EXERCISE IS TO CREATE A SENSE OF CAMARADERIE THROUGH A SUPPOSEDLY LESS RIGOROUSLY STRUCTURED OCCASION. TRUE STUDY DOES NOT OFTEN OCCUR IN THE GROVES OF ACADEME. THE LIFE TASK, WHILE BEING THE FOCUS OF WORK, DOES NOT REQUIRE THAT IT BE THE CAREER OR JOB CHOSEN BY THE FRAGMENT. OFTEN SUCH EMPLOYMENT IS THE MEANS TO AN END, NOT, IN FACT, AN END IN ITSELF.

THE PURPOSE OF THE LIFE TASK IS TO USE THE FOCUSED ENERGY OF THE ESSENCE IN THE FRAMEWORK OF

CAPABILITIES PROVIDED BY THE OVERLEAVES. IN A VERY REAL SENSE, THE OVERLEAVES ARE CHOSEN TO PERMIT THE FRAGMENT TO COMPLETE THE LIFE TASK, SHOULD THE FRAGMENT CHOOSE TO DO SO. THE PURPOSE OF TRUE REST IS TO RESTORE THE FRAGMENT SO THAT THE ENERGY IS AVAILABLE FOR THE TASK AT HAND AND THE LIFE TASK. THE PURPOSE OF TRUE PLAY IS TO "GROUND" THE FRAGMENT, SO THAT THE ENERGY IS NOT SCATTERED OR DIVERTED FROM THE LIFE TASK WHEN THE FRAGMENT CHOOSES TO PURSUE IT. THE PURPOSE OF TRUE STUDY IS TO PROVIDE FOCUS FOR THE FRAGMENT, SO THAT THE ENERGY MAY BE APPLIED IN THE WAY THAT THE FRAGMENT FINDS MOST IN ACCORD WITH THE SELECTED AT- TITUDE OF THE OVERLEAVES. THE FUNCTION OF THE LIFE TASK, OR, IF YOU WILL, TRUE WORK, IS RELATED TO THE ACTION POLARITY; THE FUNCTION OF TRUE REST IS RE- LATED TO THE INSPIRATION POLARITY; THE FUNCTION OF TRUE PLAY IS RELATED TO THE EXPRESSION POLARITY; THE FUNCTION OF TRUE STUDY IS RELATED TO THE SCHO- LAR NEUTRALITY. THOSE FRAGMENTS WHOSE POLAR- ITIES CORRESPOND TO THE REST/STUDY/WORK/PLAY FUNCTIONS WILL TEND TO PUT GREATER EMPHASIS ON THAT FUNCTION. IN OTHER WORDS, A PRIEST OR SLAVE IS MORE LIKELY TO "REQUIRE" MORE TRUE REST THAN THOSE ON OTHER POLARITIES OR IN THE NEUTRAL POSI- TION.

"I've been more willing to take time out for what I used to think of as trivial things," says Abby. "I've thought about the need for balance, and I'm coming to see that when I try to keep that balance, things really do work out better for me. I'm less rattled, I have less stress, and in spite of what I thought at first, I really do get more work done. I spend less time sitting at my desk, but when I do, more is ac- complished."

Ben adds, "I've recently joined a sketching group, and I've found it's made a tremendous difference in my general attitude about everything I do. It's not very specific; I can't point to a single instance and say, 'There it is.' But I can feel that I'm less compulsive about things, and at the same time more effective.''

"We were back East a while ago, visiting relatives, and I didn't have the chance, or the inclination, to do much of my true rest or play. And when I got home, I felt drained. It wasn't simply that my family can be like that—everyone can be like that from time to time—it was that I had lost some of my balance, and that made things difficult.'' She looks out toward the garden. "So I made a point of swimming every evening—that's part of my true rest. Everyone has three or four items in each category of rest, study, and play. Swimming is restful for me. And the funny thing is, it works. If I make a point of swimming, I feel the difference.''

What about physical exercise in general? Wouldn't that do the trick?

"I thought it might,'' says Abby. "I tried running, but that only wore me out. I didn't come away feeling restored the way I do after swimming. I tried an aerobic dance class for a while: same thing as running. Swimming does it for me. But it doesn't work for Ben. Swimming's not on his list, and when he tries it, he—''

"It's like Abby and running. All I get is tired.'' He indicates the binders. "Everyone's lists are a little different. One of the men in the group has as part of his true study the study of things with wings. We gave him a blowup pterodactyl for his birthday.''

So members of the group do socialize.

"Actually, we didn't for quite some time,'' says Ben. "Then about three years ago, we realized most of us had never had a standard party together, not as a group. So we had the First Annual All-Michael Picnic.''

"And the next year we had the Second Annual All-Michael Picnic. Now we're planning the third.'' Abby gives a sly smile. "We did desserts last time, and I think we'll do them again.''

"We make evil desserts,'' says Ben with pride.

How did the First Annual All-Michael Picnic go?

"It was strange, really. For about the first forty minutes

we all sat around staring at each other, not knowing what to say. No one had notebooks. But then Geoff showed up—leave it to an Old Sage to get people talking. We must have gone nonstop for about five hours after that." Ben shakes his head, smiling a little. "They're a lot of fun, really. And in some odd ways they do help us loosen up."

"We still don't do a lot of things together, but there is more of an openness about it when we do. A few years ago I would have hesitated to ask one of the Michael group to our New Year's Day party, but now it's pretty much a standing invitation, and for the last two years about half of them have come. Ben and I weren't sure at first that this would work—we thought maybe all the Michael group would sit in a corner and talk Michael while everyone else was puzzled or bored. It didn't turn out that way, but we had a nervous moment or two."

Is there anything about the Michael material that bothers you?

Ben answers first. "Sometimes I feel that I'm lagging, that I'm not getting *on* with it. That's impatience, I know, but there's so much I can do with my life that it bothers me when I can't do it all. There's so much information, and so many possibilities I never recognized before that now I have to stop myself from trying to do all of it at once."

"I think," says Abby, "that what troubles me occasionally is how little encouragement we get from Michael. About the strongest language Michael uses is, 'We commend you', and that doesn't happen very often. When Michael says they're indifferent, they mean it. But then," she goes on in a milder way, "I turn it around and think about what it would be like if we all spent our time trying to choose things that would bring praise, that would please Michael. That would be awful. We'd be worse than puppets. So I listen to the various choice lectures we get every session, and I keep in mind that there's nothing I can do that Michael will like or dislike, and I know that my occasional frustration is nothing compared to how I'd feel if I were trying to live up to some mid-causal expectations."

"Abby's right," says Ben with feeling. "At first I wondered if Michael really meant that 'All is chosen' stuff he keeps saying; after a while I realized that they did. That there was nothing any of us could do that would gain disapproval from Michael. We could create a lot of karma for ourselves, but Michael, in the best sense of the word, wouldn't care.''

"If anything keeps me in the group, keeps me asking questions, it's that freedom,'' says Abby. "I know I will never reach a point where I cannot get an answer because Michael doesn't like what I did with the last one they gave me. I might not like what I did with it, but Michael is truly indifferent. When they say that they love without expectations, they mean just that. No matter how puzzling it is, it's also the most persuasive aspect of Michael's teaching, at least for me. Because they don't ask anything of me, I'm more willing to listen to their comments than I would be if they wanted me to do something specific.''

"I've had a few answers that puzzled or confused me,'' says Ben. "If I thought Michael was expecting me to 'get' something out of it, I wouldn't have been willing to ask for clarification or more material. As it is, I know I can keep after something until I really do understand it.''

"Or until Milly or the Leslies can't stand channeling the answers anymore,'' Abby adds, her hazel eyes twinkling.

"That's a point,'' Ben concedes. "After all, Jessica quit; I suppose the others might . . . choose to do the same thing one day.''

"So far they haven't,'' says Abby. "In fact, the Leslies are more involved than before, taking up the slack.''

Has that made a difference in the material?

"No, not really,'' says Abby at once. "Michael has a very distinctive style, and it doesn't seem to matter who the channel is, Michael is still Michael and they still can't spell Czechoslovakia.''

Chapter 3

MICHAEL: ON LESSONS AND LIFETIMES

WE ARE AWARE THAT MANY HERE PRESENT, BELIEVING THAT SPIRITUAL EVOLUTION IS SOMEHOW LINKED WITH BEING "BETTER" OR "IMPROVED", ASPIRE TO "LEAP WHOLE CYCLES IN A SINGLE BOUND". LET US POINT OUT THAT THIS IS NEITHER POSSIBLE NOR DESIRABLE. EACH LIFE, EACH LESSON, IS APPROPRIATE TO THE PROCESS OF EVOLUTION AND LEARNING, AND THERE IS NO SHORTCUT TO TRANSCENDING.

FOR THOSE OF YOU WHO RECOGNIZE AND VALIDATE SPIRITUAL GROWTH WITHIN A GIVEN LIFETIME, THE GROWTH IS THE NATURE OF THAT CYCLE AND WILL OCCUR WITH OR WITHOUT YOUR VALIDATION WHILE ON THE PHYSICAL PLANE. THIS IS NOT TO DISCOURAGE ANY FRAGMENTS FROM SEEKING SPIRITUAL ADVANCEMENT; IT IS NOT TO ENCOURAGE THEM, EITHER. SPIRITUAL INTERESTS ARE CHOSEN, AS IS EVERYTHING ELSE IN LIFE.

WHILE IT IS TRUE, AND WE HAVE SAID THIS MANY TIMES IN THE PAST, THAT THE PHYSICAL PLANE IS THE ONLY PLANE WHERE ACCIDENTS CAN AND DO HAPPEN, UNTIL YOUR LIFE CHOICES HAVE BEEN INTERRUPTED OR DIVERTED, THE IMPACT OF ACCIDENTS IS VERY MUCH A MATTER OF CHOICE. WHERE LIFE CHOICES HAVE BEEN INTERRUPTED OR DIVERTED, SUCH AS BY WRONGFUL DEATH OR IMPRISONMENT, THEN KARMA IS THE RESULT, AND THE RIBBON WILL EXIST UNTIL IT IS BURNED. THERE ARE LESSER DEBTS, OF COURSE, THOSE THAT DO NOT HAVE THE WEIGHT OF KARMA NOR THE PREARRANGEMENT OF AGREEMENTS AND INTERFRAGMENTAL MON-

ADS, AND WE WOULD DESCRIBE THESE LESSER DEBITS AS ACTS OF RESTITUTION.

LET US PROVIDE AN EXAMPLE: A FRAGMENT, ACTING OUT OF THE NEGATIVE POLES OF THE OVERLEAVES, COMMITS AN ASSAULTIVE ACT UPON ANOTHER FRAGMENT. THERE IS DAMAGE, BUT NOT SUFFICIENT TO BRING ABOUT KARMA. NONETHELESS, THERE HAS BEEN MORE THAN BAD MANNERS, AND THE ACT WAS ONE OF FEAR, NOT LOVE. IN FUTURE CONTACT, BY WHICH WE MEAN IN FUTURE LIVES, THE OFFENDING FRAGMENT WILL BE STRONGLY INCLINED TO OFFER SOME SORT OF RESTITUTION, OFTEN IN THE FORM OF NEEDED AID.

THAT IS NOT TO SAY THAT ALL ACTS OF GENEROSITY ARE RESTITUTION. THIS IS OBVIOUSLY NOT THE CASE. SOME INSTANCES ARE NOTHING MORE THAN PRECISELY WHAT THEY SEEM—ACTS OF GENEROSITY. THERE ARE FRAGMENTS WHO POSSESS THE QUALITY OF GENEROSITY, JUST AS THERE ARE FRAGMENTS WHO POSSESS THE QUALITY OF KINDNESS AND FRAGMENTS WHO POSSESS THE QUALITY OF FAIRNESS. FOR FRAGMENTS WITH THESE QUALITIES, ACTS IN ACCORDANCE WITH THE QUALITY ARE GENERALLY ACTS FROM ESSENCE. THERE ARE ALSO ACTS OF PHILANTHROPIC KARMA. THERE ARE AGREEMENTS WHICH WILL LEAD TO GENEROUS AND/OR SUPPORTIVE ACTS. THERE ARE INTERFRAGMENTAL MONADS THAT ARE EXPRESSED THROUGH ACTS THAT MIGHT BE MISTAKEN FOR RESTITUTION. CERTAINLY THE BONDS AND LINKS OF CADENCE MEMBERS, TASK COMPANIONS, AND ESSENCE TWINS, AS WELL AS THE BONDS OF THOSE BELONGING TO THE SAME ENTITY AND/OR CONFIGURATION, CREATE A PREDISPOSITION TO RENDER SUPPORT AND ASSISTANCE. WHILE IT CAN BE WORTHWHILE TO CHOOSE TO EXPLORE SUCH RELATIONSHIPS, IT IS NEVER, OF COURSE, REQUIRED.

WHERE RESTITUTION IS IN EFFECT, THE PERCEPTIONS ARE OFTEN EXPRESSED IN THIS WAY: "I-REALLY OUGHT TO DO SOMETHING FOR THIS PERSON", THOUGH OFTEN THERE IS NO COMPREHENSION OF THE IMPULSE ITSELF. LET US OFFER AN ILLUSTRATION OF THE PROCESS WITH THIS EXAMPLE: THREE LIVES AGO, A THEN-YOUNG WAR-

RIOR, OFFENDED AT THE RADICAL PRESS RUN BY A MATURE SCHOLAR, TOOK IT UPON HIMSELF TO BEAT UP THE MATURE SCHOLAR AS A MEANS TO DISSUADE HIM FROM CONTINUING THE PRACTICES WHICH THE THEN-YOUNG WARRIOR FOUND TO BE UNACCEPTABLE. HE ALSO BURNED THE BUILDING WHERE THE PRESS ITSELF WAS LOCATED, THUS DRIVING THE MATURE SCHOLAR TEMPORARILY OUT OF BUSINESS. THIS WAS NOT THE RESULT OF A PREVIOUS AGREEMENT; THEY HAD NO MONADAL LINKS, THERE WAS NO KARMA. IN THIS LIFE, THE NOW-MATURE WARRIOR HAS TAKEN IT UPON HERSELF TO SPONSOR A SMALL AND RADICAL MUSICAL GROUP BECAUSE SHE HAS THE STRANGE SENSE THAT SHE "OUGHT" TO DO IT FOR THE CONDUCTOR, WHO IS, OF COURSE, THE MATURE SCHOLAR WHOSE PRESS THE THEN-YOUNG WARRIOR DESTROYED.

AS YOU MAY PERCEIVE, THIS ACTION IS NOT AS "COMPULSIVE" AS KARMA, AND NOT AS ONGOING AS MONADAL RELATIONSHIPS. IT CAN LEAD TO ENHANCED UNDERSTANDING, THOUGH THIS IS NOT ALWAYS THE CASE. OFTEN, WHEN THE FRAGMENT MAKING RESTITUTION IS SATISFIED THAT THE NEED HAS BEEN SATISFIED, THE RELATIONSHIP BECOMES LESS IMPORTANT IN THE LIFE.

WHERE ABDICATION OF KARMIC BURNING, MONADS, OR AGREEMENTS OCCURS, DISTANCING IS OFTEN THE RESULT. THOSE FRAGMENTS WHO "BOTCH" THE CONTACT ARE USUALLY EAGER TO GET AWAY FROM THE WHOLE THING. THERE ARE INSTANCES WHERE DIVORCED COUPLES, WHILE NOT ACTIVELY HOSTILE TO ONE ANOTHER, NEVERTHELESS END UP MOVING TO OPPOSITE ENDS OF THE COUNTRY WHILE RETAINING AN OUTWARDLY CORDIAL CONTACT WITH ONE ANOTHER. IN THESE INSTANCES—AND DIVORCE IS ONE OF THE MOST COMMON MANIFESTATIONS OF THIS SORT OF ABDICATION IN YOUR SOCIETY—ONE OR BOTH FRAGMENTS WILL SENSE THAT SOMETHING THAT WAS "SUPPOSED" TO HAPPEN, IN FACT, DID NOT. THE FRAGMENT ABDICATING IS OFTEN THE FRAGMENT MOST LIKELY TO APPEAR INJURED BY THE SEPARATION, FOR IN A SENSE THERE HAS BEEN MORE POTENTIAL "DAMAGE" DONE BECAUSE OF THE ABDICATION.

WHERE THE ABDICATION IS OF A MONAD, THE ATTEMPT WILL BE MADE AGAIN AT A LATER TIME, PROBABLY UNDER MORE "TOLERABLE" CIRCUMSTANCES. WHERE THE ABDICATION IS OF AN AGREEMENT, THERE IS NO "NEED" TO ATTEMPT THE CONTACT AGAIN, UNLESS THE FRAGMENTS CHOOSE TO "HAVE ANOTHER GO AT IT".

WE WOULD AGREE THAT THE MORE TRADITIONALLY "MAJOR" RELATIONSHIPS IN A GIVEN LIFE TEND TO HAVE A GREATER IMPACT ON THE FRAGMENTS CONCERNED. BUT THE OPERATIVE WORD HERE IS *TEND*, FOR THERE ARE RELATIONSHIPS, EVEN WITHIN "CLOSE" FAMILIES THAT HAVE LITTLE TO KEEP THEM GOING OTHER THAN GENETIC HERITAGE AND TRIBAL MYTHOLOGY. ONE OF THE REASONS THAT FEW MEMBERS OF THE SAME ENTITY ARE BORN INTO THE SAME FAMILY AT THE SAME TIME OR IN PRIMARY RELATIONSHIPS IS THAT THIS MIGHT EASILY SERVE TO DISTORT THE LESSON OF BEING IN A FAMILY. IT IS NOT UNUSUAL, HOWEVER, TO SEE OCCASIONAL FAMILIAL LINKS WITH ENTITY MEMBERS THAT ARE OFFSET IN SOME WAY; GRANDPARENTS AND GRANDCHILDREN, SECOND COUSINS, FIRST COUSINS WITH AT LEAST ONE REMOVE, MORE RARELY AUNT/UNCLE/NIECE/NEPHEW. WHEN SUCH TIES EXIST, IT IS NOT USUAL FOR THE FAMILIAL LINKS TO BE WITH MEMBERS OF THE SAME CADENCE, SINCE WITHIN THE TERMS OF ENTITY BONDS, THE MEMBERS OF THE SAME CADENCE ARE MORE LIKE SIBLINGS THAN ANY OTHERS.

CERTAINLY WHERE THE FRAGMENTS CONCERNED ARE IN THE MID-CYCLE MATURE ONWARD, THE LIKELIHOOD OF HAVING PHYSICAL-PLANE FAMILY LINKS IS GREATER THAN IT IS FOR BABY, YOUNG, AND EARLY MATURE FRAGMENTS, WHO ARE STILL IN THE PROCESS OF EXPANDING THE RANGE OF EXPERIENCE IN THEIR LIVES. THERE ARE OCCASIONS WHEN ESSENCE TWINS ARE BORN AS PHYSICAL-PLANE TWINS, AND WHEN TASK COMPANIONS ARE BORN PHYSICAL-PLANE TWINS, OR PARENTS AND CHILDREN. THESE LIVES ARE OFTEN PARTICULARLY DEMANDING ONES, AND THE PURPOSE OF THE CLOSE BONDS BEING PRESENT IS TO PROVIDE THE SUPPORT NECESSARY TO ACCOMPLISH THE TASK AT HAND, WHATEVER IT MIGHT

BE. WE WILL PROVIDE YET ANOTHER EXAMPLE: A MATURE SLAVE, OWING SEVERAL MAJOR KARMIC DEBTS FOR A LIFE AS A SLAVE TRADER, CHOOSES TO BE BORN INTO A FAMILY WHERE IT WILL BE POSSIBLE TO BURN MUCH OF THE KARMA. BUT THE ENORMITY OF THE TASK IS TREMENDOUS, AND SO THE TASK COMPANION CHOOSES TO BE HIS PHYSICAL-PLANE TWIN FOR THAT LIFE, AIDING THE MATURE SLAVE IN ACCOMPLISHING THE TASK OF THE LIFE SO THAT THE KARMA MIGHT BE BURNED. THIS CHOICE ON THE PART OF THE TASK COMPANION DOES NOT ACTUALLY CREATE PHILANTHROPIC KARMA BETWEEN TASK COMPANIONS, BECAUSE THE CHOICE WAS A CONDITION OF THE LIFE ITSELF, NOT A RESPONSE TO THE CONDITIONS OF THE LIFE DURING ITS PROGRESS. THE MATURE SLAVE WAS ABLE TO GET AN ADVANCED DEGREE IN MEDICAL RESEARCH LARGELY BECAUSE HIS ENGINEER BROTHER DEVELOPED SEVERAL NEW PROCESSES IN HIGHWAY CONSTRUCTION THAT MADE HIM SUFFICIENTLY RICH TO BE ABLE TO SUPPORT THE MATURE SLAVE'S RESEARCH. THE MEDICAL IMPROVEMENTS WERE FOR THE MOST PART IN TISSUE RESTORATION AND MICROSURGERY FOR BURN PATIENTS, WHICH HAS ALLOWED THE MATURE SLAVE TO EARN PHILANTHROPIC KARMA IN THIS LIFE AS WELL AS TO BURN NINETEEN OF THE KARMIC RIBBONS FROM THE PAST. THE TASK COMPANION, A MATURE PRIEST, SEES HIS HIGHER IDEAL BEING FULFILLED AS MUCH IN THE WORK OF HIS TWIN BROTHER AS IN HIS OWN EFFORTS IN ENGINEERING. INCIDENTALLY, IN THE CASE OF THESE TWO TASK COMPANIONS, THE SLAVE IS CARDINAL AND THE PRIEST IS ORDINAL.

THE SUCCESSFUL COMPLETION OF A LIFE TASK OFTEN REQUIRES THE SAME THING AS THE TEST FOR A MURDER SUSPECT: METHOD, MOTIVE, AND OPPORTUNITY. THE MEANS OF ACCOMPLISHING THE LIFE TASK ON SOME LEVEL MUST BE AT LEAST ACCESSIBLE. THE FRAGMENT MUST HAVE THE DESIRE TO DO THE TASK, FOR ALL FRAGMENTS ARE FREE TO CHOOSE NOT TO WORK ON A LIFE TASK. AND THE CHANCE TO DO THE WORK MUST BE AT LEAST ATTAINABLE. THE EXCEPTION TO THE FIRST, THE QUESTION OF METHOD, DOES NOT, IN FACT, APPLY TO

SLAVE ESSENCES; THE SLAVE ESSENCE, UNLIKE ALL OTHER ESSENCES, DOES NOT REQUIRE THE MEANS OF ACCOMPLISHING A LIFE TASK. BEING PRESENT ON THE PHYSICAL PLANE IS SUFFICIENT MEANS FOR SLAVE ESSENCES, WHICH IS ONE OF THE REASONS THAT SLAVES IN GENERAL INCUR LESS KARMA DURING THEIR EVOLUTION. IT IS NOT INCORRECT TO ASSUME THAT SLAVES ARE IN MANY WAYS THE MOST FLEXIBLE OF ESSENCES, AND THAT THE FLEXIBILITY THEY POSSESS PROVIDES AN EXPERIENTIAL "EDGE" THAT THE OTHER ESSENCES, ALL OF WHOM REQUIRE GREATER OR LESSER DEGREES OF "SPECIAL CIRCUMSTANCES" IN ORDER TO ACCOMPLISH THE LIFE TASK, DO NOT SHARE.

WE WOULD WISH TO SAY HERE THAT THERE IS CONTINUITY FROM LIFE TO LIFE AND THAT ALL FRAGMENTS EXPERIENCE THIS CONTINUITY, WHETHER THERE IS ACTUAL RECOGNITION OF IT DURING ANY SPECIFIC LIFE OR NOT. THE RECOGNITION DURING A LIFE, WHILE OF GREAT USE, IS IN NO SENSE "NECESSARY". A GREAT MANY FRAGMENTS CHOOSE NOT TO HAVE RECOGNITION IN ORDER TO "KEEP THEIR MINDS" ON THE PARTICULAR LIFE BEING LED AT ONE PARTICULAR TIME. THE CONTINUITY IS NOT BASED ON ANY SORT OF "CONTINUOUS NARRATIVE", BUT RATHER ON EVOLVING CHOICES PREDICATED ON THE EXPERIENCE OF THE PAST AND BY THE CULTURAL DEMANDS AND PERSONAL EXPECTATIONS OF THE LIFE BEING CURRENTLY LIVED. IN LIVING THE LIFE, EACH FRAGMENT LEARNS AND ASSESSES THE LESSONS OF TRUE INTIMACY, BY WHICH ALL GROWTH IS ACHIEVED.

THOSE FRAGMENTS WHO CHOOSE TO IGNORE THE LESSONS OF A LIFETIME WILL NONETHELESS REMEMBER THEM AT ANOTHER TIME, OFTEN IN ANOTHER WAY. MOST FRAGMENTS ARE WILLING TO LET THEIR CULTURE DECIDE FOR THEM UNTIL THE THIRD INTERNAL MONAD, WHEN THE FRAGMENT SEPARATES ITSELF FROM THE FULL IDENTITY OF THE FAMILY AND SETS OUT ON ITS OWN. CERTAIN SOCIETIES MAKE A GREAT OCCASION OF THIS WITH RITES OF PASSAGE TO MARK THE EMERGENCE FROM CHILDHOOD INTO ADULTHOOD. OTHERS DO EVERYTHING THEY CAN TO IGNORE OR DENY IT. THIS SOCIETY OFTEN DENIES THE

STATUS OF ADULTHOOD TO THOSE REACHING THE THIRD
INTERNAL MONAD. IN MOST INSTANCES IT IS THE
FEMALES WHO ARE MOST PRESSED TO DENY THE THIRD
INTERNAL MONAD, BUT IT IS THE MALES WHO ARE THE
MOST BLIND TO ITS IMPLICATIONS.

AFTER THE THIRD INTERNAL MONAD, THERE IS MUCH
NEW MATERIAL IN THE LIFE TO ATTRACT THE ATTENTION
OF THE FRAGMENTS, AND THIS LEADS TO NEW PERCEP-
TIONS THAT ARE PART OF THE VALIDATION OF THE THIRD
INTERNAL MONAD. WHEN THE THIRD INTERNAL MONAD
HAS BEEN AVOIDED, THE FOURTH INTERNAL MONAD, OR
THE EMERGENCE OF THE TRUE PERSONALITY AS COM-
PARED TO THE FALSE PERSONALITY, BECOMES MORE DIF-
FICULT THAN USUAL, IF NOT ALMOST IMPOSSIBLE. THOSE
WHO WILL NOT ACCEPT THE TRANSITS OF THE INTERNAL
MONADS ARE OFTEN CAUGHT IN BEHAVIOR THAT IS DIAG-
NOSED AS SERIOUSLY DISTURBED. OF COURSE, MANY
FRAGMENTS UNDERGOING DIFFICULT TRANSITS THROUGH
THE INTERNAL MONADS TEND TO EXPERIENCE BEHAVIOR
SHIFTS THAT ARE VIEWED AS NEUROTIC, BUT IN MOST
INSTANCES THE BEHAVIOR ALTERS TO MORE "NORMAL"
LIMITS ONCE THE TRANSIT HAS BEEN COMPLETED AND
THE LESSONS BROUGHT TO BEAR IN THE LIFE.

YOU ARE HERE TO LIVE THE LIFE YOU HAVE CHOSEN
TO LIVE. THAT DOES NOT MEAN YOU ARE "REQUIRED"
TO LIVE IT, BECAUSE THAT WOULD DENY CHOICE, AND,
OF COURSE, ALL IS CHOSEN. PREVIOUS LIFE EXPERIENCES,
AS WELL AS IMMEDIATE LIFE TASK, TEND TO SHAPE THE
LIFE CHOICES, ALTHOUGH THE PARAMETERS OF CULTURE
CAN HAVE A PROFOUND INFLUENCE ON THE MANNER IN
WHICH THE CHOICES ARE EXPRESSED. IT IS NOT "WRONG"
TO BE INFLUENCED BY CULTURE, SINCE THOSE LESSONS
ARE IMPORTANT ONES AND CAN ONLY BE LEARNED ON
THE PHYSICAL PLANE. THOSE FRAGMENTS WHO RESIST
ANY AND ALL INFLUENCES OF CULTURE ARE MOST OFTEN
PERCEIVED—NOT INCORRECTLY—AS BEING INSANE AND
ARE TREATED ACCORDINGLY. CERTAINLY MOST FRAG-
MENTS WILL CHOOSE TO PASS ONE LIFE EXPERIENCING
JUST SUCH INSANITY, AND THE LESSON WILL BE OF TRE-
MENDOUS IMPORTANCE TO THE EVOLUTION OF THE FRAG-

MENT, BUT THAT IS NOT TO SAY THAT SUCH A CHOICE IS
THEREFORE MORE "CORRECT" THAN ANOTHER MIGHT BE.
THERE IS NO "CORRECT" OR "INCORRECT", THERE IS ONLY
CHOICE. YOU ARE RESPONSIBLE FOR YOUR CHOICES AND
YOUR ACTIONS.

IN DECIDING THE NATURE OF A LIFE TASK, THE FRAG-
MENT DURING THE ASTRAL INTERVAL, OR WHAT YOU
CALL BETWEEN-LIVES, HAS ACCESS TO FULL KNOWLEDGE
OF ALL PREVIOUS LIVES AS WELL AS THE LIVES OF ALL
MEMBERS OF THE FRAGMENT'S ENTITY. WHAT HAS BEEN
LEARNED WILL INFLUENCE, AT LEAST IN PART, WHAT A
FRAGMENT "SIGNS UP" TO DO. THESE DECISIONS ARE
MADE BEFORE THE NEW INCARNATION IS UNDERTAKEN,
AND OFTEN THERE IS A FAIR AMOUNT OF LEEWAY BUILT
INTO THE LIFE PLAN, SO THAT ALTERNATIVES WILL BE
AVAILABLE IF NEEDED. OF COURSE, NOT EVERYTHING
CAN BE ADEQUATELY ANTICIPATED, BUT WHERE THE LIFE
PLAN IS NOT TOO RIGID, THERE ARE MANY REAL OPPOR-
TUNITIES TO DO THE LIFE TASK AT SOME LEVEL.

THE OVERLEAVES PROVIDE THE FRAMEWORK FOR THE
LIFE TASK AND AS SUCH ARE CHOSEN WITH THAT IN MIND.
FOR EXAMPLE, A SAGE WHO DESIRED TO DO SOLITARY
WORK OF SOME SORT, SUCH AS SCULPTURE, MIGHT
CHOOSE A GOAL OF REJECTION FOR THAT LIFETIME SO
THAT THE NATURALLY GREGARIOUS SAGE NATURE
COULD BE SET ASIDE TO SOME DEGREE, AND THE DESIRE
FOR COMMUNICATION GIVEN TO THE ART FORM RATHER
THAN TO THE MORE SOCIAL FORMS OF COMMUNICATION,
WHERE SAGES GENERALLY OPERATE. IN SUCH A CASE,
THE SAGE WOULD HAVE TO LEARN A DEGREE OF DISCI-
PLINE, BUT THAT IS THE CASE WITH EVERY SET OF OVER-
LEAVES, NO MATTER HOW APPARENTLY POSITIVE, FOR
THE NEGATIVE POLES ARE ALWAYS PRESENT AND THERE
IS NO "REQUIREMENT" FOR ANY FRAGMENT TO ACT OUT
OF THE POSITIVE POLES.

A SCHOLAR, CHOOSING TO BE MORE OPEN IN A LIFE
AND WISHING TO OVERCOME THE NATURAL SCHOLAR
RETICENCE, MIGHT SELECT THE PASSION MODE AND A
GOAL OF ACCEPTANCE, WHICH WOULD CERTAINLY GIVE
AMPLE INCLINATION TO BE MORE FORTHCOMING, BUT

THAT DOES NOT MEAN THAT THE SCHOLAR MIGHT NOT BECOME A FANATIC OF SOME SORT, OR END UP BECOMING THE ULTIMATE SYCOPHANT; THESE OVERLEAVES MIGHT WELL TEND THE SCHOLAR IN THAT DIRECTION SHOULD THE SCHOLAR CHOOSE TO ACT OUT OF THE NEGATIVE POLES. OVERLEAVES CREATE THE GUIDELINES FOR THE TRUE PERSONALITY, BUT THAT DOES NOT MEAN THAT THEY THEREFORE LIMIT THE COURSE OF ACTION OF THE FRAGMENT: THAT WOULD ABROGATE CHOICE, AND CHOICE IS THE CRUX OF THE ISSUE OF LIFE ON THE PHYSICAL PLANE.

WE RECOGNIZE THE TENDENCY IN MANY FRAGMENTS TO SEE OVERLEAVES AS RIGID LIMITATIONS INSTEAD OF THE BASIC FRAMEWORK THEY, IN FACT, ARE. IT IS NOT AMISS TO KEEP THIS IN MIND WHEN DECIDING THAT CERTAIN OVERLEAVES ARE "BETTER" THAN OTHERS, OR THAT CERTAIN LEVELS AND CYCLES ARE "BETTER" THAN OTHERS. IT IS THE APPLICATION OF THOSE OVERLEAVES THAT DETERMINE THEIR USEFULNESS TO THE EVOLUTION OF THE FRAGMENT CHOOSING THEM.

FOR THOSE WHO HAVE MADE THE BLITHE ASSUMPTION THAT THE CHOOSING OF "GOOD" OVERLEAVES IS ALL THAT IS NEEDED TO GET THROUGH A LIFE UNSCATHED, WE REMIND ALL OF YOU HERE GATHERED THAT BEING SCATHED IS PART OF LIFE, AND THAT DELIBERATELY AVOIDING SCATHING, WHILE THAT IS A MATTER OF CHOICE, OFTEN DEFEATS THE PURPOSE OF THE LIFE IN QUESTION. ALSO, IN TERMS OF WHAT ARE SEEN AS "GOOD" OR "BAD" OVERLEAVES, WE REMIND YOU THAT HANNIBAL AND HITLER HAD THE SAME OVERLEAVES, THAT QUEEN VICTORIA OF ENGLAND AND KING PHILLIP II OF SPAIN HAD THE SAME OVERLEAVES, THAT VINCENT VAN GOGH AND CHARLES CHAPLIN HAD THE SAME OVERLEAVES, THAT ST. THOMAS AQUINAS AND KARL MARX HAD THE SAME OVERLEAVES. WE REITERATE THAT HOW EACH FRAGMENT CHOOSES TO MANIFEST THE OVERLEAVES IT HAS CHOSEN HAS AS MUCH OR MORE BEARING ON THE EVOLUTION OF ESSENCE THAN THE OVERLEAVES THEMSELVES.

THOSE OF OUR LITTLE GROUP WHO HAVE CHOSEN TO

BE STUDENTS HAVE COMPLETED THE INTERNAL MONADS APPROPRIATE TO THEIR PLACE IN LIFE. MOST OF THEM HAVE AT LEAST BEGUN THE FOURTH INTERNAL MONAD, AND AT LEAST HALF OF THEM HAVE COMPLETED IT. THOSE FRAGMENTS WHO ABDICATE THE INTERNAL MONADS, IN PARTICULAR THE FOURTH, ARE NOT LIKELY TO CHOOSE TO PURSUE THIS OR SIMILAR TEACHINGS FOR ANY LENGTH OF TIME. THAT IS NOT TO SAY THAT FRAGMENTS WHO ARE NOT INTERESTED IN ESOTERIC TEACHING HAVE THEREFORE ABDICATED THE FOURTH INTERNAL MONAD; WE DID NOT SAY THAT, AND WE DID NOT IMPLY IT. WE ARE SAYING THAT THOSE WHO CHOOSE TO ABDI-CATE THE INTERNAL MONADS ARE NOT LIKELY TO RE-MAIN ACTIVE WITH A VALID—AND WE STRESS *VALID*—ASTRAL OR CAUSAL TEACHER FOR ANY LENGTH OF TIME, AND ARE NOT LIKELY TO CHOOSE TO BE STUDENTS.

HOWEVER, THERE ARE MANY FRAGMENTS WHO ARE AVOIDING THE THIRD OR FOURTH INTERNAL MONADS WHO CHOOSE TO PURSUE APPARENT SPIRITUALITY RATHER THAN DEAL WITH THE LIVES AND PERSONALITIES THEY HAVE CHOSEN. BY "DISTRACTING" THEIR ATTEN-TION FROM THE LESSONS OF THE LIFE, MANY FRAGMENTS BLOCK INSIGHTS AND GROWTH BY IMMERSION IN VARI-OUS SPIRITUAL OR RELIGIOUS STUDIES WHICH SERVE THE PURPOSE OF PROVIDING THE ILLUSION OF GROWTH AND UNDERSTANDING RATHER THAN THE ACTUALITY.

ALMOST ALL FRAGMENTS EXTANT ON THE PHYSICAL PLANE WILL HAVE AT LEAST ONE SUCH LIFE. OF COURSE, PRIEST AND SLAVE ESSENCES ARE MORE DRAWN TO SUCH "DISTRACTIONS" THAN OTHER ESSENCES BECAUSE THE INSPIRATION POLARITY HAS THAT "SLANT" ON THE WORLD FROM THE START. SUCH DISTRACTED LIFETIMES ARE OFTEN MARKED BY DOGMATIC ATTITUDES AND BLIND DEVOTION TO A RELIGION OR SPIRITUAL DISCIPLINE THAT SUPERSEDES THE GENERAL PERCEPTIONS OF LIFE AND ITS EVOLUTION.

WE WOULD WISH TO URGE ALL HERE PRESENT TO CON-SIDER THE MOTIVATIONS FOR SPIRITUAL STUDIES, SHOULD THEY CHOOSE TO DO SO. IT IS NOT INAPPRO-

PRIATE TO DO THIS WITH OUR OR ANY OTHER TEACHING, TRADITIONAL OR NOT. IT IS OF USE TO MOST FRAGMENTS TO BE AWARE OF THE IMPACT OF THIS OR ANY SPIRITUAL TEACHING IN THE CONDUCT OF THE LIFE, AND THE DE-MANDS OF THAT TEACHING, FOR WHERE A TEACHING LIMITS CHOICE, IT IS MORE DOGMA THAN "ENLIGHTEN-MENT".

THERE IS GENUINE BENEFIT TO BE GAINED FROM REC-OGNIZING THE LESSONS OF PAST LIVES AS WELL AS THE LIFE CURRENTLY BEING LIVED, AND THOSE FRAGMENTS WHO CHOOSE TO INCORPORATE THE LESSONS OF THE PAST INTO THE CURRENT LIFE CAN ACHIEVE GREATER UNDER-STANDING. OF COURSE, NO ONE OF YOU "OUGHT" TO DO THIS; IT IS A WORTHWHILE EXPLORATION FOR THOSE WHO CHOOSE TO VENTURE INTO THE ACTS OF THE PAST, FOR THE LESSONS OF THE PAST ARE ALREADY WITH YOU AND ARE LEARNED. THEY ARE AVAILABLE TO YOU ON MANY LEVELS AND CAN BE A SOURCE OF INFORMATION AND UNDERSTANDING THAT MIGHT SERVE YOU WELL IN DIF-FICULT SITUATIONS, SHOULD YOU CHOOSE TO AVAIL YOURSELVES OF WHAT YOU HAVE ALREADY LEARNED.

FOR ALL FRAGMENTS WHO ARE ATTEMPTING TO COME TO TERMS WITH THE PARAMETERS OF A GIVEN LIFETIME, WE WOULD SUGGEST THAT IT WOULD NOT BE INAPPRO-PRIATE FOR YOU TO REMEMBER THAT EVENTUALLY YOU WILL DO ALL THINGS HUMAN, INCLUDING THE ACTS YOU MIGHT THINK OF AS REPUGNANT OR APPALLING. OFTEN, THE PERCEPTION OF ACTS HAVING SUCH INTERPRETATION COMES AFTER THE FACT, WHEN THE DEEDS HAVE BEEN DONE AND THE CONSEQUENCES DEALT WITH.

LET US EXPAND UPON THAT SUBJECT: A FRAGMENT WHO HAS BEEN A TORTURER IS LIKELY TO HAVE A GREATER HORROR OF TORTURE THAN THOSE WHO HAVE NOT BEEN, FOR THE FORMER TORTURER WILL HAVE THE KARMIC VALIDATION THAT RENDERS SUCH AN ACT UN-ACCEPTABLE TO THE FRAGMENT. WE ARE AWARE OF A FRAGMENT WITH A DEEP-SEATED AND "IRRATIONAL" DREAD OF ASSASSINATION, WHICH OFTEN MAKES IT DIF-FICULT FOR THE FRAGMENT TO APPEAR IN PUBLIC; THIS

FRAGMENT NOT SO LONG AGO WAS A HIGH-RANKING COURT OFFICIAL AND CLOSE FRIEND OF THE REIGNING MONARCH WHO JOINED A GROUP OF CONSPIRATORS AND, BEING THE FRIEND OF THE MONARCH AND THEREFORE MORE ABLE TO APPROACH HIM WITHOUT SUSPICION OR QUESTIONING BY THE MONARCH'S GUARDS, BECAME HIS ASSASSIN. ALTHOUGH THIS OCCURRED THREE LIFETIMES AGO, THE MEMORY IS STRONG. SINCE THE KARMIC RIBBON HAS NOT YET BEEN BURNED—THESE TWO FRAGMENTS HAVE NOT BEEN EXTANT ON THE PHYSICAL PLANE AT THE SAME TIME SINCE THE EVENT DESCRIBED—THE HORROR OF THE ACT REMAINS UNALTERED IN THE FRAGMENT'S MIND. UNTIL THE KARMIC RIBBON IS BURNED, THIS FRAGMENT IS LIKELY TO HAVE THIS ABIDING DREAD. OF COURSE, HE COULD CHOOSE TO CONFRONT THE MEMORY OF THE ACT AND RECOGNIZE HIS FEAR FOR WHAT IT IS, WHICH WOULD BE A GREAT ACT OF FOCUS AND GROWTH, BUT IT WOULD ALSO MEAN DEALING WITH EXPERIENCES THAT ARE STILL PRESENT IN HIS PERCEPTIONS. MOST FRAGMENTS SHY AWAY FROM SUCH SELF-DISCOVERY BECAUSE THE PROCESS IS GENERALLY PAINFUL.

HOW EACH FRAGMENT CHOOSES TO CONDUCT A LIFETIME WILL SHAPE THE LESSONS LEARNED DURING THAT LIFETIME. THE OVERLEAVES ARE ONLY THE BEGINNING, AND WITHIN THEIR FRAMEWORK, OR THE FRAMEWORK OF THE FALSE PERSONALITY, ALMOST ANY ACTS CAN BE POSSIBLE, DEPENDING ON THE CHOICES THAT THE FRAGMENT MAKES. WHATEVER THE LESSONS ARE, THE EXPERIENCES OF THE LIFETIME ARE VALID, AND THE LESSONS LEARNED REMAIN WITH THE FRAGMENT THROUGH ALL LIVES FROM THAT TIME ON. WHETHER OR NOT THE "PERSONALITY" REMEMBERS, THE ESSENCE DOES.

THERE ARE FRAGMENTS WHOSE OVERLEAVES PERMIT GREATER ACCESS TO MEMORY THAN OTHERS. THAT IS PART OF THE CHOICES MADE IN TERMS OF PLANNING THE COURSE OF A LIFE. IT IS ALSO VERY MUCH INFLUENCED BY THE CULTURE WHERE THE FRAGMENT LIVES. IN CULTURES WHERE REINCARNATION IS REGARDED AS "PROP-

ER" AND "ORDINARY", THE ACCESS TO THE PAST IS MORE EASILY DEVELOPED AND VALIDATED THAN IN THOSE CULTURES—SUCH AS YOUR OWN—THAT GENERALLY DENY THE POSSIBLITY OF REINCARNATION. EVEN THOSE WHO CHOOSE TO ACCEPT THE "REALITY" OF REINCARNATION IN A SOCIETY SUCH AS THIS ONE ARE APT TO ENCOUNTER DERISION OR HOSTILITY FROM OTHERS.

IT IS NOT AMISS TO BE AWARE OF WHAT THE SOCIETY AND THE CULTURE THINKS OF AS "NORMAL" IN ORDER TO ASSESS THE DEGREE OF DIFFICULTY ONE MIGHT ENCOUNTER IF ONE CHOOSES TO EXPLORE CONCEPTS NOT CONSIDERED APPLICABLE TO THE MAIN PHILOSOPHIES OF THE CULTURE. FOR THOSE WHO ARE WILLING TO MAKE THIS EVALUATION, THERE CAN BE MORE POTENTIAL FOR PROGRESS AND GROWTH WITHOUT THE DISTRESS OF SOCIETAL RESISTANCE THAT OFTEN MARKS SUCH VENTURES INTO THE REALMS OF THE ARCANE. THAT IS NOT TO SAY THAT ALL FRAGMENTS MIGHT THEREFORE "IMPROVE" IF THEY CHOOSE TO ACT AGAINST THE CULTURAL "NORMS"; WE MERELY WISH TO POINT OUT THAT THE EXPERIENCE OF A LIFE LIVED "AGAINST THE CURRENT" IS OFTEN SIGNIFICANTLY DIFFERENT THAN ONE LIVED WITHIN THE CULTURAL AND SOCIETAL "NORMS", AND THAT PART OF THE LESSON OF THAT LIFE, NO MATTER WHAT THE OVERLEAVES, LIFE TASK, OR ANY OTHER CONSIDERATIONS MAY BE, WILL REFLECT THE EXPERIENCE OF MOVING COUNTER TO THE GENERAL PERCEPTIONS OF THE CULTURE.

THOSE WHO CHOOSE TO EXPLORE THEIR PAST LIVES OFTEN DISCOVER THAT THIS ENTAILS DEALING WITH THE PRESENT LIFE AS WELL, WHICH CAN LEAD TO GENUINE PROGRESS WHEN THERE IS RECOGNITION. TO DEAL WITH THE TRUE PERSONALITY—THAT IS, THE MANIFESTATION OF THE OVERLEAVES—THE FRAGMENT MIGHT WISH TO ASSESS THE NEGATIVE POLES OF THE OVERLEAVES, FOR THAT IS THE SOURCE NOT ONLY OF ALL MAYA AND DISTORTION, IT IS THE MEANS BY WHICH FEAR WORKS IN THE LIFE AND IN THE WORLD.

LET US SAY THAT ANY CONFIRMATION OF THE NEGA-

TIVE POLES OF THE OVERLEAVES AND/OR CHIEF FEATURE OF NECESSITY REQUIRES THE MOST STALWART COURAGE, IN THAT THE CHIEF FEATURE AND NEGATIVE POLES BY DEFINITION HAVE DIRECT ACCESS TO ALL NEGATIVE POLES AS WELL AS "POWER" OVER THEM. WHILE WE AGREE THAT EXTERNAL CONDITIONS MAY OR MAY NOT BE ADVANTAGEOUS TO ALL FRAGMENTS, THE PERCEPTIONS OF SUCH CONDITIONS ARE DIRECTLY RELATED TO THE DEGREE IN WHICH THE CHIEF FEATURES HAS DOMINANCE OVER ALL THE OTHER OVERLEAVES, AND BY WHICH IT CAN BRING ABOUT ACTION AND PERCEPTION FROM THE NEGATIVE RATHER THAN POSITIVE POLARITIES. IN OTHER WORDS, WHEN THE NEGATIVE POLES OF THE OVERLEAVES ARE IN OPERATION, SO IS THE CHIEF FEATURE, NO MATTER HOW MUCH IT MAY APPEAR OTHERWISE.

WE DO NOT MEAN TO DISCOURAGE ANY FRAGMENT FROM RECOGNITION OF THE MACHINATIONS OF THE CHIEF FEATURE, BUT WE WOULD THINK THAT IT IS OF INTEREST TO NOTE THAT SUCH SELF-EXPLORATION REQUIRES DETERMINATION AND FOCUS. WHILE IT IS PHYSICALLY LESS HAZARDOUS, IT IS PSYCHOLOGICALLY MORE HARROWING TO CONFRONT THE CHIEF FEATURE THAN TO CONFRONT A DOZEN HIGH-SPEED ARMORED TANKS, FOR CHIEF FEATURE TURNS ALL THAT IT TOUCHES TO DREAD: A HIGH-SPEED ARMORED TANK, THOUGH CERTAINLY DANGEROUS, IS JUST A HIGH-SPEED ARMORED TANK.

IN A SENSE, ALL FRAGMENTS ON THE PHYSICAL PLANE HAVE "SIGNED UP" FOR VARYING DEGREES OF DIFFICULTIES. THOSE ARE PART OF THE LESSONS GAINED THROUGH LIFE EXPERIENCES ON THE PHYSICAL PLANE, AND MANY OF THEM CAN BE FOUND NOWHERE ELSE. IF YOU HAD NOT CHOSEN TO DEAL WITH PHYSICAL-PLANE DIFFICULTIES, YOU WOULD NOT BE THERE. DIFFICULT TIMES ARE INTRINSIC TO GROWTH AND WE WOULD HAVE TO SAY THAT IF "ALL" YOU DO IN A LIFE IS IDENTIFY THE DISTORTIONS AND LIES OF THE CHIEF FEATURE, YOU WILL HAVE ACCOMPLISHED MORE THAN OVER NINETY-SEVEN PERCENT OF THOSE FRAGMENTS INCARNATE UPON THE PHYSICAL PLANE ANYWHERE IN THE PHYSICAL UNIVERSE.

THIS DOES NOT MEAN THAT THE TASK IS OVERWHELM-
ING OR IMPOSSIBLE, ONLY THAT IT IS DAUNTING. THERE
ARE THOUSANDS OF FRAGMENTS WHO UNDERTAKE THE
RECOGNITION WITH A GOOD DEGREE OF SUCCESS EVERY
YEAR. BUT AGAIN, WE WOULD WISH TO POINT OUT THAT
IT IS THE NATURE OF THE CHIEF FEATURE TO EMPLOY
EVERY ASPECT OF NEGATIVITY THAT THE FRAGMENT POS-
SESSES IN ORDER TO REMAIN IN CHARGE. TO SEE THIS,
TO UNDERSTAND THE FAR-REACHING CONSEQUENCES,
REQUIRES STEADFAST PURPOSE AND A DEDICATION TO
SELF-DISCOVERY THAT NOT ALL FRAGMENTS ARE WILL-
ING OR ABLE TO APPROACH. THERE IS ABSOLUTELY NO
"ERROR" IN THIS. MOST FRAGMENTS ARE WILLING TO
LET THE CHIEF FEATURE CONTINUE TO "RUN THINGS" BE-
CAUSE THERE ARE OTHER DIFFICULTIES IN THE LIFE THAT
DEMAND THE ATTENTION AND ENERGY OF THE FRAG-
MENT'S ESSENCE AND OVERLEAVES, AS WELL AS REQUIR-
ING TIME AND RESOURCES IN A MANNER THAT MIGHT BE
PERCEIVED AS PREEMPTORY. USING THE "BATTLE" WITH
THE CHIEF FEATURE AS AN EXCUSE TO AVOID AGREE-
MENTS, MONADS AND OTHER SUCH ASPECTS OF LIFE,
WHILE OF GREATER CURIOSITY THAN MOST SUCH EX-
CUSES, ARE STILL EXCUSES AND ONES THAT CAN SERVE
TO INTERRUPT THE WORK ON THE LIFE TASK.

OF COURSE, THIS DOES NOT SAY THAT SUCH ASPIRA-
TIONS ARE NOT USEFUL, OR THAT ATTEMPTS TO EXTIN-
GUISH THE CHIEF FEATURE ARE FUTILE. WE DID NOT SAY
THAT AND WE DID NOT IMPLY IT. WE ARE SEEKING ONLY
TO MAKE IT CLEAR TO ALL HERE GATHERED THAT WHEN
THE CHIEF FEATURE IS THE TARGET, THERE ARE MANY,
MANY OBSTACLES TO BE OVERCOME, INCLUDING EVERY
NEGATIVE POLE OF THE OVERLEAVES, FOR THOSE ARE
THE "KEY" TO THE STRANGLEHOLD OF THE CHIEF FEA-
TURE. WE OFFER A DISINTERESTED WARNING TO THOSE
FRAGMENTS CONSIDERING A CAMPAIGN AGAINST THE
CHIEF FEATURE THAT SUCH PROJECTS ARE NOT AC-
COMPLISHED QUICKLY OR EASILY, AND THERE IS NO
SHORTCUT TO THE GOAL.

VALIDATION OF LESSONS *AS THEY ARE EXPERIENCED* IS
OFTEN THE MOST SUCCESSFUL MEANS OF RECOGNIZING

PROGRESS AND EVOLUTION WITHIN THE LIFE. TO BE WILL-
ING TO ACCEPT THE LESSON DURING THE EXPERIENCE,
WHILE RARE, IS VERY GOOD WORK INDEED. THAT IS NOT
TO SAY THAT THERE IS SOME "FAULT" IF A FRAGMENT
FAILS TO DO THIS: MOST FRAGMENTS EXTANT UPON THE
PHYSICAL PLANE DO NOT CHOOSE SUCH THINGS. MOST
FRAGMENTS EXTANT UPON THE PHYSICAL PLANE ARE
CAUGHT UP IN THE PERSONAL AND WORLD TRUTHS OF
THEIR DAILY LIVES, AND THERE IS LITTLE INCLINATION
OR DESIRE TO "TAKE ON" ANOTHER LEVEL OF ACTIVITY.
HOWEVER, WHEN A FRAGMENT IS ABLE TO VALIDATE A
LESSON WHILE THE LESSON IS OCCURRING, RATHER THAN
PERCEIVING IT IN RETROSPECT, THE LESSON BRINGS TO
BEAR MORE POWERFUL INSIGHTS THAN AT OTHER TIMES.

WE WOULD WISH TO SAY THAT EVERY LIFE HAD VALUE,
EVERY EXPERIENCE HAS MERIT. THAT DOES NOT MEAN
THAT ANY FRAGMENT IS "REQUIRED" TO "LOOK FOR THE
SILVER LINING".THAT WOULD NOT BE A VALIDATION;
MORE LIKELY IT WOULD BE THE CHIEF FEATURE IN YET
ANOTHER OF ITS SEDUCTIVE DISGUISES, MAKING FEAR
MORE PALATABLE THAN LOVE. SOME EXPERIENCES ARE
HIDEOUS. THERE IS NO "SILVER LINING" IN MOST KARMA-
RELATED DISASTERS, SUCH AS BEING BETRAYED BY AN
AMBITIOUS RELATIVE AND, BECAUSE OF THAT, SEN-
TENCED TO AN OAR IN A ROMAN BIREME, AS HAPPENED
TO ONE OF THE FRAGMENTS NOW ACTIVE IN OUR LITTLE
GROUP. LET US POINT OUT THAT SUCH TRAGEDIES HAPPEN
WITH FAIRLY GREAT REGULARITY, AND ONLY WHEN THE
PLANET HAS EVOLVED TO LATE-MATURE AND OLD-SOUL
LEVELS WILL THIS TEND TO DECREASE. THAT DOES NOT
MEAN IT WILL OF NECESSITY DISAPPEAR ENTIRELY, BUT
THAT IT WILL NOT BE THE RELATIVELY COMMON OCCUR-
RENCE THAT IT IS AT THIS TIME IN YOUR EVOLUTION.

CONSIDER, IF YOU WILL, THE PLIGHT OF THREE WOMEN,
ALL SISTERS IN THE SAME CHARITABLE SOCIETY, LIVING
IN SOUTH AMERICA, WHO JOINED A GROUP OF OTHER
WOMEN WHO WERE GOOD CATHOLIC WOMEN AND THERE-
FORE DESIROUS OF AIDING THE RELATIVES OF FRIENDS
WHO HAD BEEN "DETAINED" BY THE AUTHORITIES. THEY

HAD NO ANTIGOVERNMENTAL SENTIMENTS, NO POLITI-
CAL MOTIVES IN WHAT THEY DID. THEIR TROUBLE BEGAN
WHEN THEY ATTEMPTED TO LOCATE THE MISSING RELA-
TIVES OF FRIENDS AND DISCOVERED TO THEIR DISMAY
THAT THERE WERE NO RECORDS OF WHERE OR WHY THESE
FRAGMENTS HAD BEEN INCARCERATED. ON THE ADVICE
OF THEIR PRIEST, THEY PERSEVERED. WARNED BY THE
POLICE THAT HIS WIFE WAS AIDING DANGEROUS REV-
OLUTIONARIES, THE HUSBAND OF ONE OF THESE WOMEN
SUPPLIED ALL THE EVIDENCE THE AUTHORITIES WANTED
IN REGARD TO HIS WIFE AND HER TWO FRIENDS,
EXAGGERATING THEIR PURPOSE AND THEIR MOTIVATIONS
SO THAT NO SUSPICION MIGHT FALL UPON HIM. THE
THREE WOMEN "DISAPPEARED" OVER FOUR YEARS AGO.
THERE IS NO "SILVER LINING" TO THEIR VERY REAL
PLIGHT. ONE HAS THE GREAT MISFORTUNE TO BE STILL
ALIVE, THOUGH SHE WOULD BE DIAGNOSED AS INSANE,
WHICH WE AGREE IS VALID. THE HUSBAND IN QUESTION
NOW HAS A KARMIC RIBBON TO BURN WITH EACH OF
THESE WOMEN. HAD THE WOMEN BEEN MORE EDUCATED
OR MORE SOCIALLY "AWARE" THEY MIGHT NOT HAVE
TAKEN THE ACTION THEY DID, BUT THEIR NAÏVETÉ DOES
NOT IN ANY WAY MITIGATE THE RESPONSIBILITY OF THE
HUSBAND'S BETRAYAL.

IT IS NOT INAPPROPRIATE FOR THOSE FRAGMENTS
EVALUATING THEIR OPTIONS FOR CHOICE TO BE AWARE
THAT EACH AND EVERY ONE OF YOU IS RESPONSIBLE FOR
YOUR ACTIONS; YOU ARE ACCOUNTABLE TO YOURSELF
AND FOR YOURSELF. BEFORE YOU EVOLVE FROM YOUR
INCARNATIONS ON THE PHYSICAL PLANE, ALL RIBBONS
WILL BE BURNED. IT DOES NOT MATTER TO ESSENCE HOW
LONG SUCH EVOLUTION TAKES, OR THE CIRCUMSTANCES
UNDER WHICH THE EVOLUTION OCCURS. YOU, AS THE
SUM TOTAL OF ALL YOUR EXPERIENCES AND KNOWL-
EDGE, HAVE ACCESS TO LESSONS ALREADY LEARNED,
SHOULD YOU CHOOSE TO AVAIL YOURSELF OF THEM, BUT
OF COURSE, NO ONE OF YOU IS "REQUIRED" TO DO SO.

Chapter 4

"SAMUEL AND LOUISE FISHER"

Again, these are not real names; their occupations have been shifted to related fields rather than their actual areas of work. They have been in the Michael group for over five years and were introduced by a Mature Priest who works with Sam, but who is no longer active in the group himself. They were high-school sweethearts, have been married for twenty-six years, have three children. Sam (in *MORE MESSAGES FROM MICHAEL*, Sam is part of the composite character Henry Ingvesson) is the head of his department at a Bay Area college; Louise (in *MORE MESSAGES FROM MICHAEL*, she is part of both Kim Ingvesson and Alex Squire) is a career guidance counselor.

"I think that what has made the biggest difference in my life where the Michael teaching is concerned," says Louise, "is what it has taught me about chief feature. I knew for years that there was always something getting in my way, something that I couldn't see, but I sensed was interfering with my life. I had no idea what it was, but I wanted to find out, so I could do something about it." She is a slender woman, and when she slumps to indicate the discouragement she felt, she looks a bit more angular than usual. "And, at that time, I wasn't doing work on careers yet, I was just working as a receptionist in one of the large local medical clinics. In a way that fed into my chief feature—self-deprecation—because there was always so much pressure on us, and often those of us who weren't 'real' medical personnel took the brunt of it. Well, self-dep laps that up, and that underlying fear of inadequacy runs amok. And until I quit that job—and when I quit, I was thoroughly convinced I could never find anything better—I never realized the hold all the negativity had over me. Michael had warned me several times that I had become trapped in the hold of the chief feature, but I didn't see it. Oh, I knew that the stress was undermining my confidence, but I didn't understand how much else was going on."

Sam nods as she speaks. "I don't have self-dep, but I know the feeling, though I find it harder to deal with the secondary chief feature than I do the primary. It wasn't always the case, but now I'm starting to look at what the secondary does to me, and I can't say I like it a lot."

IN AREAS OF PERSONAL RELATIONSHIPS, WE WOULD HAVE TO SAY THAT THE SECONDARY CHIEF FEATURE, WHICH INFLUENCES THE ATTITUDE AS THE PRIMARY INFLUENCES THE GOAL, IS MORE OFTEN THE CULPRIT THAN IS THE PRIMARY. HOWEVER, WHERE THE SECONDARY IS MOST STRONGLY APPARENT, THERE IS ALMOST A REVERSAL OF ORDER, IN THAT THE PRIMARY FUNCTIONS MORE AS THE SECONDARY AND THE SECONDARY AS THE PRIMARY. WHAT IS CRUCIAL HERE IS THE PERCEPTION THAT IT IS THE ATTITUDE, NOT THE GOAL, THAT DETERMINES THE FOCUS OF THE SECONDARY CHIEF FEATURE. WE WOULD URGE ALL FRAGMENTS TO BE AWARE THAT THE SECONDARY CHIEF FEATURE, WHILE OFTEN FAR LESS OBVIOUS IN ITS MACHINATIONS, HAS AS DISTORTING AN EFFECT ON THE ATTITUDE AS THE PRIMARY CHIEF FEATURE HAS ON THE GOAL. WE CAN ILLUSTRATE IN THE FOLLOWING WAY: A FIRST-LEVEL OLD SCHOLAR IN THE PASSION MODE WITH A GOAL OF DOMINANCE, A REALIST IN THE INTELLECTUAL PART OF EMOTIONAL CENTER WITH A PRIMARY CHIEF FEATURE OF ARROGANCE AND A SECONDARY CHIEF FEATURE OF GREED FIXATED ON EXPERIENCE IS GOING TO HAVE THE UNDERLYING FEAR OF VULNERABILTY (ARROGANCE) IN REGARD TO THE GOAL (DOMINANCE), WHICH WILL TEND TO MAKE THE FRAGMENT APPEAR SHY AND HARD TO KNOW, SINCE THAT IS MOST

OFTEN THE INTERACTION OF DOMINANCE/ARROGANCE. ON THE RELATIONAL AREA, HOWEVER, THE REALIST, WHICH PERMITS THE FRAGMENT TO PERCEIVE ALL ASPECTS OF A SITUATION, IS DISTORTED BY GREED FIXATED ON EXPERIENCE. SINCE THE UNDERLYING FEAR OF GREED IS THE FEAR OF LACK OR WANT, THE FRAGMENT WILL ALWAYS FEEL THAT HE HAS NOT HAD ENOUGH EXPERIENCE, AND THEREFORE WILL CONSTANTLY BE ASSESSING AND EVALUATING EVERY PERSONAL RELATIONSHIP IN HIS LIFE. THE ARROGANCE CERTAINLY DOES NOT HAVE THIS ASPECT, BUT IN THE SECONDARY CHIEF FEATURE HERE, THERE IS MUCH TO BE LEARNED, AND THERE ARE ASPECTS OF THIS TRUE PERSONALITY THAT WILL MAKE SUSTAINED PERSONAL RELATIONSHIPS MORE THAN USUALLY DIFFICULT, SINCE THE FRAGMENT WILL CONTINUALLY HANKER AFTER NEW EXPERIENCES. ONLY WHEN FRAGMENTS HAVE TRULY FACED THE LIES OF THE PRIMARY CHIEF FEATURE IS THE SMOKE SCREEN LIFTED ENOUGH TO PERMIT AN APPROACH TO THE SECONDARY CHIEF FEATURE, AND ALMOST ONLY THOSE FRAGMENTS WHO HAVE SUCCESSFULLY TRANSITED THE FOURTH INTERNAL MONAD ARE SUFFICIENTLY FREE OF FALSE PERSONALITY TO BE ABLE TO PERCEIVE THE LIES OF BOTH CHIEF FEATURES.

"Michael told me that because I was learning more about how my primary and secondary chief features worked, I had finally validated the transit of the infamous Fourth Monad," Sam explains. "I still don't see it very clearly—chief feature at work again, both of 'em."

"The entire question of the Fourth Monad has been very important to us, and to almost everyone in the group, I think," says Louise. "At least half the group members got involved in the teaching about the time they entered the Fourth Monad, or were on the verge of it. Some of those who've left have gone because they don't really want to face completion of the Fourth Monad. And about twenty percent of the personal-agenda questions we ask have bearing on the Fourth Monad, I'd guess."

"That sounds about right," agrees Sam. "There was a time when about eighty percent of my questions were about the Fourth Monad, but that was while I was still trying to get through it."

"For a while both of us were having a rough time." Louise exchanges a quick, shy glance with Sam. "Fenella asked a very good question about anger that helped me to understand what was going on, not only with me but also with others who were caught up in anger."

THERE ARE LEVELS OF ANGER. BASICALLY AND MOST "ESSENTIALLY", WHEN THE PHYSICAL BODY IS THREATENED, ANGER IS THE MEANS BY WHICH THE BODY PREPARES TO DEFEND ITSELF AGAINST IMMINENT PHYSICAL HARM. SECONDARILY, ANGER GROWS IN CHILDREN OUT OF FRUSTRATION AND FEAR. WE ARE HOPEFUL THAT MOST OF YOU HERE GATHERED REALIZE BY NOW THE NEGATIVE TRIGGER OF FEAR. IN MORE "ADULT" CIRCUMSTANCES ANGER IS THE RESULT OF DISAPPOINTMENT. CERTAINLY THAT DISAPPOINTMENT CAN RANGE OVER A WIDE TERRITORY FROM ILL MANNERS TO OUTRAGE. HOWEVER, WHILE IT IS TRULY A "LEGITIMATE" FEELING, IT IS ALSO MOST OFTEN A STRONG HOLD OF CHIEF FEATURE, AND WORDS SPOKEN IN ANGER THAT ARE MOST LIKELY TO COME FROM CHIEF FEATURE THAN FROM ESSENCE. THAT IS NOT TO SAY THAT YOU ARE NOT FREE TO CHOOSE TO SPEAK, FOR, OF COURSE, ALL IS CHOSEN, BUT THERE IS A QUESTION OF DEGREE AND HOW MANY BRIDGES YOU WANT BURNED. SINCE YOU HAVE THE LEISURE FOR THIS ASSESSMENT, YOU MIGHT WISH TO CONSIDER THE IMPACT OF ANGER. IT IS ALSO NOT AMISS TO POINT OUT TO THE FRAGMENT IN QUESTION THAT THE SOONER A RESOLUTION IS REACHED, THE LESS ANGER IS LIKELY TO BE EXPENDED. FOR THOSE FRAGMENTS WHO CHOOSE TO "NURTURE" ANGER, THERE IS OFTEN LITTLE THAT CAN BE DONE FOR THEM, FOR THAT ALLEGIANCE TO ANGER CREATES A BARRIER THAT FEW CAN PENETRATE, AND ONLY THEN WITH THE MOST PERSISTENT EFFORTS WITH FEW OR LITTLE REWARDS. THE CLAIM THAT ANGER GIVES STRENGTH IS, OF

COURSE, INVALID, AND THOSE WHO SEEK RAGE AS A SUB-
STITUTE FOR PASSION OF ANY NATURE WHATEVER HAVE
ACCEPTED THE MOST DEVASTATING LIE OF THE CHIEF
FEATURE, WHICH LEADS TO MANY SORTS OF DESTRUC-
TION.

"What I found very interesting along those lines," says
Sam, "was what Michael had to say about the seven levels
of love and the seven levels of conflict. It helped me understand not only how things get out of hand but how we—
people, fragments—get closer to each other."

THERE ARE, OF COURSE, SEVEN LEVELS OF CONFLICT,
AND THEY ARE: ONE: DISAGREEMENT. WHEN TWO OR
MORE FRAGMENTS ARE DEALING WITH MINOR CONFLICT-
ING ISSUES, NOT PRIMARILY PERSONAL IN NATURE, RES-
OLUTION CAN BE ACHIEVED BY FINDING OUT ON WHICH
POINT OR POINTS THEY DISAGREE, DEFINING A MUTUALLY
ACCEPTABLE GOAL THEY ARE WORKING TOWARD, AND
DISSOLVING OR RESOLVING THE POINTS OF DISAGREE-
MENT BASED ON THE GOAL. TWO: AGGRAVATION. PRO-
LONGED DISPUTES BETWEEN INDIVIDUAL FRAGMENTS
SUCH AS CONTINUING COMPETITION OR "GRUDGE
MATCHES" ARE THE SECOND LEVEL OF CONFLICT. WHAT
HAS TO BE DETERMINED IN INSTANCES OF THIS TYPE IS
WHAT THE BASIC ISSUE OF THE GRUDGE IS, AND WHAT IT
WOULD TAKE FOR THE INVOLVED PARTIES TO BE WILLING
TO SET THE DISPUTE ASIDE; THERE IS A CERTAIN ASPECT
OF A BOARD GAME ABOUT THIS LEVEL ("IF I GIVE YOU
MY HOTELS ON PARK PLACE, WILL THAT DO IT?"). THE
THIRD LEVEL IS CIVIL DISPUTE. THIS IS FORMALIZED, BY
WHICH WE MEAN IT USES THE COURTS. UNDERSTANDING
IS ACHIEVED THROUGH INTERMEDIARIES, SINCE THE CON-
FLICTED PARTIES ARE NO LONGER IN A POSITION TO DEAL
DIRECTLY. THE INTERMEDIARIES ARE MOST OFTEN AT-
TORNEYS, ADVOCATES, MAGISTRATES, OR SIMILAR OF-
FICERS. AND SINCE THE ARGUMENTS CAN NO LONGER BE
RESOLVED TO MUTUAL SATISFACTION, WHAT IS OFFERED
IN ITS PLACE IS COMPENSATION. FOUR: CRIMINAL DIS-

PUTES. AGAIN, THESE CONFLICTS ARE SETTLED IN THE COURTS, IN WHICH THE FRAGMENT WRONGED IS CONSIDERED TO BE "THE PEOPLE" BECAUSE THE "SOCIAL INSULT" HAS PASSED BEYOND ACCEPTABLE SOCIAL CONDUCT, EVEN UNDER STRESS. THE MORE VIOLENT THE ACTION OF THE CONFLICT, THE MORE IMPOSING THE PROCESS OF THE COURT, EXCEPT WHEN SOCIAL POSITION IS A FACTOR, AND IN SUCH CASES THE PROCESS OF THE COURT IS DETERMINED MORE BY THE DEGREE OF SOCIETAL "PULL" BROUGHT TO BEAR IN THE CONFLICT. BEYOND CRIMINAL DISPUTES ARE REGIONAL DISPUTES. HERE THE COURTS ARE NO LONGER CONSIDERED APPROPRIATE TO RESOLVE THE CONFLICTS. MINOR VERSIONS: THE HATFIELD/ MCCOY FEUD. MAJOR VERSIONS: THE GUELPHS AND GHIBELINES WHOSE FEUD LASTED FOR MORE THAN FIVE GENERATIONS AND INVOLVED SEVERAL CITY-STATES BEFORE IT WAS CONCLUDED. IN GENERAL, THESE CONFLICTS HAVE NO IMMEDIATE SOLUTION IN LAW BECAUSE THE NATURE OF THE DISPUTE TRANSCENDS THE SOLUTIONS OF THE LAW WHERE LAWS ARE ADDRESSED TO INDIVIDUAL ACTS, NOT CONTINUING CONFLICTS. RESOLUTION IS ACHIEVED THROUGH SYMBOLIC OR TOTEMIC GESTURES AND SOME FORM OF COMPENSATORY SACRIFICE. THE GENERAL POPULATION IS OFTEN INDIRECTLY CONCERNED IN THIS LEVEL OF CONFLICT, AND IT WILL OFTEN HAVE A PROLONGED IMPACT ON SOCIETAL CODES. LEVEL SIX IS CALLED WAR, AND IT IS ADJUDICATED THROUGH NEGOTIATION AND REPARATION OF A "DIPLOMATIC" NATURE: THIS CAN BE FINANCIAL, SOCIAL, MILITARY, AND/OR SACRIFICIAL. THE CONFLICT ITSELF AND ITS AFTERMATH WILL IMPINGE ON THOSE FRAGMENTS NEVER DIRECTLY INVOLVED IN THE CONFLICT, AND THE IMPACT WILL EXTEND WELL BEYOND THE ACTUAL DURATION OF THE WAR ITSELF. TO TELL WHO REALLY WON A WAR, SINCE THIS IS OFTEN IN DOUBT, DETERMINE WHO PAYS "BLOOD MONEY" TO WHOM. WILLINGNESS TO ACCEPT THE GESTURE ACKNOWLEDGES THE VALIDITY OF THE DEBT. THE NATURE OF WAR IS, OF COURSE, NEGATIVE, AND THE NEGATIVITY CAN LAST FOR GENERATIONS AND TOUCH

FRAGMENTS FAR REMOVED FROM THE EVENTS. AT LEVEL SEVEN THERE IS ANNIHILATION. THE SOLUTION TO THE WHOLE DESTRUCTION OF THE ENVIRONMENT IS THE SELECTION OF THE NEW SPECIES FOR THE FRAGMENTS DEPRIVED OF "HOME" TO INHABIT. ALTHOUGH PLANETARY DESTRUCTIONS OR COLLAPSE OF THE ENVIRONMENT IS RELATIVELY COMMON—ROUGHLY THIRTY PERCENT OF ALL ENSOULED SPECIES DO NOT FINISH THEIR REINCARNATIONS IN THE SAME SPECIES AND IN THE SAME ENVIRONMENT THAT THEY BEGAN—THE DESTRUCTION CAUSED BY ARMED CONFLICT ACCOUNTS FOR A THIRD OF THE DESTRUCTION. IT MIGHT BE OF INTEREST TO KNOW THAT THOSE FRAGMENTS RESPONSIBLE FOR THE DESTRUCTION CHOOSE TO RETURN TO THE WRECKAGE AS LONG AS LIFE IS VIABLE, NO MATTER HOW DIFFICULT SUCH LIVES MIGHT BE. THIS IS NOT A QUESTION OF BEING COMPELLED; IT IS SIMILAR TO PAYING KARMA, IN THAT THE DESTRUCTION WAS CHOICE, AND LIVING WITH THE RAMIFICATIONS OF CHOICE IS THE CLOSEST THING THAT ANY ENSOULED FRAGMENT HAS TO A "PURPOSE" IN LIFE.

"The seven levels of love are much more pleasant," says Sam with an ironic smile.

THERE ARE, OF COURSE, SEVEN LEVELS OF LOVE AS EXPERIENCED ON THE PHYSICAL PLANE. FIRST IS NURTURING. HERE THE EMPHASIS IS ON SURVIVAL, AND IT IS SEEN NOT ONLY IN CREATURES OF REASON BUT IN ALL CREATURES WITH A SENSE OF INDIVIDUAL SURVIVAL. ONE OF THE INDICATIONS OF THE DEGREE OF SPECIES EVOLUTION IS THE DEGREE OF NUTURING AND THE LENGTH OF TIME THE NURTURING IS PROVIDED. THE SECOND LEVEL IS ALLIANCE. THE EMPHASIS IS NOW ON THE FAMILY/TRIBE/CLAN AND HAS A STRONG "US-VERSUS-THEM" FLAVOR TO IT. THOSE WHO ARE "US" ARE OKAY; THOSE WHO ARE "THEM" ARE NOT OKAY. THERE IS A HIGH VALUE PLACED ON OBLIGATION AND DUTY AT THIS LEVEL. THIRD IS RECIPROCITY. FOR THE FIRST TIME THOSE NOT DIRECTLY KNOWN TO THE FRAGMENT DOING THE LOVING ARE IN-

CORPORATED IN THE FEELING. THE SENSE EXTENDS TO THOSE OF A COMPANY OR RELIGION OR NATION AND OFFERS GOODWILL ON THE STRENGTH OF THE MUTUALITY. THE EMPHASIS IS ON INITIATIVE, FOR AT THIS LEVEL EXPERIENCES ARE ACTIVELY SOUGHT AND CONNECTIONS ARE PURSUED BEYOND THE PREVIOUSLY ACCEPTED LIMITS. APPRECIATION IS THE FOURTH LEVEL OF LOVE. THIS PUTS EMPHASIS ON DIVERSITY AND CAN RANGE FROM ACADEMIC PASSIONS FOR THE LIVES OF THE ANCIENT MINOANS TO PEACE CORPS VOLUNTEERS IN BOTSWANA, AND OFTEN SHOWS ITSELF IN THE DELIBERATE SEEKING OUT OF FRIENDS AND ASSOCIATES OF VARIOUS CULTURAL OR SOCIOECONOMIC BACKGROUNDS. THIS LEVEL CAN LEAD TO SERIAL SEXUAL RELATIONSHIPS WHEN OTHER OUTLETS ARE NOT AVAILABLE. THE FIFTH LEVEL IS COMPREHENSION. THIS IS ACCOMPLISHED THROUGH INTERACTION, WHICH IS, OF COURSE, THE AREA OF EMPHASIS. THERE ARE INTENSE INVOLVEMENTS OF MANY SORTS FOR THE PURPOSE OF DISCOVERING THE UNDERLYING "TRUTH" OF OTHERS. THE SIXTH LEVEL IS ALTRUISM. THIS BRINGS COMPASSION FOR THE HUMAN CONDITION ON THE WHOLE AND A GENERAL SENSE OF GOOD FELLOWSHIP WITH ALL FRAGMENTS. THE EMPHASIS HERE IS ON PERSPECTIVE, BOTH PERSONAL AND EXPERIENTIAL. AT THE SEVENTH LEVEL THERE IS AGAPE. THERE IS NO EMPHASIS OF ANY KIND; RATHER, LOVE IS A STATE OF ACCEPTING THE TOTALITY OF FRAGMENTS WITH EMPATHETIC-BUT-DISENGAGED WHOLEHEARTED AFFECTION WHICH IS GIVEN UNCONDITIONALLY. IN TERMS OF EXPRESSING THE VARIOUS LEVELS OF LOVE, MOST FRAGMENTS RISE TO A GENERAL LEVEL THROUGH THE PROGRESS OF A LIFE AND MAY ACHIEVE ONE OR TWO LEVELS HIGHER FOR BRIEF PERIODS DURING INTIMATE RELATIONSHIPS.

"This isn't one of those answers that you just read over and forget," says Sam. "I've looked it through now more than a dozen times, and I'm just starting to appreciate what it says. Not that I have any direct idea of what kind of difference it might make in my life as such.'' He indicates a stack of papers on the desk. "It's certainly not going to help me figure out my semester-end evaluations, though there is a chance that I might try to keep my personal opinions from getting in the way of what I have to say about the way individual faculty members performed.''

"And you might not,'' adds Louise. "The trouble is, these evaluations go against the grain in so many ways.''

"Yes,'' agrees Sam. "Every time I have to do them, I end up procrastinating because I think they're so . . . so unrealistic. I'm not the one the administration ought to be talking to, it's the students, but the administrators don't trust students. Heavenly days! the students might actually say something useful, and then where would we be?'' He stops. "Actually,'' he goes on in a more subdued way. "Michael warns about this kind of sarcasm because they say that it pulls you into the negative poles of the Overleaves.''

"I didn't think that was so when it first came up,'' Louise elaborates. "And there are times when I can't resist getting in a good, witty zinger. Most of the time the opportunity is too tempting. But I think I've begun to see what Michael means about the negativity of that kind of remark. I won't say I've done much in stopping myself, but I'm a little less eager to jump in with a really good one-liner than I used to be.'' She has a very gentle smile, and it isn't easy to imagine her using sarcasm the way she describes.

"Oh, all us Scholars have a little of that in us,'' says Sam. "Some of us have a lot of it.'' He folds his arms. "I don't supress the urge nearly as well as Louise does; recently I've come to think that I ought to—''

"Don't say *ought*,'' Louise interrupts.

"Or *should*. 'Don't *should* on me.' I remember; I remember.'' He opens his hands. "All those 'engage brain before opening mouth' reminders. Louise is conscientious about language, more than I am.''

"Or maybe it's just the self-dep,'' Louise says quietly. "I won't rule out that possibility. It's too easy to tell myself that I really have the self-dep under control and that I'm just too *evolved* for wit and sarcasm, when in fact all I'm doing is finding a better disguise for my chief feature.''

"I don't know if this sounds very enthusiastic about the Michael teaching, but I really am. It's been useful for us, and helpful in a couple of very difficult situations in our lives.'' Sam looks toward a number of framed photographs on the wall. "Our middle child, our daughter, married a man who belongs to one of the stricter Fundamentalist sects, and . . . well, you can imagine the problems we've had. She was very upset that we weren't willing to be converted, and her husband was very apprehensive about us because we didn't share his religious convictions. When he found out how far away from his view of religion we actually are, he wanted Anne to break with us completely. We hoped it wouldn't come to that.''

"Michael gave us some suggestions about ways we might be able to minimize the stress, and it seems to be working so far,'' says Louise. "Knock wood.''

SHOULD YOU WISH TO ENTER INTO THE DEBATE ON THE RELIGIOUS CONVICTIONS, SUCH A STANCE OR CONFRONTATION IS, OF COURSE, YOUR CHOICE, BUT WE WOULD THINK THAT IT MIGHT PROVE A COSTLY ONE IN TERMS OF THE RELATIONSHIP WITH THE FRAGMENT WHO IS NOW ANNE. SINCE SHE IS A WARRIOR, HER SENSE OF LOYALTY IS EXTREMELY IMPORTANT TO HER, AND FORCING THE ISSUE WITH HER AND HER HUSBAND CAN ONLY GIVE HER STRESS, WHICH WOULD NOT TEND TO IMPROVE THE CURRENT IMPASSE, IT WOULD NOT BE AMISS, IF YOU CHOOSE TO DO SO, TO EVALUATE YOUR OWN ATTITUDES AND PERCEPTIONS FIRST, SO THAT IF YOU ARE CHALLENGED ON ANY POINT, YOU WILL BE PREPARED TO MAKE A REASONABLE—AND WE EMPHASIZE *REASONABLE*—RESPONSE TO THE MATTER IN CONTENTION IN SUCH A WAY THAT IT WILL NOT TEND TO ESCALATE THE DISAGREEMENT. BOTH OF YOU MIGHT WANT TO DISCUSS HOW MUCH YOU ARE WILLING TO "ENDURE" IN RELATION TO THIS VERY DETERMINED YOUNG SLAVE'S EFFORTS AT YOUR SALVATION. THERE IS NO SENSE IN MAKING A SYMBOLIC SACRIFICE; IT MIGHT BE MORE WORTHWHILE TO ENCOUR-

AGE COMMUNICATION ON THOSE ISSUES WHERE THERE IS ALREADY AGREEMENT, SUCH AS ADMIRATION FOR THE FRAGMENTS WHO ARE NOW ANNE'S CHILDREN, THE COMPETENCE OF HER HUSBAND'S TRULY EXPERT CARPENTRY AND FINE WOODWORK. THE NATURAL BEAUTY OF THEIR HOME, THE RECENT ACHIEVEMENTS THE FRAGMENT WHO IS NOW ANNE HAS MADE IN HER WORK WITH PHYSICALLY HANDICAPPED CHILDREN. THERE IS NO DISAGREEMENT IN THESE AREAS, AND THE LINES OF COMMUNICATION WHICH HAVE BECOME FEWER AND MORE QUESTIONABLE MAY BE RESTORED ALONG AN "ALTERNATE ROUTE", SHOULD YOU CHOOSE TO TRY ANOTHER APPROACH.

"We've been trying this, and so far we're optimistic," says Sam. "Anne isn't as defensive as she was a year ago, and her husband, while he doesn't approve of us, doesn't disapprove as much as he used to. He considers us 'misled'. If he knew about Michael, he'd probably decide we're damned."

TO ANTICIPATE THE REACTION OF OTHERS, NO MATTER HOW WELL CONSIDERED, STILL COMES UNDER THE HEADING OF SCRIPTING, WHICH, OF COURSE, IS NOT GOOD WORK, IN THAT IT CREATES AN IRONCLAD FORMAT FOR THE CONDUCT OF OTHERS, WHICH THEY ARE NOT LIKELY TO KNOW OF OR TO FOLLOW. IF A FRAGMENT IS DRAWN TO SCRIPTING—AS SAGES AND SCHOLARS ARE—THEN IT IS NOT AMISS, SHOULD YOU CHOOSE TO DO SO, TO CREATE A MULTIPLICITY OF SCRIPTS, SO THAT EVERY ANTICIPATABLE EVENTUALITY HAS BEEN CONSIDERED. THIS HAS THE ADVANTAGE THAT IT DOES NOT LOCK THE FRAGMENT INTO ONE PARTICULAR EXPECTATION OR PERCEPTION, AND AT THE SAME TIME IT MAKES IT POSSIBLE FOR THE FRAGMENT TO INDULGE IN A FALSE SENSE OF PREPAREDNESS THAT CAN DO MUCH TO CALM THE FRAGMENT ENTERING A DIFFICULT SITUATION. OF COURSE, WHEN A FRAGMENT HAS REACHED THE STAGE WHERE NEITHER SCRIPTING NOR MULTIPLE SCRIPTING IS REQUIRED, THEN THERE HAS BEEN VALID PROGRESS AGAINST THE INCURSIONS OF THE CHIEF FEATURE.

"I'm at the multiple-script stage right now," says Louise. "And it does help when I'm really apprehensive. I've even learned to make a game out of it, to dream up the very, very worst script I can think of, and run it all the way through, and then the absolute best script, and run *that* through. By the time I'm finished, I'm about ready for anything, even a sermon from my son-in-law."

"I think one of the things that makes our position here so awkward," Sam continues when Louise does not, "is that he's clearly a wonderful match for Anne. They have a wonderful understanding, and they have done more together then they could possibly have done apart; I'm convinced of it. So when I think about her, I try to keep my opinion of him out of it, because my daughter is happy with him and he treats her splendidly. If I ever thought otherwise, it would mean a complete reevaluation."

"Sam," Louise protests, "I feel the same way, but there's no point in borrowing trouble about him."

"It's hard," he admits. "But the funny thing is that when I keep Michael's suggestions in mind and stick to those areas where we have some common interests and very few conflicts, I like him better, and I think we all get along better. The disagreements don't vanish into the air, but they aren't so obtrusive that we can't work our way around them."

"Our relationship with Anne is a bit cobbled together right now, but it's getting better, and I'm not sure we could have done that without Michael's aid and insights." Louise puts her hand to her forehead. "I was in a real stew about this for weeks before I worked up the nerve to ask about it at a session. It wasn't that I didn't want the help, that's not it. It was more a problem of wondering what the rest of the group would say. You'd think by now I would have outgrown that, but it's still present in me."

"It does take time to feel trusting enough to ask the questions that are really important. But increasingly that's what's happening in the group, and the answers are becoming more comprehensive than they were, say, five years ago." Sam falters. "It's probably the group that's changed, but it's hard to tell. We're used to one another now, and there's a definite sense of balanced energy; I'm not sure I know what that means in terms of the group dynamic.''

"Maybe it doesn't mean much of anything?" Louise suggests, only half-kidding.

"Or it means what we choose to make of it?" Sam adds in the same light, teasing tone, then becomes more serious. "I think it has something to do with what Michael has called forbearance, in that we're all more or less tolerant—no, it's more than that—tolerance implies a superiority on the part of the tolerator, doesn't it?—we're more or less accepting of each other. I suppose when you come right down to it, in a strange way we all like each other. We come from very different backgrounds, and most of us don't have a great deal in common in terms of our specific work, but there are aspects of our lives that really do touch. I feel very close to most of the core group, and even the call-ins, but in a way that isn't the way I feel close to, say, my friends or my colleagues. It's a little bit the way I feel toward my family but without the complex histories.''

"There are times Sam can't forget that he's a teacher," says Louise. "This has been one of them.''

Sam holds up his hands in mock surrender. "I admit it, I admit it.''

THOSE FRAGMENTS CONCERNED WITH INSTRUCTION OF VARIOUS SORTS OFTEN FIND THAT THE PATTERN OF IN- STRUCTION "CARRIES OVER" INTO LESS APPROPRIATE AREAS OF LIFE AND CAN LEAD TO CONFUSION OR OTHER DIFFICULTIES WHERE THE FRAGMENTS ON THE "RECEIV- ING END" OF THE INSTRUCTION ARE NEITHER DESIROUS OF THE INSTRUCTION NOR "EXPECTING" IT. WHILE IN GENERAL THE ESSENCE MOST PRONE TO THIS IS PRIEST, BOTH SCHOLARS AND SAGES ARE NOT IMMUNE TO THE PROBLEM. FOR EXAMPLE, PRIESTS ARE PRONE TO SER- MONIZE TO THE "HIGHER SIGNIFICANCE" OF ALMOST ANYTHING, AND OFTEN THE OCCASIONS THEY CHOOSE ARE NOT TRULY EFFICACIOUS TO THEIR PURPOSE, FOR NOT ALL FRAGMENTS ARE INCLINED TO BE CONCERNED

ABOUT THE COSMIC IMPORTANCE OF—TO SELECT ONE
EXAMPLE KNOWN TO OUR LITTLE GROUP—ANTS AT A PIC-
NIC. SAGES, BEING THE GREATEST COMMUNICATORS AND
THEREFORE THE GREATEST ENTERTAINERS, ARE PRONE
TO OFFER PERFORMANCES AT "THE DROP OF THE HAT",
AND THEREFORE TO PERFORM RATHER THAN EXPERIENCE
THEIR LIVES. THIS NEED TO PERFORM CAN "BACKFIRE"
WHEN IT BECOMES INTRUSIVE INSTEAD OF COMMUNICA-
TIVE. ONE OF THE MOST EXTREME EXAMPLES WE CAN
OFFER IS THAT OF THE TECHNICALLY ACCOMPLISHED
LOVER WHO CAN ORCHESTRATE GREAT PHYSICAL PLEA-
SURE—WHICH IS A VALID EXPERIENCE—FOR A LOVER,
BUT USES THE PERFORMANCE NOT FOR COMMUNICATION
AND BY EXTENSION INTIMACY, BUT FOR THE "APPLAUSE"
OF ACKNOWLEDGED SEXUAL GRATIFICATION. OFTEN
SUCH PERFORMANCES PALL WHEN IT BECOMES APPARENT
TO THE LOVER INVOLVED WITH SUCH A SAGE THAT THE
CONTACT BETWEEN THEM—NO MATTER HOW PHYSI-
CALLY SATISFACTORY—IS LIMITED TO THE PERFOR-
MANCE; GREATER COMMUNICATION IS RENDERED NEXT
TO IMPOSSIBLE BY THE DEMANDS OF THE SAGE FOR THE
APPLAUSE OF THE "AUDIENCE". IN THE CASE OF SCHO-
LARS, THE NEED TO ACCESS AND ANALYZE IS VERY
STRONG, AND WE WOULD HAVE TO SAY THAT IT IS NOT
UNCOMMON FOR SCHOLAR ESSENCES TO USE THE "NAT-
URAL" SCHOLAR DISTANCE, BROUGHT ABOUT BY THE
NEUTRALITY OF THE POLAR POSITION, TO KEEP FROM DI-
RECT PARTICIPATION. SCHOLARS ARE PRONE TO "STAND-
ING BACK" IN ORDER TO EVALUATE A SITUATION, AND
TO LECTURE RATHER THAN ENTER THE RISKY REALMS OF
CONVERSATION AND CONTACT. IT IS NOT UNUSUAL FOR
SCHOLARS TO TRY TO BRING A LESSON TO BEAR IN THE
LIFE, NOT BY PERMITTING THE EXPERIENCE TO BE
REALIZED BUT TO "COMPARE AND CONTRAST" THE CUR-
RENT EXPERIENCE WITH OTHER PREVIOUS EXPERIENCES.
WHILE THIS IN ITSELF IS NOT BAD WORK, IT CAN SERVE
TO BLOCK THE VALIDATION BY MAKING IT APPEAR THAT
THE EXPERIENCE CAN BETTER BE UNDERSTOOD WITHOUT
"ENTANGLEMENT". INSTEAD OF PERMITTING THE EXPERI-

ENCE ITS RANGE AND EXPRESSION, THE SCHOLAR WILL
TEND TO TRY TO TURN THE EXPERIENCE TO A "LECTURE
AND LAB" STUDY FORMAT, WHICH ALSO TENDS TO BLOCK
RECOGNITION AND INTIMACY. BE AWARE THAT NO MAT-
TER HOW "UNTIDY" OR "DISORGANIZED" AN EXPERI-
ENCE MAY BE, IF THAT IS ITS FORM, THEN THIS IS NOT
INAPPROPRIATE.

THAT IS NOT TO SAY THAT OTHER ESSENCES DO NOT
HAVE THEIR OWN SORTS OF BLIND SPOTS AND MISAP-
PREHENSIONS TO CONTEND WITH, OR THAT THESE PAT-
TERNS DO NOT SHOW UP IN MODIFIED VERSIONS IN OTHER
FRAGMENTS AS THE RESULT OF PARENTAL PATTERNING
OR CULTURAL CONDITIONING: WE INTEND ONLY TO POINT
OUT THAT THE ESSENCES OF PRIEST, SAGE, AND SCHOLAR
ARE MORE INCLINED TO VERBAL EXPRESSIONS AS THE
PRIMARY REVELATION OF ESSENCE THAN ARE OTHERS.
PLEASE NOTE THAT THE OPERATIVE WORD HERE IS *IN-
CLINED*. OVERLEAVES AND CULTURE EXERT A TREMEN-
DOUS INFLUENCE ON THE NATURE OF THE PERSONALITY,
BOTH TRUE AND FALSE, AND AS A RESULT, THE MANNER
IN WHICH A FRAGMENT MANIFESTS OVERLEAVES CAN
VARY WIDELY; A MAORI AND A PRUSSIAN, THOUGH THEY
HAVE IDENTICAL OVERLEAVES, ARE MOST LIKELY TO
SEEM DRAMATICALLY DIFFERENT, ONE FROM THE OTHER,
BECAUSE OF CULTURE AND FAMILIAL PATTERNS.

"Michael often cautions and qualifies answers," says
Louise, "and I think the reason is that we're all eager to
find some kind of absolutes. I know when I first got into
the group, I went through a period when I assumed that all
Scholars acted in a very proscribed way; otherwise they
weren't showing their true personality. After a while I
realized that all the Overleaves play a part: I'm first-level
Old, in perseverance mode with a goal of dominance, a
skeptic in the intellectual part of emotional center, primary
chief feature of self-deprecation, a secondary of impatience.
After a while I started to see that all the Overleaves made
a difference, and that no matter what Essence I had, the
rest was as important and valid for this life as being a

Scholar. It's hard to learn that, but once you do, understanding is a bit easier.''

"I'd have to agree about that," says Sam. "And I think that in the last year or so I've become much more relaxed in terms of the Michael teaching. I'm a mid-cycle Mature Scholar, by the way, caution mode, goal of dominance—''

"Two dominances in the same house," Louise reminds both of them, "is a lot of dominance.''

"It is," he agrees. "I'm a spiritualist in the moving part of emotional center with a primary chief feature of stubbornness and a secondary of arrogance. I find that I can see how they work together, how they can gang up on me.''

"That doesn't mean that once you figure out a few things everything else falls into place," Louise says. "It's not that easy, and there have been some hard things along the way. That's when having such a solid group can help almost as much as what Michael has to say.''

"Two years ago when Jessica quit," Sam says a bit awkwardly, "I felt almost as if she had betrayed me. Now, if the Leslies or Milly quit, while I would be disappointed, it wouldn't have the same impact on me." He leans back in his chair. "Not that I want any of them to give it a try to find out. But when and if they decide to stop, well, I'd be more able to let it happen. It's not easy for someone with a goal of dominance to say that, you know, but I'm learning. Slowly." This last word has a feeling of philosophical resignation.

"I have some of the same feeling myself, surprise, surprise," Louise says, "but because of the self-dep, I was convinced that it was because of something I had or had not done that she chose to stop channeling. That's not true, but it took me a while to deal with it.''

Sam reaches out and takes Louise's hand. "Don't be so hard on yourself.''

"I'll try if you'll try," Louise says, leaning against the sofa arm in order to hold Sam's hand more tightly.

"Yeah," Sam goes on reflectively after a pause. "Yeah, it upset all of us, but Louise and I . . . it was a year after Anne's marriage, and on top of that, both of us were in the

final throes of Fourth Monad. Not that we had any means
to stop Jessica. I'd like to think that even if we had, we
would have had the good sense not to interfere. The Leslies
and Milly handled the change-over very well, and when it
comes right down to it, the group kept going pretty steadily.
I think that what bothered me the most, that is personally,
is that I'd love to be able to channel, but I can't; I find it
hard to accept that someone who can would ever want to
stop.''

"I had to convince myself that we didn't drive her away.
She made it very clear that we didn't, but it was several
months before I really believed that.'' Louise looked out
toward the sliding glass doors to the deck beyond. "In a
way I think it helped us. I know that it was the most sensible
thing for Jessica to do, given how she was feeling.''

When Sam speaks this time, he sounds a bit wistful. "It
was fun with Jessica. It's fun with Milly and the Leslies,
don't get me wrong, but when Jessica left, it was almost
as if a special phase had ended.''

"I feel that way whenever a member of the group leaves,
too,'' says Louise. "When Geoff moved south, when Sandra
moved east, it got to me. I wondered each time if we could
keep the same quality of balance we've had in the group.''

"It's not exactly the same from session to session, though
I will say that there is an over-all kind of energy level,''
says Sam. "When a core-group regular leaves, it does take
a while for a new equilibrium to be established. So far we've
been lucky, I think.''

THE QUESTION OF THE DYNAMICS OF OUR LITTLE
GROUP IS NOT A MATTER OF WHAT YOU CALL LUCK.
THOSE OF YOU WHO ARE HERE HAVE GOOD REASON—AG-
REEMENTS, MONADS, AND THE LIKE—TO BE HERE. THAT
BALANCE IS MAINTAINED THROUGH VARIOUS TRANSI-
TIONS REFLECTS THE BASIC COHERENCE OF THE GROUP.
TO PURSUE THE TEACHING IN OUR LITTLE GROUP RE-
QUIRES A DEGREE OF INVESTMENT—BY WHICH WE MEAN
TIME AND ENERGY, NOT FINANCIAL—THAT NOT ALL
FRAGMENTS ARE PREPARED TO MAKE. WHEN THE GROUP

CHOOSES TO EXTEND AN INVITATION, ACCEPTANCE IS NOT REQUIRED. THOSE WHO CHOOSE TO ACCEPT ARE MOST OFTEN WILLING TO EXTEND THEMSELVES ON BEHALF OF THE GROUP. SUCH WILLINGNESS IS HARDLY LIMITED TO ARCANE STUDIES, BUT IN THIS INSTANCE IT IS PRESENT IN ALL FRAGMENTS HERE GATHERED. THOSE WHO ARE AT A GEOGRAPHICAL DISTANCE ARE NOT AT "FAULT" BECAUSE THEY CANNOT ATTEND SESSIONS WITH ANY REGULARITY. THOSE WHO CHOOSE TO ATTEND NO LONGER ARE NOT AT "FAULT" FOR TAKING ANOTHER PATH TO THE GOAL. THOSE WHO CHOOSE TO FOCUS THEIR ATTENTION ON OTHER MATTERS ARE NOT AT "FAULT", EITHER, NO MATTER WHAT THEIR FUNCTION WITHIN THE GROUP.

"That was a wrist-slap," says Sam cheerfully. "I don't know about anyone else, but I earned it."

"We all got something out of that answer," Louise reminds him. "That's one of the things I really like about the group—how much we gain from the questions others ask."

"There are times it feels like theme night," Sam agrees. "You'd think we'd all got together over supper and decided to ask about one subject. We don't. The questions and the quality of the answers grow out of one another."

"When Michael gets caught up in a subject, it's almost as if everything anyone asks relates back to the main issue Michael is discussing." Louise pulls a stray lock of hair out of her eyes. "It's probably because, on some level we can't understand, all questions are the same question and all answers apply."

"When we're advanced enough to figure that out," he says, more wistfully than ever, "I suppose we won't be here any longer."

CHAPTER 5

MICHAEL: ON TIME AND WHAT IT IS FOR

THOSE FRAGMENTS EXTANT ON THE PHYSICAL PLANE, NO MATTER IN WHAT PART OF THE PHYSICAL PLANE, OR IN WHAT FORM, EXPERIENCE THE PASSAGE OF TIME. TIME AS A SEQUENTIAL PHENOMENON CAN ONLY BE EXPERIENCED ON THE PHYSICAL PLANE; IT DOES NOT EXIST AS YOU UNDERSTAND IT ON OTHER PLANES. IF THE SEQUENTIAL NATURE OF TIME ON THE PHYSICAL PLANE DID NOT EXIST, EVOLUTION FOR FRAGMENTS EXTANT ON THE PHYSICAL PLANE WOULD ALSO NOT EXIST.

LET US EXPLICATE: IT IS THE NATURE OF THE PHYSICAL PLANE TO EVOLVE THROUGH PHYSICAL MEANS, WHICH REQUIRES A PASSAGE OF TIME FOR WHAT YOU CALL AGING. ALL FRAGMENTS EXTANT ON THE PHYSICAL PLANE ANY AND EVERYWHERE IN THE PHYSICAL UNIVERSE EXPERIENCE SOME SORT OF AGING, WHICH IS PART OF THE NATURE OF THE PHYSICAL PLANE ITSELF. SOME FRAGMENTS AGE VERY, VERY SLOWLY, SOME EXTREMELY QUICKLY. YOU, ON YOUR PLANET, AGE PROPORTIONALLY FAIRLY QUICKLY. FOR MOST ENSOULED INDEPENDENTLY MOBILE SPECIES, LIFETIMES TEND TO AVERAGE SOMEWHAT LONGER THAN YOURS. WE ARE AWARE OF AT LEAST THREE INDEPENDENTLY MOBILE ENSOULED SPECIES, HOWEVER, WHOSE LIFE SPANS IN TERMS OF YOUR UNDERSTANDING OF MEASURING TIME AVERAGE ABOUT FIVE OF YOUR YEARS. FOR THESE FRAGMENTS, PASSAGE THROUGH THE INTERNATAL MONADS COMPRISE A SIGNIFICANT PART OF THE EXPERIENCE OF LIFE WITH

LITTLE CHANCE TO REFLECT. ON THE OTHER HAND, THERE ARE SOCIETAL PATTERNS TO MARK THESE MONADAL PASSAGES SO THAT THE FORMALITY OF THE ACKNOWLEDGMENT BRINGS THE LESSONS OF THE MONADAL TRANSITS TO BEAR FAR MORE CLEARLY THAN IS THE CASE IN YOUR SPECIES AND CULTURE.

TIME AS YOU EXPERIENCE IT, CAN BE CALLED A "UNIVERSAL" WORLD TRUTH IN THAT IT APPLIES THROUGHOUT THE PHYSICAL PLANE. AGING IS A WORLD TRUTH TO THE DEGREE THAT ALL LIVING CREATURES AGE, AND A PERSONAL TRUTH IN THAT AGING HAPPENS TO EVERY SINGLE ONE OF YOU. TO IGNORE TIME IS NOT ONLY IMPOSSIBLE, IT BLOCKS MANY USEFUL LESSONS THAT CAN ONLY BE EXPERIENCED WHILE ENSOULED. WHEN A FRAGMENT CHOOSES TO RESIST THE NATURE OF TIME, IT IS GENERALLY MORE DUE TO THE DISTORTIONS OF THE CHIEF FEATURE THAN ANY VALID INSIGHT.

BECAUSE THIS IS A YOUNG SOUL WORLD AND THE UNITED STATES OF AMERICA IS A YOUNG SOUL COUNTRY, YOUNG PERCEPTIONS AND EXPECTATIONS ARE MORE PROMINENT THAN IN OLDER-SOUL COUNTRIES AND/OR PLANETS. THE NATURE OF THE YOUNG SOUL TENDS TO AGGRANDIZE THE PROCESS OF YOUTH—WHICH IS NOT REMARKABLE—BUT DOES SO AT THE COST OF APPRECIATION OF THE ASSET OF AGE, EITHER IN TERMS OF INDIVIDUAL CHRONOLOGY OR IN THE EVOLUTION OF THE SOUL. FOR THOSE YOUNG FRAGMENTS WHO LEARN TO "APPRECIATE" THE MERITS OF CHRONOLOGICAL AGE AND OLD SOUL PERCEPTIONS, THERE ARE OPPORTUNITIES FOR EVOLUTION THAT ARE NOT ACCESSIBLE TO THOSE YOUNG SOULS WHO CHOOSE NOT TO EXPLORE THE POSSIBILITIES OF AGE, NO MATTER WHAT ITS FORM.

THERE ARE THOSE WHO HAVE A SENSE OF SOUL EVOLUTION AND WHO ARE WILLING TO "LET NATURE TAKE ITS COURSE" IN TERMS OF THE PHASES OF BODILY AGING; WHEN SUCH SOULS ARE STILL IN THE YOUNG CYCLE, THE PROGRESS MADE, WHERE THE RECOGNITION IS VALID, CANNOT BE UNDERESTIMATED. AS THE SOUL EVOLVES, THE PROCESS OF AGING LOSES SOME OF ITS TERRORS—UN-

LESS THE FRAGMENT CHOOSES TO ACT FROM THE NEGA-
TIVE POLES OF THE OVERLEAVES—AND THE RABID DE-
NIAL OF AGE IS REDUCED. NEITHER POSITION IS "COR-
RECT" OR "INCORRECT", BUT IN GENERAL PERCEPTIONS
THAT ARE UNHAMPERED WITH THE DISTORTIONS OF FEAR
ARE OF GREATER VALIDITY THAN THOSE DERIVED FROM
FEAR.

THAT IS NOT TO SAY THAT ALL FRAGMENTS AT ALL
TIMES UNDER ALL CIRCUMSTANCES EXPERIENCE TIME IN
PRECISELY THE SAME WAY. AS ALL OF THOSE HERE PRES-
ENT ARE AWARE, THERE ARE DAYS THAT "FLY" AND MI-
NUTES THAT TAKE "FOREVER". IN SUCH ACTIVITIES AS
SPORTS, DANCE, AND MARTIAL ARTS, THERE ARE FRAG-
MENTS WHO, WHILE ACTING WITH "UNCANNY" SWIFT-
NESS APPEAR TO BE MOVING ALMOST LAZILY, AS IF THEY
HAD THE MEANS TO "STRETCH" TIME. THIS IS NOT INAC-
CURATE IN ITS PERCEPTUAL FRAMEWORK, FOR THOSE
FRAGMENTS WHO HAVE ACHIEVED THAT LEVEL OF MAS-
TERY HAVE ACCOMPLISHED THE REALIZATION ABOUT
THE PERSONAL TRUTH OF TIME. TIME AS IT IS EXPERI-
ENCED ON THE PHYSICAL PLANE IS A WORLD TRUTH; PER-
CEPTION OF TIME IS A PERSONAL TRUTH. THE *APPEARANCE*
OF TIME "SLOWING DOWN" OFTEN OCCURS TO THOSE "UN-
SKILLED" FRAGMENTS DURING TIMES OF PERSONAL
CRISIS OR PERIL, SUCH AS THE FRAGMENT ON THE FRINGES
OF AN EXPLOSION, WHO REMEMBERS THE EVENT AS HAP-
PENING SLOWLY. THIS IS THE RESULT OF A LEVEL OF CON-
CENTRATION POSSIBLE IN THE HIGHER INTELLECTUAL
CENTER. WHAT IS SEEN IN FILM WHEN AN AUTOMOBILE
HURTLES OVER A BARRIER IN SLOW MOTION TO DROP
GRACEFULLY AS A FEATHER INTO THE WATER IS, IN FACT,
AN ACCURATE REPRESENTATION OF WHAT IS EXPERI-
ENCED BY THOSE CAUGHT UP IN THE ENHANCED CONCEN-
TRATION OF THE HIGHER INTELLECTUAL CENTER.

LET US REITERATE: ALL "ASTRONOMICAL" BODIES EX-
PERIENCE SOME SORT OF "TIME"—THAT IS, MEASURABLE
PHYSICAL PROGRESS THROUGH A PREORDAINED COURSE
THROUGH THE UNIVERSE. THIS IS NOT MERELY DUE TO
THE ROTATION OF A PLANET AROUND THE SUN OR COMBI-

NATIONS OF SUNS, BUT THE MOVEMENT OF THE VARIOUS SOLAR SYSTEMS THROUGH THE GALAXY AND THE EBB AND FLOW OF THE GALAXIES IN THE VASTNESS OF SPACE. INCIDENTALLY, THE SUPPOSITION THAT YOUR SUN HAS A BINARY IS VALID, THOUGH THE BINARY HAS CONSIDERABLY LESS MASS AND HEAT THAN THE PRIMARY, THAT IS, THE SUN.

ALL CREATURES OF REASON ENSOULED WITHIN A SPECIES DEVELOP A CONCEPT AND METHOD FOR MEASURING TIME. WHERE MULTIPLE STARS ARE INVOLVED, THE DEFINITION OF A "YEAR" OR ANY SIMILAR MEASUREMENT IS FAR MORE DIFFICULT THAN IN THE CASE OF AN APPARENT SINGLE STAR SYSTEM SUCH AS YOUR SYSTEM. WE ARE AWARE OF INHABITED PLANETS WITHIN THIS GALAXY WHOSE ROTATIONAL PATTERNS ARE MORE FIGURE-EIGHT-LIKE THAN ELLIPTICAL: THE CONCEPT OF TIME FOR THE THREE ENSOULED SPECIES ON TWO OF THESE GIDDY PLANETS WOULD BE ALMOST INCOMPREHENSIBLE NOT ONLY TO YOU BUT TO ALMOST ALL FRAGMENTS LIVING ON PLANETS WITH SIMPLER ASTRONOMICAL ARRANGEMENTS.

IT IS NOT AMISS TO BE AWARE THAT TIME HAS VALIDITY. IT BRINGS MANY LESSONS INHERENT ON THE PHYSICAL PLANE TO BEAR IN WAYS THAT CANNOT EASILY BE ACQUIRED IN OTHER WAYS OR IN OTHER PLACES. TIME IS A GREAT TEACHER, IF YOU CHOOSE TO REGARD IN THAT LIGHT. THOSE OF YOU WHO CHOOSE TO EXPERIENCE THE PHYSICAL EVOLUTION OF THE LIFE WILL TEND TO HAVE FAR MORE UNDERSTANDING OF THE NATURE AND FOCUS OF A LIFETIME THAN THOSE WHO CHOOSE NOT TO RECOGNIZE SUCH EXPERIENCES. BETWEEN LIVES MUCH UNDERSTANDING IS AVAILABLE THAT IS NOT GENERALLY POSSIBLE TO THOSE ON THE PHYSICAL PLANE, BUT THERE ARE BENEFITS TO COMPREHENDING WHAT YOU ARE DOING AS YOU ARE DOING IT THAT CANNOT ONLY REDUCE THE MAYA IN A LIFE, IT CAN AID IN VALIDATING THE EVOLUTION OF THAT LIFE WHILE THE LIFE IS PROGRESSING. IN MOST CASES THOSE WHO CHOOSE TO HAVE THIS RECOGNITION ARE MATURE AND OLD SOULS, AND THAT CHOICE

IS RELATED TO THE NATURE OF THOSE TWO CYCLES. THAT DOES NOT MEAN THAT MATURE AND OLD SOULS *MUST* HAVE SUCH EXPERIENCES, OR THAT OTHERS BY DEFINITION *CANNOT*. THAT DENIES CHOICE, WHICH, AS WE HAVE SAID MANY TIMES BEFORE, IS THE PURPOSE OF LIFE, INSOFAR AS LIFE HAS A PURPOSE.

WHEN THE QUESTION OF THE VALIDITY OF TIME ARISES, THERE ARE MANY FRAGMENTS WHO SEEK TO "ESCAPE" IT, WHICH, OF COURSE, IS DONE "AUTOMATICALLY" WHEN THE PHYSICAL PLANE IS LEFT, EITHER BETWEEN LIVES, OR WHEN THE CYCLES OF LIVES ON THE PHYSICAL PLANE IS AT AN END. TO SOME DEGREE, THOSE ENTITIES WITH FRAGMENTS BOTH ON THE PHYSICAL PLANE AND ON THE ASTRAL PLANE BETWEEN LIVES TEND TO HAVE A GREATER AWARENESS OF TIME WHILE ON THE ASTRAL PLANE DUE TO THE LINK WITH THE FRAGMENTS ON THE PHYSICAL PLANE. THAT IS NOT TO SAY THAT THE ASTRAL PLANE HAS THE SAME SORT OF TIME—AS WE HAVE SAID BEFORE, IT DOES NOT. HOWEVER, FRAGMENTS WITH LINKS TO THE PHYSICAL PLANE FROM THE ASTRAL PLANE WILL PERCEIVE THE LIVES OF THOSE ON THE PHYSICAL PLANE AS PASSING THROUGH TIME, WHICH IS THE NATURE OF THE PHYSICAL PLANE. THOSE FRAGMENTS ON THE ASTRAL PLANE DO NOT IN THE USUAL SENSE PARTICIPATE IN TIME ON THE PHYSICAL PLANE, BUT THERE IS A LEVEL OF UNDERSTANDING IN THOSE ASTRAL FRAGMENTS THAT IS NOT SHARED BY REUNITED ENTITIES EITHER ON THE ASTRAL OR CAUSAL PLANES.

EACH PLANE OF EXISTENCE—PHYSICAL, ASTRAL, CAUSAL, AKASHIC, BUDDHIC—HAS ITS OWN PARAMETERS OF EXPERIENTIAL PERCEPTION. IT WOULD NOT BE ENTIRELY INCORRECT TO ASSUME THAT ALTHOUGH WE DO NOT EXPERIENCE TIME AS YOU DO, WE DO PARTICIPATE IN THE NATURE OF THE TAO, AS DO ALL THINGS. BECAUSE WE MOVE TOWARD THE TAO, THERE IS AN EVOLUTION NOT UNLIKE THE PASSAGE OF TIME. FOR EXAMPLE, WE ARE AWARE OF THE TOTALITY OF TIME *UP TO THIS POINT* IN ITS EXPERIENTIAL ENTIRETY. WE ARE ALSO AWARE OF WHAT YOU CONSIDER TO BE THE FUTURE IN ALL ITS *POS-*

SIBLE MANIFESTATIONS. UNTIL CHOICES ARE MADE, ALL POSSIBLE MANIFESTATIONS OF WHAT YOU CONSIDER THE FUTURE ARE EQUALLY VIABLE, ALTHOUGH WE ADMIT THAT SOME EVENTUALITIES ARE MORE LIKELY THAN OTHERS. WE HAVE ACCESS TO ALL THE POSSIBILITIES OF WHAT MIGHT BE CHOSEN BY YOU AND EVERY FRAGMENT ON THE PHYSICAL PLANE, BOTH IN REGARD TO PERSONAL CHOICE AND LIFE PLANS, AND IN REGARD TO THE HAZARDS INHERENT ON THE PHYSICAL PLANE. FOR EXAMPLE: WHILE IT IS EXTREMELY UNLIKELY, IT IS NOT IMPOSSIBLE FOR YOUR SUN TO GO NOVA, OR FOR A STAR NEARBY TO GO NOVA, WITH SIMILAR VAST REPERCUSSIONS FOR ALL FRAGMENTS AND ALL CREATURES CURRENTLY EXTANT ON YOUR WORLD. THERE ARE OTHER "ACCIDENTS" OF AN ASTRONOMICAL NATURE THAT CONSTITUTE A HAZARD TO BEING ON THE PHYSICAL PLANE, JUST AS CROSSING THE STREET AGAINST THE LIGHT IN HEAVY TRAFFIC ALSO CONSTITUTES A HAZARD OF BEING ON THE PHYSICAL PLANE.

THOSE OF YOU WHO ARE DRIVEN TO MARK THE ACHIEVEMENTS OF YOUR LIFE AGAINST YOUR CHOSEN "RACE WITH THE CLOCK" OFTEN DO NOT HAVE THE OPPORTUNITY TO SAVOR THE DELIGHTS OF GENUINE ACCOMPLISHMENTS BECAUSE OF THE DEADLINE YOU HAVE CHOSEN. LET US ENLARGE UPON THIS: A FRAGMENT CHOOSES TO STUDY FOR AN ADVANCED DEGREE WHICH THE FRAGMENT IS DETERMINED TO ACQUIRE IN A SET LENGTH OF TIME—FOR THE SAKE OF THIS EXPLANATION, LET US SAY SIX YEARS—WHICH, DUE TO CIRCUMSTANCES "BEYOND THE FRAGMENT'S CONTROL" IS SUBJECT TO DELAY, AND INSTEAD OF TAKING SIX YEARS, THE COVETED DEGREE IS NOT OBTAINED FOR BETWEEN SEVEN AND EIGHT YEARS. THE FRAGMENT FEELS KEEN DISAPPOINTMENT AT THIS DELAY, AND TAKES LITTLE OR NO SATISFACTION FROM THE DEGREE BECAUSE IT WAS NOT ATTAINED IN THE PRESELECTED AND ARBITRARILY SET PERIOD OF TIME. THIS, OF COURSE, IS LARGELY THE RESULT OF CHIEF FEATURE DISTORTIONS AND "SHOULD" SERVE AS A REMINDER TO ALL HERE PRESENT THAT MOST

SUCH LIMITS, WHEN IMPOSED, EXPECIALLY WHEN SELF-IMPOSED, TEND TO COME NOT FROM ESSENCE BUT FROM CHIEF FEATURE.

WHEN UNDERTAKING A PROJECT, PARTICULARLY AN EXTENSIVE OR COMPLEX ONE, WE WOULD SUGGEST THAT ALL FRAGMENTS MAKE A REALISTIC ASSESSMENT OF HOW MUCH TIME IS GENERALLY NEEDED TO ACCOMPLISH SUCH TASKS, UNDER THE MOST FAVORABLE CIRCUMSTANCES, UNDER ORDINARY CIRCUMSTANCES, AND UNDER UNFAVORABLE CIRCUMSTANCES, AND USE THOSE GUIDELINES TO DETERMINE PROGRESS. UNLESS THERE ARE OVERWHELMING REASONS TO DO SO, WE WOULD THINK THAT THE INSTALLATIONS OF DEADLINES WOULD SERVE LITTLE PURPOSE BUT TO ADD ADDITIONAL STRESS TO THE PROJECT, AND TO INTRODUCE AN ELEMENT OF FRUSTRATION WHERE IT MIGHT NOT OTHERWISE BE PRESENT.

WE REALIZE THAT THIS YOUNG SOUL CULTURE SETS GREAT STORE BY TIME. PROJECTS TAKING GREAT QUANTITIES OF TIME *THAT ARE SUCCESSFUL* ARE SEEN AS MORE SIGNIFICANT BECAUSE OF TIME USED TO ACCOMPLISH THEM. IF THE PROJECTS ARE NOT SUCCESSFUL, THEN THEY ARE DISMISSED AS FOLLY AND "CRACKPOT" WASTES OF TIME. NOTHING IS EVER WASTED, AND THAT INCLUDES TIME. CONVERSELY, WHEN A PROJECT DOES NOT TAKE MUCH TIME, OR AS MUCH TIME AS IT IS THOUGHT TO REQUIRE, THEN IT IS ASSUMED THAT THE ACCOMPLISHMENT IS NOT AS GREAT BECAUSE IT DIDN'T TAKE "LONG ENOUGH". FOR EXAMPLE, THERE WAS A PERIOD WHEN IT WAS ASSUMED THAT COMPOSERS, BEING INSPIRED, COMPLETED WORKS QUICKLY, AND WORKS THAT TOOK "TOO LONG" WERE REGARDED WITH SUSPICION BECAUSE IT WAS SUSPECTED THAT THE WORK IN QUESTION WAS NOT SUFFICIENTLY "INSPIRED". LATER, WHEN PROFUNDITY OF THOUGHT WAS CONSIDERED TO BE MORE IMPORTANT THAN INSPIRATION IN COMPOSITION, WORKS WERE ASSUMED TO REQUIRE GREAT PERIODS OF TIME TO COMPLETE, AND WHEN THEY DID NOT TAKE LONG PERIODS OF TIME, THEY WERE REGARDED WITH SUSPICION BECAUSE THE BREVITY OF THEIR COMPOSITIONAL TIME APPEARED

TO RENDER THEM "TRIVIAL" OR "UNFORMED". IT MAY BE APPARENT TO SOME OF YOU BY NOW THAT THE WORK TAKES AS LONG AS IT TAKES TO BE FINISHED. THERE ARE TIMES WHEN THIS IS DONE QUICKLY AND TIMES WHEN IT IS DONE SLOWLY. THERE IS NO "CORRECT" LENGTH OF TIME FOR ANY EXPERIENCE OR PROJECT. THE IMPOSITON OF TIME FACTORS, ESPECIALLY IN AREAS OF LEARNING FOR CHILDREN, LIMITS THE OPPORTUNITIES FOR THE CHILDREN AND THEIR TEACHERS ALIKE AS WELL AS SERVING ONLY TO CREATE A COMPULSION ABOUT TIME IN MANY FRAGMENTS WHO MIGHT OTHERWISE SHOW SURPRISING ABILITY IF PERMITTED TO STUDY AND DEVELOP AT THEIR OWN RATE.

WHILE WE AGREE THAT TIME IS VALID FOR THE PHYSICAL PLANE AND THAT MEASURING IT IS "NATURAL" TO ENSOULED SPECIES, WE WOULD HAVE TO ADD THAT THE PREOCCUPATION WITH TIME IS A MAJOR DISTORTION. THAT DOES NOT MEAN WE PERCEIVE ANYTHING "WRONG" IN PUBLISHING A DAILY NEWSPAPER DAILY, OR IN HAVING BIRTHDAY PARTIES OR ANNIVERSARY CELEBRATIONS. THE FORMER IS A CONTRACTUAL AGREEMENT BEING FULFILLED; THE LATTER ARE EXAMPLES OF VALID CULTURAL LANDMARKS IN INDIVIDUAL LIVES. HOWEVER, THOSE WHO ARE CONVINCED THAT THEY *MUST* READ THE MORNING PAPER BY EIGHT-FIFTEEN SO THAT THEY CAN HAVE THE NECESSARY SEVEN MINUTES FOR BREAKFAST ARE PERMITTING TIME TO DOMINATE THEIR LIVES IN A WAY THAT ULTIMATELY SERVES TO HAMPER RATHER THAN BENEFIT THE FRAGMENTS IN QUESTION.

OF COURSE, THERE ARE MANY INSTANCES WHEN TIME AND/OR THE LACK OF IT IS USED AS A CONVINCING EXCUSE. ONE FRAGMENT SAYS TO ANOTHER: "I CANNOT GET ENOUGH VACATION TIME TO SAIL TO TAHITI WITH YOU". THIS MAY BE AN ACCURATE STATEMENT OF CIRCUMSTANCES, BUT IT IS MORE A QUESTION OF PRIORITIES THAN OF VACATION TIME. WHAT THE FRAGMENT IS REVEALING IS THAT MAINTAINING THE JOB HE OR SHE HAS IS, IN FACT, A HIGHER PRIORITY THAN SAILING TO TAHITI WITH THE FRAGMENT REQUESTING HIS OR HER COMPANY. THE

PRIORITY MAY BE THE RESULT OF MANY FACTORS. IT MAY
BE THAT THE FRAGMENT BEING ASKED DOES NOT LIKE
TO SAIL. IT MAY BE THAT HE OR SHE DOES NOT WANT TO
GO TO TAHITI. IT MAY BE THAT HE OR SHE DOES NOT
WANT TO SAIL WITH THE FRAGMENT ASKING. IT MAY BE
THAT THE WORK THIS FRAGMENT IS DOING IS TREMEN-
DOUSLY SATISFYING AND THE FRAGMENT DOES NOT
WANT TO GIVE IT UP IN ORDER TO SAIL TO TAHITI. IT MAY
BE THAT THE FRAGMENT FEARS THAT BEING GONE FROM
THE JOB FOR ANY LENGTH OF TIME MIGHT SERVE AS AN
EXCUSE TO BE TERMINATED, AND THEREFORE THE OFFER
HAS LITTLE ALLURE. IT MAY BE THAT THE FRAGMENT
ALREADY HAS VACATION PLANS TO DO SOMETHING ELSE
SOMEWHERE ELSE. THERE ARE MANY OTHER POS-
SIBILITIES AS WELL, BUT TIME IS THE EXCUSE, NOT THE
REASON FOR THE REFUSAL.

BECAUSE OF THE POTENCY THIS SOCIETY BESTOWS ON
TIME, ALMOST ALL FRAGMENTS ARE PROFOUNDLY CON-
SCIOUS OF ITS PASSAGE. IT IS NOT INAPPROPRIATE TO
VIEW THE PREOCCUPATION WITH YOUTH AS A DIRECT RE-
SPONSE TO THIS OBSESSION WITH TIME. MANY FRAG-
MENTS ARE FASCINATED BY THOSE WHO APPEAR TO BE—
HOWEVER BRIEFLY—IMMUNE TO TIME. IT IS TRUE THAT
CULTURAL ROLES ARE INCLINED TO DEMAND THAT
WOMEN—OTHER THAN MOTHER—REMAIN UNTOUCHED
BY THE "BLIGHT OF AGE", FOR THE MOST PART TO ASSURE
THE SOCIETALLY DOMINANT MALES THAT THEY ARE NOT
"FATALLY TAINTED" BY THE PASSAGE OF TIME. LET US
POINT OUT THAT THOSE FRAGMENTS WHO SURVIVE ANY
SIGNIFICANT NUMBER OF YEAR—THESE NUMBERS VARY
FROM FRAGMENT TO FRAGMENT, FROM ERA TO ERA,
FROM CULTURE TO CULTURE—ARE ALMOST CERTAINLY
GOING TO AGE. IN MANY SOCIETIES WHERE SURVIVAL IS
MORE DIFFICULT, AGE IS VALUED, EVEN IN WOMEN.

THOSE FRAGMENTS HERE GATHERED ARE NOT AS MUCH
"IN THE GRIP" OF THE DREAD OF AGE TO THE DEGREE
THAT MANY OF YOUR SPECIES ARE. THAT IS NOT TO SAY
YOU HAVE ESCAPED IT ENTIRELY, FOR THAT IS PART OF
FUNCTIONING WITHIN A CULTURE. MOST OF YOU ARE

AWARE THAT AGE IS A "NATURAL" OUTCOME OF LIVING, AND THAT IT IS NOT "EVIL", AS MANY OTHERS ASSUME IT IS. YOU ARE PREPARED TO ACCEPT THE PASSAGE OF TIME AS A VALID EXPERIENCE, AND THE AGING OF THE BODY AS THE COUNTERPART TO LIFETIME EVOLUTION. THE CULTURAL PRESSURES THAT IMPINGE ON ALL OF YOU ARE NOT REGARDED AS BEING BINDING AND VALID IN THE WAY THAT MANY FRAGMENTS "ACCEPT" THEM. WE SAY "ACCEPT" IN THIS SENSE ONLY: THAT THEY ARE TAKEN IN WITHOUT QUESTION AND WITH THE ASSUMPTION THAT THEY ARE "PART OF THE NATURAL ORDER OF THE UNIVERSE". THIS IS, OF COURSE, NOT THE CASE. TO UNDERSTAND THE IMPACT OF THE PASSAGE OF TIME, WE WOULD URGE THOSE FRAGMENTS WHO CHOOSE TO DO SO TO EXAMINE THE CHARACTERISTICS OF AGING IN TRUSTED ANIMALS, WITH EMPHASIS ON THE EXPERIENCE THE ANIMALS HAVE. MOST ANIMALS DO NOT "MIND" GETTING OLDER, AND WHILE MOST OF THEM REACH A POINT WHERE THE BODY NO LONGER FUNCTIONS AS WELL AS IT USED TO, THE ANIMAL DOES NOT "RESENT" THE PASSAGE OF TIME OR BECOME "INFERIOR" BECAUSE OF IT.

LET US DIGRESS ON THE MATTER OF AGING AND MENOPAUSE—AND YES, THERE IS A HORMONAL SHIFT IN MALES AS WELL AS FEMALES—AND THE CULTURAL MYTHOLOGY THAT SURROUNDS IT. BECAUSE FERTILITY WAS REGARDED AS A HIGH PRIORITY IN WOMEN FOR A VERY LONG PERIOD OF TIME, THE CESSATION OF THAT ASPECT OF FEMALENESS WAS GIVEN EXAGGERATED IMPORTANCE, BOTH IN THE EYES OF MEN AND WOMEN. AS A RESULT, ATTITUDES ABOUT THE "IMPORTANCE" OF WOMEN WAS HIGHLY INFLUENCED BY WHETHER OR NOT THEY WERE ABLE TO BEAR CHILDREN. THIS HAS LONG SINCE CEASED TO BE A SOCIOLOGICALLY VALID POSITION, BUT IT CONTINUES WITHIN THE CULTURE, BRINGING ABOUT MANY NEEDLESSLY ADVERSE MISPERCEPTIONS ON THE PART OF ALMOST ALL FRAGMENT CURRENTLY EXTANT IN YOUR SPECIES AND CULTURE. TO EQUATE MENOPAUSE, EITHER MALE OR FEMALE, WITH DEATH, EITHER DIRECTLY OR BY IMPLICATION, IS AT THE VERY

BEST MISLEADING. AS PART OF ITS PASSAGE THROUGH TIME, THE BODY UNDERGOES MANY CHANGES. PUBERTY DOES NOT, IN FACT, START LIFE. MENOPAUSE DOES NOT, IN FACT, END IT. BOTH ARE PART OF THE REPRODUCTIVE PHASES OF LIFE, AND THAT IS ALL.

IT IS VALID THAT BODIES POSSESS "CLOCKS". VARIOUS SYSTEMS WEAR OUT AT DIFFERENT RATES, IN PART DETERMINED BY USE, IN PART BY THE SYSTEM "CLOCK". THOSE WITH SLOW METABOLIC RATES TEND TO POTENTIALLY LONGER LIVES. THOSE WITH VERY FAST METABOLIC RATES TEND TO POTENTIALLY SHORTER LIVES. THE OPERATIVE WORDS HERE ARE *TEND* AND *POTENTIALLY*. ALL THESE PHYSICAL ASPECTS ARE INFLUENCED BY THE PHYSICAL PLANE. NO MATTER WHAT SORT OF METABOLIC RATE A FRAGMENT HAS, IF THE FRAGMENT IS EXPOSED REPEATEDLY TO TOXIC WASTES, FOR EXAMPLE, THE LIFETIME WILL TEND TO BE SHORTENED NO MATTER WHAT THE "CLOCKS" ARE SET TO DO. BY COMPARISON, A FRAGMENT WITH A VERY FAST METABOLIC RATE LIVING IN LOW-STRESS AND HEALTHFUL SURROUNDINGS AND MAINTAINING AN OPTIMISTIC FRAME OF MIND WILL TEND TO GET THE MOST OUT OF THE "CLOCKS".

OF COURSE, THE REFERENCE TO METABOLISM IS NOT USED IN ITS MOST LIMITED CLINICAL SENSE HERE, BUT AS A FRAME OF REFERENCE FOR THE RATE OF FUNCTION OF THE BODY AS A TOTALITY. WE HAVE SAID BEFORE THAT FROM OUR PERSPECTIVE ALL BODILY FUNCTIONS INTERACT IN SUCH A WAY THAT STRICT ISOLATION OF ONE FROM ANOTHER IS NOT, IN FACT, WHOLLY POSSIBLE. TO US, ATTITUDE IS PART OF BODILY FUNCTIONS.

WE WOULD WISH TO RECOMMEND TO FRAGMENTS WHO FEAR AGING THAT A PERIOD OF TIME BE SET ASIDE TO OBSERVE THE OPPORTUNITIES OF AGE, AND BY THAT WE DO NOT MEAN RETIRED FRAGMENTS PUTTERING AROUND THE GOLF COURSE. THERE ARE WORKS OF ARTISTS THAT DEVELOPED WITH AGE. THERE ARE MAJOR MUSICAL WORKS THAT WERE COMPOSED LATE IN THE COMPOSER'S LIFE, WHEN THE COMPOSER WAS "READY" FOR THEM. THERE ARE INVENTIONS AND ENTERTAINMENTS THAT

ARE ENJOYED IN AGE, NOT AS A SOP AND SUBSTITUTE FOR "THE REAL THING", BUT AS GENUINE AND ENJOYABLE PURSUITS. TO SAY THAT AGE MUST BE BURDENSOME DENIES THE MERITS OF YOUTH. TO ASSUME THAT AGE IS WITHOUT BENEFIT OR HONOR RENDERS BOTH EXPERIENCE AND LEARNING WORTHLESS, AS WELL AS DENYING ONE OF THE MOST BASIC WORLD TRUTHS EXPERIENCED THROUGHOUT THE PHYSICAL PLANE: ALL THAT LIVES AGES.

WHILE IT IS NOT EASY FOR US TO EXPRESS HOW WE EXPERIENCE TIME ON THE MID-CAUSAL PLANE, WE WILL ATTEMPT TO PROVIDE A FRAME OF REFERENCE THROUGH A SERIES OF METAPHORS. ASSUME, IF YOU WILL, THAT ALL TIME ON THE PHYSICAL PLANE IS A MULTI-MILLION-STRAND "BRAID". THE POINT WHERE THE BRAID IS BEING BRAIDED IS WHAT IS PERCEIVED BY YOU AS THE PRESENT. THE UNBRAIDED STRANDS ARE THE CHOICES OF THE FUTURE, THE BRAIDED STRANDS ARE THE PAST. THIS IS NOT A STATIC IMAGE, HOWEVER, FOR THE PERCEPTION IS ONLY PARTLY PHYSICAL. THOSE ASPECTS THAT PARTAKE OF OTHER PLANES OF EXISTENCE AND PERCEPTION ARE WITHIN THE FRAMEWORK OF THOSE PLANES AND ARE THEREFORE NOT THE CONCRETE MATTER ASSOCIATED WITH THE PHYSICAL PLANE. TO SAY THAT WE ARE "ABOVE" THE BRAID IS NOT WHOLLY CORRECT, BUT WE ARE NOT WITHIN IT. WE HAVE REFERRED TO THE TAPESTRY, THE WEAVING THAT IS THE PHYSICAL-PLANE MANIFESTATION OF THE TAO. THAT WEAVING IS ALL THE BRAIDS MOVING TOGETHER, THEIR INTERSECTIONS AND THEIR PATTERNS. EACH BRAID PASSES FROM PHYSICAL PLANE TO ASTRAL PLANE AND BACK AGAIN MANY, MANY TIMES, AS LIVES ARE UNDERTAKEN. WHILE THE BRAID IS OFF THE PHYSICAL PLANE, IT IS PARTIALLY REMOVED FROM TIME. IT IS CONTINUOUS, HOWEVER, AND UNINTERRUPTED, WHICH IS WHY NO FRAGMENT IS ABLE TO "RETURN" AS ITS OWN GRANDPARENT. EVOLUTION MOVES ONLY ONE WAY; OTHERWISE IT WOULD NOT BE EVOLUTION.

TO CONTINUE THE METAPHOR. WE ARE NOT THE

WEAVER. EACH STRAND, EACH BRAID, IS ITS OWN
WEAVER. THE NATURE OF THE LOOM IS ESTABLISHED AT
THE CASTING OF FRAGMENTS FROM THE TAO. BEYOND
THAT, CHOICE IS THE ONLY WEAVER. WE PARTICIPATED
IN OUR OWN WEAVING WHEN WE WERE EXTANT ON THE
PHYSICAL PLANE, AND IN OUR ASTRAL INTERVALS. NOW
THAT WE ARE AT THE MID-CAUSAL PLANE, WE ARE AWARE
THAT THE TAPESTRY IS A TOTALITY, BOTH FINISHED AND
UNFINISHED. WE ARE AWARE OF WHAT THE PHASES OF
BRAIDING ARE ON INDIVIDUAL BASES AS WELL AS IN RE-
LATION TO THE EVOLUTION OF FRAGMENTS, CADENCES,
ENTITIES, CADRES, AND BEYOND.

ANOTHER WAY TO CONSIDER THE PASSAGE OF TIME AS
WE EXPERIENCE IT IS IN REGARD TO THAT VAST PARTICLE
RELEASE KNOWN AS THE SOLAR WIND. AS THE SUN PUTS
OUT ENORMOUS ENERGY, VISIBLE AS LIGHT, IT ALSO PUTS
OUT PARTICLES WHICH ARE NOT AS EASILY PERCEIVED.
ONLY IN THE FAR NORTH AND SOUTH OF THE PLANET CAN
THEY BE PERCEIVED AS THE AURORA BOREALIS AND AUS-
TRALIS. FOR ALMOST ALL FRAGMENTS, THE VALIDITY OF
THE SUN IS ITS LIGHT. FOR US, THE VALIDITY OF THE SUN
IS THE POLAR AURORAS.

WHILE THE ROTATION OF THE PLANET IS REGULAR AND
PREDICTABLE, TIME IN THE SUBJECTIVE SENSE, IS NOT.
THIS IS THE DIFFERENCE BETWEEN PERSONAL AND
WORLD TRUTHS. THE ROTATION OF THE EARTH IS THE
WORLD TRUTH. THE SUBJECTIVE PERCEPTION OF THE PAS-
SAGE OF TIME IS A PERSONAL TRUTH. THAT LIVING
THINGS AGE IS A WORLD TRUTH. THE NUMBER OF YEARS
AND DAYS YOU HAVE LIVED IS A PERSONAL TRUTH, AND
ONE THAT IS WITH YOU CONSTANTLY.

ANOTHER PERSONAL TRUTH DIRECTLY RELATED TO
TIME AND TO THE "CLOCKS" WE HAVE PREVIOUSLY MEN-
TIONED IS THE MATTER OF THE ACTIVE AND INACTIVE
CYCLES WITHIN AN INDIVIDUAL FRAGMENT; THAT IS TO
SAY, WHAT IS TRIVIALLY DESCRIBED AS THE DIFFERENCE
BETWEEN "MORNING PEOPLE" AND "NIGHT PEOPLE".
THERE ARE INDIVIDUAL CYCLES THAT ARE BY NO MEANS
AS CUT-AND-DRIED AS THOSE BASIC TERMS SUGGEST.

EVERY FRAGMENT HAS HIGHLY INDIVIDUALIZED CYCLES IN LIFE, AND THE CYCLES ARE OFTEN SUBJECT TO CHANGE DURING THE LIFE AS THE FRAGMENT AGES AND OTHER IMPOSITIONS ARE MADE ON THE AGENDA OF THE LIFE.

THERE WAS A TIME WHEN EARLY RISING MADE A MODICUM OF SENSE IN A LARGELY AGRARIAN CULTURE WITH LIMITED POWER RESOURCES. THEN THERE WERE COGENT REASONS TO BE "UP WITH THE LARK" IN ORDER TO MAKE THE MOST OF THE AVAILABLE DAYLIGHT AS WELL AS TO DEAL WITH THE DEMANDS OF LIVESTOCK AND FIELD. THOSE DAYS ARE, OF COURSE, LONG PAST, EVEN IN A NUMBER OF AGRARIAN SITUATIONS. WITH MORE AVAILABLE POWER THE WORKING DAY CAN BE AND HAS BEEN EXTENDED. BUT THE NEXT STEP BEYOND THAT HAS NOT BEEN TAKEN. INSTEAD OF FOLLOWING THE ARMY, AS IT WERE, THE ONLY CONCESSION THAT HAS DEVELOPED IS FOLLOWING THE NAVY. IN OTHER WORDS, IN PLACE OF ONE LONG, LIGHT-DEFINED WORKING DAY, THE PATTERN NOW IS TO STAND WATCHES, OTHERWISE KNOWN AS SHIFTS, BUT STILL RIGIDLY DEFINED IN LENGTH, BEGINNING, ENDING, AND SIMILAR WAYS. ONLY THE PERFORMING ARTS HAVE BECOME A BIT MORE FLEXIBLE, BUT EVEN SUCH THINGS AS REHEARSALS ARE, TO SOME DEGREE OF NECESSITY, DEFINED IN TERMS OF LENGTH AND WORK TO BE ACCOMPLISHED.

BECAUSE EACH FRAGMENT HAS INDIVIDUAL CLOCKS, AND BECAUSE IT IS POSSIBLE FOR THE EMPLOYMENT PATTERN TO ACCOMMODATE THIS, IT IS OFTEN PUZZLING TO US WHY MORE HAS NOT BEEN DONE. THERE WOULD BE AN INCREASE OF PRODUCTIVITY AS A RESULT OF SUCH CHANGES, AND WE WOULD NOT BE SURPRIZED TO NOTICE A DECREASE IN VARIOUS STRESS-RELATED CONDITIONS, INCLUDING IN THE AREAS OF MENTAL HEALTH. WE WOULD WISH TO POINT OUT THAT FRAGMENTS WORKING DURING WHAT IS ACTUALLY AN INACTIVE CYCLE FOR THE BODY ARE MORE PRONE TO DEPRESSION AND ADDICTIVE BEHAVIOR THAN ARE FRAGMENTS WORKING IN THE ACTIVE CYCLES.

WE DO NOT MEAN TO IMPLY THAT PERMITTING FRAG-

MENTS TO FOLLOW THE DICTATES OF INDIVIDUAL BODILY
"CLOCKS" WILL THEREFORE ELIMINATE ADDICTIVE BE-
HAVIOR AND DEPRESSION. WE DID NOT SAY THAT AND
WE DID NOT IMPLY IT. WE DO SAY THAT SUCH PROBLEMS
WOULD BE *REDUCED,* NOT ELIMINATED. AND WE WOULD
ALSO SUSPECT THAT SOME OF THE DIFFICULTIES WITHIN
THE "SYSTEM" IN TERMS OF INTERPERSONAL CLASHES
WOULD ALSO BE REDUCED.

SUCH AWARENESS OF CYCLES IS NOT EASILY DETER-
MINED. BY THE TIME AN INFANT IS TWO, AT THE VERY
OLDEST, THE REQUIRED ACTIVE AND INACTIVE PERIODS
APPROVED BY THE SOCIETY HAVE ALREADY BEEN SO
RIGOROUSLY ENFORCED THAT THE FRAGMENT'S INDI-
VIDUAL PATTERNS ARE OFTEN CONCEALED OR DIS-
TORTED, OCCASIONALLY ALMOST COMPLETELY FORGOT-
TEN. THE PATTERNS ARE APT TO REAPPEAR IN SUCH
FORMS AS STRESS-RELATED DISEASE, INCLUDING SUCH
THINGS AS ASTHMA AND ALLERGIES; IN PERSONALITY
"DISORDERS" INCLUDING BUT NOT LIMITED TO DEPRES-
SION; IN COMPULSIVE BEHAVIOR RESULTING FROM THE
TIME-USE COMPULSION ALREADY IMPOSED ON THE FRAG-
MENT. WE WOULD THINK THAT THERE WOULD BE MANY
BENEFITS TO ALL CONCERNED IF THERE WERE A GENERAL
REASSESSMENT ON THE CONCEPT OF WHAT CONSTITUTES
A WORKING DAY, AND THE MANNER IN WHICH IT IS CON-
DUCTED. ACCOMMODATION FOR INDIVIDUAL ACTIVE
AND INACTIVE PATTERNS IS NOT IMPOSSIBLE, FOR THERE
IS NO REASON FOR MOST ASPECTS OF YOUR CURRENT SO-
CIETY AND THOSE OF TECHNOLOGICALLY SOPHISTICATED
COUNTRIES TO RUN "ROUND THE CLOCK". THERE ARE
OTHER BENEFITS THAT MIGHT BE DERIVED FROM SUCH
AN ADJUSTMENT, SUCH AS A MORE EFFECTIVE USE OF
RESOURCES AND TRANPORTATIONAL FACILITIES.

SUCH A TRANSITION WOULD NOT BE EASILY AC-
COMPLISHED, AT LEAST AT FIRST, FOR MOST FRAGMENTS
WOULD REQUIRE A CONSIDERABLE LENGTH OF TIME—
THREE YEARS AT A MINIMUM—TO DETERMINE THEIR OWN
TRUE ACTIVE AND INACTIVE CYCLES. ONCE DETERMINED,
IT WOULD THEN REQUIRE A FAIRLY LONG TIME TO WORK

OUT THE MOST EFFECTIVE ACCOMMODATION FOR THOSE FRAGMENTS DESIRING TO ALTER THEIR PATTERN FROM WHAT YOU THINK OF AS THE "NORMAL" ONE, WHICH SIMPLY MEANS, IN THIS CASE, THE MOST TRADITIONALLY CONVENIENT ONE. THERE IS NOTHING "NORMAL" IN RISING AT A SPECIFIC TIME OF DAY; IT IS MERELY A HABIT.

WE DO NOT WISH TO SUGGEST THAT WE ARE "RECOMMENDING" ANY CHANGE. THAT WOULD PRESUME TO IMPOSE, WHICH ABROGATES CHOICE. WHAT WE HOPE TO POINT OUT IS THAT THE CONCEPT OF A WORKING DAY IS NOT ABSOLUTE LAW, AND THAT THE NATURE OF HOW THAT WORKING DAY IS DEFINED NEED NOT BE AS RIGIDLY CONSTRAINED AS IT HAS BEEN IN THE PAST. WE WOULD WISH TO ENCOURAGE THOSE WHO CHOOSE TO DO SO, TO EXAMINE THEIR NATURAL ACTIVE AND INACTIVE CYCLES, FOR MUCH USEFUL INFORMATION MAY BE GAINED FROM THIS EXERCISE.

WE REMIND YOU THAT THESE CYCLES DO CHANGE DURING LIFE, AND WHAT MIGHT BE A PERSONAL TRUTH FOR A FRAGMENT AT FIFTEEN IS APT NOT TO BE PERSONALLY TRUE AT FIFTY. TAKING SUCH TRANSITIONS INTO CONSIDERATION CAN DO MUCH IN AIDING FRAGMENTS TO DETERMINE HOW THEY VIEW THE PROSPECT OF AGING, WHICH IS NOT A MATTER OF CONSTANT LOSS BUT OF CONSTANT CHANGE. THOSE WHO VIEW THE NATURE OF AGE AS ONE OF LOSS WILL HAVE DIFFICULTY IN PERCEIVING THE ADVANTAGES AND IMPROVEMENTS OF AGE, WHICH, IN TURN, WILL TEND TO LIMIT CHOICES UNNECESSARILY.

THERE IS PERHAPS NO AREA IN LIFE WHERE THE CHIEF FEATURE CAN GAIN A SURER HOLD OF THE PERSONALITY THAN THROUGH THE PERCEPTIONS OF TIME, FOR THE CONCEPT OF LIMITATION THROUGH TIME, OR BY A "DEADLINE" CAN GIVE THE CHIEF FEATURE MORE POTENCY WITHOUT APPARENT MANIPULATION THAN CAN ANY OTHER ASPECT OF DAILY LIFE. BY MEASURING ACCOMPLISHMENT AGAINST TIME, THE CHIEF FEATURE IS CAPABLE OF CONVINCING A FRAGMENT THAT THE ONLY POSSIBILITY IS FAILURE ANDD THAT THE ONLY ACCOMPLISHMENTS ARE TOO LATE AND FORGOTTEN. WE WOULD WISH

TO POINT OUT THAT DEADLINES ARE AT BEST A CONVEN-
IENCE, AND THAT MOST OF THEM, WHEN THEY ARE NOT
SELF-IMPOSED, ARE NEGOTIABLE TO A GREATER OR LES-
SER DEGREE. WHERE THE DEADLINE IS SELF-IMPOSED
THERE ARE PROBLEMS DEVELOPING FROM THE BELIEF OF
THE INDIVIDUAL FRAGMENT THAT TIME HAS PERSONAL
SIGNIFICANCE BEYOND ITS ACTUAL IMPACT. TO REGARD
TIME AS SOMETHING OTHER THAN THE CONVENIENCE IT
IS SERVES LITTLE PURPOSE FOR ANY FRAGMENT.

THAT IS NOT TO SAY THAT IT IS THEREFORE "PROPER"
TO BE LATE FOR APPOINTMENTS OR TO IGNORE TIME-RE-
LATED CELEBRATIONS, ALTHOUGH, OF COURSE, YOU MAY
CHOOSE TO DO SO IF THAT IS WHAT YOU WISH. TIME IS
ONE OF THE STANDARD SOCIAL CONTRACTS INDEPEN-
DENTLY MOBILE ENSOULED SPECIES ADOPT WHENEVER
POSSIBLE, AND IT IS NOT INAPPROPRIATE TO REGARD IT
IN THAT WAY. THERE ARE "GOOD" REASONS TO USE
CALENDARS AND TEND TO APPOINTMENTS, BUT THEY ARE
THE RESULT OF PERSONAL CHOICES, NOT IMMUTABLE
LAWS. VALIDATING THIS DIFFERENCE CAN BE OF GREAT
USE FOR THOSE OF YOU WILLING TO MAKE SUCH A
CHOICE.

Chapter 6

"ALISON AND RODERICK BROMLEY"

As before, the names are changed. Since Alison and Roderick were not in the Michael group at the time the last book (*More Messages From Michael*) was written, they were not used as composites of any of the people in that book. They are both near fifty, have been married for twenty-seven years, have two children.

"We really are the newcomers," says Alison. She is sitting in a wing-back chair under one of her own large canvases. She has been an artist for fifteen years. "Actually, I've been an artist most of my life," she amends, "but the money didn't start coming in for work like this"—a nod toward the canvas overhead—"until just over fifteen years ago. Now things are looking decidedly encouraging."

Roderick, a long, lean fellow, is a chemist. "I still can't quite believe I'm involved in something like this. I'm simply not what anyone would think of as typical of people who get involved in this sort of thing."

"How would you characterize people who get involved in something like this?" Alison asks. "Robes? Candles? Incense?"

"You know what I mean," Rod says. "I don't like to think of myself as credulous, or . . . or gullible."

"You aren't," Alison says serenely. "Though I must confess if someone had told me five or six years ago that you'd be in a group like the Michael group, I would have laughed them out of the house."

Rod pours out a second glass of wine for all of us. "That's

precisely what I mean,'' he says emphatically. "I am not
the sort of man who goes to sessions and asks questions of
something calling itself a mid-causal reunited teaching entity. I mean, really!'' His indignation is mixed with sardonic
humor. "But we've been going regularly for almost two
years, and so far, every answer I've gotten has rung true,
even the very speculative and nonpersonal material.''

Alison nods slowly. "I think part of the appeal is that
there isn't any fuss made about the channeling. Milly or
one of the Leslies sits there with the rest of us, looking a
bit distant and hollow-eyed some of the time. Each of us
asks our questions in turn, and our medium turns either red
or white, and answers.''

"Just like that,'' says Rod. "There's no moaning or thrash-
ing about or . . .''

"Trumpets or tambourines,'' Alison supplies when Rod
falters.

"Yes, that's what I was getting at. It's all very . . . very
ordinary. You'd think that it was standard procedure for
one member of a discussion group to go off in light trance.''

"When we first started coming,'' Alison says, picking up
the story, "Milly was still doing automatic writing, and the
Leslies were still using the board. But shortly after we joined
the group—and I'm not implying that our joining had anything to do with it—they began to switch over to light
trance.''

"Lately the trances seem to have gotten deeper,'' Rod
adds. "And the information is growing more . . . complex
is the best way to describe it, I think. There's more meat
to it, and that's astonishing, considering the quality of information that was present from the start.''

"We were both very much intrigued,'' says Alison in a
contemplative way as she looks toward the window. It is
near sunset, and the western sky has turned a deep golden-
orange color. "Now that's a shade I wish I could put on
canvas,'' she muses.

"We're still intrigued,'' Rod says. "If for no other reason
that so far we've yet to discover any inconsistencies in
Michael. When you think of the number of perfectly normal

inconsistencies you discover about your friends in the space of two years, it's amazing that Michael has not deviated at all in that time. It's one of the most convincing factors in the material, that consistency. From what we've seen of the transcripts of earlier sessions, to say nothing of what we've read in the two books, the consistency has been going on for a lot longer than two years. I find that quite remarkable." He has set out some duck pâté, and he busies himself spreading it on crackers before offering it around.

"I think I was more prepared for this material, at least at first," says Alison. "I had fewer assumptions to deal with. Rod took more time because he had more to adjust to." She shakes her head at the memory. "But he never rejected it outright. That's what impresses me the most."

"You're the one with rejection, not me," Rod reminds her.

"True enough," she agrees. "Not that I understood that at first. I never thought of myself as a rejecting sort of person, but that was because I didn't have the same perspective that Michael has."

KINGS OFTEN CHOOSE REJECTION AS A GOAL WHEN THEY SEEK TO BE ABLE TO WORK ALONE, WITHOUT THE USUAL REGAL ENTOURAGE. THERE IS ALSO THE QUESTION OF AUTHORITY, WHICH IT IS NOT ALWAYS THE KING'S CHOICE TO USE. WHEN A KING FRAGMENT WISHES TO RELEASE THE BURDEN OF AUTHORITY, THE GOAL OF REJECTION IS ONE OF THE MOST OBVIOUS WAYS, ESPECIALLY WHEN THE KING IS WORKING IN AN ISOLATED WAY. EVEN KINGS IN SUBMISSION CAN EXERCISE AUTHORITY, BUT ON BEHALF OF OTHERS. WE ARE AWARE OF SEVERAL NURSES AND ONE POPULAR ACTOR WHO ARE MATURE KINGS WITH GOALS OF SUBMISSION. IN THE CASE OF THE FRAGMENT WHO IS NOW ALISON, THE CRITICAL ACUMEN THAT CAN BE DEVELOPED FROM REJECTION WAS PREFERRED OVER THE DEDICATION THAT IS PART OF SUBMISSION. IN GENERAL WE WOULD HAVE TO SAY THAT THIS OLD KING HAS DONE MUCH TO ACHIEVE ACCESS TO THE POSITIVE POLES OF HER OVERLEAVES.

"That was encouraging," says Alison. "I remembered being a girl, when they were looking for captains of sports teams and things like that: I was always being asked to be captain and I was always doing it badly. Now I can appreciate what was going on; at the time I simply hated always being asked to be captain because I knew I'd do it wrong."

"It's rather strange, actually," says Rod. "Here we are, two Action polarity fragments—I'm a Mature Warrior—and we have two Expression polarity kids. Our boy is a Mature Sage and our girl is a Young Artisan. That was one of the things I accepted about Michael right away; they called that one. And it's been a great deal of help in understanding what the kids are like. I'll admit that they baffled me many times. They still do, but now I have some concept of the nature of the bafflement, and that is helpful."

"I'm sure it's been helpful to them as well," says Alison. "They've been insisting since they were very young that Rod and I never really understood, and now I can see that in a way they're right."

"True," Rod concurs. He keeps his transcripts in a leather portfolio, which he opens now. "Not long ago Michael was going on about the process of reaction in the various Essences, and that was very useful to me, though it was Stu Gradiston's question."

IT IS NOT AMISS TO REMEMBER THAT FRAGMENTS BY NATURE OF ESSENCE HAVE DIFFERENT FRAMES OF REFERENCE FOR RESPONSE. THOSE SCHOLARS, BEING IN THE NEUTRAL POSTION, OFTEN WAIT AND EVALUATE WHEN DEALING WITH UNEXPECTED SITUATIONS. THEY STUDY AND EXPERIMENT. BECAUSE OF THE SINGLE CHANNEL OF INPUT, THEY HAVE TO DIGEST THE WHOLE THING BEFORE "GETTING A HANDLE" ON IT. THE SAME IS TRUE TO SOME DEGREE OF THE ACTION POLARITY, BECAUSE THEY SHARE THE SINGLE-CHANNEL INPUT; HOWEVER, BOTH KINGS AND WARRIORS ARE APT TO BE INCLINED TO ACT AS PART OF THE PROCESS OF GAINING UNDERSTANDING, FOR THE ACTION POLARITY—AS THE NAME IMPLIES—REQUIRES

ACTION IN ORDER TO BE ENGAGED. FOR ACTION POLARITY FRAGMENTS, DOING NOTHING IS OFTEN THE MOST DIFFICULT OF ALL TASKS. ON THE INSPIRATION POLARITY, WHERE THERE ARE TWO CHANNELS OF INPUT, THE PRIEST AND SLAVE FRAGMENTS HAVE TWO POINTS OF FOCUS ON GAINING UNDERSTANDING. ONE IS THE REAL-WORLD LEVEL, THE HERE-AND-NOW PHYSICAL PLANE LEVEL. FOR PRIESTS THE OTHER CHANNEL IS THE HIGHER IDEAL, WHATEVER THE PRIEST HAS DECIDED THE HIGHER IDEAL IS, AND ALL PROJECTS ARE ASSESSED IN RELATIONSHIP TO THAT HIGHER IDEAL, AND ARE ASSIGNED IMPORTANCE IN TERMS OF THE HIGHER IDEAL. SLAVES SERVE THE COMMON GOOD, WHATEVER THE SLAVE CHOOSES THE COMMON GOOD TO BE, AND ASIDE FROM THE FIRST CHANNEL OF REAL-WORLD CONCERN, THERE IS THE LARGER ISSUE OF COMMON GOOD, WHICH IS ALWAYS A FACTOR IN HOW A SLAVE WILL UNDERSTAND SITUATIONS. WE HAVE POINTED OUT BEFORE THAT THE SLAVES ARE THE ONLY ESSENCES THAT NEED NO SPECIAL CIRCUMSTANCES IN ORDER TO FULFILL THEIR LIFE TASKS, AND THAT AIDS THEM CONSIDERABLY IN TERMS OF ACQUIRING UNDERSTANDING. THE EXPRESSION POLARITY IS MORE COMPLEX IN MANY WAYS. THE SAGES HAVE THREE CHANNELS OF INPUT, AND THE ARTISANS FIVE. IT IS OFTEN DIFFICULT FOR THE EXPRESSION POLARITY TO KEEP ON ANY ONE CHANNEL FOR ANY LENGTH OF TIME, ESPECIALLY WHEN UNDER STRESS, AND BECAUSE OF THAT THE ATTENTION CAN BE DIVERTED TO OTHER CHANNELS AND CONCEPTS. OFTEN THE EXPRESSION POLARITY WILL "TUNE OUT" STRESS AND RELOCATE TO ANOTHER CHANNEL UNTIL THE REASON FOR THE STRESS HAS DIMINISHED. FRAGMENTS ON THE EXPRESSION POLARITY OFTEN HAVE TROUBLE DISTINGUISHING BETWEEN PERSONAL AND WORLD TRUTHS BECAUSE ON ONE OF THE CHANNELS, WORLD TRUTHS AND PERSONAL TRUTHS CAN OVERLAP. INTEGRAL UNDERSTANDING IS NOT EASILY ACHIEVED BY THESE FRAGMENTS. FOR EXPRESSION POLARITY FRAGMENTS THERE CAN BE MORE PROBLEMS WITH DISTRACTIONS THAN THERE ARE WITH OTHER ES-

SENCES BECAUSE CONCENTRATION IS A MORE COMPLI-
CATED PROCESS FOR EXPRESSION POLARITY FRAGMENTS
THAN FOR OTHER FRAGMENTS. IN DEALING WITH THE
YOUNG ARTISAN, STUART, WE WOULD SUGGEST THAT
YOU KEEP IN MIND THE MULTIPLICITY OF CHANNELS
WORKING IN HER UNDERSTANDING IF YOU WISH TO BE
ABLE TO ATTAIN THE DEGREE OF COMMUNICATION YOU
INDICATE YOU WANT TO HAVE.

"That multiplicity of channels certainly describes dealing
with our kids," says Alison with a sense of resignation. "I
thought when they were younger it was simply because they
were kids. But they're both teenagers now, and I can see
that this isn't going to stop because they're older."

"I used to get angry with Wendy because she never seemed
to be able to concentrate. Mind you, some of that was
definitely the way she was being taught, and I'm more aware
than ever now that attempting to give a uniform education
to kids is a losing proposition. She never developed the kind
of skills I was certain she"—he makes quotes signs with
his fingers—"ought to have done, and that worried me."

"Worried you?" Alison says with a trace of surprise.
"Why worry? I can see why you might be annoyed and
frustrated, but not worried."

"Well, what it comes down to," Rod admits with awkward candor, "I didn't want her turning into a flake."

"But sometimes she is a bit of a flake." Alison points
out. "She's always been."

Rod shrugs. "No argument. The thing is, it used to bother
me a great deal more than it does now. I will say that is
one difference the Michael material has made that has real
and immediate application: I have a much better understanding of my children and I don't fret about them as I used to."

"Wendy's been doing much better now that she's got
interested in stage lighting," Alison says. "She has a real
knack for it, and she truly enjoys it. Her high school drama
teacher has got her working with one of the local theater
groups, and she is doing very well with them. They're
talking about letting her do the entire lighting design for

Macbeth next year. She's enthusiastic about it. And the amazing thing is that now she's finally reading. She has had trouble with reading in the past, and wasn't much motivated to do it. Michael told us that Artisans often have trouble learning to read and do not take to it easily. Now that she has to know *Macbeth* inside and out, she's improving her skills.''

"She told me years ago when I asked her why she didn't like reading that there wasn't enough going on. At the time I thought it had something to do with attention spans and television and all the usual explanations. Now, I think it was the observation of a Young Artisan trying to deal with multi-channel input.'' Rod stares up at the ceiling. "She's been good at gymnastics, too, and that is definitely an Artisan skill.''

"David, on the other hand,'' says Alison, talking around a pâté-smeared cracker, ''has this desire to be a great film director. He wants to write and direct and produce. He's not very attracted by acting—he says that it doesn't give him enough scope.'' Her laughter is kind and indulgent. "David's a bright kid. He has this need for applause; he's had it since he was a little baby. He needs it all along the way, too, not just as a curtain call. It puzzled me at first, this constant seeking of applause. I don't mean approval, incidentally, I mean the clapping and bravos. He absolutely thrives on adulation, and without it he wilts.''

"I have trouble with that,'' Rod admits. "I'm trying to be more forthcoming with David, but it goes against the grain for me. Some of it is the way I was raised, but some of it is the Warrior nature.''

MOST WARRIORS ARE SUSPICIOUS OF APPLAUSE, EVEN WHEN THEY ENJOY IT. THAT IS NOT TO SAY THAT THEY DO NOT WISH TO HAVE THEIR ACCOMPLISHMENTS ACKNOWLEDGED: ALL WARRIORS WANT THEIR BATTLE STRIPES AND MEDALS. HOWEVER, THE SAGE NEED FOR APPLAUSE IS "FOREIGN'' TO THE WARRIOR NATURE, AND THEY TEND TO INTERPRET IT AS GRANDSTANDING AT BEST. IN THIS INSTANCE, RODERICK, WE WOULD HAVE

TO SAY THAT YOUR DISCOMFORT IS RECOGNIZED BY THE FRAGMENT WHO IS NOW DAVID, AND HAS BEEN FROM THE FIRST. THERE HAS BEEN A LEVEL OF PROFOUND MIS- UNDERSTANDING THAT IS THE RESULT OF THIS DICHOT- OMY. IT WOULD NOT BE AMISS, SHOULD YOU CHOOSE TO DO SO, TO TAKE THE TIME TO LISTEN TO THE PLANS OF THIS SAGE REALIZING THAT THE SAGE DOES NOT, IN FACT, REGARD ALL OF THEM AS FEASIBLE. SAGES ARE NOT IN- CLINED TO STRATEGY, JUST AS WARRIORS ARE NOT IN- CLINED TO EXTRAPOLATION. WARRIORS TEND TO HOLD TO THE "CREDIT WHERE CREDIT IS DUE" PHILOSOPHY, WHILE SAGES PREFER "I DON'T CARE WHAT THEY SAY ABOUT ME SO LONG AS THEY SPELL MY NAME RIGHT." THERE IS MUCH THAT MIGHT BE LEARNED, EACH FROM THE OTHER, SHOULD YOU CHOOSE TO LISTEN WITHOUT JUDGMENT.

"I think I got that answer at the fourth or fifth session we attended, and as a result I really tried to see what David was telling me from his point of view. I'm not saying I've succeeded. For one thing, we have a fourteen-year history of misconceptions to get through. In general, however, I think we're both more aware of how each of us sees each other, and that's a definite improvement."

"We're luckier than many of the parents we know," Ali- son goes on. "So far we haven't had any real problems with either Wendy or David with either drugs or sex. We've always made it a point not to lecture them. I know that all it took was a lecture when I was a kid for me to want to do the thing they were lecturing me against."

"Sounds right," says Rod.

"If you're referring to my rejection," Alison says with prim defiance, "I don't think my response was all that un- usual for any kid growing up."

"I didn't say it was," Rod counters. "You brought up your goal." He pulls out his transcripts. "Of course, it may be obvious to say this, but much of what Michael has said has been a great help to our relationship. I have learned a lot, not just about Alison but about relationships in general.

This one is the most important to me, and so I have spent more time finding out about it.''

"I'd agree, though what has made the biggest difference to me," Alison says, helping herself to another cracker, "has been finding out about primary and secondary chief features. That has made all the difference in the world to me, knowing that these things really do exist, that there is a name for them and a pattern to them and that they can be accurately described and dealt with. What Michael calls 'photographing the chief feature' is a very useful exercise: I have finally been able to see what it is that my chief feature does to me while it is doing it. That doesn't mean I can stop it, but at least I know what's going on.''

"I've found that *very* useful," Rod says. "Not just for myself, but in regard to the people I work with. I kept running afoul of one of them, and the more I tried to resolve things, the worse they seemed to get. It was the most frustrating situation, and nothing I did made it improve. Finally I got the fellow's Overleaves, and that made a tremendous difference to me.''

THIS IS A SECOND-LEVEL MATURE PRIEST IN THE CAUTION MODE WITH A GOAL OF DOMINANCE, A PRAGMATIST IN THE MOVING PART OF INTELLECTUAL CENTER WITH A CHIEF FEATURE OF STUBBORNNESS AND A SECONDARY OF MARTYRDOM.

"Well, the primary stubbornness really does hook into the dominance in this man, I can tell you. Also those are my two chief features, and I know what they do to me. He absolutely refuses to deal with new situations in any way, shape, or form. But it was the secondary that was the root of the problem in my dealing with him. That martyrdom distorting the pragmatism made it almost impossible to persuade him that it was worth trying something different or new. I have that martyrdom/pragmatist action going on, and I am very much aware, thanks to Michael, how it pulls you off the track. Add to that the squirrelliness some Priests have, and you can see why I never managed to get through

to him.'' He looks at the Overleaf sheet again. ''If I hadn'
found out about him, I know I would have made thing
even worse than they were in my dealing with him. I
retrospect, I'm a bit surprised he didn't fire me. I think tha
he recognized my ability to get things done, and that made
sense to him. That's my assessment, incidentally, no
Michael's.''

Alison gets up and draws the draperies across the window
''It's getting dark enough for this. Rod, start the fire, wil
you?'' While he busies himself with long matches and cu
lengths of wood, she takes her seat again and goes on. ''I'v
always had a sense about people, ever since I was a very
little child. I couldn't account for it, but I knew it was there
I was always sensitive to the motives people around me
had, as compared to what they said they had. Some of that
I gather from Michael's comments, is typical of the Ol
soul cycle. The rest has something to do with Kings.''

''She is a pretty impressive King,'' says Rod as he con
tinues to work on the fire. ''It's funny; she was a little pu
off to find out about being a King, but I wasn't the leas
surprised.''

''Given the way he acts, you might suppose Rod was the
King instead of the Warrior. He certainly has a way o
taking charge of things.'' She takes her glass and tastes the
wine. ''That was one of the things I liked about him at the
first, how forthright he is. That doesn't mean I was entirely
favorably impressed when we first met.''

''Oh, don't say that,'' protests Rod in mock dismay. ''
was entirely captivated by you from the first and you know
it.''

''Um.''

The fire is going well; Rod gets up, brushes off his knees,
and resumes his place on the sofa. ''You're being non-com-
mittal again,'' he tells her.

''I am?''

''Stop that,'' he says, trying not to laugh.

''Why?'' She gives him the blandest of smiles, and he
guffaws. ''And they say Warriors have no sense of humor.''

Rod makes himself stop laughing. ''When we were first

married, I used to call her Duchess—''

"Which I disliked very much," Alison interjects.

"—because it suited her. But I was underestimating her, wasn't I? She outranks me more than that, and in soul cycle as well as Essence. She's a first-level Old King, observation mode, goal of rejection, an idealist, in the intellectual part of emotional center, chief feature of stubbornness with a secondary of arrogance."

"Sam Fisher and I had a long talk one evening about that chief feature combination, since we share it. By the way, Rod's a fifth-level Mature Warrior in the caution mode— though you'd hardly guess it—goal of growth, a pragmatist in the moving part of intellectual center with a primary chief feature of stubbornness, like me, and a secondary of martyr- dom, the 'natural' Warrior chief feature. Come to think of it, there are two other Warriors in the group who have martyrdom as a secondary." This last is said after a short pause.

"Lucky us," says Rod, pausing as the phone rings. "I'll get it."

"Thanks, love," says Alison. "One of the things I liked about him from the first is that he's always been willing to do things."

"Warriors are like that," I say.

"And very convenient for Kings," Alison finishes with a smile. "Yes, there is that."

Rod comes back into the room. "Wendy and David will be ready for a ride home in half an hour," he announces. "Shall we finish up quickly, or wait?"

"Let's get this out of the way," says Alison, indicating Rod's place on the couch. "There are those who find our match puzzling, and have from the first. After all, there's Rod, a hardheaded, practical chemist married to a painter who likes to do strange, very large paintings. Aside from the parents of our children's schoolmates, we have few groups of friends in common. Our professional interests are quite separate and our colleagues are extremely diverse."

"There is the Michael group," Rod says with a trace of a smile.

"There certainly is, but I'm not certain it counts," Alison says when she has given it her consideration. "I suppose it does, in a very strange way. It is odd, though. We've been in the group for some little time, and I admit I still don't know for sure what everyone else in the group does. It was only a couple months ago that I finally learned Bill Dutton's last name, and that was an accident."

"And I didn't learn where Sam teaches until we'd been coming to sessions for almost a year," Alison says. "I knew he was a teacher, but I didn't know where."

"That's the strange thing about the group," Rod goes on. "We have very close associations with each other in one sense, but in another, we're almost unknowns. Stu Gradiston didn't find out I was a chemist until I asked the question about that new lab procedure we were trying."

"It's a unique experience, being in a group like this," Alison says for both of them. "It would be difficult to say what difference it's made, since I don't know how things would have gone for us if we hadn't *chosen* to accept the invitation to participate. But I know that I feel more comprehension about my life and my work than I did two years ago. Maybe that's Michael, and maybe I'm getting more sensible as I get older, and maybe it's some of both."

"I know I'm enjoying the group and the sessions," says Rod. "I look forward to the sessions and I think that what I've learned so far has been useful. I'm occasionally surprised at how mundane some of the questions can be, but it doesn't bother me now, the way it did at first."

IT IS NOT INAPPROPRIATE FOR FRAGMENTS TO ASK QUESTIONS ABOUT WHAT IS OF CONCERN TO THEM. LET US REMARK THAT IN MANY INSTANCES THE ISSUES OF CONCERN APPEAR "MUNDANE" TO OTHERS BECAUSE THE ISSUES BEING ASKED ABOUT DO NOT DIRECTLY IMPINGE ON THE LIVES OF THE FRAGMENTS CONSIDERING THE QUESTION "MUNDANE". IT IS EASY TO DISMISS A HEADACHE AS MINOR WHEN IT IS NOT YOUR HEADACHE. BY THE SAME TOKEN, QUESTIONS THAT SEEM "MUNDANE" ARE OFTEN MISUNDERSTOOD BY THOSE NOT ASK-

ING THE QUESTION. IT IS GOOD WORK TO BE WILLING TO ACCEPT THE VALIDITY OF THE QUESTIONS OF OTHER FRAGMENTS AND TO GIVE THEM SERIOUS ATTENTION. FOR THOSE WHO CANNOT "COME TO TERMS" WITH THE QUESTIONS ASKED BY OTHERS, WE WOULD SUGGEST THAT THE CHIEF FEATURE BE EXAMINED FOR CREATING STATIC. REGARDING THE QUESTIONS OF OTHERS AS INTRINSI-CALLY LESS IMPORTANT THAN ONE'S OWN IS A TYPICAL DISTORTION OF CHIEF FEATURE, AND ONE OF THE MOST PERNICIOUS, FOR IT BLOCKS MUCH OF THE MEANS FOR INTIMACY, WHICH IS, OF COURSE, THE PROCESS OF ES-SENCE CONTACT AND THE ONLY MEANS BY WHICH FRAG-MENTS EVOLVE.

"Back to chief feature again," says Rod with resignation. "It's a very real force in life, isn't it?"

WE HAVE SAID MANY TIMES BEFORE, BUT WE WILL REPEAT: THERE ARE ONLY TWO FORCES IN THE UNI-VERSE—LOVE AND FEAR. LOVE IS INFINITELY STRONGER BUT FEAR IS INFINITELY MORE SEDUCTIVE. FEAR IS RARELY PRESENTED AS ALL-OUT TERROR, BUT AS APPAR-ENTLY REASONABLE POSITIONS AND REASONS FOR A PER-SON TO BLOCK THE PROGRESS OF ESSENCE OR THE VAL-IDATION OF PROGRESS THROUGH THE LIFE. FEAR COMES IN COUNTLESS DISGUISES AND DISTORTIONS. LOVE IS ITSELF ONLY. FEAR OFFERS ENDLESS APPARENT ADVANTAGES. LOVE IS NOT A BARGAIN OR CONTRACT; IT IS A UNIVERSAL TRUTH. FEAR IS ULTIMATELY COERCIVE AND MENDA-CIOUS. LOVE IS THE SOURCE OF TRUTH. FOR THOSE WORK-ING UNDER THE SPELL OF CHIEF FEATURE, IT IS DIFFICULT TO BREAK AWAY FROM ITS PRISON, AND OFTEN, WHEN SUCH BREAKAWAY HAS OCCURRED, NO MATTER HOW BRIEFLY, THEN THE CHIEF FEATURE EXACTS A PRICE FOR THIS "LAPSE" IN ORDER TO REESTABLISH ITS DOMINATION OF THE FRAGMENT IN QUESTION.

"When we've done the nonpersonal agenda session, we've had some fascinating questions, and none of them have

personal significance, as such, for any of us," Rod says
with enthusiasm. "In a way, I enjoy those the most. We
had one not long ago that was largely about the problems
of handling information."

THERE BEING SO MANY SOURCES OF INFORMATION,
AND SO MUCH ACTUAL MATERIAL ON ALMOST ANY "REC-
OGNIZED" SUBJECT, THE PROCESS OF SELECTION TENDS
TO BECOME INCREASINGLY IMPORTANT: TO ASSUME THAT
THE NARROWEST VISION IS ONE AREA ONLY WILL PRO-
VIDE THE SOLUTION FOR THE GATHERING OF INFORMA-
TION IS, OF COURSE, NOT VALID, BUT LIKEWISE, THE
"SAMPLING" OF ALL AREAS OF STUDY AND AVAILABLE
INFORMATION WILL TEND TO BE BASICALLY UNSATISFY-
ING UNLESS THE PROFESSION OF THAT FRAGMENT IS THAT
OF POPULAR JOURNALIST. WHILE IN GENERAL WE WOULD
HAVE TO SAY THAT ECLECTICISM HAS MORE BENEFITS
THAN SINGLE-MINDED PURSUIT OF ONE SOLITARY DISCIP-
LINE, WE ARE AWARE THAT TAKEN TO EXTREMES ECLEC-
TICISM IS AT THE LEAST SELF-DEFEATING. WE WOULD
WISH TO POINT OUT THAT LEARNING TO ASSESS THE "RE-
LATIVE MERIT" OF INFORMATION IS BECOMING A MAJOR
CONSIDERATION FOR ALL FRAGMENTS EXTANT ON THE
PHYSICAL PLANE OF THIS PLANET AND SPECIES FOR ALL
BUT THE MOST "THIRD WORLD" COUNTRIES, AND EVEN
IN THOSE COUNTRIES MANY CITY DWELLERS ARE BEGIN-
NING TO FACE THE SAME BEWILDERING MOSAIC AS THOSE
IN MORE TECHNOLOGICALLY ADVANCED COUNTRIES. TO
ASSESS THE RELATIVE IMPORTANCE OF INFORMATION, IT
IS GENERALLY "BEST" TO DETERMINE HOW MUCH IF ANY
BEARING THIS INFORMATION HAS IN RELATION TO THE
FOCUS OF THE SPECIFIC LIFE IN QUESTION. CURIOSITY
AND AMUSEMENT ARE, OF COURSE, VALID PARTS OF THE
FOCUS. THE GREATER THE SIGNIFICANCE OF THE INFOR-
MATION IN TERMS OF THE FOCUS OF THE LIFE, THE
GREATER THE AMOUNTS OF ACTUAL MATERIAL WOULD
TEND TO BE OF IMPORTANCE AND USE. FOR EXAMPLE,
THE SPECIFIC KNOWLEDGE OF DENTISTRY IS NOT NECES-
SARY IN ORDER TO GET YOUR TEETH CLEANED. IF, ON

THE OTHER HAND, YOUR PROFESSION IS THAT OF DENTIST, THEN IT IS GENERALLY "INCUMBENT UPON YOU" TO GATHER AS MUCH INFORMATION, OLD AND CURRENT AND EMERGING, AS IS APPROPRIATELY AVAILABLE. LIKEWISE, NOT EVERY FRAGMENT HAS REASON OR DESIRE TO BE INVOLVED IN THE MAKING OF FISHING FLIES, BUT FOR THOSE FRAGMENTS FOR WHOM FLY CASTING IS AN IMPORTANT PART OF LIFE, KNOWLEDGE IN DEPTH IN THIS AREA CAN BE VERY USEFUL INDEED.

IT IS NOT UNWISE TO BE AWARE THAT VAST AREAS OF KNOWLEDGE OVERLAP, SO THAT WHAT IS OF INTEREST TO A FORENSIC SCIENTIST MAY ALSO BE OF INTEREST TO A STRUCTURAL ENGINEER OR A SPECIAL-EFFECTS DESIGNER. THE PERCEPTION OF RIGIDLY BLOCKED OUT AREAS OF EXPERTISE IS NOT ONLY INAPPROPRIATE TO GROWTH AND UNDERSTANDING, BUT OFTEN DETRIMENTAL TO PROGRESS AND EVOLUTION OF ENSOULED SPECIES. IT IS NOT UNCOMMON ON YOUNG SOUL PLANETS TO SEE AREAS OF KNOWLEDGE DOGMATICALLY DEFINED AND SORTS OF STUDY BE CONSIDERED MORE OR LESS LEGITIMATE GIVEN ANY SET OF PREVAILING ACADEMIC AND SOCIAL FANCY. WE WOULD DESCRIBE YOUR APPLICATION TO THIS MATERIAL AS GENERALLY DOGMATICALLY UNACCEPTABLE IN THE TRADITIONAL ACADEMIC COMMUNITY, JUST AS FIVE HUNDRED YEARS AGO METALLURGY WAS GENERALLY RELEGATED TO ALCHEMISTS WHO AT THAT TIME WERE ON BEGINNING THEIR "FALL" FROM ACADEMIC "GRACE". IN GENERAL, THE FERVID BELIEF IN DEDUCTIVE REASONING AND THE SCIENTIFIC METHOD HAS BEEN EXTENDED TO SUCH WILDLY INAPPROPRIATE AREAS AS MUSIC AND PHILOSOPHY BECAUSE OF ITS PREEMINENT POSITION IN INTELLECTUAL ESTEEM IN THE OCCIDENTAL WORLD. TO INSIST THAT ALL INFORMATION AND STUDY ACCOMMODATE ITSELF TO THE SCIENTIFIC METHOD IS, OR COURSE, ABSURD. BY EXTENSION OF SUCH CONCEPT, ANY WELL-TRAINED TENNIS PLAYER IS "PERFECTLY CAPABLE" OF PERFORMING *SWAN LAKE*. EVEN IN ASSESSING THE STRUCTRUAL REQUIREMENTS OF SKYSCRAPERS, MOST BUILDING DESIGNERS HAVE AN AES-

THETIC STANDARD AS WELL AS AN ENGINEERING STANDARD IN MIND, OR THERE WOULD NOT BE CLEARLY DIVERGENT STYLES IN THE BUILDINGS.

"I'm especially interested in the answer Michael gave regarding the validity of some kind of space warp for traveling at speeds greater than light, and if they required particle disassembly and reassembly; the old 'Beam me up, Scotty' method."

THERE ARE METHODS THAT EMPLOY THAT PARTICULAR TECHNIQUE. THERE ARE OTHERS THAT DO NOT. MATTER NEED NOT BE ENDLESSLY ATTENUATED IN ORDER TO BE "WARPED". ONE ANALOGY MIGHT BE THE CASE OF A SWIFTLY MOVING ICE SKATER WHO SUDDENLY TURNS FRONT TO BACK BUT CONTINUES TO MOVE IN THE SAME DIRECTION AT UNDIMINISHED AND/OR INCREASING SPEED. THIS "FLIP" CAN BE APPLIED IN TERMS OF EXCEEDING THE SPEED OF LIGHT IN THAT ACCELERATING TO THE POINT THAT BY GOING BACK TO FRONT YOU CONTINUE TO ACCELERATE INDICATES THE KEY. WHILE PARTICLE DISASSEMBLY AND REASSEMBLY IS EMPLOYED BY A NUMBER OF ENSOULED SPECIES, IT IS IN FACT MORE HAZARDOUS AND LESS EFFICIENT THAN HYPERACCELERATION AND IS IN PART CONSTRAINED BY THE MAGNETIC LINES OF FORCE EMANATING FROM THE CENTER OF THE GALAXY. PLUS-LIGHT SPEEDS HAVE NO SUCH LIMITATION, SO WHAT THEY LACK IN CHRONOLOGICAL EFFICIENCY THEY MAKE UP FOR IN PRACTICALITY. ONE OF THE HAZARDS OF PARTICLE DISASSEMBLY AND REASSEMBLY IS THE POTENTIAL RISK OF THE ENVIRONMENT AT THE REASSEMBLY POINT, WHICH IF INIMICAL TO THE PARTICLES COMING CAN PROVE UNPLEASANT AT BEST AND DISASTROUS AT MOST FOR THE TRANSPORTED FRAGMENT BEING REASSEMBLED. WHILE THE PARTICLE DISASSEMBLY AND REASSEMBLY IS EVEN FASTER THAN THE "FLIP" IT WORKS MOST EFFICIENTLY ON "LIVE" GOODS AND IS THEREFORE NOT MUCH USE FOR COMMERCE OR SIMILAR VENTURES.

• • •

"Don't you sometimes feel that questions about things like space travel are wasting Michael's time?" Alison asks speculatively.

"I don't think so," Rod answers. "Michael has said that all questions are valid, and, frankly, I'm interested in the workings of space flight, even if it's only theoretical."

"Still, we *are* contributing to the information glut, aren't we?" she asks mischievously, clearly not interested in an answer.

CHAPTER 7

MICHAEL: INTIMACY AND EVOLUTION

ALL FRAGMENTS EXTANT ON THE PHYSICAL PLANE ARE LINKED THROUGH THE PROCESS OF ENSOULMENT. THIS IS NOT LIMITED TO YOUR PLANET AND YOUR SPECIES; IT APPLIES TO ALL SPECIES THROUGHOUT THE UNIVERSE. AS AN ENSOULED FRAGMENT, THE CASTING FROM THE TAO AND THE EVOLUTION OF RETURN TO THE TAO IS NEVER COMPLETELY "OUT OF TOUCH" WITH THAT UNIVERSAL TRUTH. THIS DOES NOT MEAN, HOWEVER, THAT THERE IS AN ACKNOWLEDGMENT OF THIS EXCEPT AT ESSENCE LEVEL; SUCH PERCEPTION RARELY ENTERS THE REALMS OF THE OVERLEAVES AND/OR THE PERSONALITY.

HOWEVER, THIS LINK IS SOMETIMES SENSED DURING THE TIMES OF RECOGNIZED AND VALIDATED INTIMACY. THERE ARE REFERENCES TO LOVERS WHO DURING PHYSICAL INTIMACY HAVE A SENSE OF "FLOATING IN THE UNIVERSE". THIS IS NOT THE SAME THING AS BODY-TYPE ATTRACTION WITH ITS PHYSICAL "FIREWORKS", THIS IS SOMETHING THAT APPROACHES OUT-OF-BODY EXPERIENCES. OFTEN SUCH EXPERIENCE IS FRIGHTENING TO FRAGMENTS UNPREPARED FOR IT, AND CAN SERVE TO INTERFERE WITH THE RELATIONSHIP THROUGH THE CHIEF FEATURE. THAT SENSE OF BEING OUT IN THE UNIVERSE IS THE USUAL WAY FRAGMENTS OF YOUR SPECIES AND OF THE CETACEAN SPECIES VALIDATE THAT UNIVERSAL LINK.

IT MIGHT BE APPARENT THAT SUCH CONTACT IS MORE EASILY ACHIEVED WITH FRAGMENTS WITH WHOM THERE

ARE BONDS, LINKS, TIES, PAST ASSOCIATIONS, AND SIMILAR RELATIONAL ASPECTS. FOR THE MOST PART, THAT IS AN ACCURATE PERCEPTION, ALTHOUGH THERE ARE EXCEPTIONS OF MANY SORTS. TO LIMIT THE NATURE OF VALIDATED INTIMACY IS TO DEFEAT THE CONTACT AT THE OUTSET.

BY INTIMACY WE MEAN, OF COURSE, VALID ESSENCE CONTACT. THIS IS THE ONLY SOURCE OF GROWTH AND EVOLUTION, FOR IT IS THE ONLY FUNCTION OF LOVE. ESSENCE CONTACT IS THE PURPOSE OF LOVE, IF IT IS NECESSARY FOR LOVE TO BE PERCEIVED AS HAVING A PURPOSE. IT IS MORE ACCURATE THAT ESSENCE CONTACT *IS* LOVE, UNTRAMMELED BY THE DISTORTIONS OF SPECIES OR THE CHIEF FEATURE OR THE NEGATIVE POLES OF THE OVERLEAVES. WHEN TRUE INTIMACY OCCURS, ALL THAT IS "THERE" FOR THE CONTACT IS ESSENCE AND CASTING ORDER. ALL ELSE IS "SET ASIDE".

OF COURSE, SEXUAL CONTACT IS NOT THE SOLE AND ONLY PLACE THAT VALID ESSENCE CONTACT CAN AND DOES OCCUR. ESSENCE CONTACT IS POSSIBLE AT ALL TIMES AND ALL PLACES, EVEN WHEN THE FRAGMENTS IN QUESTION ARE NOT, IN FACT, PHYSICALLY PRESENT AT THE SAME PLACE, ALTHOUGH WE WOULD HAVE TO SAY THAT SUCH INTIMATE-BUT-PHYSICALLY-ABSENT, CONTACT ALMOST ALWAYS IS LIMITED TO ESSENCE TWINS, TASK COMPANIONS, AND, OCCASIONALLY, MEMBERS OF THE SAME CADENCE. THE PROCESS OF ESSENCE CONTACT IS THE VALIDATION OF THE LINK THAT EXISTS BETWEEN ALL FRAGMENTS AND THE TAO, AS WELL AS THE CONTACT WITH THE FRAGMENTS. WE DO NOT INTEND TO REPRESENT THIS AS DIFFICULT OR COMPLICATED. ESSENCE CONTACT IS, IN FACT, UTTERLY SIMPLE, WHICH IS ONE OF THE REASONS IT IS DIFFICULT TO ATTAIN AND TO MAINTAIN. THERE ARE NO "TRICKS" TO IT, EXCEPT THAT THERE ARE NO TRICKS. WE DO NOT POSE A RIDDLE IN THIS STATEMENT, WE ARE ATTEMPTING TO EXAMINE THE NATURE OF ESSENCE CONTACT IN A WAY THAT WILL AID YOU IN YOUR SEARCH.

TWO MEMBERS OF OUR LITTLE GROUP HAVE DESCRIBED

A CONVERSATION HELD AT LUNCH ON A SUNNY AFTER-
NOON IN A QUIET CORNER OF A POPULAR RESTAURANT.
BOTH FRAGMENTS REMARKED THAT FOR A WHILE THEY
WERE BOTH SO WHOLLY CAUGHT UP IN THE CONVERSA-
TION, SO VERY PRESENT IN WHAT THEY WERE SAYING TO
EACH OTHER, AND THE VERY CLEAR QUALITY OF THEIR
LISTENING TO ONE ANOTHER THAT IT WAS ODDLY DIF-
FICULT TO REMEMBER THE CONVERSATION AFTERWARD;
THEY WERE SO FOCUSED ON WHAT WAS GOING ON AS IT
WAS GOING ON THAT IT "BURNED CLEAN" AND LEFT VERY
LITTLE "RESIDUE". WHAT OCCURRED, OF COURSE, WAS
VALID ESSENCE CONTACT. IT IS NOT UNUSUAL FOR SUCH
MOMENTS TO BE "STORED" INCOMPLETE IN THE MEMORY,
FOR THE CHIEF FEATURE INTERVENES TO DISTORT THE
OCCASION, AND, AS THE STUDENT WHO IS NOW FENELLA
SO CORRECTLY OBSERVED, THE MOMENT "BURNED
CLEAN" SO THAT MOST OF THE MEMORY WAS OF TANGEN-
TIAL ASPECTS, NOT THE CONTACT ITSELF.

THIS IS NOT MEANT TO BE DEFEATING IN ANY WAY.
ESSENCE CONTACT IS THE SINGLE GREATEST ACHIEVE-
MENT OF ANY FRAGMENT EXTANT ON THE PHYSICAL
PLANE, AND NO MATTER HOW FLEETING THE CONTACT
OR HOW POORLY REMEMBERED, THE CONTACT ITSELF
HAS LASTING SIGNFICANCE IN THE LIFE BEING LED *AND
ALL LIVES TO COME*. EVERY INSTANCE OF ESSENCE CON-
TACT IS ANOTHER STEP IN ESSENCE EVOLUTION AND THE
EVOLUTION OF ALL FRAGMENTS.

WHAT MANY FRAGMENTS FIND PERPLEXING ABOUT ES-
SENCE CONTACT IS THAT IT DOES NOT RESPOND TO WHAT
YOU CALL THE SCIENTIFIC METHOD—DUPLICATE THE AP-
PARENT CIRCUMSTANCES AND IT MAY OR MAY NOT HAP-
PEN AGAIN, AND THE EXPERIENCE IS LIKELY TO BE PER-
CEIVED DIFFERENTLY EACH TIME IT OCCURS. WHILE WE
BASICALLY WOULD CAUTION ALL FRAGMENTS AGAINST
THE VERY "HUMAN" TENDENCY TO LEAP TO PREMISES AS
WELL AS CONCLUSIONS, WE WOULD ENCOURAGE INDUC-
TIVE REASONING AS BEING ON A PAR WITH DEDUCTIVE
REASONING, WITH THE EXPERIENCES AND CONCLUSIONS
PERCEIVED AS VALID AS THOSE OBTAINED THROUGH

"ARISTOTELIAN" THINKING.

WHILE WE REALIZE THAT CURRENT PHILOSOPHIES OF ACADEMIC CLASSROOM INSTRUCTION DO NOT EASILY ACCOMMODATE INDUCTIVE REASONING, NONETHELESS STUDENTS, AND BY THIS WE MEAN WITHIN THE FORMAL SOCIO-ACADEMIC FRAMEWORK, DO NOT TRULY LEARN TO "THINK" IF THEY ARE NOT AT LEAST CONVERSANT WITH THE INDUCTIVE PROCESS AS WELL AS THE DEDUCTIVE ONE. THE ATTITUDE OF SKEPTIC IS THE MOST "NATURALLY" DRAWN TO INDUCTIVE REASONING, AND AS WE HAVE SAID BEFORE, ALMOST ALL INFORMATIONAL ADVANCES HAVE COME FROM FRAGMENTS WITH THE ATTITUDE OF SKEPTIC. BEYOND INDUCTIVE REASONING ARE THE "WONDERLANDS" OF ART AND AESTHETICS, AND WE HASTEN TO POINT OUT THAT NEITHER CAN BE "COMFORTABLY" ATTAINED WITHOUT FIRST ACQUIRING THE "KNACK" OF INDUCTIVE REASONING AND NONLINEAR LOGIC.

THE WILLINGNESS OF A FRAGMENT TO QUESTION ITS PERCEPTIONS OF THE SURROUNDINGS IS THE FIRST STEP TOWARD SELF-AWARENESS, AND IN VALIDATING THE EVOLUTION WITHIN A GIVEN LIFE, OR ALL LIVES, THE QUESTIONING OF PERCEPTIONS BRINGS THE LESSONS TO BEAR. ONLY WHEN THE QUESTIONS HAVE BEEN ASKED AND THE AWARENESS OF SELF HAS BEGUN CAN TRUE ESSENCE CONTACT BE VALIDATED AND RECOGNIZED DURING THE ACTUAL COURSE OF THE LIFE. ALL ESSENCE CONTACT IS RECOGNIZED, AND THE COURSE OF THE LIFE AND EVOLUTION VALIDATED DURING THE ASTRAL INTERVAL, AND IT IS NOT NECESSARY THAT YOU CHOOSE TO DO OTHER THAN VALIDATE BETWEEN LIVES. HOWEVER, SHOULD YOU CHOOSE TO EXAMINE YOUR LIFE AND ACHIEVE A LEVEL OF SELF-AWARENESS—AND WE WISH TO POINT OUT THAT SELF-AWARENESS IS NOT SELF-CONCIOUSNESS OR SELF-INVOLVEMENT—THEN THE EXPERIENCES OF VALID ESSENCE CONTACT ARE WITHIN YOUR UNDERSTANDING DURING THE LIFE.

THAT IS NOT TO SAY THAT YOU ARE THEREFORE URGED TO CHOOSE SUCH A PATH. FOR MANY FRAGMENTS THE

NATURE OF THE LIFE TASK LIES ALONG OTHER ROUTES,
AND FOR SUCH FRAGMENTS VALIDATION BETWEEN LIVES
IS THE MORE "SENSIBLE" CHOICE. THE VALIDATION OF A
LIFE NEED NOT BE ENTIRELY THE PRODUCT OF DELIBER-
ATE SELF-AWARENESS; THAT IS ENTIRELY A MATTER OF
CHOICE. WE WOULD WISH TO POINT OUT, HOWEVER, THAT
THE GREATER THE COMPREHENSION ACHIEVED DURING
A LIFETIME THE GREATER THE DEGREE OF ACCESS TO
COMPREHENSION IN THE LIVES TO COME.

COMPREHENSION IS VERY MUCH A TOOL OF VALIDA-
TION AND RECOGNITION AND IT CAN PLAY A ROLE IN
MANY ASPECTS OF THE LIFE. OF COURSE, ACHIEVING ES-
SENCE CONTACT IS ONE OF THE POSSIBILITIES THAT CAN
RESULT FROM SELF-AWARENESS AND THE RESULTANT
COMPREHENSION. THERE ARE MANY OTHER APPLICA-
TIONS OF COMPREHENSION ONCE IT IS BROUGHT TO BEAR:
THE FRAGMENT WHO HAS SELF-AWARENESS IS MORE
ABLE TO MOVE THROUGH THE INTERNAL MONADS WITH-
OUT THE HIGH DEGREE OF STRESS EXPERIENCED BY SO
MANY FRAGMENTS. THAT DOES NOT MEAN THAT SUCH
MONADS ARE THEREFORE ENTIRELY WITHOUT STRESS,
BUT THAT WITH SELF-AWARENESS THE STRESS AND UP-
HEAVAL IS REDUCED. THERE IS ALSO THE QUESTION OF
WORKING ON THE LIFE TASK, WHICH IS MORE EASILY AC-
COMPLISHED WHEN SELF-AWARENESS IS PRESENT IN THE
LIFE.

SELF-AWARENESS IS A GREAT ASSET WHEN TRUE INTI-
MACY IS SOUGHT, FOR THE COMPREHENSION OF THE EX-
PERIENCE LESSENS THE FRIGHT OF THE EXPERIENCE SO
THAT THE TENDENCY TO FLEE IS MUCH REDUCED. FOR IT
IS OFTEN THE CASE WHEN TRUE ESSENCE CONTACT HAS
OCCURRED THAT ONE OR BOTH FRAGMENTS WILL SUC-
CUMB TO THE INSISTENCE OF CHIEF FEATURE AND REJECT
THE RELATIONSHIP, AVERTING THE DANGER OF GREATER
INTIMACY, OR PUTTING SUCH DEMANDS ON THE RE-
LATIONSHIP THAT IT CANNOT SUSTAIN INTIMACY.

LET US ADD HERE THAT FOR MANY FRAGMENTS SEXUAL
ACTIVITY IS A MEANS TO AVOID ACTUAL INTIMACY, SUB-

STITUTING THE PHYSICAL CONTACT FOR ESSENCE CON-
TACT. WE DO NOT LIMIT THIS TO SEX-FOR-HIRE, ORGIAS-
TIC EVENTS, ONE-NIGHT STANDS, OR SIMILAR PHYSICAL
CONTACTS, AND WE DO NOT RULE OUT THE POSSIBILITY
OF ESSENCE CONTACT CURING SUCH PHYSICAL ARRANGE-
MENTS; IT IS, IN FACT, MORE COMMON IN CONTINUING
SEXUAL RELATIONSHIPS, SUCH AS, BUT NOT LIMITED TO,
MARRIAGE, FOR THE RISK OF INTIMACY IS MUCH GREATER
WHEN TWO FRAGMENTS HAVE TIME TO EVOLVE TO-
GETHER, AND THEREFORE THE TEMPTATION TO ESTAB-
LISH A "NICE, SAFE" SEXUAL ROUTINE IS VERY GREAT,
AND LARGELY GETS RID OF THE SPECTER OF TRUE INTI-
MACY.

ONCE TRUE INTIMACY HAS OCCURRED BETWEEN FRAG-
MENTS, THERE IS A SUBTLE CHANGE IN THE NATURE OF
THE RELATIONSHIP, NOT ALWAYS A BENEFICIAL ONE.
MANY FRAGMENTS ARE DRIVEN TO "EXPLAIN" WHAT
HAPPENED AND, IN SO DOING, DENY IT. THE CHANGE IN
THE RELATIONSHIP IS THE RESULT OF THE PERCEPTION
OF ESSENCE. IN OTHER WORDS, ON MANY LEVELS EACH
FRAGMENT IS TRULY AWARE OF WHO THE OTHER FRAG-
MENT *IS*.

FOR YOUNG AND BABY SOULS, SUCH RECOGNITION IS
NOT OFTEN EASILY ACCEPTED, FOR BABY AND YOUNG
SOULS ARE JUST LEARNING TO UNDERSTAND THAT EACH
AND EVERY FRAGMENT EXTANT UPON THE PHYSICAL
PLANE IS AS PRESENT AND VALID AS EVERY OTHER FRAG-
MENT. FOR BABY AND YOUNG SOULS, THIS IS A VERY
DISQUIETING CONCEPT, ONE THAT IS GENERALLY DIS-
TURBING AND/OR DISTRESSING. TO HAVE THE ADDED
SHOCK OF ESSENCE CONTACT IS MORE THAN SUCH SOULS
ARE GENERALLY WILLING TO HANDLE.

OF COURSE, ESSENCE CONTACT OCCURS FOR ALL FRAG-
MENTS AT ALL LEVELS, OR THERE WOULD BE NO EVOLU-
TION. HOWEVER, UNTIL THE VERY END OF THE YOUNG
CYCLE, VALIDATION AND RECOGNITION OF THE ESSENCE
CONTACT IS "SHELVED" UNTIL THE ASTRAL INTERVAL BE-
TWEEN LIVES WHERE THE CONSTRAINTS OF PERSONAL-

ITY, OVERLEAVES, AND THE REST DO NOT INFLUENCE THE FRAGMENT. AS THE VALIDATION PROGRESSES, SO DOES THE FRAGMENT.

WE WOULD WISH TO DIGRESS ON THE MATTER OF ESSENCE CONTACT, IN ORDER TO EXPAND UPON THE EXPERIENCE FOR THOSE STUDENTS WHO MAY BE CURIOUS ABOUT IT. ESSENCE CONTACT RARELY OCCURS BECAUSE IT IS "SOUGHT" ACTIVELY; IN MOST INSTANCES ESSENCE CONTACT OCCURS WHEN THE RELATIONSHIP THROUGH WHICH IT IS ACCOMPLISHED IS ONE WITH *NO EXPECTATIONS* TO COLOR IT OR TO QUALIFY THE NATURE OF THE LOVE PRESENT. WHEN THERE ARE CONDITIONS AND EXPECTATIONS, THEN IT IS VERY DIFFICULT FOR THE ESSENCE CONTACT TO TAKE PLACE, SIMPLY BECAUSE CONDITIONS AND EXPECTATIONS ARE THE PRODUCT OF FEAR—THE MORE FEAR PRESENT, THE MORE DIFFICULT IT IS TO VALIDATE ESSENCE CONTACT. FRAGMENTS WHO ARE TRULY WILLING TO "BE IN THE MOMENT" WITHOUT EXPECTATIONS HAVE A GREATER CHANCE OF ACHIEVING ESSENCE CONTACT THEN THOSE WHO HAVE "COME PREPARED FOR A MOMENTOUS EVENT". FOR MOST FRAGMENTS, TRUE INTIMACY IS A STILLNESS, NOT A MASSIVE FANFARE. THIS IS THE CONSIDERATION THAT MAKES THE ACHIEVEMENT OF TRUE INTIMACY MORE DIFFICULT THAT MANY FRAGMENTS BELIEVE IT IS; THAT IT IS QUIET AND RESTFUL, THOUGH OFTEN ACCOMPANIED BY PERCEPTIONS OF THE VASTNESS OF THE UNIVERSE. FRAGMENTS WHO ARE SEEKING "THRILLS" RARELY FIND IT IN TRUE INTIMACY, BUT INSTEAD ARE MORE CAPTIVATED BY THE "ROLLER-COASTER" THRILLS OF BODY-TYPE ATTRACTION.

THAT DOES NOT MEAN THAT BODY-TYPE ATTRACTION IS NOT VALID OR THAT THE CONTACT IS LESS GENUINE THAN OTHER CONTACT. WHILE SIMPLE BODY-TYPE ATTRACTION DOES NOT OFTEN LEAD AUTOMATICALLY TO TRUE INTIMACY, THE EXPERIENCE OF BODY-TYPE ATTRACTION IS A VALID AND VERY USEFUL ONE, WHETHER OR NOT IT HAS ANY APPLICATION BEYOND THE OBVIOUS ONE OF BODY-TYPE ATTRACTION AND PHYSICAL VALIDA-

ION. TO VALIDATE THE REALITY OF THE PHYSICAL PRES-
ENCE IS GOOD WORK.

THERE ARE THOSE OF YOU WHO TEND TO BELIEVE THAT
IF THE RELATIONSHIP—NO MATTER HOW EXPRESSED—IS
NOT THE MOST DEVELOPED POSSIBLE, THEN THE RE-
LATIONSHIP IS NOT VALID. A LOVE AFFAIR TO BE A LOVE
AFFAIR *MUST* BE WITH THE ESSENCE TWIN. A PARTNER-
SHIP TO BE A PARTNERSHIP *MUST* BE WITH THE TASK COM-
PANION. A PROJECT IN ORDER TO BE A TRUE PROJECT
MUST BE WITH THE MEMBERS OF THE CONFIGURATION. A
SHARED PERCEPTION IN ORDER TO BE A REAL SHARED
PERCEPTION *MUST* BE WITH MEMBERS OF THE SAME CA-
DENCE. THIS IS, OF COURSE, RIDICULOUS. A LOVE AFFAIR
IS POSSIBLE WITH ALMOST ANY OTHER FRAGMENT WITH
SIMILAR SEXUAL ORIENTATION. A PARTNERSHIP IS POSSI-
BLE WITH ALMOST ANY FRAGMENT WITH SOMEWHAT
COMMON GOALS. A PROJECT CAN BE ACCOMPLISHED
WITH ANY GROUP OF FRAGMENTS PROVIDED THEY SHARE
A COMMON PURPOSE FOR THE PROJECT. A SHARED PER-
CEPTION CAN BE SHARED WITH ANY FRAGMENT WILLING
TO BE OPEN TO A PARTICULAR EXPERIENCE OR INSIGHT.
THESE ARE THE CONNECTIONS THAT ARE OF IMPORTANCE
IN THE LIFE AND THE ONES THAT LEAD TO EVENTUAL
SIGNIFICANT PAST ASSOCIATIONS. WE WOULD ENCOUR-
AGE ALL FRAGMENTS HERE PRESENT TO CONSIDER WHAT
WE HAVE SAID, FOR THE TENDENCY TO LIMIT THE VALID-
ITY OF AN EXPERIENCE IN THE ARBITRARY WAY SOME OF
YOU HAVE CHOSEN IS, IN FACT, SELF-DEFEATING; AND WE
WOULD HAVE TO SAY THAT THOSE FRAGMENTS WHO FALL
INTO THE TENDENCY TO DEFINE VALIDITY "BEFORE THE
FACT" ARE BLOCKING THEIR OWN ADVANCEMENT AND
DENYING MUCH OF MERIT. THIS IS ANOTHER CASE OF THE
TRIUMPH OF THE CHIEF FEATURE WHERE GOOD SENSE
MIGHT OTHERWISE PREVAIL.

THE ATTRACTIONS OF INTIMACY ARE MANY AND VARI-
ED, AND IT IS OFTEN DIFFICULT FOR FRAGMENTS TO ADMIT
TO THE DESIRES BROUGHT ABOUT BY THE RECOGNITION
THAT ESSENCE SEEKS ONLY JOY, WHICH, ON THE PHYSI-

CAL PLANE, IS MOST OFTEN ACHIEVED BY INTIMACY
PLEASE NOTE THAT WE SAY MOST OFTEN, FOR THERE ARE
OTHER CIRCUMSTANCES WHEN JOY IS WITHIN THE GRAS
OF FRAGMENTS THAT IS NOT DIRECTLY CONNECTED WITH
TRUE INTIMACY, AT LEAST NOT IN THE WAY YOU UNDER
STAND THE TERM.

ONE OF THE MOST PROFOUND SOURCES OF JOY ON THE
PHYSICAL PLANE IS WHAT YOU ON THE PHYSICAL PLANE
CALL THE ARTS. THE ARTS IN GENERAL DIFFERENTIATE
WORLD AND PERSONAL TRUTHS. THIS ELUCIDATION IS A
SOURCE NOT ONLY OF INSIGHT BUT OF JOY AND VERY
POWERFUL EMOTIONAL RESPONSES THAT ARE CAPABLE
OF REACHING ESSENCE AS WELL AS ALL OF THE OVER
LEAVES.

LET US EXPLICATE: FOR ALMOST ALL FRAGMENT
WORKING IN WHAT YOU ON THE PHYSICAL PLANE CALL
THE ARTS, THERE IS A GENUINE ASPECT OF PASSION FOR
THE WORK. FOR MOST ARTISTS, THE WORK CANNOT BE
SUSTAINED WITHOUT THE PASSION TO SUPPORT IT
THEREFORE, THE WORK OF NECESSITY REFLECTS THE PAS
SION AS WELL AS THE INSIGHT WHICH BROUGHT IT INTO
BEING. THOSE FRAGMENTS WITH A DEGREE OF SENSITIV
ITY NOT ONLY RESPOND TO THE INSIGHT, THEY RESPOND
AS WELL TO THE PASSION, ALLYING THE ENERGY AND
THE WORK IN THEIR RESPONSE.

WE WILL DIFFERENTIATE HERE BETWEEN THE DI
RECTLY CREATIVE ARTS—THAT IS, PAINTING AND ALL
FINE ARTS, LITERATURE, MATHEMATICS, ARCHITECTURE
AND COMPOSITION—AND THE INTERPRETIVE ARTS—
MUSIC, THEATER, DANCE, MEDICINE, ANIMAL HUSBAN
DRY, AND COMMUNICATIONS—WHICH, BY DEFINITION
REQUIRE EITHER DIRECT OR INDIRECT RESPONSES. WE
REALIZE THAT OUR DESCRIPTIONS OF ARTS DO NOT EN
TIRELY CORRESPOND WITH THE TRADITIONAL LISTS, BUT
THAT IS DUE TO YOUR CULTURAL PERCEPTIONS, NOT TO
VALID UNDERSTANDING.

THOSE FRAGMENTS WHO COMPOSE MUSIC DO NOT HAVE
THE SAME EXPERIENCE AS THOSE WHO PERFORM IT, NOR
DO THOSE WHO HEAR IT HAVE THE SAME EXPERIENCE O

T THAT EITHER THE COMPOSER OR THE PERFORMERS HAVE. THAT IS NOT TO SAY THAT ANY RESPONSE IS MORE VALID THAN ANY OTHER RESPONSE. EACH LEVEL OF APPRECIATION IS A VALID ONE, AND EACH KIND OF APPRECIATION HAS ITS PLACE IN THE ARTISTIC PROCESS. FOR EXAMPLE, A FRAGMENT WHO IS A COMPOSER MAY CHOOSE TO ATTEND A SYMPHONY CONCERT TO HEAR THE WORKS OF THE OLD SCHOLAR HAYDN. THAT DOES NOT MEAN THAT THE COMPOSER IS LOOKING TO COMPARE HIS OR HER WORK TO HAYDN'S, OR THAT HE OR SHE BELIEVES THAT LISTENING TO HAYDN MIGHT INSPIRE HIS OR HER — ALTHOUGH BOTH THINGS ARE POSSIBLE. THE COMPOSER TENDS TO BE ESPECIALLY SENSITIVE TO THE HIGHER EMOTIONAL CENTER AND OFTEN SEEKS THE OPPORTUNITY TO REACH IT. COMPOSITION IS ONE VERY PERSONAL AND DIRECT MEANS TO REACH THE HIGHER EMOTIONAL CENTER, BUT IT DOES NOT HAVE THE QUALITY OF RECIPROCITY THAT LISTENING TO MUSIC OR PERFORMING IT HAS.

THE SAME THING CAN BE SAID OF THOSE DOING THEATRICAL MATERIAL, SUCH AS PLAYS OR SCENARIOS FOR THE SCREEN. THIS IS A PROCESS THAT REQUIRES AN INTERPRETIVE PHASE FOR THE ART TO BE REALIZED. THOSE WHO WORK WITH THIS ASPECT OF WHAT YOU ON THE PHYSICAL PLANE CALL THE ARTS HAVE A KEEN AWARENESS OF THE MUSICAL IMPLICATIONS OF THE SOUNDS OF WORDS, SINCE THE WORDS ARE INTENDED TO BE SPOKEN. INCIDENTALLY, THEATER AND PLAYS GREW NOT OUT OF LITERATURE BUT OUT OF DANCE, STARTING WITH SACRED DANCE RITUALS THAT REPEAT CERTAIN "MAGICAL" PATTERNS, AND FROM THERE BECOMING MORE ELABORATE SPOKEN OR CHANTED RITUALS FOR DANCERS. EVENTUALLY ONE OF THE DANCERS SPOKE — HE IS REMEMBERED IN SOME OF YOUR MYTHS AS THESPIS — AND THEATER WAS "INVENTED".

FOR THOSE WORKING WITH THE WRITTEN WORD OR THE FINE ARTS, THE SECOND INTERPRETIVE PHASE IS UNDERTAKEN NOT BY PERFORMERS BUT DIRECTLY BY THE AUDIENCE, THOSE SEEING THE WORK EITHER AS VIEWERS OR

AS READERS. THEREFORE THERE IS AN INCREASED TEN-
DENCY FOR THE INTERACTION BETWEEN AUDIENCE AND
ARTISTS TO BE SHARPENED TO A MUCH HIGHER DEGREE
THAN WHERE INTERPRETATION PLAYS A PART IN THE FUL-
FILLMENT OF THE ARTISTIC VISION. THOSE WORKING IN
FINE ARTS ARE, OF COURSE, CONNECTED TO THE HIGHER
EMOTIONAL CENTER, AND THOSE WITH WORDS WITH THE
HIGHER INTELLECTUAL CENTER.

THESE HIGHER CENTERS ARE ONE MEANS FOR ACHIEV-
ING INTIMACY. THAT DOES NOT MEAN THAT TRUE INTI-
MACY IS "EASIER" FOR THOSE CAUGHT UP IN ARTISTIC
VISIONS, BUT RATHER THAT WHERE THERE HAS BEEN
SOME SENSE OF THE HIGHER CENTERS ACHIEVED, THE
OPENNESS OF INTIMACY CAN BE MORE READILY ACCESSI-
BLE, SHOULD THE FRAGMENT CHOOSE TO BE OPEN TO THE
HIGHER CENTER. OF COURSE, WHEN THE MEANS TO TRUE
INTIMACY IS THROUGH SEXUAL CONTACT, THE HIGHER
CENTER IS THE MOVING CENTER, THE ONLY HIGHER
CENTER THAT YOUR SPECIES, AND ALL INDEPENDENTLY
MOBILE ENSOULED SPECIES, HAVE REGULAR ACCESS TO.

ONCE THERE HAS BEEN A VALIDATED RECOGNITION OF
HIGHER CENTERS, THE FRAGMENT MAY THEN CHOOSE TO
DEVELOP THAT RECOGNITION. THOSE WHO PRACTICE AN
INTERPRETIVE ART OFTEN TAKE A GREAT DEAL OF TIME
AND ENERGY TO LEARN TO OPERATE IN THE APPROPRIATE
HIGHER CENTER FOR LONG PERIODS AT A STRETCH, AND
IN A STRANGE WAY BECOME WHAT MIGHT BE CALLED
"HOOKED" ON THE ATTAINING OF THE HIGHER CENTER
BECAUSE OF THE HEIGHTENED AWARENESS SUCH CEN-
TERING BRINGS WITH IT. FRAGMENTS AT THIS LEVEL OF
SELF-AWARENESS ARE MUCH MORE CAPABLE OF SUSTAIN-
ING VALIDATED INTIMATE CONTACT WITH ANOTHER
FRAGMENT. THAT DOES NOT MEAN THAT THEREFORE
THEY *DO* SUSTAIN VALIDATED INTIMATE CONTACT WITH
OTHER FRAGMENTS. IN FACT, THERE ARE THOSE WHO
FIND INTIMATE CONTACT A THREAT TO THEIR HIGHER
CENTERING, AND THEREFORE THEY WILL TEND TO AVOID
OR DENY THE INTIMACY AND ESSENCE CONTACT IN

ORDER TO PRESERVE THE "PURITY" OF THE HIGHER
CENTER.

WHEN FEAR HAS BEEN SUFFICIENTLY OVERCOME TO
PERMIT ESSENCE CONTACT TO BE VALIDATED AND REC-
OGNIZED WHEN IT HAPPENS, FRAGMENTS OCCASIONALLY
ESTABLISH REQUIREMENTS FOR THE CONTACT THAT REN-
DERS IT DIFFICULT OR IMPOSSIBLE BECAUSE THE LIMITA-
TIONS IMPOSED DISTORT THE PERCEPTIONS. THIS IS AN
EXAMPLE OF HOW SEDUCTIVE FEAR CAN BE, AND HOW
MANY FORMS IT CAN TAKE IN ITS EFFORT TO SUBVERT
THE CAPACITY OF THE ESSENCE TO LOVE. NO MATTER
WHAT THE ROLE OF ESSENCE, THE ESSENCE ITSELF IS
COMPOSED WHOLLY OF LOVE. ESSENCE IS WITHOUT FEAR.
ESSENCE, WHICH SEEKS ONLY UTTER JOY, IS ALWAYS
CAPABLE OF CONTACT WHEN THE FEAR EXPERIENCED BY
THE FRAGMENT HAS BEEN SUBDUED ENOUGH FOR THE
CONTACT TO OCCUR. ONCE THE CONTACT HAS OC-
CURRED, THEN ESSENCE HAS FULL AWARENESS AND VAL-
IDATION OF THE CONTACT NO MATTER WHAT PERSONAL-
ITY AND DENIAL MAY CONVINCE THE FRAGMENT. THE
FRAGMENT MAY CHOOSE TO TRY AGAIN, "JUST IN CASE
SOMETHING REALLY DID HAPPEN" AND WILL TAKE THE
SECOND APPARENT LACK OF SUCCESS AS AN INDICATION
THAT THE FIRST ESSENCE CONTACT DID NOT, IN FACT,
OCCUR.

FOR THOSE FRAGMENTS WHO HAVE STRIVEN TO ESTAB-
LISH CONTACT ONLY TO "SHY OFF" AT THE CRITICAL MO-
MENT, WE WOULD SUGGEST THAT THERE BE SOME PERIOD
OF REFLECTION, SHOULD THE FRAGMENT CARE TO UN-
DERTAKE SUCH A PROJECT. BY THIS WE MEAN THAT THE
FRAGMENT MIGHT DISCOVER A PATTERN OF BEHAVIOR
THAT WOULD REVEAL WHY AND HOW THE CHIEF FEATURE
BRINGS FEAR TO BEAR, AND WHAT LIES ARE SUFFI-
CIENTLY CONVINCING TO CAUSE THE FRAGMENT TO
ABANDON THE PURSUIT OF ESSENCE CONTACT. THE FRAG-
MENT MAY WISH TO TRY TO DISCOVER WHAT IT IS THAT
THE CHIEF FEATURE IS THREATENING THE FRAGMENT
WITH. IN MOST CASES, THE UNDERLYING FEAR OF THE

CHIEF FEATURE IS DISGUISED TO BE POSSIBLE REJECTION
OR DAMAGE TO THE EGO. OCCASIONALLY THE CHIEF FEA-
TURE DREDGES UP ALL THE HATEFUL MEMORIES THE
FRAGMENT HAS BEEN CARRYING AROUND, AND FROM
THEM EXTRACTS THOSE INSTANCES MOST DAMAGING TO
SELF-ESTEEM WHICH THEN ARE USED TO PRESENT THE
FRAGMENT WITH A PICTURE THAT IS REPELLENT TO THE
FRAGMENT, WHO THEN IS NOT WILLING TO "FOIST" SUCH
A TERRIBLE PERSON OFF ON THE FRAGMENT WITH WHOM
ESSENCE CONTACT IS DESIRED.

WE DO NOT INTEND TO LIMIT THESE PROBLEMS TO
AREAS OF SEXUAL INTIMACY. WE ARE NOT DISCUSSING
"ROMANTIC" PROBLEMS ALONE, ALTHOUGH THERE ARE
OFTEN SHARPER PERCEPTIONS IN THAT AREA THAN IN
OTHERS. IT IS AS DAUNTING FACING CERTAIN FRIENDS AS
IT IS FACING A POTENTIAL OR CURRENT LOVER, AND THE
CHIEF FEATURE CAN BE AS MENDACIOUS ON THOSE OCCA-
SIONS AS IT CAN DURING THE MORE OBVIOUS ENCOUN-
TERS. WE WOULD URGE THOSE FRAGMENTS CHOOSING
TO EXAMINE THIS ASPECT OF THEIR LIVES TO BE AWARE
THAT THE BLOCKAGE OF TRUE INTIMACY CAN TAKE
PLACE ON MANY LEVELS AND DURING MANY SORTS OF
ENCOUNTERS. WE ARE AWARE OF MANY FRAGMENTS
WHO ARE MORE CONFIDENT WITH A LOVER THAN THEY
ARE WITH A FRIEND. THAT IS NOT TO SAY THAT THERE-
FORE THERE IS A GREATER SENSE OF TRUE INTIMACY WITH
A LOVER THAN WITH A FRIEND; WE WOULD TEND TO BE-
LIEVE THE REVERSE TO BE THE CASE. THE REACTION TO
THE LOVER REVEALS THAT THE FRAGMENT HAS VERY LIT-
TLE SENSE OF "RISK" WITH THE LOVER AND THEREFORE
IS NOT APT TO BE SEEKING ESSENCE CONTACT THROUGH
THE RELATIONSHIP WITH THE LOVER. IT IS NOT INAPPRO-
PRIATE FOR FRAGMENTS TO TAKE A LITTLE TIME TO
ASSESS THESE PERCEPTIONS IN TERMS OF THE RISKS PER-
CEIVED AS INDICATIVE OF THE AREAS WHERE THE CHIEF
FEATURE IS MOST THREATENED. WHERE THE GREATEST
THREAT TO CHIEF FEATURE EXISTS, THERE THE GREATEST
POTENTIAL FOR ESSENCE CONTACT MAY BE FOUND.

THE RESULTS OF ESSENCE CONTACT ARE NOT OFTEN

"WORLD-SHAKING" EXCEPT WHEN OCCURRING TO FRAG-
MENTS WHO DO NOT "BELIEVE IN" THE VALIDITY OF SUCH
CONTACTS. WHEN DISBELIEVING—AND WE MEAN
WHOLLY DISBELIEVING, NOT SKEPTICAL—FRAGMENTS
EXPERIENCE ESSENCE CONTACT, THE EXPERIENCE IS
OFTEN SO DISRUPTIVE THAT IT IS FLED. THOSE WHO ARE
SEEKING IT OFTEN REACT WITH GENUINE LAUGHTER.
WHEN A FRAGMENT CAN ACCEPT ESSENCE CONTACT, IT
IS QUITE JOYOUS. TRUE INTIMACY IS FUN. FREEING THE
OVERLEAVES FROM THE BONDAGE OF THE CHIEF FEA-
TURE, EVEN BRIEFLY, IS ALWAYS A SOURCE OF HAPPINESS
IF THE INTIMACY IS RECOGNIZED.

THROUGH THE MOMENTS OF ESSENCE CONTACT THERE
CAN BE MUCH OF VALUE ACHIEVED. WHEN THE ESSENCE
CONTACT OCCURS, AND IS RECOGNIZED AND VALIDATED,
THEN THE FRAGMENT ADVANCES PERCEPTUALLY. WHEN
THIS IS ACHIEVED DURING THE LIFETIME, THE PERCEP-
TUAL ADVANCES ARE PART OF THE LIFE PROGRESS AND
CONTRIBUTE TO THE CHOICES MADE DURING THE LIFE,
AS WELL AS INCREASING THE PERCEPTUAL PARAMETERS
OF THE FRAGMENT FOR THAT LIFE AND ALL FUTURE LIVES.
WE EMPHASIZE THIS IN ORDER TO SHOW THE REASONS IT
IS WORTHWHILE TO OVERCOME FEAR. FOR THOSE FRAG-
MENTS WHO CANNOT BRING THEMSELVES TO STRIVE FOR
ESSENCE CONTACT, OR, HAVING DONE SO, BLOCK IT TO
KEEP IT FROM HAPPENING, OR, HAVING HAD IT OCCUR,
FLEE IT, THE TRIUMPH OF FEAR HAS DISTORTED MUCH OF
MERIT IN THE LIFE. WHEN THE CHIEF FEATURE IS ABLE
TO TURN A FRAGMENT AWAY FROM ESSENCE CONTACT,
OR TO DENY IT HAS OCCURRED, OR CONVINCES THE FRAG-
MENT THAT SUCH CONTACT IS "DANGEROUS," THEN THE
HOLD OF THE CHIEF FEATURE INCREASES IN THE LIFE. IT
IS NOT INACCURATE TO SAY THAT FEAR FEEDS ON FEAR,
AND THE MORE THE FRAGMENT IS WILLING TO ACQUIESCE
TO FEAR, THE STRONGER THE HOLD THE FEAR WILL HAVE
ON THE FRAGMENT, AND THE MORE DISTORTED WILL BE
THE PERCEPTIONS OF THE NATURE OF THE LIFE BEING
LIVED, AS WELL AS THOSE LIVED BEFORE.

LET US SAY THERE THAT CHIEF FEATURE CAN BE VERY,

VERY, VERY, VERY SUBTLE ABOUT HOW IT MANIPULATES
THE PERCEPTIONS OF THE FRAGMENT. FEAR, AS WE HAVE
SAID MANY TIMES BEFORE, IS SEDUCTIVE. IT CAN PRESENT
THE MOST APPEALING PICTURES TO DISGUISE THE "DUN-
GEON" THAT IS THE ACTUALITY OF FEAR. MOST FRAG-
MENTS ARE NOT TRULY AWARE THAT FEAR IS OPERATING
WHEN CHIEF FEATURE IS AT WORK. OFTEN CHIEF FEATURE
REPRESENTS ITSELF AS GOOD SENSE AND REALISTIC UN-
DERSTANDING. CHIEF FEATURE IS ADEPT AT CONVINCING
FRAGMENTS THAT ESSENCE CONTACT AND SOUL EVOLU-
TION IS "BAD FOR YOU", AND PRESENTS ITSELF AS PRO-
TECTION AND SUPPORT RATHER THAN RAVENING FEAR.
IT IS MOST DISTORTING WHEN CLOAKED IN RELIGION, AND
WE WOULD WISH TO POINT OUT THAT MOST ORGANIZED
RELIGION HAS GREAT SKILL IN TURNING CHIEF FEATURE
TO ITS ADVANTAGE: "I CANNOT LOVE THAT PERSON BE-
CAUSE LOVING THAT PERSON IS IMMORAL", "I MUST NOT
PERMIT THAT PERSON TO INTERFERE WITH MY LOVE AF-
FAIR WITH GOD", "I MUST RESTRICT HOW I RELATE TO
PEOPLE SO THAT SANCTITY IS PRESERVED", "I MUST NOT
BE LIKE THOSE PEOPLE WHO DO THINGS THAT MAKE ME
UNCOMFORTABLE BECAUSE THEN I WILL NOT BE WORTHY
OF BEING COMFORTABLE", "I MUST NOT LET OTHERS SEE
THE SINS I HAVE HIDDEN IN MY SOUL", "THIS PERSON IS
UNACCEPTABLE BECAUSE HE OR SHE IS UNCLEAN/UNAC-
CEPTABLE/OF ANOTHER FAITH/OF ANOTHER CULTURE/OF
AN INAPPROPRIATE GROUP". THESE AND MANY OTHER
CONVINCING LIES ARE PRESENTED AS MORAL TRUTHS.
THE RESULTANT MORBID PREOCCUPATION WITH THE FOR-
BIDDEN, AS WELL AS THE THRILL OF GUILT, SERVES TO
ENMESH THE FRAGMENT MORE AND MORE IN THE HOLD
OF THE CHIEF FEATURE. THE CHIEF FEATURE HAS THE
ADDED "ADVANTAGE" OF NEVER HAVING TO REVEAL IT-
SELF AS BEING THE MANIFESTATION OF FEAR. IN MOST
INSTANCES FRAGMENTS CAUGHT UP IN THIS PATTERN
WILL NOT BE ABLE TO RECOGNIZE AND VALIDATE ES-
SENCE CONTACT EXCEPT IN THE ASTRAL INTERVAL.

THIS DOES NOT MEAN, OF COURSE, THAT A FRAGMENT
CANNOT CHOOSE TO STRIVE TOWARD ESSENSE CONTACT,

TOWARD RECOGNITION AND VALIDATION OF IT, BUT THAT IF THE FRAGMENT HAS HAD MUCH RELIGIOUS TRAINING, PARTICULARLY IN OCCIDENTAL RELIGIONS, THERE IS APT TO BE A GREAT DEAL OF STRUGGLE WITH CHIEF FEATURE MANIPULATIONS AS WELL AS SIGNIFICANT DISTORTIONS OF PERCEPTION. ONE OF THE MOST DISTORTING DISSERVICES THAT RELIGION PERPETRATES IS THE ENSHRINEMENT OF EXPECTATIONS: BY CREATING A RIGID FRAMEWORK FOR THE "PROPER" WAY FOR EXPERIENCES TO BE PERCEIVED, IT BLOCKS MANY OF THE LESSONS AND VALIDATIONS IN LIFE, WHICH IS NOT GOOD WORK AND CARRIED OUT TO SUFFICIENT EXTREMES CAN LEAD TO KARMA.

FOR MANY FRAGMENTS, PERCEPTION OF ESSENCE— THAT IS, THE CORE OF THEMSELVES—IS MISTAKEN FOR "SEEING GOD". ESSENCE IS A VASTNESS WITHIN THE LITTLE CONFINES OF THE "SELF", AND, AS SUCH, EXTENDS FAR BEYOND THE PHYSICAL-PLANE AWARENESS OF SELF. MOST FRAGMENTS TEND TO PERCEIVE ESSENCE, WHEN THEY CHOOSE TO APPLY THE INNER-LOOKING DISCIPLINES, AS AN ENORMOUS AREA OF LIGHT. THAT LIGHT IS EXPRESSED IN PHYSICAL TERMS AS THE AURA, WHICH IS THE NARROW BAND OF LIGHT WHICH SOME FRAGMENTS CAN PERCEIVE OUTLINING THE BODIES OF PHYSICALLY EXTANT FRAGMENTS. THE LARGER, EGG-SHAPED MANIFESTATION THAT IS SOMETIMES "SEEN" IS THE ENERGY FIELD OF THE BODY ITSELF. LEARNING TO RECOGNIZE THE ESSENCE, AND THEN VALIDATING THAT IT IS, IN FACT, THE CORE OF THIS AND EVERY OTHER LIFE THE FRAGMENT HAS LIVED IS VERY GOOD WORK AND LEADS TO MUCH VALIDATED GROWTH IN A LIFE. THE WILLINGNESS TO ACCEPT THE ENORMITY OF ESSENCE IS NOT EASILY COME BY, AND CHIEF FEATURE WILL GO TO GREAT LENGTHS TO PROVIDE "REASONS" TO DISOWN ESSENCE, AND ARGUMENTS TO DENY THE VALIDATION. FOR THOSE FRAGMENTS WHO HAVE ENCOUNTERED ESSENCE, WE WOULD THINK THAT THERE IS COMPREHENSION AND VALIDATION OF THIS PROBLEM, WHICH IS ONGOING NOT ONLY IN THIS LIFE BUT FROM LIFE TO LIFE AS WELL.

THE DISCOVERY OF ESSENCE CAN PROVIDE ACCESS TO PAST EXPERIENCES AS WELL AS BRING TO BEAR THE LESSONS OF THE CURRENT LIFE. THIS, IN TURN, CAN AID IN THE RECOGNITION OF THE PATH AND THE CHOICES THAT HAVE CONTRIBUTED TO THE LIFE TASK. PERCEPTION OF ESSENCE CAN ALSO, WHEN THERE HAS BEEN VALIDATION, AID IN ESSENCE CONTACT. THOSE WHO HAVE PERCEIVED AND VALIDATED ESSENCE "WITHIN" THEMSELVES ARE MORE CAPABLE OF PERCEIVING AND VALIDATING ESSENCE "WITHIN" OTHERS, WHICH IS A SIGNIFICANT PART OF ACHIEVING ESSENCE CONTACT. IT IS EASIER TO "SEE" A THING WHEN YOU KNOW WHAT YOU ARE "LOOKING" FOR.

OF COURSE, WITH OR WITHOUT VALIDATION, ESSENCE CONTACT WILL TAKE PLACE, AND NO MATTER WHAT THE REACTION OF THE PERSONALITY TO IT, THE ASTRAL INTERVAL WILL PROVIDE THE RECOGNITION AND VALIDATION THAT IS PART OF GROWTH. EVENTUALLY MOST CARDINAL FRAGMENTS WILL HAVE ACHIEVED SOME VALIDATED AND RECOGNIZED ESSENCE CONTACT DURING A LIFETIME. OFTEN ORDINAL FRAGMENTS WILL BE ABLE TO ACCEPT AND INCULCATE THE LESSONS OF TRUE INTIMACY WITHOUT THE RECOGNITON AND VALIDATION, FOR AMONG ORDINAL CAST FRAGMENTS THE PERCEPTION CAN BE ACHIEVED IN MANY WAYS OTHER THAN DIRECT RECOGNITION AND VALIDATION; THE INTIMACY WILL HAVE BEARING ON THE LIFE WITHOUT THE ORDINAL CAST FRAGMENT CONSCIOUSLY "PROCESSING" THE EXPERIENCE. FOR CARDINAL FRAGMENTS, OF COURSE THE "PROCESSING" IS PART OF THE VALIDATION.

THAT IS NOT TO SAY THAT THEREFORE THERE IS NO POINT TO ORDINAL CAST FRAGMENTS TO PURSUE VALIDATION AND RECOGNITION OF THE EXPERIENCE OF ESSENCE CONTACT. WE DID NOT SAY THAT AND WE DID NOT IMPLY IT. WE WISH ONLY TO CLARIFY THE NATURE OF THE EXPERIENCE AS IT IS MANIFEST IN THE LIFE FOR CARDINAL AND ORDINAL CAST FRAGMENTS. ANY AND ALL FRAGMENTS ARE CAPABLE, SHOULD THEY CHOOSE TO DO SO, OF VALIDATION AND RECOGNITION OF ESSENCE CONTACT

AND TRUE INTIMACY. ALL FRAGMENTS ARE CAPABLE, SHOULD THEY CHOOSE TO DO SO, OF BRINGING ESSENCE CONTACT TO BEAR IN THE LIFE. ALL FRAGMENTS ARE CAPABLE, SHOULD THEY CHOOSE TO DO SO, OF PERCEIVING THEIR OWN ESSENCE. THAT MOST FRAGMENTS ARE UNWILLING TO UNDERTAKE THE TASK IS NOT ENTIRELY SURPRISING, SINCE IN ORDER TO ACHIEVE ESSENCE CONTACT, WITH EITHER ONE'S OWN ESSENCE OR THE ESSENCE OF ANOTHER FRAGMENT, THE CHIEF FEATURE MUST BE CONFRONTED, WHICH IS, OF COURSE, THE MOST FRIGHTENING THING ANY FRAGMENT EVER UNDERTAKES.

WHERE THE PAST ASSOCIATIONS OR BONDS, TIES AND THE LIKE ARE PRESENT, THE "DOOR" FOR ESSENCE CONTACT CAN MORE EASILY BE OPENED THAN WITH A "COMPARATIVE STRANGER", BUT THAT IS NOT TO SAY THAT THEREFORE ESSENCE CONTACT "OUGHT" TO BE LIMITED TO "SAFER" FRAGMENTS. PUTTING LIMITATIONS ON THE POSSIBILITIES OF ESSENCE CONTACT SERVES TO LESSEN THE CHANCE OF ACHIEVING IT, AND DEFEATS ITS "PURPOSE" AS WELL, WHICH IS TO FREE THE FRAGMENT FROM THE SHACKLES OF FEAR. WHERE CHIEF FEATURE IS STRONGEST, THE PROSPECT OF TRUE LIBERTY IS THE MOST TERRIFYING, WHICH IS WHY THE EXPERIENCES OF ESSENCE CONTACT IS SO OFTEN "EPHERMERAL".

TWO FRAGMENTS, BOTH WARRIORS, ONE OLD, ONE MATURE, GOOD FRIENDS—WITH THIRTY-ONE PAST ASSOCIATIONS, NINETEEN AS COMRADES-AT-ARMS—ONE IN OUR LITTLE GROUP, ONE A GOOD-HEARTED "DISBELIEVER" RECENTLY HAD A VALIDATED EXPERIENCE OF ESSENCE CONTACT. BOTH HAVE SOME SKILL AT PLAYING THE PIANO AND WERE AMUSING THEMSELVES WHILE WAITING FOR WORK TO RESUME BY TAKING TURNS AT THE PIANO. AFTER A WHILE, THEY DECIDED TO TRY A DUET AND "FOR SOME REASON" SELECTED THE SCHUBERT *MILITARY MARCH*, WHICH THEY FOUND IN A BOOK OF PIANO DUETS. ORDINARILY IF PLAYING DID NOT GO WELL, THESE PERFECTIONISTIC FRAGMENTS—BOTH ARE IDEALISTS— WOULD HAVE STOPPED, BUT IN THIS INSTANCE, THOUGH THEY PLAYED BADLY, THEY PERSEVERED AND ENDED UP

LAUGHING FOR "PURE ENJOYMENT", WHICH WAS MORE THE RESULT OF THE ESSENCE CONTACT THAN THEIR DISASTROUS PLAYING. BOTH FRAGMENTS LATER ACKNOWLEDGED THAT "SOMETHING HAPPENED" TO THEM WHILE THEY WERE PLAYING, AND BOTH HAVE FELT A MUCH DEEPER SENSE OF MUTUAL UNDERSTANDING SINCE THAT OCCASION. THE MATURE WARRIOR HAS NOT ATTEMPTED TO DEFINE THE EXPERIENCE, ALTHOUGH HE IS CONTENT TO ACCEPT ITS VALIDITY IN HIS LIFE. THE OLD WARRIOR, OUR STUDENT, HAS VALIDATED AND RECOGNIZED ESSENCE CONTACT, ALTHOUGH SHE HAS NOT "INSISTED" THAT THE MATURE WARRIOR "SEE IT HER WAY", SINCE SHE IS AWARE THAT VALIDATION DOES NOT REQUIRE AGREEMENT ON THE SPECIFIC VOCABULARY.

THOSE OF YOU WHO ARE ABLE TO ACHIEVE VALIDATION OF ESSENCE CONTACT MAY FIND THAT THE GENERAL LEVEL OF PERCEPTIONS LOSE A LITTLE OF THE PERVASIVE DISTORTION OF CHIEF FEATURE; THOSE WHO CHOOSE TO PURSUE ESSENCE CONTACT *WITHOUT EXPECTATIONS* CAN REACH THE POSITIVE POLES OF THE OVERLEAVES MORE CONSISTENTLY, FOR ESSENCE FUNCTIONS *ONLY* IN THE POSITIVE POLES OF THE OVERLEAVES. WHEN THE NEGATIVE POLES ARE OPERATIVE, THEN FEAR AND CHIEF FEATURE PREVAIL. THE LIES OF FEAR SERVE TO BLOCK RECOGNITION AND VALIDATION IN THE LIFE NOT ONLY OF ESSENCE CONTACT BUT OF ALL OTHER FORMS OF GROWTH AS WELL.

Chapter 8

LONG-DISTANCE MICHAEL

There are many members of the Michael core group who are now living away from the Bay area and participate either through phone-in questions or through occasional attendance at sessions when they are in the area. In *More Messages From Michael*, these various people were combined into Katherine Gerrard, and Sally and Ed Rogers. There are actually about a dozen core-group members who phone in questions with great regularity. There are others who have less frequent contact with the group but who are still very much a part of it. Their comments, of necessity, were taken from phone interviews.

Miriam O'Brian lives and works on the East Coast. She is a third-level Mature Scholar in the caution mode with a goal of dominance, a realist in the moving part of intellectual center with a chief feature of impatience and a secondary of arrogance.

"And if you don't think that's a handful to deal with," she says. "Luckily I work with my TC, and that's a very stabilizing influence. Before that happened, I tended to go off in every direction at once. All the caution seemed to do was make me worry if I had done the right thing—after I did it." She considers a moment. "I think about the best think Michael has done for me, and the reason I keep asking questions, is that what I get from them seems to work. Most of the time I'm curious about relationships—all kinds of relationships: business, personal, familial, speculative, you name it—and sometimes about the past. I mean the past-past.''

How did she get into the group?

"Well, it was one of those strange things. I was living right where I live now, and aside from some interest in this kind of studies, I wasn't in any hurry to find a teacher. But I'm a friend of Joan Standish, and she was in the group. We got to talking about it, and I asked a few questions through her and got back my answers. When Joan and Mark moved out of the Bay Area, I kept in contact with Leslie Adams, whom I'd met on a couple of business trips. Now I call Leslie with my questions. Once in a while, when there's a real emergency, I'll call for special comments, like the time my daughter had emergency surgery. Leslie, who doesn't usually do any channeling except at sessions, dropped everything and got back to me in less than an hour. I can't tell you how much that meant to me.''

THE FRAGMENT WHO IS NOW AUGUSTA HAS A SERIOUS FRACTURE OF THE COLLARBONE AS WELL AS A CONCUSSION AND NUMEROUS MINOR CONTUSIONS AND ABRASIONS. HOWEVER, THERE HAS BEEN SOME DAMAGE DONE TO THE RIGHT EYE, AND WE WOULD THINK THAT CAREFUL ATTENTION WOULD BE IN ORDER IF THE VISION IS TO REMAIN UNIMPAIRED. THERE ARE SEVERAL SERIOUS BRUISES, BOTH TO THE RIBS AND TO THE LEFT LEG, AND ONE OF THEM MAY CAUSE CLOTTING PROBLEMS IF NOT ATTENDED TO AT THIS TIME. WE WOULD THINK THAT REPAIR OF THE COLLARBONE IS THE FIRST ORDER OF BUSINESS, BUT THAT IS BY NO MEANS THE ONLY CONSIDERATION HERE. LET US ALSO RECOMMEND THAT THE FRAGMENT WHO IS NOW AUGUSTA BE ALLOWED TO VENT HER ANGER, FOR THE ALTERNATIVE HERE IS DEPRESSION, WHICH WOULD BE MORE DANGEROUS TO HER, FOR IT WOULD TEND TO PRESS HER TO OVERLOOK SYMPTOMS NEEDING ATTENTION, WHICH IS ALREADY A PROBLEM WITH WARRIORS, WHO ARE VERY RELUCTANT AS A GROUP TO ACKNOWLEDGE INJURIES OR ILLNESS.

"Well, that was very useful advice, because as it turns out, Augusta did have some problems after the surgery, some of them from depression and in one case from symptoms she was determined to ignore. She's fine now, but I was pretty worried for a couple months. She's back in college and doing fine. She hasn't given up mountain climbing, which I would have done after a fall like that. That's what comes of having a Warrior in the family, I guess." Miriam pauses. "Another thing Michael helped me out with a couple years ago was a vacation I went on. The whole thing went badly, and I wanted to get a handle on it."

ONE OF THE DIFFICULTIES OF THE RITUALS YOU CALL VACATIONS IS THAT THEY ARE SO INEXORABLY SET IN CERTAIN FORMS: TWO OR THREE WEEKS, MOST OFTEN IN A LUMP, ONCE A YEAR. OCCASIONALLY THE VACATION CAN BE SPLIT FOR TWICE A YEAR, BUT THIS IS NOT USUAL. IN HAVING VACATIONS SO FIXED, IT MAKES IT AWKWARD WHEN THE BREAK IN ROUTINE IS ACTUALLY NEEDED AT A DIFFERENT TIME. ALSO, FRAGMENTS PRONE TO SCRIPTING ARE NEVER MORE ACTIVE THAN WHEN SETTING OUT TO "GET THE MOST" OUT OF A VACATION, AND THERE-FORE ORDER THE OCCASION SO COMPULSIVELY THAT THERE IS LITTLE ROOM FOR SPONTANEITY, WHICH, OF COURSE, DEFEATS MUCH OF THE PURPOSE IN "GETTING AWAY".

IN THIS CASE, MIRIAM, THERE WAS A COMBINATION OF ELEMENTS AT WORK. FIRST, AGREEMENTS THAT HAD BEEN MADE FOR THE JOURNEY WERE NOT KEPT FOR A VARIETY OF REASONS, AND THEREFORE CONTACTS YOU WERE "ANTICIPATING" DID NOT OCCUR, WHICH LEFT YOU FEELING "OUT OF TOUCH". THEN, BECAUSE OF THE TEN-DENCY OF DOMINANCE/IMPATIENCE TO REQUIRE THE FRAGMENT BE IN CONTROL AT ALL TIMES AND TO ANTICI-PATE EVERY EVENTUALITY, SCRIPTING ENTERED THE PIC-TURE IN A VERY EMPHATIC WAY. THE SCRIPTING MADE IT DIFFICULT FOR YOU TO ADJUST YOUR SET EXPECTA-TIONS IN ORDER TO BE FLEXIBLE ENOUGH TO ENJOY THE CHANGE OF PLANS. BECAUSE OF THAT LACK OF FLEXI-

BILITY, DISAPPOINTMENT RESULTED AND YOU, MIRIAM, WERE LEFT WITH THE SENSATION OF HAVING "WASTED" YOUR VACATION TIME.

FOR MANY FRAGMENTS, THE FOCUS OF A VACATION IS THE IMPACT IT WILL HAVE AFTER-THE-FACT, IN RETELLING TO THOSE WHO WERE NOT ALONG ON THE OCCASION. MANY FRAGMENTS CHOOSE TO SPEND THEIR VACATIONS NOT IN PLACES THEY TRULY WISH TO VISIT, BUT IN PLACES AND SURROUNDINGS THEY BELIEVE WILL IMPRESS OTHERS. THIS, OF COURSE, IS CONTRARY TO THE SUPPOSED PURPOSE OF THE VACATION. THAT IS NOT TO SAY THAT FRAGMENTS "SHOULD" NOT MAKE RECORDS OF THEIR VACATIONS AND SHARE THEM, BUT IF THE RECORDS AND THE AFTEREFFECTS ARE WHAT ARE CHIEFLY DESIRED, THEN THE VACATION ITSELF IS NOT APT TO HAVE THE DESIRED EFFECT, AND NO MATTER HOW OUTWARDLY "SUCCESSFUL" WILL TEND TO BE DISAPPOINTING IN STRANGE WAYS, IN THAT IT WAS NOT APPRECIATED WHILE IT WAS GOING ON. FOR THOSE WHO KNOW WHAT THEIR TRUE REST AND TRUE PLAY ARE, VACATIONS WHICH ACCOMODATE TRUE REST AND TRUE PLAY CAN BE ESPECIALLY USEFUL, FOR THE OPPORTUNITY TO HAVE TRUE REST AND TRUE PLAY IN A SETTING ALREADY CONCEIVED FOR SUCH ACTIVITIES IS ONE THAT IS NOT OFTEN ENCOUNTERED IN YOUR OBSESSIVE AND COMPULSIVE YOUNG SOUL CULTURE.

"So on my next vacation, I thought I wouldn't plan anything, and that didn't work out, either."

FOR THOSE WITH GOALS OF DOMINANCE, SOME STRUCTURE IS USUALLY NEEDED FOR THE FRAGMENT TO FEEL "SECURE". WHILE WE COMMEND YOU, MIRIAM, FOR UNDERTAKING TO SET BOTH CHIEF FEATURES AND THE GOAL ASIDE, WE WOULD HAVE TO SAY THAT IT MAY BE YOU "BIT OFF MORE THAN YOU COULD CHEW". IT WOULD NOT BE AMISS TO HAVE SOMETHING OF AN AGENDA, BUT ONE THAT IS NOT SO FIXED THAT IT CANNOT BE SHIFTED AND

CHANGED AS UNEXPECTED OPPORTUNTIES ARISE. LET US SUGGEST THAT SHOULD YOU CHOOSE TO DO SO, YOU WORK OUT WHAT YOU WOULD LIKE TO DO ON YOUR NEXT VACATION, BUT NOT DECIDE IN ADVANCE UNLESS NECESSARY FOR THINGS LIKE TICKETS, WHEN YOU WILL DO THEM. SINCE YOUR TRUE REST CONSISTS OF WINDOW-SHOPPING AMONG ANTIQUES, READING POETRY OF THE ROMANTIC PERIOD, AND BUBBLE BATHS, AND YOUR TRUE PLAY CONSISTS OF RESTORING AND REFINISHING FURNITURE AND ACCESSORIES, GOING ON CARNIVAL RIDES, AND WINE TASTINGS, WE WOULD ENCOURAGE YOU TO CONSIDER THESE FACTORS WHEN YOU PLAN YOUR NEXT VACATION TIME.

"I don't know for sure if I'm going to do that," Miriam says reflectively. "For one thing, I can't abide the thought of spending vacation time fixing up furniture—I do that most weekends. But the carnival rides and wine tastings sound like a lot of fun. I think I might give them a try. Maybe I'll go to the Bahamas or take a trip to Italy. According to Michael, life before last I spent quite a lot of time in Italy and Greece. It might be fun to see it again."

Does being unable to attend sessions bother Miriam?

"Well, sometimes. There are other times when I feel a little relieved. I don't have to see the reaction when I ask yet another set of Overleaves. I'm sure half the group is sick and tired of my endless lists of Overleaves and related comments. Since I have contact with Joan and Mark on a pretty regular basis and I've met five of the group members while they or I were traveling, I don't think of myself as a stranger. And when Leslie comes to town on business, she's usually willing to do a short session for me, as a favor for a friend, and I really appreciate that." Again she pauses. "There are times when I think it would be fun, naturally, but for the most part, I think I get useful information. It's true I don't get the group support that those who attend sessions regularly get, but since I'm working with my Task Companion, I have a lot of support from him. That makes a difference, I think."

THE TASK COMPANION BOND IS ONE OF THE TWO STRONGEST EXPERIENCED BY FRAGMENTS EXTANT ON THE PHYSICAL PLANE AND HAS FAR-REACHING EFFECTS FOR THOSE WHO HAVE DIRECT PERSONAL ACCESS TO THE TASK COMPANION. THE FOCUS OF THE RELATIONSHIP IS OUTWARD, ON THE COMPLETION OF THE LIFE TASK FOR EACH FRAGMENT. WHETHER OR NOT THE TASK COMPANIONS HAVE DIRECT CONTACT, THE WORK EACH DOES WILL COMPLEMENT THE WORK OF THE OTHER, AND BY WORK IN THIS INSTANCE WE MEAN THE LIFE TASK. IN ALMOST ALL INSTANCES THERE IS A QUALITY OF RECIPROCITY IN THE WORK, ALTHOUGH IT IS RARELY CARRIED OUT IN THE SAME FIELD. FOR THE FRAGMENT WHO IS NOW MIRIAM AND HER TASK COMPANION, THE OPPORTUNITY TO HAVE A PROFESSION DIRECTLY ASSOCIATED WITH THE LIFE TASK IS AN ADVANTAGE RARELY ENCOUNTERED ON THE PHYSICAL PLANE. WE WOULD AGREE THAT THE QUALITY OF MUTUAL SUPPORT HERE IS VERY HIGH AND THAT THE RESULTANT PROGRESS IS FAR GREATER THAN IT WOULD BE WITHOUT THE CONTACT.

"If anything happens to my TC, who knows how I'll feel about being away from the group. I may have to move to the West Coast." Although she laughs, there is an underlying seriousness that is most revealing.

Dominique Long lives and works in Southern California and is able to attend sessions perhaps three or four times a year. She is a mid-cycle Mature Scholar in the observation mode with a goal of submission, an idealist in the intellectual part of emotional center with a chief feature of stubbornness and a secondary of self-deprecation. She has been associated with the group for almost nine years. Again, her comments were given over the phone.

"I think one of the hardest things to remember when you're a call-in, like me, is how much energy the channeling takes. When I'm at a session, I'm always amazed at the energy expended by the mediums. When I'm at home, it doesn't seem real. That's one of the reasons I try not to abuse the privilege of getting to call in for answers. I don't like to use up energy for minor things, and I don't want to make too many demands on Milly or both the Leslies.'' She breaks off to call out to her housemate—"Will you take the chicken out of the freezer ?''—and then continues. "I'm planning to come up for a　 ssion next month, and I'm already working on my questions, weeding out the things that I don't want to waste time on. I know that Michael says nothing is wasted, and I accept that, but I want to make the most of my chance to ask questions.''

IT IS NOT AMISS FOR STUDENTS TO CONSIDER THEIR INQUIRIES BEFORE MAKING THEM; OFTEN THE ANSWERS ARE ALREADY AT HAND, AND WHEN THE QUESTION IS CLARIFIED, THE ANSWER IS KNOWN. WE HAVE SAID BEFORE THAT ONE OF THE MOST DIFFICULT SKILLS FOR FRAGMENTS TO DEVELOP IS THE WAY IN WHICH QUESTIONS ARE ASKED FOR MAXIMUM INFORMATION. OUR STUDENT DOMINQUE IS MORE SENSITIVE TO THIS ISSUE THAT SOME OTHERS, AS MUCH BECAUSE HER VERY HIGH CARINALITY GIVES HEIGHTENED SENSITIVITY TO THE ENERGY REQUIRED TO CHANNEL THE ANSWERS. FOR THOSE FRAGMENTS WHO CHOOSE TO EXAMINE THEIR QUESTIONS AND "HONE" THEM, WE WOULD THINK THAT THE QUALITY OF OUR RESPONSES WOULD REFLECT THEIR SHARPER FOCUS.

"I took that answer to heart,'' says Dominique. "I've tried to review my questions, and to approach the material in terms of verification. Recently, for example, I had some business dealings with a man who seemed 'familiar' to me, though in this life we come from very divergent backgrounds. He admitted that he felt something about me, not necessarily a sexual attraction thing, but something very persuasive—that was his word. I gave the whole thing some serious consideration, and when I was through, I was pretty sure there were past connections, but I didn't think he was a Scholar. I was aware that there was some energy in the relationship, but I didn't think it was anything pertaining to this life. I asked Michael to comment on my impressions and to correct any errors I might make in terms of getting the impressions right.''

FIRST WE WOULD HAVE TO SAY THAT THE IMPRESSIONS ARE GENERALLY ACCURATE. THE FRAGMENT IN QUESTION IS A SIXTH-LEVEL YOUNG SLAVE IN THE PERSEVERANCE MODE WITH A GOAL OF GROWTH, A SKEPTIC IN THE EMOTIONAL PART OF INTELLECTUAL CENTER WITH A CHIEF FEATURE OF ARROGANCE AND A SECONDARY CHIEF FEATURE OF STUBBORNNESS. THERE ARE FOURTEEN PAST ASSOCIATIONS OF NOTE, AND IN THE LIFE BEFORE LAST, THESE TWO FRAGMENTS COMPLETED A PARTNERSHIP MONAD. IN THAT LIFE THE FRAGMENT WHO IS NOW DOMINIQUE WAS THE EQUIVALENT OF A POLICE LIEUTENANT AND HE DEDICATED MOST OF HIS PROFESSIONAL LIFE TO PURSUING ONE PARTICULAR CRIMINAL WHO IS NOW THE FRAGMENT THOMAS. IT IS INTERESTING TO NOTE HERE THAT THE MONAD WAS COMPLETED IN THIS WAY, FOR THE INTENSE INVOLVEMENT OF LAW OFFICER AND CRIMINAL CAN BE A VERY COMPLEX RELATIONSHIP. WE WOULD THINK THAT SOME OF THE "ENERGY" CURRENTLY PERCEIVED COMES FROM THAT LIFE, FOR ALTHOUGH THE MONAD IS FINISHED, THERE ARE RESONANCES THAT ARE VERY STRONG FOR BOTH FRAGMENTS.

"I haven't said anything to Tom about this,'' Dominique goes on.' "I wouldn't know how to broach the subject with him. He's pretty strict Greek Orthodox and I don't think he'd be very comfortable with this material. But I feel better about the relationship. I have a better perspective about it.'' She pauses to light a cigarette. "Don't tell me that these things aren't good for me. Hell, Southern California air isn't good for me. One of these days I'll stop. I mean that, incidentally. About ten years ago I quit smoking entirely. It wasn't until we hired three smokers last year that I started up again.''

Has Michael made any observations about her smoking?

"I haven't asked. I know I'll get a health warning and one of the variations on the choice lecture. I know it's up to me. I can't see the point in asking about smoking when there are many other more important things to ask about."

EACH FRAGMENT IS FREE TO PURSUE WHATEVER AREA OF INFORMATION THE FRAGMENT DESIRES TO PURSUE. THERE IS NO "RIGHT" OR "WRONG" APPLICATION OF THIS INFORMATION. WE DO NOT CARE WHAT OR HOW OR IF YOU USE THE MATERIAL. WE GIVE OUR ANSWERS WHOLLY UNCONDITIONALLY, AND OUR ANSWERS ARE AS CLEAR AS WE CAN MAKE THEM, GIVEN THE LIMITATIONS OF LANGUAGE AND THE NATURE OF THE QUESTIONS ASKED. WE HAVE NEVER REFUSED TO ANSWER A QUESTIONS, FOR THAT WOULD IMPOSE SOME ASPECT OF CONDITIONS ON THE MATERIAL, WHICH IS FAR FROM THE PURPOSE OF OUR TEACHING. AS YOU VALIDATE AND ADVANCE THROUGH LEARNING, LESSONS ARE BROUGHT TO BEAR FOR US AS WELL AS FOR YOU, AND LIKE YOU, WE ATTAIN GROWTH.

"I think about that from time to time. I know that Michael gets something out of teaching, but I know that what they tell us about it has to be metaphorical. Also, to me it is important that Michael does not refuse to answer questions, although from time to time the mediums block on the answers. One of the Leslies has a great deal of difficulty getting material having to do with abused children—and not because he was an abused child but because he worked with abused children during and after college. Milly has trouble getting material having to do with health and medical matters, and the female Leslie sometimes blocks on material having to do with divorce, because she is divorced herself. So is Milly. So am I, for that matter. When the mediums know there is a chance they'll block, they often turn the question over to one of the other mediums, to enable Michael to give a complete answer. Sometimes the mediums warn us to be sure we want answers to certain questions, because Michael is not one to soften the blow."

Has Dominique ever had such an answer?

"Several times. I think we all have. When I decided to try to do something about my chief feature, I worked out a very elaborate scheme for finding ways of getting around it. I asked Michael for comments, thinking I would get an endorsement. I didn't."

WHEN THE CHIEF FEATURE IS THE ISSUE, THE MORE "CEREMONY" THAT IS DEVELOPED AROUND IT, THE LESS LIKELY THE OPPORTUNITY TO BREAK ITS HOLD. THE BELIEF THAT RITUALIZING THE CHIEF FEATURE IS ANOTHER ONE OF ITS SEDUCTIVE LIES: THE CHIEF FEATURE IS, AS WE HAVE STATED BEFORE BUT WILL REITERATE, A MASTER OF DISGUISES, AND NEVER MORE SO THAN WHEN IT IS UNDER ATTACK.

"I'm still thinking about that one," Dominique admits. "I know that there have been a few times when I've been able to consciously hold the chief feature at bay—never for very long, and always with difficulties later. Other people in the group have had the experience as well; the chief feature beats you up for having the audacity to oppose it."

THE EXPERIENCE YOU DESCRIBE HERE IS ONE OF THE MORE BLATANT EXAMPLES OF THE CHIEF FEATURE ATTEMPTING TO MAINTAIN ITS HOLD. WHEN FRAGMENTS ARE ABLE TO BREAK THE HOLD OF CHIEF FEATURE, EVEN FOR VERY BRIEF PERIODS OF TIME, IT WEAKENS THE HOLD IN GENERAL. THE CHIEF FEATURE MUST THEREFORE STRIVE TO REASSERT ITS AUTHORITY IN THE LIFE, AND THIS IS DONE BY MAKING THE EXPERIENCE OF BREAKING ITS HOLD NOT WORTH IT. MOST OF THE TIME THE CHIEF FEATURE GOES TO GREAT LENGTHS TO HIDE ITS TYRANNY, THE "IRON FIST IN VELVET GLOVE" TECHNIQUE. BUT WHEN A FRAGMENT HAS SUCCESSFULLY SUPPRESSED THE CHIEF FEATURE, SUBTLETY IS OUT OF THE QUESTION, AND THE CHIEF FEATURE SHOWS ITS TRUE "COLORS" IN EVERY WAY POSSIBLE. CHIEF FEATURE, BEING MADE OF FEAR, IS RUTHLESS, AND ITS ATTEMPT TO DOMINATE THE LIFE

IS RELENTLESS. IT WILL USE EVERY MEANS AT ITS DIS-
POSAL TO KEEP THE FRAGMENT FROM BREAKING FREE OF
ITS RULE.

"I can't say that the information made things much easier
for me, but I will agree that I try to keep it in mind when
I'm having an especially bad time with chief feature. It does
help to know that most of what I'm responding to is distorted.
I find that gives me more comprehension. Michael also gave
me some advice about learning to deal with the distortions.
They've said much the same thing to others, but it came at
just the right time for me to realize what they meant, and
that's important."

WHEN FRAGMENTS ARE IN DOUBT ABOUT THE WORK-
INGS OF CHIEF FEATURE, OR THE UNDERSTANDING OF
OTHERS, WE WOULD RECOMMEND THE DIRECT AP-
PROACH, WHAT MIGHT BE TERMED A "REALITY" CHECK.
SPEAK TO THE FRAGMENT IN QUESTION AND ASK IF THIS
IS, IN FACT, HOW THE FRAGMENT PERCEIVED THE SITUA-
TION OR REACTION. FOR EXAMPLE, SAY YOU, DOMINIQUE,
ATTEND A SOCIAL FUNCTION AND WHILE THERE MEET A
CASUAL FRIEND. DURING CONVERSATION, AS OCCASION-
ALLY HAPPENS, THE SUBJECTS TURN SERIOUS AND PER-
SONAL, AND FOR TWO HOURS THERE IS MUCH VALID COM-
MUNICATION. LATER, OF COURSE, CHIEF FEATURE SEEKS
TO DISTORT THIS, PERHAPS SUGGESTING THAT YOU WERE
INTRUDING INTO THE OTHER FRAGMENT'S LIFE, OR WERE
IMPOSING, AND HAVE IN SOME UNDISCLOSED MANNER
OFFERED THE FRAGMENT AN UNFORGIVABLE INSULT. IF
IT IS POSSIBLE TO CHOOSE TO DO SO, WE WOULD THINK
THAT A SIMPLE TELEPHONE CALL AND A FEW QUESTIONS
WOULD SERVE TO CLEAR UP THE MISUNDERSTANDING,
FOR IN ALMOST ALL INSTANCES THERE IS MISUN-
DERSTANDING. LET US ENCOURAGE YOU AND ALL FRAG-
MENTS HERE PRESENT TO CONSIDER MAKING A "REALITY"
CHECK WHEN SUCH CIRCUMSTANCES ARISE, ALTHOUGH
YOU ARE FREE TO DO AS YOU CHOOSE, AND THERE IS NO
REQUIREMENT THAT YOU MAKE A "REALITY" CHECK, OR

DO ANYTHING ELSE, FOR THAT MATTER.

"One of the things I like about Michael is the way they constantly lean over backward to keep from telling anyone what to do, or make it appear that they are telling you what to do. I find that one of the most . . . well, endearing aspects of the teaching. As long as I'm certain they have no requirements to make of me, I know I'll keep asking questions, because as long as they have no expectations of me—to use their words—I'll know they're giving me the straight goods. There's little enough of that in the world."

Jake Reston has been exclusively a call-in group member for about nine years. A Southerner, Jake had contact to the group through Jessica Lansing.

"Yeah, Jessica and I met about ten years ago, while she was attending a conference in New Orleans. I was there—we do similar public-relations jobs—and we got to talking. You know how it is. The panels are boring, you don't want to hang out with people from the office, so you look for someone who seems interesting. I wasn't looking for a pickup, incidentally, and if I had been, it wouldn't have been Jessica, since I'm gay. I saw this woman from California, and I knew a little about her organization, and it started there. What got us from PR to Michael was a question about astrology. She didn't tell me she was a medium; that came much later. She simply told me she was in an esoteric study group and wanted to know if I had any questions. We must've talked for six hours." He stops. "What time is it out there in California?"

"Six-thirty."

"I can never keep the time difference straight. I called Jessica a couple of times much too early. You know how much she hates getting early calls." He falls silent for a short while. "When Jessica stopped channeling, I went through a period when I didn't ask any questions. I thought that without Jessica to answer the questions, I was . . . I don't know, intruding. But about a year ago, the female Leslie called me and asked if I was still interested in the group and the teaching. I said, 'hell, yes.' And since then I've kept in contact.''

Has Jake had direct contact with any members of the group other than Jessica?

"Well, I met the male Leslie when he was out here visiting family. I met Martin Keir a couple years ago. That's about it.'' He chuckles. "We suffer from culture shock, the Michael group and I. There's a big difference between the South and California.''

"Northern California,'' I remind him.

"Yeah, *North*ern California. You know what north any-thing sounds like to a Southerner.'' He chuckles again. "I'll say this about Michael: he sure called it about why Jessica and I got along so well. That was one of my first questions, why we did. You know, I gotta say I miss that lady.''

"So do all of us,'' I agree.

He gets back on the subject. "Anyway, I asked first about the connection with Jessica and me.''

THE FRAGMENT WHO IS NOW JACOB IS A SIXTH-LEVEL MATURE SCHOLAR IN THE OBSERVATION MODE WITH A GOAL OF DOMINANCE, A SPIRITUALIST IN THE MOVING PART OF INTELLECTUAL CENTER WITH A CHIEF FEATURE OF ARROGANCE. THERE ARE ELEVEN PAST ASSOCIATIONS OF NOTE HERE, PRIMARILY AS FELLOW MARINERS AND SIBLINGS OF THE CLOTH. THE OVERLEAVES ARE VERY COMPATIBLE, AND SO ARE BODY TYPES. THE ONLY POSSI-BLE ABRASION IN THE OVERLEAVES IS THE POTENTIAL CONFLICT BETWEEN ATTITUDES; SPIRITUALIST AND PRAG-MATIST.

"Actually, with the exception of soul age and the attitude, our Overleaves are the same,'' Jake says. "Jessica's second-level Old.'' There is the sound of shuffled papers. "I dug out something that meant a great deal to me at the time. I was on a serious health kick; my father had just died and I was feeling my mortality.''

AS REGARDS MATTERS OF HEALTH, WE WOULD HAVE

TO SAY THAT ANYTHING DONE TO EXCESS, INCLUDING
"HEALTHY" EXERCISE DOES NOT CONTRIBUTE TO WELL-
BEING. THOSE WHO CHOOSE TO DEVOTE TIME TO A SPE-
CIFIC FITNESS PROGRAM WOULD DO WELL TO EXAMINE
WHAT THEY DESIRE TO ACHIEVE FROM SUCH A PROGRAM
AND TO ASSESS WHAT THE GOAL THEY HAVE IN MIND IS
LIKELY TO REQUIRE, NOT ONLY IN TERMS OF TIME, BUT
EQUIPMENT AND OTHER EXPENSES. PURSUING THE IDEAL
OF FITNESS WITHOUT SUCH AN ASSESSMENT CAN LEAD
TO DISAPPOINTMENT AND DAMAGE TO THE BODY, WHICH
IS NOT GOOD WORK. LET US ALSO REMARK THAT DEVOT-
ING TIME AND ENERGY TO FITNESS WITHOUT ATTENDANT
PERIODS OF TRUE REST, TRUE STUDY, AND TRUE PLAY IS
LIKELY TO PRODUCE LITTLE BUT EXHAUSTION FOR THE
FRAGMENT IN THE LONG RUN. FRAGMENTS WHO ARE PAR-
TICIPATING IN PHYSICAL CONDITIONING OF VARIOUS
SORTS MIGHT RECALL THAT THE BODY IS NOT, IN FACT,
A MACHINE, AND THAT CERTAIN BODIES LEND THEM-
SELVES TO CERTAIN FORMS OF EXERCISE MORE READILY
THAN OTHERS. WHEN UNDERTAKING TO DETERMINE
WHAT A FRAGMENT CHOOSES TO DO TO REMAIN FIT, IT
IS NEVER AMISS TO HAVE A LONG, HARD, PRACTICAL
LOOK AT THE BODY AND ACCOMMODATE THE EXERCISE
TO THE BODY RATHER THAN THE BODY TO THE EXERCISE.

"That wasn't quite what I was expecting, and I said so
at the time. You got to understand that I was turning my
whole life upside down, going from meat-eater to vegetarian
and all the rest of it."

JUST AS THERE ARE GREAT FADS IN EXERCISE, THERE
ARE ALSO FADS IN SUCH MATTERS AS NUTRITION. EVERY
FRAGMENT CAN EVALUATE HIS OR HER INDIVIDUAL RE-
QUIREMENTS AND WOULD BE WISE TO REGARD ALL FADS
WITH A DEGREE OF SKEPTICISM. FRAGMENTS OFTEN USE
PHYSICAL FITNESS AS THE MEANS TO AVOID CONFRONT-
ING DOUBTS, CONFLICTS, AND CRISES IN THE LIFE, AND
THAT, IN ALMOST ALL CASES, SERVES TO INCREASE IN-
STEAD OF LESSEN STRESS.

• • •

"Well, that one hit home, I can tell you," Jake says. "There were all kinds of things I was avoiding, and old Michael put a finger right on it. I hadn't let myself deal with my father dying. I was doing everything I could think of to keep from dealing with it. Michael can really rock you back on your heels."

FOR MANY FRAGMENTS, DEALING WITH GRIEF IS DIF- FICULT BECAUSE THERE IS A LARGE ELEMENT OF ANGER IN GRIEF. THE ANGER IS SEEN AS "WRONG" AND "UNAC- CEPTABLE", AND THEREFORE MOST FRAGMENTS DENY IT. THERE ARE CULTURES THAT ACCEPT GRIEF AND HAVE THE MEANS TO DEAL WITH THE ANGER THAT ACCOM- PANIES IT, BUT WE WOULD HAVE TO SAY THAT FEW IF ANY OCCIDENTAL CULTURES ARE "REALISTIC" ABOUT THE ANGER IN GRIEF. LET US ASSURE YOU, JACOB, THAT THERE IS NO "FAULT" IN BEING ANGRY AT YOUR FATHER FOR LEAVING YOU. THERE IS NO "FAULT" IN BEING ANGRY AT YOUR FATHER FOR BECOMING ILL AND DYING. ALL FRAGMENTS, NO MATTER WHAT THEIR SPECIES, FEAR ABANDONMENT; AND DEATH, IN A VERY REAL PHYSICAL PLANE SENSE IS ABANDONMENT. THE ESSENCE RETURNS, BUT, OF COURSE, NOT THE PERSONALITY. WE WOULD THINK THAT SHOULD YOU CHOOSE TO RELEASE YOUR ANGER, MUCH OF THE PAIN OF YOUR GRIEF WOULD SUB- SIDE, AND THE GUILT YOU NOW EXPERIENCE SO KEENLY AND DENY SO ADAMANTLY WOULD LOSE ITS POWER.

"Jessica told me about someone in the group who had described indulging the chief feature as hugging a cactus. Well, where my father's death was concerned, I was hugging a whole yard full of cacti. What Michael told me made a lot of sense, and it helped me get through that bad time. My lover and I have lived together for almost fifteen years, and I can't remember a time we were closer to breaking up than in the first six months after my father died. I was taking it out on everyone. I know what it took for him to hang in. Michael helped me find ways to acknowledge that, without getting caught in the old gratitude trap.''

WHILE WE WOULD AGREE THAT GRATITUDE FOR
GENUINE SERVICE IS A REASONABLE EXPRESSION OF AP-
PRECIATION, WE WOULD WARN THE FRAGMENT WHO IS
NOW JACOB THAT CONTINUING GRATITUDE FOR AID
WHEN THE AID IS FREELY GIVEN SUBVERTS THE GIFT. THE
FRAGMENT WHO IS NOW HOWARD HAS CHOSEN TO EX-
TEND HIS EMOTIONAL SUPPORT DURING THIS DIFFICULT
TIME. IT IS WHAT HE WISHES TO DO. IT IS HIS CHOICE TO
DO IT; YOU DID NOT DEMAND OR REQUIRE IT OF HIM. LET
US SUGGEST THAT SOME FORM OF ACKNOWLEDGMENT
BE AGREED UPON *AS A ONETIME GESTURE,* AND SHOULD
YOU CHOOSE TO DO THIS, IT WOULD "CLEAR THE AIR"
FOR BOTH OF YOU. TO CONTINUE TO EXPRESS GRATITUDE
AND A SENSE OF BEING "BEHOLDEN" IS NOT ONLY UN-
NECESSARY, IT SERVES ONLY TO KEEP THE PAIN AND DIF-
FICULTY ALIVE BETWEEN YOU, WHICH WILL NOT AID THE
RELATIONSHIP IN ANY FAVORABLE WAY. WHATEVER YOU
CHOOSE TO DO, JACOB, WE WOULD WISH TO POINT OUT
THAT HOWARD WILL MAKE HIS CHOICES AS WELL.

"So I took part of the inheritance and we spent three
weeks in Europe. That was my last thank-you, and I made
a point of telling Howard that it was my last thank-you. It
seems to have worked pretty well. I don't feel so weighed
down, and neither does he.''

Does Jake think the Michael information has helped him?

"Lordy, Lordy, you bet I do,'' he says with feeling. "Just
that business of going on a trip with Howard. I'd never have
thought of that in a million years; it worked. We were in
pretty bad shape until we did that. And the things Michael
told me about grief, while I didn't like them, helped me get
through it. Chances are I would have got through anyway,
but you never can tell. I know I wouldn't have got through
as well.'' When he speaks again, his tone is more quiet. "I
don't say that Michael changed my life. There's no way to
be sure about that. But I know that I see things differently,
and maybe that's the real key to changing a life. Maybe the

way you see things is what matters most.''

Geoffrey Clifford is a fifth-level Old Sage who was in the core group for two years before he moved out of the Bay Area. He is part of Larry Herron and John Verano in *More Messages From Michael*. Recently married, he has a new career as well as a new home. Geoff is in his mid-thirties.

"I get to sessions whenever I'm in the Bay Area at the right time," he says, adding, "which isn't often enough. It's odd to think that without Michael's insight, I wouldn't have made the move and changed careers, even though I wanted to. And now that I've moved, I don't get much opportunity to get information from Michael. It's a strange feeling." He pauses before going on with more enthusiasm. "Michael warned me once about fragments with goals of growth. I didn't pay much attention at the time; I was new to the group and still trying to get my footing. Now I know just what Michael was talking about.''

LET US SAY TO THOSE WITH GOALS OF GROWTH THAT IT IS "TYPICAL" OF THAT GOAL TO SEEK OUT CHANGE, TO SHIFT GEARS IN THE LIFE, TO DEVELOP NEW INTERESTS. GROWTH DOES NOT LIKE TO REPEAT ITSELF, NOR DOES IT WANT TO REMAIN IN THE SAME PLACE. THOSE WHO HAVE GOALS OF GROWTH AND CHIEF FEATURES OF IMPATIENCE TEND TO HAVE THE MOST DIFFICULTY WITH "LEAPING WITHOUT LOOKING". WE REMIND YOU THAT THE NEGATIVE POLE OF GROWTH IS CONFUSION, AND THAT IF CONFUSION IS PRESENT, CHIEF FEATURE IS PRESENT ALSO. IN THE CASE OF THE FRAGMENT WHO IS NOW GEOFFREY, WE WOULD REMIND HIM THAT BECAUSE OF THE CHIEF FEATURE OF ARROGANCE, THERE IS CONSTANT FEAR OF VULNERABILITY WHICH TENDS TO MAKE GROWTH APPEAR THREATENING SINCE GROWTH BY ITS VERY NATURE HAS AN ASPECT OF "EXPOSURE" ABOUT IT. LET US SUGGEST THAT SIMPLIFICATION IS IN ORDER WHEN THE CONFUSION LEVEL RISES. IT IS NOT UNUSUAL FOR THOSE FRAGMENTS WITH GROWTH TO BE TEMPTED TO CHANGE

ONLY THE EXTERNALS AND NEGLECT THE INTERNALS, WHICH IS ULTIMATELY UNSATISFYING. AS THIS OLD SAGE COMPLETES THE TRANSIT OF THE FOURTH INTERNAL MONAD, WE WOULD THINK HE MIGHT CHOOSE TO KEEP THIS IN MIND.

"According to Michael, I finally made it through the damned thing. I admit I feel more at home in my own skin now, and I don't thrash around looking for a role to play. I'm glad I didn't move until I was almost finished with the infamous Fourth Monad. That's all one word: infamousfourthmonad," he says, illustrating. "Michael helped me identify the areas in my life where I had got stuck in False Personality; that was a big help."

Has Geoff changed the sorts of questions he asks?

"Yes and no. Since I'm not able to be with the group at sessions, I find I don't get the chance to spark off of other people's questions. I wish I did. That's the part I miss; you see, everyone is supportive and concerned for the others in the group. It's a great feeling. I'll say this for the mediums— they work very hard on keeping the group really balanced. It makes a difference when that level of care is taken." He is more reluctant when he goes on. "Michael told me when I asked that I could develop an ability to channel, and in a way I can sense that in myself. But I look at Milly or the Leslies while they work, and I see what they go through, and I have to admit I'm not ready to do that. It's exhausting work. Leslie-female tells me that it feels wonderful while she does it, at least when the information is not too dreadful. But you ought to see her afterward. She's worn to a frazzle. Milly is more careful; she limits herself and knows how to stick by it. Leslie-male doesn't do as much channeling as the other two, so it doesn't get to him the same way, I don't think. Still, I hope I'll reach the point someday when I'll want to channel. Not now, but maybe before I'm forty. Maybe."

What does Michael have to say about that?

"The usual—'all is chosen'. I know that. It took me almost two years to get it. I heard it all the time at sessions, but I didn't really get it for some time. That's probably why Michael repeats it so often. What finally did it for me was my dealing with a repair service. They declared my home computer fixed, even though it wasn't, and refused to do anything more about it. I asked Michael for advice and recommendations.''

WE WOULD AGREE THAT THE COMPUTING MACHINE IS NOT WORKING PROPERLY AND THAT THE TERMS OF THE AGREEMENT IN REGARD TO MAINTENENCE HAVE NOT BEEN MET. THAT IS NOT TO SAY THAT THEREFORE THE FRAGMENTS IN QUESTION *MUST* REPAIR THE MACHINE, FOR THEY HAVE CLEARLY CHOSEN NOT TO. THERE IS NO REASON FOR YOU TO ACCEPT THIS, IF YOU CHOOSE NOT TO. THERE ARE VARIOUS MEANS TO DEAL WITH THE PREDICAMENT. YOU MAY WISH TO SPEAK TO THE SENIOR FRAGMENT OF THE REPAIR COMPANY, ASKING THAT FRAGMENT TO CHECK OUT THE COMPUTING MACHINE FOR HIMSELF. YOU MAY WISH TO CALL IN ANOTHER COMPANY WITH THE UNDERSTANDING THAT YOU ARE TRANSFERRING YOUR BUSINESS. THERE IS ALSO THE POSSIBILITY OF SMALL-CLAIMS COURT. IT IS UP TO YOU WHICH OF THESE APPROACHES YOU SELECT, IF ANY. YOU MAY CHOOSE TO IGNORE THE ISSUE, OR TO TRADE THE COMPUTING MACHINE IN ON A MORE RELIABLE ONE. YOU MAY CHOOSE TO REQUEST A REPLACEMENT MACHINE FROM THE REPAIR COMPANY.

"I hadn't really considered the possibilities until I got that answer. I also hadn't really understood about choice. After that, I did, and life got a lot easier. Incidentally, I traded in the computer for a more versatile one.''

Was there any one thing Michael told Geoff that has turned out to be more important than the other messages?

"There is one thing that does stand out,'' he says when he has thought about it. "I didn't pay much attention to it at first, but like a lot of what Michael says, it sneaks up on you. This one is still sneaking.''

FOR THOSE WHO ARE ATTUNED TO THE CONCEPT OF HARMONICS, NOT ONLY IN THE MUSICAL SENSE BUT IN THE CASTING SENSE, THERE IS MUCH OF MERIT THAT CAN BE ACHIEVED WHEN THAT PERCEPTION IS BROUGHT TO BEAR IN THE LIFE. WE WOULD THINK THAT EXPLORING THE ACCESS TO THE HIGHER EMOTIONAL CENTER WOULD PROVIDE MUCH FOOD FOR THOUGHT FOR THIS OLD SAGE. WE WOULD ALSO SUGGEST TO THIS FRAGMENT THAT HE CONSIDER MORE ADVANCED STUDIES IN THE AREA OF MUSIC, FOR SHOULD HE CHOOSE TO ADVANCE HIS KNOWL- EDGE IN THAT ART, HE MAY FIND OTHER VISTAS OPENING FOR HIM AS WELL. IT IS NOT INAPPROPRIATE TO RECALL THAT SIX IS THE NUMBER OF HARMONY, AND THIS OLD SAGE IS SIXTH CAST IN HIS CADRE. RESONANCES OCCUR IN MANY PLACES AND IN MANY WAYS; THIS FRAGMENT IS ONLY NOW BECOMING AWARE OF THE POTENTIALS FOR HARMONY, LITERALLY AND FIGURATIVELY, IN HIS LIFE.

"I can't say that I've undertaken to write immortal music, but I have got back into writing songs. Who knows what might come next?" He laughs once. "I won't ask Michael, because Michael never predicts." He sighs.

Of the fourteen phone-in group members, eight of them call regularly, the other six more sporadically. Their ques- tions cover as wide a range as those of the rest of the group. With the exception of Jeanette Pierce, who is working in Europe for the next two years, most phone-in group members make contact with the group at least once every six to eight weeks.

CHAPTER 9

MICHAEL: THE REALITIES OF INCARNATION

ALL FRAGMENTS EXTANT UPON THE PHYSICAL PLANE AT ANY PLACE IN THE PHYSICAL UNIVERSE HAVE CERTAIN THINGS IN COMMON, THE MOST OBVIOUS BEING THAT THE FRAGMENTS, EITHER INDEPENDENTLY OR INTERDEPENDENTLY, HAVE SOME PHYSICAL FORM, BETTER KNOWN AS BODIES. THERE ARE FRAGMENTS WHO WOULD APPEAR TO BE MORE LIKE BUDS AND BLOSSOMS TO YOU, FRAGMENTS WHO ARE PHYSICALLY LINKED WITH OTHER FRAGMENTS IN INTERDEPENDENT WAYS, EITHER SYMBIOTIC OR PARASITIC OR "SYNERGETIC." ALL FRAGMENTS ENSOULED ARE SUBJECT TO THE HAZARDS OF THE PHYSICAL PLANE, AND ALL HAVE AN ASPECT OF BODILY MAINTENANCE IN THEIR LIVES. YOUR SPECIES IS, OF COURSE, NO DIFFERENT THAN THE OTHERS.

IN THE CASE OF ENSOULED FRAGMENTS ON THIS PLANET AS WELL AS OTHER SPECIES OF HIVE-SOUL NATURE, ONE OF THE MOST OBVIOUS CHARACTERISTICS OF YOUR PLANET IS THAT ALMOST ALL INDEPENDENTLY MOBILE SPECIES HAVE ONLY TWO SEXES, AND THOSE SEXES REMAIN FIXED THROUGHOUT LIFE—AT LEAST IN THE GENETIC SENSE. BECAUSE OF THIS, YOUR SPECIES HAS BECOME FAR MORE RIGID IN ITS SEXUAL PERCEPTIONS THAN MANY OTHERS EXTANT ON THE PHYSICAL PLANE. YOUR SPECIES ALLOWS GENDER AND SEXUAL ORIENTATION TO INFLUENCE A MUCH LARGER PART OF THE LIFE THAN MANY OTHER ENSOULED SPECIES DO, AND THE RESULTANT SOCIALIZATION OF FRAGMENTS ALONG

RIGIDLY DEFINED GENDER AND SEXUAL ORIENTATION LINES OFTEN SERVES TO DISTORT MANY OF THE LIFE PERCEPTIONS. OCCIDENTAL ACCULTURATION HAS CREATED A SERIES OF SEXUAL EXPECTATIONS THAT NOW INFLUENCE SOCIAL BEHAVIOR IN MOST OF THE WORLD, AND HAS PROVIDED A MODEL FOR "ACCEPTABLE" BEHAVIOR AND APPEARANCE THAT HEAVILY INFLUENCE SOCIAL PATTERNS.

IN REGARD TO THE MATTER OF SEXUALITY AND CULTURATION, WE WOULD HAVE TO SAY THAT THERE IS AN EXTENSIVE AND NOT ALWAYS CONSTRUCTIVE INTERACTION HERE THAT CAN BRING ABOUT COMPLEX MISUNDERSTANDINGS AS WELL AS CREATING EXPECTATIONS WHICH ARE NOT IN ANY SENSE OF THE WORD VALID. THE IMPOSED STANDARDS AS PRESENTED TO THE "COSMOPOLITAN" AUDIENCE ARE ENSHRINED AS CULTURAL IKONS, AND EMULATION IS REGARDED AS WORTHY AND "ESSENTIAL" FOR MANY VARIETIES OF SOCIAL SUCCESS.

AS WE HAVE INDICATED BEFORE, WHETHER A FRAGMENT IS HETEROSEXUAL, HOMOSEXUAL, BISEXUAL AND/OR ASEXUAL IS DETERMINED BY THE TIME THE FRAGMENT IS THREE, AND IS OFTEN CHOSEN BY THE FRAGMENT BEFORE INCARNATION AS PART OF THE LIFE PLAN. OFTEN THERE ARE PRIOR AGREEMENTS THAT TEND TO MOVE A FRAGMENT TOWARD ONE ORIENTATION OR ANOTHER. BY THE TIME SEXUAL BEHAVIOR IS CONSIDERED MANIFEST— BY WHICH WE MEAN OVERT—THE FRAGMENT HAS HAD SEVERAL YEARS IN WHICH TO BECOME INFLUENCED BY SOCIAL ATTITUDES TOWARD THE FRAGMENT'S INDIVIDUAL SEXUALITY. INCIDENTLY, WE WOULD SAY THAT SEXUAL BEHAVIOR BEGINS AT BIRTH, FOR UNLIKE THE EXPECTATIONS OF THIS CULTURE, WE SEE ALMOST ALL FORMS OF PHYSICAL EXCITATION AS HAVING A SEXUAL ASPECT. THIS IS NOT TO SAY THAT WE AGREE WITH THE MATURE PRIEST WHO WAS SIGMUND FREUD THAT SEX IS THE BASIC FORCE BEHIND ALL BEHAVIOR IN LIFE. CERTAINLY SEXUALITY IS A SIGNIFICANT ASPECT OF THE PERSONALITY, BOTH THE TRUE AND THE FALSE—WHICH IN PART IS THE RESULT OF HAVING FIXED GENDERS—AND IS

VERY MUCH LINKED TO THE EXPERIENCES OF THE PHYS-
ICAL PLANE, BUT IT IS NOT WHAT IS THE DRIVING FORCE
IN ALL EXPERIENCES AND UNDER ALL CIRCUMSTANCES
FOR ALL FRAGMENTS.

PHYSICAL EXCITATION CAN BE EXPERIENCED IN MANY
WAYS THAT ARE NOT OFTEN REGARDED AS SEXUAL, SINCE
THEY HAVE LITTLE TO DO WITH EROTIC STIMULUS, SUCH
AS HIKING, SKIING, MOST FORMS OF SPORT, COOKING,
AND INDEED MOST PHYSICAL ACTIVITY THAT IS NOT
SENSELESSLY REPETITIOUS. THIS PHYSICAL EXCITATION
IS PRESENT IN ALMOST ALL SEXUAL MANIFESTATIONS EX-
CEPT THOSE THAT ARE ABUSIVE. TO ASSUME THAT THERE-
FORE SEXUALITY IS THE UNDERLYING PURPOSE IS FAR
FROM THE POINT, HOWEVER. WE WOULD SAY RATHER
THAT PHYSICAL EXCITATION IS THE UNDERLYING PUR-
POSE OF SEXUALITY.

IT IS NOT INAPPROPRIATE TO REMEMBER THAT THE SEX-
UAL CENTER AND THE MOVING CENTER ARE ON THE AC-
TION POLARITY AND THEREFORE ARE DIRECTLY CON-
CERNED WITH ACTION. IT IS THE APPLICATION AND FOCUS
OF THE ACTION THAT DETERMINES THE DEGREE OF PHYS-
ICAL EXCITATION EVOKED BY THE ACTION.

ONE OF THE ASPECTS OF BEING ENSOULED IN A BODY
IS THAT THE BODY IS A LARGE PART OF THE LESSONS TO
BE LEARNED. BODIES, AND BY EXTENSION, GENDERS, DO
NOT EXIST EXCEPT ON THE PHYSICAL PLANE. THERE ARE
EXPERIENCES THAT CAN ONLY BE HAD IN A BODY, AND
FOR THAT REASON WE WOULD WISH TO POINT OUT THAT
THOSE WHO SEEK TO GET "BEYOND" THE BODY ARE SET-
TING ASIDE AN IMPORTANT LESSON THAT IS INTRINSIC TO
BEING EXTANT ON THE PHYSICAL PLANE. WE WOULD EN-
COURAGE ALL FRAGMENTS TO LEARN WHAT THE BODY
HAS TO TEACH AND AND TO COME TO APPRECIATE THE
SENSE OF THE LESSONS AND EXPERIENCES AS UNIQUE TO
THE PHYSICAL PLANE, SHOULD YOU CHOOSE TO DO SO.

THE EXPERIENCE OF SEXUALITY IS, OF COURSE, PART
OF THAT LESSON, AND ONE OF THE MOST COMPLICATED
THAT THE BODY HAS TO TEACH, FROM THE CHANGING
FUNCTIONS OF THE BODY'S SEXUAL CAPACITIES TO THE

VERY AMBIVALENT SOCIAL ATTITUDES TOWARD ALL FORMS OF SEXUALITY. THIS IS MADE EVEN MORE COMPLEX THROUGH THE PROCESS OF ACCULTURATION—THAT IS THE TRANSFER OF CULTURE FROM ONE ETHNIC GROUP TO ANOTHER, SO THAT THE MOST DESIRED FORM, ESPECIALLY OF FEMALES, IS ENCOUNTERED IN AREAS WHERE IT WOULD APPEAR MOST INAPPROPRIATE.

IT WOULD BE MISLEADING TO SAY THAT ALL FRAGMENTS SEEK SOME FORM OF SEXUAL EXPRESSION IN EACH AND EVERY LIFE. THIS IS CLEARLY NOT THE CASE; THERE ARE MANY FRAGMENTS WHO ARE TO ALL INTENTS AND PURPOSES ASEXUAL AND HAVE CHOSEN THAT. THERE ARE MANY OTHERS WHO ARE ASEXUAL AS A RESULT OF PRESSURE AND CONFUSION BROUGHT ABOUT BY THE VERY CONFLICTING REPRESENTATIONS OF SEXUALITY, WHICH IS OFTEN REGARDED BOTH AS SUBLIME AND BENEFICIAL AND UPLIFTING, AS WELL AS DEGRADING AND ANIMALISTIC AND BRUTAL. MOST OF THESE PERCEPTIONS COME FROM VARIOUS AREAS OF ACCULTURATION AND ARE THE RESULT OF SEVERAL LAYERS OF FEELINGS AND ATTITUDES BEING PILED TOGETHER, ONE ON TOP OF THE OTHER, AND THEN PRESENTED AS A "COHERENT" WHOLE, WHICH IS OBVIOUSLY NOT THE CASE.

BECAUSE OF THE POTENTIAL FOR INTIMACY AND THEREFORE ESSENCE CONTACT THROUGH SEXUAL EXPERIENCES, THE CHIEF FEATURE SEEKS OUT THE MOST DISTORTING OF THE ACCULTURATED MYTHS WITH WHICH TO DENY THE CONTACT AND EVEN THE POTENTIAL FOR THE CONTACT WHICH SUCH CLOSENESS MAY PROVIDE. CHIEF FEATURE WITHOUT EXCEPTION DISTORTS THE WHOLE REALM OF INTIMACY, AS WE HAVE DESCRIBED ALREADY, ESPECIALLY WHERE SEXUALITY IS INVOLVED IN PART BECAUSE THERE IS SO MUCH SOCIAL PRESSURE AND MISUNDERSTANDINGS AROUND THE NATURE OF SEXUAL RELATIONSHIPS. WE WOULD THINK THAT MOST FRAGMENTS HAVE HAD THE EXPERIENCE OF BEING CONVINCED THAT A POTENTIAL LOVER WOULD BE DISGUSTED OR APPALLED IF HE OR SHE DISCOVERED SOME PARTICULAR THING ABOUT THE FRAGMENT, AND THAT THINGS

OFTEN HAS MUCH TO DO WITH THE CHIEF FEATURE AND LITTLE TO DO WITH THE VALID NATURE OF SEXUAL AND/ OR BODY-TYPE ATTRACTION.

SEXUAL ATTRACTION IS ONE ASPECT, BUT NOT, WE HASTEN TO ADD, THE ONLY ASPECT, OF BODY-TYPE ATTRACTION. MOST OF THE TIME SEXUAL EXPERIENCES ARE MORE SATISFYING WHEN BODY TYPES ATTRACT OR ARE AT LEAST COMPATIBLE. THAT DOES NOT MEAN THAT IT IS IMPOSSIBLE TO HAVE SATISFYING AND PROFOUNDLY INTIMATE CONTACT WITHOUT BODY-TYPE ATTRACTION OR COMPATIBILITY, BUT THAT IF THE BODY-TYPE ATTRACTION IS NOT PRESENT, THEN THERE WILL HAVE TO BE OTHER ASPECTS OF ATTRACTION THAT FUNCTION IN ITS PLACE, SUCH AS COMPATIBLE OVERLEAVES, ESSENCE TWIN OR TASK COMPANION BONDS, CADENCE BONDS, MULTIPLE PAST ASSOCIATIONS OF A BENEFICIAL SORT, AND SIMILAR CONDITIONS.

WHEN SEXUALITY HAS COME UNDER COMPLETE CULTURAL MANIPULATION, THEN THERE IS A GREATLY REDUCED CHANCE FOR TRUE INTIMACY, FOR THE CULTURAL EXPECTATIONS ALMOST ENTIRELY RULE OUT THE CHOICES THAT MAKE VALIDATION POSSIBLE. FOR EXAMPLE, IN CULTURES WHERE THE SEXES ARE KEPT APART FOR MOST OF YOUTH, MARRIAGES ARE ARRANGED AND THE PRIMARY GOAL IS PROCREATION: THIS CREATES SUCH RIGOROUS EXPECTATIONS AND SUCH LIMITED OPPORTUNITY FOR COMMUNICATION THAT THERE IS LITTLE OR NO CHANCE FOR THE FRAGMENTS TO PERCEIVE THE TRUE NATURE OF THE PARTNER. WHEN A FRAGMENT HAS SEXUAL IDENTITY AND SOCIAL ROLE IMPOSED BEFORE PERSONALITY, THE DISTORTIONS WROUGHT, NOT ONLY BY CHIEF FEATURE BUT BY THE CULTURAL PRESSURES ARE SO ACUTE THAT MANY TIMES THERE IS NO REAL SENSE THAT TRUE INTIMACY EXISTS, OR THAT ESSENCE CONTACT IS POSSIBLE.

IN GENERAL IN THIS SOCIETY MATTERS ARE NOT SO RESTRICTIVE. HOWEVER, THERE IS A VERY LIMITING SENSE OF ROLE MODEL THAT PUTS SUCH STRINGENT LIMITS ON ATTRACTIVENESS THAT MANY FRAGMENTS

ARE NOT ABLE TO FUNCTION EFFECTIVELY IN GENERAL
SOCIAL SETTINGS AND LACK CONFIDENCE TO ENTER INTO
A POTENTIALLY PHYSICALLY INTIMATE CONTACT. THAT
IS NOT TO SAY THAT WE ADVOCATE CASUAL SEXUAL EN-
COUNTERS. WE DID NOT SAY THAT AND WE DID NOT
IMPLY IT. WHAT WE DO SAY IS THAT FOR MANY FRAG-
MENTS, THE LEVEL OF SELF-ESTEEM IN REGARD TO AT-
TRACTIVENESS IS SO LOW THAT THE FRAGMENT RARELY
IF EVER HAS THE OPPORTUNITY TO GIVE FULL RANGE TO
SEXUAL INTIMACY AND OCCASIONALLY ENDS UP PREFER-
RING "KINKY" SEX WITH ITS RITUALS AND LACK OF
GENUINE CONTACT TO THE MORE DANGEROUS POTENTIAL
OF TRUE SEXUAL INTIMACY, WITH ITS THREAT OF "SOME-
THING MORE". THE PREOCCUPATIONS WITH THE "PER-
FECT 10" IN THE MALE AND FEMALE FORM CLOUDS THE
ISSUE—NOT EVERYONE IN FACT IS TRULY ATTRACTED TO
WHAT THE SOCIETY SEES AS A "PERFECT 10" THIS "SEA-
SON" OR WOULD BE COMFORTABLE WITH ONE IF HE OR
SHE HAD THE OPPORTUNITY TO BE PHYSICALLY INVOLVED
WITH A DESIGNATED "PERFECT 10". ALSO, WE WISH TO
EMPHASIZE THAT IT IS NOT AMISS TO BE AWARE THAT
WHAT CONSTITUTES A "PERFECT 10" CHANGES FROM
YEAR TO YEAR, SO WHAT IS THE IDEAL ONE DECADE WILL
NOT BE THE IDEAL IN ANOTHER. WE WOULD REFER YOU
TO PAINTINGS AND STATUES AS WELL AS FASHION
MAGAZINES AND FILMS IF YOU DOUBT THIS. THE "PER-
FECT 10" ALSO CHANGES FROM COUNTRY TO COUNTRY
AND FROM SOCIAL LEVEL TO SOCIAL LEVEL AS WELL,
AND WHILE INTERNATIONAL COMMUNICATIONS CON-
TRIBUTE TO THE ACCULTURATIVE PROCESS WE HAVE
MENTIONED, REGIONAL DIFFERENCES ARE ALWAYS PRES-
ENT.

MOST FRAGMENTS LEARN VERY EARLY IN LIFE WHAT
BEHAVIOR IS SEEN AS SEXUALLY INVITING AND WHAT
BEHAVIOR IS SEEN AS SEXUALLY DISINTERESTED. MOST
PARENTS TEND TO REWARD ONE SORT OF BEHAVIOR OR
ANOTHER, NOT NECESSARILY CONSISTENTLY. OFTEN
IN FAMILIES THERE ARE SOME CHILDREN WHO ARE EN-
COURAGED TO BE SEXUALLY INVITING AND OTHERS WHO

ARE DISCOURAGED FROM THIS. THIS PATTERN, ONCE
LEARNED, TENDS TO STAY WITH THE FRAGMENT AT LEAST
UNTIL THE FOURTH INTERNAL MONAD AND OFTEN
THROUGHOUT THE ENTIRE LIFE. MOST FRAGMENTS TAKE
THE EARLY FAMILIAL ASSESSMENT OF SEXUAL ATTRAC-
TIVENESS AS BINDING AND VALID, AND EVEN WHEN
LATER EXPERIENCE SUGGESTS THAT FAMILIAL CONCEPTS
WERE INACCURATE, THE FRAGMENT WILL TEND TO HOLD
TO WHAT WAS TAUGHT FIRST. WHICHEVER FORM OF BE-
HAVIOR BROUGHT GREATER PARENTAL APPROVAL WILL
CONTINUE TO BE THE MOST COMFORTABLE AND "NATU-
RAL" FOR THE FRAGMENT BECAUSE OF EARLY PATTERN-
ING.

BECAUSE OF SOCIAL EXPECTATIONS, OFTEN BEHAVIOR
IS INTERPRETED AS BEING SEXUAL IN CONTEXT WHEN, IN
FACT, IT IS NOT. THIS MOST OFTEN IS THE CASE WHERE
GENUINE AFFECTION IS PRESENT BETWEEN MALES AND
FEMALES, SINCE CERTAIN ASPECTS OF THE CULTURAL
MYTHS REGARD IT AS IMPOSSIBLE FOR MALES AND
FEMALES TO BE FRIENDS, EVEN VERY CLOSE FRIENDS,
WITHOUT ACTUAL SEXUAL ACTIVITY "ACCOUNTING" FOR
IT. THIS, OF COURSE, IS NOT VALID, BUT OFTEN INTER-
FERES WITH MALE/FEMALE FRIENDSHIPS TO A GREAT DE-
GREE, EVENTUALLY RENDERING THEM UNTENABLE FOR
THOSE WHO ARE ESPECIALLY SENSITIVE TO SOCIAL PRES-
SURES AND EXPECTATIONS. OCCASIONALLY SUCH
FRIENDSHIPS WILL TURN SEXUAL BECAUSE IT IS ASSUMED
TO BE THE "NATURAL DEVELOPMENT" WHEN MALES AND
FEMALES LIKE EACH OTHER. HAVING SUCH RIGID PRE-
CONCEPTIONS DOES MUCH TO OBSCURE THE VARIOUS AS-
PECTS OF ANY RELATIONSHIP.

IT IS NOT AMISS TO EXAMINE THE NATURE OF YOUR
EXPECTATIONS IN REGARD TO YOUR COMPANIONS AND
FRIENDS IN TERMS OF CULTURE, ACCULTURATION AND
SOCIAL MORES AS WELL AS IN TERMS OF PERSONAL AT-
TRACTION, SHOULD YOU CHOOSE TO DO SO.

FRAGMENTS ARE, BY DEFINITION, BORN INTO A FAM-
ILY, NO MATTER HOW SMALL OR HOW BRIEF THE ASSOCI-
ATION MAY BE. A NEWBORN INFANT ABANDONED IN A

DITCH DID, IN FACT, HAVE A MOTHER, AND TO THAT EXTENT WAS PART OF A FAMILY. INCIDENTALLY, DO NOT ASSUME THE MOTHER WAS "WRONG" TO ABANDON A CHILD UNDER SUCH CIRCUMSTANCES—TWO OF THE FRAGMENTS NOW STUDENTS IN OUR LITTLE GROUP HAVE BOTH ABANDONED AND BEEN ABANDONED INFANTS, AND NEVER OUT OF CHOICE. IN ONE INSTANCE THE MOTHER WAS A SLAVE BEING TAKEN TO A NEW WORK AREA; IN ANOTHER INSTANCE THE MOTHER WAS FLEEING FROM THE ENEMY AND WAS SUFFERING FROM THE BEGINNING OF CHOLERA; IN A THIRD INSTANCE THE MOTHER WAS ORDERED BY THE FATHER TO ABANDON THE INFANT ON PAIN OF SEVERE HARM TO BOTH HER AND HER CHILD, AND ON THE FOURTH CASE THE MOTHER WAS A GYPSY EN ROUTE TO TREBLINKA AND DEATH.

FOR MOST FRAGMENTS, THE FAMILY IS THE FIRST "SOCIETY" THE FRAGMENT EXPERIENCES, AND ITS PERCEPTIONS AND INSTRUCTION ARE THE MOST LASTING OF ANY THE FRAGMENT RECEIVES DURING LIFE. THE ATTITUDE AND CHARACTER OF THE FAMILY WILL INEVITABLY LEAVE THEIR MARKS ON THE FRAGMENT. THOSE FRAGMENTS WHO DO NOT SHOW ANY FAMILIAL PATTERNING AND INFLUENCES ARE TERMED INSANE BY ALMOST ALL CULTURES THROUGHOUT YOUR SPECIES AND IN MOST ENSOULED SPECIES WHERE THE YOUNG ARE RAISED IN "FAMILIES". INFANTS ARE, AS MANY "EXPERTS" HAVE DECLARED, HIGHLY IMPRESSIONABLE, AND THEY ALSO KNOW THE TRUTH WHEN THEY HEAR IT. NO MATTER WHAT A PARENT OR SIBLING SAYS, THE INFANT, UNTIL IT LEARNS TO RECOGNIZE THE MEANING OF WORDS, WILL RESPOND ONLY TO WHAT THE PARENT OR SIBLING TRULY FEELS. A PARENT WHO IS AMBIVALENT ABOUT A CHILD AT THE BEGINNING WILL NEVER WHOLLY CONVINCE THE CHILD OF ANYTHING ELSE, NO MATTER HOW THE RELATIONSHIP DEVELOPS.

IN MOST FAMILIES, AND IN MOST CULTURES, CHILDREN ARE ASSIGNED CERTAIN FAMILIAL "ROLES" VERY EARLY, WHICH MAY OR MAY NOT ACCURATELY REFLECT THE ESSENCE AND OVERLEAVES OF THE INFANT. ONE CHILD

MAY BE "A FLIRT" OR "A BRAT" OR "A SPACE CADET" WHILE ANOTHER MAY BE "A WHIZ" OR "A WIGGLER" OR "A WHINER". WE WOULD AGREE THAT ALL THOSE WORDS CAN BE ACCURATELY DESCRIPTIVE OF HOW A PARTICULAR INFANT BEHAVES, BUT IT WILL ALSO SERVE TO TEACH THE CHILD HOW HE OR SHE IS *EXPECTED* TO BEHAVE. IF A CHILD SEES THAT THE WAY TO GAIN ATTENTION IN A FAMILY IS TO HAVE AN ILLNESS, THEN THE CHILD WILL TEND TO GET SICK. IF A CHILD GAINS ATTENTION ONLY WHEN PROTESTING, IT WILL BECOME CONTRARY. THIS IS HOW FALSE PERSONALITY BEGINS, AND IS NOT NECESSARILY A NEGATIVE EXPERIENCE, FOR IT IS ONE OF THE MOST PROFOUND LESSONS OF THE PHYSICAL PLANE, ESPECIALLY FOR THOSE INCARNATE IN INDEPENDENTLY MOBILE SPECIES.

LET US RECOMMEND, FOR THOSE WISHING TO BETTER UNDERSTAND THE NATURE OF FALSE PERSONALITY, THAT FAMILY IKONOGRAPHY BE OBSERVED. WHAT ARE THE ATTRIBUTES, VIRTUES, AND VICES OF EACH MEMBER OF THE FAMILY AS THE FAMILY DEFINES THEM? WHAT KIND OF TALES ARE TOLD ABOUT WHAT MEMBER? OF THOSE TALES, WHICH EVOKES DERISION AND WHICH EVOKES ADMIRATION? WHAT DOES THE MEMBER DO THAT IS SOCIALLY APPROPRIATE BUT FAMILIALLY INAPPROPRIATE? HOW DO THE SIBLINGS RESPOND TO EACH OTHER? HOW MUCH DIFFERENT IS THAT RESPONSE WHEN ADULTS ARE PRESENT? WHAT DOES THE FAMILY TALK ABOUT AT MEALS? WHAT ARE THEY FORBIDDEN TO TALK ABOUT AT MEALS? WE REMIND YOU THAT BEING SIMIAN MAMMALS, HOW AND WHERE AND WITH WHOM YOU TAKE MEALS HAS A VERY STRONG SIGNIFICANCE. FOR CETACEANS, FEEDING IS NOT THE ISSUE, BUT "PLAYING" IS. CONDUCT WITH MEALS IS OFTEN THE KEY TO THE TRUE NATURE OF A FAMILY, BOTH WHEN ENTERTAINING AND THEREFORE ON "COMPANY BEHAVIOR" AND WHEN LIMITED TO FAMILY MEMBERS. OFTEN THE FIRST SIGN OF THE START OF THE THIRD INTERNAL MONAD IS THE FRAGMENT'S TENDENCY NOT TO HAVE MEALS WITH THE FAMILY.

ANOTHER RELIABLE CLUE TO FAMILY MYTHOLOGY IS

BASED ON HOW THE CHILDREN ARE DRESSED. THIS IS NOT
SIMPLY AN ECONOMIC ISSUE, NOR IS IT A MATTER OF THE
"REALITIES" OF RAISING CHILDREN. NO MATTER WHAT
THE ECONOMIC AND SOCIAL POSITION OF THE FAMILY,
EACH CHILD IS DRESSED DIFFERENTLY. FOR EXAMPLE,
ONE CHILD WILL TEND TO HAVE THE MOST ATTRACTIVE
CLOTHES AVAILABLE, AND EVEN IF THEY ARE PASSED ON
FROM OTHERS, THEY ARE MADE TO FIT THE CHILD RECEIV-
ING THEM AND ARE "DISGUISED" FROM WHAT THEY WERE
SO THAT THEY ARE LESS APPARENT "HAND-ME-DOWNS".
OTHER CHILDREN WILL HAVE NEW CLOTHING THAT DOES
NOT FIT PROPERLY, ON THE STATED THEORY THAT THEY
WILL "GROW INTO THE GARMENTS" OR THAT "THEY WEAR
OUT SO QUICKLY, ANYWAY" OR "FIT ISN'T IMPORTANT
AT THAT AGE". ALL FAMILY MEMBERS ARE KEENLY
AWARE OF THESE DIFFERENTIATIONS, AND THEY CAN
PLAY A LARGE ROLE IN HOW FALSE PERSONALITY IS EX-
PRESSED, AS WELL AS HOW "INFLUENCE" IS ESTABLISHED
WITHIN THE FAMILY. WE WOULD WISH TO RECOMMEND
A PROJECT TO THOSE PARENTS WHO CHOOSE TO UNDER-
TAKE A REASSESSMENT OF THIS "DRESS CODE" PAT-
TERNING: WHEN A CHILD IS GETTING DRESSED, AS MUCH
AS POSSIBLE, PERMIT THE CHILD TO CHOOSE WHAT IT
WILL WEAR, AND WHEN GETTING NEW OR REPLACEMENT
CLOTHES, ALLOW THE CHILD TO SELECT FOR ITSELF WHAT
GARMENTS IT PREFERS—WITHOUT PASSING JUDGMENT
ON THE CHILD'S CHOICE BEYOND REASONABLE CAVEATS,
SUCH AS, "YOU MIGHT WANT SOME LONG-SLEEVED
SHIRTS, TOO, FOR COLD DAYS" WITHOUT SAYING WHICH
LONG-SLEEVED SHIRTS THE CHILD IS TO SELECT. WE
REALIZE THAT NOT ALL PARENTS ARE WILLING OR ABLE
TO DO THIS, AND THAT IS, OF COURSE, A MATTER OF
CHOICE. HOWEVER, FOR THOSE WHO WISH TO LESSEN THE
FALSE PERSONALITY IN CHILDREN, THIS IS ONE PLACE TO
BEGIN, IF IT IS A CHOICE THAT THE PARENTS CHOOSE TO
MAKE. SELECTING CLOTHING IS A GOOD PLACE FOR CHIL-
DREN TO PRACTICE MAKING CHOICES, INCIDENTALLY,
FOR IT TENDS TO HAVE LIMITED REPERCUSSIONS. WE
WOULD WISH TO ADD ONE NOTE OF WARNING BEYOND

WHAT WE HAVE SAID ALREADY, WHICH IS THAT CHILDREN ARE VERY SENSITIVE TO PARENTAL OPINION, AND THE OPINION OF OTHER FAMILY MEMBERS, AND THIS EXERCISE IS BOUND TO BE COLORED BY A DESIRE FOR CERTAIN REACTIONS FROM THE PARENTS AND OTHER FAMILY MEMBERS, NOT ENTIRELY ON PERSONAL PREFERENCE. EVEN FROM SUCH PATTERNS THERE IS MUCH TO BE LEARNED IF YOU CHOOSE TO PAY ATTENTION.

THERE ARE FRAGMENTS WHOSE BEHAVIOR CHANGES MARKEDLY WHEN TAKEN FROM THE FAMILY SETTING. THIS MAY REVEAL MANY UNRESOLVED CONFLICTS WITH THE FAMILY; IT MAY INDICATE THE FALSE PERSONALITY IS SIGNIFICANTLY DIFFERENT THAN THE TRUE PERSONALITY OF THE OVERLEAVES. IT MAY ALSO INDICATE A CHIEF FEATURE EMERGING EARLY. WHERE SUCH DIVERGENCE EXISTS, AND OTHERS CHOOSE TO EXPLORE THE REASON, WE WOULD THINK THAT A DIRECT RESPONSE IS NOT LIKELY TO SHOW MUCH OF THE CONFLICT. INCIDENTALLY, WHEN WE DESCRIBE SIGNIFICANT BEHAVIOR CHANGES, WE DO NOT NECESSARILY MEAN THE YOUNGSTER WHO BECOMES A "HOLY TERROR" OUTSIDE THE FAMILY, BUT ALSO THE SUDDEN "GOODY-TWO-SHOES", NEITHER OF WHICH ROLES ARE APT TO REFLECT ANY TRUE PERSONALITY.

THE NATURE OF FAMILIES IS DEFINED AS MUCH BY CULTURE AS BY ANYTHING ELSE, BUT WE WOULD HAVE TO ADD HERE THAT CULTURE TENDS TO SHAPE FAMILIES AS MUCH THROUGH SOCIAL STATUS AS THROUGH ENVIRONMENTAL AND ECONOMIC DEMANDS, ALTHOUGH ALL THREE ARE MAJOR INFLUENCES ON THE FAMILY WITHIN THE CULTURE. IT IS AMISS, HOWEVER, TO EXTEND THE FAMILIAL CONCEPT TO THE CULTURE AS WELL. SOCIETY AND CULTURE ARE *NOT* EXTENDED FAMILIES. THE TIES OF WHAT YOU CALL BLOOD ARE NOT TRULY PRESENT IN A CULTURE AND ALTHOUGH THE CULTURE SHAPES PERCEPTIONS AND BEHAVIOR, IT IS NOT SEEN AS THE "FORCE OF DESTINY" THAT A FAMILY, ESPECIALLY FOR YOUNG SOULS, IS OFTEN ASSUMED TO BE. LATE BABY AND MOST YOUNG SOULS ARE OFTEN PREOCCUPIED WITH FAMILY

HERITAGE, AS IF THERE ARE ANSWERS TO THE "MYSTERY OF SELF" IN THE BEHAVIOR OF ONE'S ANCESTORS. IN A VERY LIMITED GENETIC SENSE THERE IS SOME ASSOCIATION, BUT IT IS SO TENUOUS THAT ITS BEARING HAS LITTLE IMPORTANCE EXCEPT IN PATTERNS OF LONGEVITY AND PREDISPOSITION TO CERTAIN DISEASES. IN NO SENSE OF THE WORD IS BIOLOGY THE ONLY SOURCE OF "DESTINY".

MATURE AND OLD SOULS TEND TO BE INTERESTED IN THEIR FAMILY HISTORIES IN DIFFERENT WAYS—MANY TIMES THEY ARE NOT PARTICULARLY INTERESTED AT ALL—HAVING MORE TO DO WITH THE NATURE OF THE FRAGMENTS WHO HAVE LIVED BEFORE AS KEYS TO THE PAST RATHER THAN AS KEYS TO THEMSELVES. THIS IS A DISTINCTION THAT MAY NOT APPEAR SIGNIFICANT, BUT IT HAS A BEARING ON HOW THE FRAGMENT PERCEIVES ITS PARTICIPATION WITHIN A FAMILY. FOR YOUNG SOULS, BEING A CREDIT TO THE FAMILY IS TO LIVE UP TO AND EXCEED THE ACCOMPLISHMENTS OF PREVIOUS FAMILY MEMBERS. FOR MATURE SOULS, BEING A CREDIT TO THE FAMILY IS TO DO SOMETHING UNIQUE OR DISTINCTIVE. MATURE SOULS OFTEN REGARD THEIR ANCESTORS WITH MORE AFFECTION AND LESS AWE THAN THE YOUNG AND BABY SOULS DO—"AH, YES, THAT'S WICKED GREAT-GREAT-GREAT UNCLE PHILLIP; HE KEPT THREE WOMEN IN THREE DIFFERENT PARTS OF THE CITY AND PAID FOR IT BY EMBEZZLING FROM THE GUILD TREASURY"—AND SENSE THEM AS PERSONALITIES, NOT UNLIKE CHARACTERS IN A PLAY. OLD SOULS TEND NOT TO RESIST FAMILY IDENTITIES ACTIVELY; THEY OFTEN GO THEIR OWN WAY UNOBTRUSIVELY AND COMPARATIVELY EARLY IN LIFE. OLD SOUL REBELLION AGAINST FALSE PERSONALITY IS USUALLY PRESENT TO SOME DEGREE FROM EARLY YOUTH, AND WHEN THIS IS SUFFICIENTLY THREATENING WITHIN AUTHORITARIAN FAMILY STRUCTURES CAN LEAD TO CHILD ABUSE. THAT IS NOT TO SAY THAT EVERY OLD SOUL IS AN ABUSED CHILD, OR THAT EVERY ABUSED CHILD IS AN OLD SOUL. WE DID NOT SAY THAT AND WE DID NOT IMPLY IT. WE HAVE SAID THAT SINCE OLD SOULS

TEND TO RESIST FALSE PESONALITY RELATIVELY EARLY
IN LIFE, IF THEY ARE IN AN AUTHORITARIAN FAMILY, AND
IF THEIR TRUE PERSONALITY IS SUFFICIENTLY UNLIKE THE
FALSE ONE BEING IMPOSED, THEN ONE OF THE FAMILY
RESPONSES TO THIS RESISTANCE MAY BE EITHER OVERT
OR COVERT ABUSE. IN SOME SOCIETIES AND AT CERTAIN
SOCIAL LEVELS, SUCH A CHILD IS TURNED OVER TO A
PERSON OR INSTITUTION TO BE "STRAIGHTENED OUT".

THE NATURE OF SIMIAN MAMMALS AND THEIR SOCIAL
INTERACTION IS THE BASE OF THE HUMAN FAMILY UNIT.
OF COURSE, BECAUSE OF SOCIETAL VARIATIONS, CUL-
TURAL EXPECTATIONS, AND PATTERNS, AS WELL AS THE
NATURE OF ENSOULMENT, THERE HAVE BEEN MANY DIS-
TORTIONS OF THAT BASIC, MAMMALIAN BEHAVIOR. WE
WOULD THINK THAT THERE ARE A FEW THINGS MANY
HUMAN FAMILIES MIGHT DO WELL TO OBSERVE AND RE-
VERT TO, HOWEVER, FOR THE BENEFIT OF THE YOUNG IN
QUESTION. FIRST, ALMOST ALL HUMAN INFANTS NEED TO
BE HELD BY OTHER HUMANS. THAT DOES NOT MEAN
LUGGED ABOUT IN A CARRYALL ON SOMEONE'S BACK; IT
MEANS HELD SECURELY BUT UNCONFINEDLY IN SOME-
ONE'S ARMS. NOTE THAT WE STRESS UNCONFINEDLY; A
HUG IS NOT A RESTRAINT, AND THOSE CHILDREN WHO
ARE HELD TO BE RESTRAINED QUITE JUSTIFIABLY TEND
TO FIND IT FRIGHTENING AND RESIST BEING HELD. A
CHILD NEEDS TO BE HELD WHENEVER IT SEEKS HOLDING,
BY EITHER PARENT. MANY VERY YOUNG CHILDREN
LEARN TO MANIPULATE THEIR PARENTS BECAUSE THE
PARENTS DO NOT RESPOND TO THE CHILDREN'S DEMANDS
TO BE HELD AND THEN FEEL GUILTY ABOUT IT. THE CHIL-
DREN, OUT OF DESPERATION—AND MAKE NO DOUBT
ABOUT IT, FOR VERY YOUNG CHILDREN, NOT BEING HELD
IS CAUSE FOR DESPERATION—"GET EVEN" WITH THE PAR-
ENTS BY USING THE GUILT THE PARENTS EXPERIENCE,
AND STRIVE TO INCREASE THE GUILT IN ORDER TO GAIN
MORE CONTROL OVER THE BEHAVIOR OF THE PARENTS.

LET US DIGRESS ON CHIEF FEATURES AND EARLY
TREATMENT OF VERY YOUNG CHILDREN, FOR ALTHOUGH
THE CHIEF FEATURE USUALLY DOES NOT EMERGE UNTIL

AROUND AGE TWENTY IN THIS CULTURE, IT IS MOST OFTEN
PREDICATED ON THE EXPERIENCES OF EARLY CHILD-
HOOD. THOSE CHILDREN WHO ARE MADE TO FEEL THAT
THEY HAVE NO CONTROL IN THEIR LIVES, WHO ARE
TREATED TO ALTERNATING PERIODS OF ABUSE THROUGH
NEGLECT, AND ABUSE THROUGH RIGIDITY, EITHER THE
RESULT OF SOCIOECONOMIC OR RELIGIOUS OR PSYCHO-
LOGICAL PRESSURES ARE LIKELY TO BE TERRIFIED OF LOS-
ING CONTROL AND WILL EVENTUALLY TEND TO ACQUIRE
A CHIEF FEATURE OF SELF-DESTRUCTION. THOSE CHIL-
DREN WHO ARE NEVER "DESERVING ENOUGH" OF WHAT-
EVER THEY WANT, WHO ARE REQUIRED TO DEFER TO
OTHER FAMILY MEMBERS, WILL BE TERRIFIED OF WORTH-
LESSNESS AND WILL EVENTUALLY TEND TO ACQUIRE A
CHIEF FEATURE OF MARTYRDOM, ESPECIALLY IF DAMAGE
DONE TO THE CHILD IS NEVER REDRESSED. THOSE CHIL-
DREN WHO DON'T "QUITE LIVE UP" TO WHAT IS EXPECTED
OF THEM, WHO ARE CONSTANTLY "DAMNED WITH FAINT
PRAISE," WILL HAVE A DREAD OF INADEQUACY AND WILL
TEND TO ACQUIRE A CHIEF FEATURE OF SELF-DEPRECA-
TION. THOSE CHILDREN WHO ARE NEVER PREPARED FOR
CHANGES IN THEIR LIVES, WHO ARE PLACED IN UNFAMIL-
IAR AND THEREFORE FRIGHTENING POSITIONS WITHOUT
ANY PREPARATION, WILL BE TERRIFIED BY NEW SITUA-
TIONS AND WILL TEND TO ACQUIRE THE CHIEF FEATURE
OF STUBBORNNESS, PARTICULARLY IF THE CHILD IS
MOCKED FOR BEING FRIGHTENED. THOSE CHILDREN WHO
ARE DEPRIVED OF PERSONAL CONTACT IN THEIR LIVES,
AND ARE OFFERED "SUBSTITUTES" OR "REWARDS" IN
PLACE OF ATTENTION AND PHYSICAL CONTACT WILL
HAVE A CONSTANT SENSE OF EMPTINESS OR WANT AND
WILL TEND TO ACQUIRE THE CHIEF FEATURE OF GREED.
THOSE CHILDREN WHO ARE CRITICALLY OR MALICIOUSLY
TEASED, WHOSE DIFFERENCES ARE REGARDED WITH DERI-
SION OR CONTEMPT OR DELIBERATE LACK OF UNDER-
STANDING, WILL HAVE A CONSTANT SENSE OF VULNERA-
BILITY AND WILL TEND TO ACQUIRE ARROGANCE AS A
CHIEF FEATURE. THOSE CHILDREN WHO ARE RARELY AL-
LOWED TO PARTICIPATE IN EVENTS, OR WHOSE PARTICI-

PATION IS SEVERELY RESTRICTED EITHER THROUGH FAMILY IKONOGRAPHY OR SOCIAL PRESSURES, WILL HAVE A CONSTANT INNER SENSE OF "MISSING SOMETHING" AND WILL TEND TO ACQUIRE THE CHIEF FEATURE OF IMPATIENCE. WHILE THERE IS NOT AN ABSOLUTE RULE ABOUT THESE MISTREATMENTS AND CHIEF FEATURES, THE PATTERN IS STRONG ENOUGH THAT WE WOULD SAY THE PATTERN HOLDS TRUE IN ROUGHLY EIGHTY PERCENT OF ALL FRAGMENTS. LET US ALSO REMARK HERE THAT THE THREE ORDINAL CHIEF FEATURES—SELF-DESTRUCTION, MARTYRDOM, SELF-DEPRECATION—ARE ALL THE RESULT OF A SPECIFIC FOCUSED DREAD. THE CARDINAL CHIEF FEATURES—GREED, ARROGANCE, IMPATIENCE—ARE ALL THE RESULT OF A "SENSE" OF A LACK. FOR THE ORDINAL CHIEF FEATURES, THE FEAR ACTS OVERTLY: IN THE CARDINAL CHIEF FEATURES, THE FEAR ACTS COVERTLY. IN THE CASE OF STUBBORNNESS, THE REACTION IS, OF COURSE, A FIXED ONE.

ANOTHER CONCERN OF THOSE INCARNATE IS THE "CARE AND FEEDING" OF THE BODY. BODIES ARE UNIQUE TO THE PHYSICAL PLANE. ASTRAL MATTER MAY BE FORMED INTO PHYSICAL BEINGS, SINCE IT IS WHOLLY MALLEABLE AND MAINTAINED IN THAT FORM FOR AS LONG AS THE CONCENTRATION AND ENERGY CAN SUPPORT THEM, BUT THE PHYSICAL MANIFESTATION OF ASTRAL MATTER IS NOT THE SAME THING AS HAVING A BODY. BODIES, BY THEIR VERY NATURE, ENDURE "WEAR AND TEAR", WHICH IS PART OF THE NATURE OF THE PHYSICAL PLANE. THEY ALSO REQUIRE "UPKEEPING", SUCH AS FOOD, SLEEP, WATER—BOTH INTERNAL AND EXTERNAL—EXERCISE, AND GROOMING, IF THEY ARE GOING TO FUNCTION WELL. THAT DOES NOT MEAN THAT ONE *MUST* CARE FOR THE BODY. ALL FRAGMENTS MAY CHOOSE TO TREAT THEIR BODIES IN WHATEVER WAY THEY WISH; THEY WILL ALSO INHABIT THE CONSEQUENCES. THAT IS NOT TO SAY THAT WE ENCOURAGE A PREOCCUPATION WITH THE BODY. WE HAVE SAID MANY TIMES BEFORE THAT THIS IS NEITHER NECESSARY NOR ADVISABLE IN ALMOST ALL CASES. WE DO, HOWEVER, SUGGEST THAT REASONABLE

MAINTENANCE IS NOT INAPPROPRIATE. CARING FOR THE BODY SO THAT IT FUNCTIONS WITH REASONABLE EFFICIENCY IS GENERALLY THE MOST "SENSIBLE" APPROACH TO MAINTAINING IT. FOR THOSE WHO HAVE CHOSEN OCCUPATIONS THAT REQUIRE A GREATER DEGREE OF PHYSICAL PRECISION, SUCH AS BALLET STUDENTS AND MARTIAL-ARTS PRACTITIONERS, OR TREETOPPERS AND MARINE SALVAGE WORKERS, OR LARGE-SCALE MURALISTS OR TRAPEZE ARTISTS, AN ADJUSTMENT IN THE LEVEL OF MAINTENANCE CAN BE MADE, JUST AS A MECHANIC CARING FOR A FAMILY SEDAN HAS A DIFFERENT STANDARD OF PERFORMANCE BOTH DESIRABLE AND ATTAINABLE THAN WHEN TENDING A HIGH-SPEED EXPERIMENTAL RACING VEHICLE.

HEALTH IS PART OF THE ISSUE OF MAINTENACE. CLEARLY, IF A BODY IS IMPAIRED, IT CANNOT FUNCTION EFFICIENTLY, NOR CAN IT BE MAINTAINED AT A "SENSIBLE PERFORMANCE" LEVEL. WE AGREE THAT THERE ARE VERY MANY FACTORS CONTRIBUTING TO HEALTH AND THAT THEY ARE NOT ALL AS APPARENT AS MIGHT SEEM THE CASE.

IN REGARD TO THE MANNER IN WHICH OPTIMISM, PESSIMISM AND PHYSICAL WELL-BEING ARE INTERRELATED, WE WOULD HAVE TO BEGIN WITH SAYING THAT MUCH OF THE ROOT OF THE PROBLEM STEMS FROM THE BASIC MEDICAL ASSUMPTION THAT SOMETHING IS ALWAYS "WRONG" WITH THE PATIENT. WHILE IN PART THIS GROWS OUT OF THE MEDICAL TENDENCY TO TREAT BODIES ONLY IN TIMES OF CRISIS, WE WOULD WISH TO REMARK THAT EVEN IN CASES OF SIX-WAY BYPASS SURGERY, MOST OF THE TIME THE REST OF THE BODY IS IN TOLERABLY GOOD CONDITION; OTHERWISE; THE SURGICAL RISKS WOULD BE RELEGATED TO THE POSITION OF INVALID.

TO PLACE EMPHASIS ON THE "WRONGNESS" OF ILLNESS IMMEDIATELY STRESSES NEGATIVITY AND CREATES A "NEUROTIC" RELATIONSHIP BETWEEN PHYSICIAN AND PATIENT IN WHICH THE PATIENT IS ENCOURAGED TO BECOME INCREASINGLY DEPENDENT ON THE PHYSICIAN'S ABILITY

TO PROVIDE "TRANSITORY" RELIEF FOR VARIOUS FORMS OF PHYSICAL DISTRESS. IN THIS RELATIONSHIP CONFLICT AND TENSION ARE PROVIDED, AS IN CLASSICAL DRAMA, BY HOURLY ANTICIPATION OF THE NEXT DISASTER— "THEY'VE CURED MY HEMORRHOIDS, BUT WHEN ARE THEY GOING TO DO SOMETHING ABOUT MY PANCREAS?"— "DURING MY LAST GALLBLADDER ATTACK; I WAS IN A PRE-STROKE CONDITION."—"IF THEY HADN'T GONE IN IN TIME, I WOULD HAVE DIED OF PERITONITIS"—ALL OF WHICH CONTRIBUTE TO AN UNDERLYING SENSE OF BE-TRAYAL. THE PESSIMISM PRESENTS THE BODY AS SOME-THING THAT HAS BEEN "SUBVERTED", OR EVEN WORSE, BEEN "SCUTTLED" THE HEALTH OF THE FRAGMENT EN-SOULED.

IT SHOULD BE READILY APPARENT THAT THE PERCEP-TION OF SELF AS A BIOLOGICAL TIME BOMB—WHILE IN CERTAIN RESPECTS VALID, SINCE BODIES DO WEAR OUT— IS PESSIMISTICALLY NARCISSISTIC IN THE EXTREME AND LEADS TO A SOAP-OPERA-LIKE PREOCCUPATION WITH EVERY ASPECT AND FUNCTION OF THE BODY PERCEIVED AS CYPHERS OR CLUES IN THE PUZZLE OF SELF-DESTRUC-TION.

WHILE WE WOULD UNDERSTAND THE LURE OF THIS PREOCCUPATION, WE WOULD HAVE TO SAY THAT HEALTH IN ANY SENSE OF THE WORD IS HEAVILY RELATED TO OPTIMISM, NOT ONLY IN TERMS OF SPECIFIC BODILY FUNC-TIONS OR LACK THEREOF BUT IN APPRECIATION OF THE COMPLEXITY OF THE MECHANISM ITSELF, AS WELL AS THE RECOGNITION AND REALIZATION THAT THE HUMAN BODY, BY ITS VERY NATURE—AND APPROPRIATELY— DOES, IN FACT, WEAR OUT. TO PASS A LIFE WHERE THERE IS NO IMPINGMENT ON THE BODY IS TO PASS A LIFE OF DENIAL. THE BODY IS THE GAUGE OF GROWTH, FOR THE PHYSICAL AND THE "SPIRITUAL" ARE INTERRELATED IN MANY WAYS. ALL AGE IS GROWTH, INCIDENTALLY, WHETHER RECOGNIZED OR NOT DURING THE INCARNA-TION. FOR FRAGMENTS WHO LEARN TO ACCEPT THE MERITS OF AGE, AND THEREBY VALIDATE GROWTH, WE

WOULD THINK THERE MIGHT BE MUCH LIBERATION FROM
THE SOCIAL PRESSURES THAT DO SO MUCH TO REINFORCE
PESSIMISM.

AGING IS NOT A DISEASE. DYING IS NOT A DISASTER.
ILLNESS IS NOT A "COMMUNIST PLOT". TO BE OLD IS NOT
TO BE "UGLY". TO BE ILL IS NOT TO BE "WRONG". TO BE
PHYSICALLY DAMAGED IS NOT TO BE "FLAWED". ALL
FRAGMENTS ARE TOUCHED BY THE LIVES THEY LEAD,
AND THAT TOUCHING, ONE WAY OR ANOTHER, LEAVES
ITS MARK. THERE IS NOTHING AMISS IN THE "SOUVENIRS"
FRAGMENTS CHOOSE TO COLLECT ALONG THE WAY.

FOR THOSE WHO ARE DISSATISFIED WITH THE BODIES
THEY HAVE CHOSEN, OR WHO HAVE HAD EXTERNAL CON-
DITIONS IMPOSED ON THEIR BODIES, WE WOULD HAVE TO
SAY THAT MUCH OF THE DEGREE IN WHICH THIS AFFECTS
YOU IS IN THE NATURE OF YOUR PERCEPTION OF THE
BODY. THERE ARE FRAGMENTS FOR WHOM A MISSING
FINGERTIP IS PERCEIVED AS A MAJOR MUTILATION, AND
THOSE FOR WHOM A MISSING LEG IS PERCEIVED AS AN
INCONVENIENCE. NEITHER PERCEPTION IS "CORRECT" OR
"INCORRECT". HOWEVER, THOSE WHO ARE WILLING TO
COME TO TERMS WITH THE NATURE AND CONDITION OF
THE BODY ARE APT TO ACCOMPLISH MORE WITH IT THAN
THOSE WHO ARE NOT, IN PART BECAUSE THOSE WHO
ACCEPT WILL HAVE AVAILABLE TO THEM THE ENERGY
OTHERS ARE USING FOR DENIAL OR REJECTION. IF THE
BODY DOES NOT FUNCTION "PERFECTLY"—AND WE
WOULD WISH TO REMIND YOU THAT FEW BODIES DO SO,
LET ALONE FOR ANY EXTENDED LENGTH OF TIME—THAT
DOES NOT MEAN THAT IT IS THEREFORE A "FAILURE".
THE BODY, LIKE THE PHYSICAL PLANE, IS SUBJECT TO
HAZARDS. THE MOST SUPERB ATHLETES CAN SUFFER
FROM ALLERGIES AND/OR INDIGESTION. THE MOST PHYS-
ICALLY IMPAIRED CAN LEARN TO USE WHAT IS AVAILABLE
FOR ACCESS TO THE EXPRESSION OF LIFE.

THE SOCIALLY DEFINED LIMITS OF PHYSICAL ATTTRAC-
TION, ALTHOUGH A VALID EXPRESSION OF CULTURE AND
SOCIETAL EXPECTATIONS, PARTICULARLY FOR YOUNG
SOUL WORLDS, SERVES TO ENMESH THE FRAGMENT IN

MAYA MORE THAN ALMOST ANY OTHER OUTWARD FAC-
TOR. IF YOU CHOOSE TO DOUBT IT, NOTICE THAT SO-
CIALLY DEFINED "ATTRACTIVE" FRAGMENTS ARE OFTEN
GIVEN PREFERENTIAL ADVANCEMENT, EITHER SOCIALLY
OR ECONOMICALLY OR BOTH, OVER FRAGMENTS WHO
ARE NOT SO "GIFTED". THIS PATTERN HOLDS THROUGH-
OUT YOUR WORLD, ALTHOUGH IN SOME SOCIETIES IT IS
LESS OBVIOUS THAN IN OTHERS. WE WOULD WISH TO
POINT OUT THAT THIS PERCEPTION IS ONE OF THE GREAT-
EST BARRIERS TO REAL COMMUNICATION. ESSENCE CON-
TACT, AND VALIDATED INTIMACY THAN ANY OTHER GEN-
ERALLY ENCOUNTERED.

ALL CULTURES OF THE PHYSICAL PLANE THROUGHOUT
THE UNIVERSE HAVE STANDARDS OF ATTRACTIVENESS.
THIS IS ONE OF THE OUTCOMES OF HAVING BODIES, AND
ONLY ON THE PHYSICAL PLANE CAN THIS BE EXPERI-
ENCED. IT IS A VALID LESSON. TO RECOGNIZE THAT THERE
ARE STANDARDS OF ATTRACTION IS TO RECOGNIZE A
WORLD TRUTH. WHATEVER THE STANDARD IS, CHANGES
FROM CULTURE TO CULTURE AND FROM TIME TO TIME,
BUT THE STANDARD IS PRESENT, TO A GREATER OR LESSER
DEGREE. ALL BUT VERY OLD SOUL WORLDS POSSESS
SUCH STANDARDS, AND WE WOULD HAVE TO SAY THAT
IN GENERAL THEY ARE DISTORTING, AND AS SUCH CAN
DO MUCH TO REINFORCE THE HOLD OF CHIEF FEATURE.
IT IS NOT AMISS TO EXAMINE THE STANDARDS IN THIS
LIGHT, SHOULD YOU CHOOSE TO GAIN A DIFFERENT PER-
SPECTIVE ON THE PROCESS OF PARTICIPATING IN A CUL-
TURE.

WHEN CONFRONTED WITH SOCIETAL AND CULTURAL
PATTERNS UNFAMILIAR, IT MAY BE OF HELP FOR ALL
FRAGMENTS TO RECALL THAT NO MATTER WHAT THE
"PACKAGING", EVERY ENSOULED FRAGMENT ON THE
PHYSICAL PLANE IS ONE OF SEVEN ESSENENCES: SLAVE,
ARTISAN, WARRIOR, SCHOLAR, SAGE, PRIEST, AND KING.
IT OCCUPIES ONE OF SEVEN LEVELS IN FIVE EVOLUTION-
ARY CYCLES: INFANT, BABY, YOUNG, MATURE, AND
OLD. IT HAS ONE OF SEVEN MODES: REPRESSION, CAU-
TION, PERSEVERANCE, OBSERVATION, POWER, PASSION.

AND AGGRESSION. IT HAS ONE OF SEVEN GOALS: RETAR-
DATION, REJECTION, SUBMISSION, STAGNATION, ACCEP-
TANCE, GROWTH, AND DOMINANCE. IT HAS ONE OF SEVEN
ATTITUDES: STOIC, SKEPTIC, CYNIC, PRAGAMIST,
IDEALIST, SPIRITUALIST, AND REALIST. IT HAS ACCESS TO
FIVE OF SEVEN CENTERINGS: EMOTIONAL, INTELLECTUAL,
SEXUAL, INSTINCTIVE, HIGHER INTELLECTUAL, HIGHER
EMOTIONAL, AND MOVING. AND IT ACQUIRES ONE PRI-
MARY AND ONE SECONDARY OF SEVEN CHIEF FEATURES:
SELF-DEPRECATION, SELF-DESTRUCTION, MARTYRDOM,
STUBBORNNESS, GREED, ARROGANCE, AND IMPATIENCE.
ESSENCE AND OVERLEAVES ARE THE ENDURING REALITY,
NOT THE BODY HOUSING THEM. THOSE WHO CHOOSE TO
VALIDATE THIS PERCEPTION ARE GOING A LONG WAY TO-
WARD DIMINISHING THE MAYA IN LIFE.

CHAPTER 10

LINKS, BONDS, AND TIES

Michael often discusses the ways in which fragments related to one another (see *More Messages From Michael*, Chapter 4). Three of the strongest bonds are those of Essence Twin, Task Companion, and Cadence Member. Those in the core group who have had contact with one or more of these very basic and compelling associations have a number of reactions to the experience.

Joan Standish, who now lives about a thousand miles away from the group and is one of the phone-in members of the group, is part of the same cadence as Fenella Thilman (in *More Messages From Michael* she is part of Lizzy Roarke). She has this to say about her relationship with Fenella.

"I don't really know how I would have reacted to her without the Michael framework. But I probably wouldn't have got the chance, because I probably would never have met her. We work in very different fields, we live in different parts of the country, we have different interests. On the other hand, when we did meet, it was very, very comfortable."

"Yeah," says Fenella. "I've met my Essence Twin, and let me tell you, I'd rather hang out with a Cadence Member any day of the week. The Essence Twin association is so inward and so damned intense that it's about as comfortable as a bed of hot coals. But Cadence Members, it's like a favorite chair."

"Hey, thanks a lot," protests Joan in mock horror.

"Anytime." Fenella laughs. "That's one of the things we do a lot of—laugh. We whoop and holler and get rowdy and make bad puns. And we're a couple of staid, Mature Scholars."

"In passion," Joan adds, as if it is an explanation. "That accounts for it."

"Uh-huh," says Fenella. "One of the things that struck me from the first was that I knew I could tell Joanie anything. Anything at all."

"True enough," says Joan. "I've got some comparison, since I'm married to my Task Companion. That relationship has a different kind of focus. It has a sense of having something to *do*. It has a purpose, a direction, a thrust. This stuff with Fenella is just . . . fun."

"You're lucky with Mark," says Fenella. "I've had an on-again, off-again thing with my Essence Twin for the last six years, and that takes so much energy, and it's so demanding, that I come away from it exhausted. I'm addicted to it, in a weird way, but I wouldn't call it fun in any sense of the word. Hanging out with Joanie is fun."

Other Cadence Members agree: Bill Dutton and Stuart Gradiston (who was part of John Verano and Henry Ingvesson in *More Messages From Michael*) are also Scholars, Bill late-cycle Mature, Stu early-cycle Old.

"I wouldn't say there was any startling recognition," says Stu. "Bill had been coming to sessions for several months before he asked about his place in casting, and that's when I went back over my notes. I thought something sounded familiar."

"Stu was the one who commented on the Cadence bond." Bill is a tall man, gregarious and outgoing. "It's my six-ness. Those of us sixth cast are always making connections. It's the job."

"Bill's one of those very hospitable Southerners," says Stu. "I'm a laid-back Californian."

"Ho-ho," Bill interjects.

"We have some strange similarities, even though we don't have anything but Michael in common," Stu goes on. "My wife and Bill's lady are both Young Artisan. They get on real well, which is nice for all of us.''

"I was going to say that at first I didn't notice much about Stu," Bill says, "but that's not really true. What was interesting was that I didn't notice something that in anyone else, I would have noticed. That brought me up short when I realized what was happening. You know I don't usually like people dropping in; it breaks up my working day.''

"And I don't usually drop in on people. It's very much against the way I was raised,'' says Stu. "And if I might want to pay an impromptu visit, I call first, to give the other person a chance to say no.''

"Except me,'' adds Bill. "He and Sabrina drop by from time to time, no warning, they just show up, and I put my work aside and we have a great time together. Stu even has more than one glass of wine at dinner.''

Stu shakes his head and heaves an exaggerated sigh. "You're leading me into terrible errors, Bill.''

"Won't be the first time,'' Bill says. "We've had many, many, many past associations.''

"It was life before last, wasn't it, that you were shooting at me?'' Stu asks, faintly amused.

"That's the Sepoy Mutiny life,'' Bill confirms. "Stu was the wife of a British officer and I was on the other side—a risaldar, with the Indian troops—and we ended up on opposite sides of the war. No hard feelings,'' he adds to Stu. "I probably didn't mean for you to have to dodge my bullets.''

Stu shrugs. "I've done it before, and I'll probably do it again if I have to.'' He chuckles. "When Michael told us about that life, we both knew, beyond doubt, who was what. I *knew* I was the army wife, Bill *knew* he was the mutineer. No question.''

"What about that life with the cannon?'' Bill asks enthusiastically. "I designed this cannon, an improved model, I thought. Stu cast it and blew himself and it up.''

Both of them laugh.

"God,'' says Stu when he quiets down. "The things we do for our friends.''

ALTHOUGH NOT AS COMPELLING AS EITHER THE ES-

SENCE TWIN OR THE TASK COMPANION BOND, THE CA-
DENCE BOND IS PERHAPS THE MOST ENDURING. MEMBERS
OF THE SAME CADENCE PASS A GREAT NUMBER OF THEIR
INCARNATIONS TOGETHER. THE CADENCE IS THE SMALL-
EST TOTALITY WE PERCEIVE. ALL SEVEN FRAGMENTS OF
A CADENCE ARE THE FIRST COMPLETE UNIT THAT IS NOT
FRAGMENTARY. CADENCE MEMBERS SEEK EACH OTHER
OUT FOR PURPOSES OF EXPERIMENTAL AND PERCEPTUAL
COMPLETION, AND FOR THE CONTACT OF ESSENCE. FOR
CADENCE MEMBERS, ESSENCE CONTACT CAN BE EASILY,
ALMOST ROUTINELY, ACHIEVED AFTER THE MID-CYCLE
MATURE LEVELS. THE RELATIONSHIP IS, BY THEN, NOT
ONLY WELL ESTABLISHED AND "COMFORTABLE", IT IS
ALMOST SELF-SUSTAINING.

"I want to keep the relationship going," says Stu. "That's
one of the things I'm aware of. I take the time to call Bill,
and if I were in a real, serious jamb, the kind when you
call someone at three in the morning to meet you at the
hospital, I wouldn't hesitate to ask Bill."

"I'd be offended if you didn't," says Bill seriously. "I
know I'd do the same if the situation was reversed."

"We have the kind of friendship that feels as if we'd lived
next door to each other all our lives."

"It's the kind of feeling the group makes jokes about, the
feeling that Leslie calls the 'Where were we before we were
so rudely interrupted?' sense. I don't get the feeling that I
have to watch myself around Stu because he might judge
me poorly for anything I say or do. It doesn't occur to me
that could happen." He looks to Stu, who nods agreement.
"We have an extra going for us. We know a third member
of our Cadence."

"So far as we know, we're the only ones in the group to
have such contact," Stu adds. "It was quite an experience."

Since it is Bill's story, Stu lets him tell it. "Years ago,
long before I met Barbara, when I was living in another
part of the country, I lived with a woman for about four
years; she was divorced, with a two-year-old daughter. I
really loved that kid, and I don't mean that I'm kinky for

little girls. In fact, it bothered me that I felt so close to that kid. She was like a part of my family. Anyway, her mother and I are still friends, more because of Roxanne than anything else. I've kept in touch with her all these years. And I do things for her I wouldn't do for anyone else. When she needed tutoring when she changed schools, Maggie couldn't afford it, so I paid for it. I volunteered to pay for it. When Roxanne turned sixteen, I made sure she got the sweet sixteen pearl earrings and necklace that girls always got back where I grew up.''

"How did Maggie feel about all this largesse?'' Stu asks, prompting deliberately.

"Occasionally she gets a little worried, not because of my relationship with Roxanne but because she doesn't want to be beholden to me. I appreciate that—and I know how Warriors are about obligations. Maggie's a Mature Warrior, and she has a very big need to keep her obligations in balance. Anyway, after a while I asked Michael what my connection with Roxanne is. I thought if I had connections with anyone, it was with Roxanne. And it turns out that she's—''

"—part of our Cadence,'' Stu finishes for him. "Another Old Scholar like me. Bill here is the junior member.''

"Snob,'' Bill says lightly. "Anyway, Roxanne was out for part of the summer. She stayed with Barbara and me for about two weeks. Barbara says it's like having a very nice niece or stepdaughter. Of course, while she was here, Stu and I made it a point that all three of us get together.''

"I don't mind admitting I was apprehensive at first,'' says Stu. "What on earth do I have in common with an eighteen-year-old girl? I'm forty-two, and I've got a kid in grammar school. Teenagers are a foreign country to me. I was also a little nervous that I might find her attractive in a way I wouldn't like. I don't think of myself as a man who gets turned on by cute kids.''

"Roxanne said she wasn't nervous, and I think that was probably true,'' says Bill. "She spent about twenty minutes fussing with her hair, but she does that all the time; it doesn't mean very much.''

"Well, my apprehension disappeared as soon as we met. It was like finding out I had a kid sister I'd forgotten about. She was as comfortable as Bill is. More so—she's Old."

"That was something I was very aware of," Bill says, picking up the thread. "We got together, and I could really sense the difference between Mature, even late-cycle Mature, and Old. Boy, you give those guys a chance and they'd sit still so long they'd grow moss."

"You're just a whippersnapper," Stu says, and both men laugh again. "We had a great day. Bill here was full of plans of what we ought to do, and all kinds of activities we could choose. Trouble is, what we really wanted to do, Roxanne and I, was sit still and talk. And after a very nice drive and lunch over at Muir Beach, we ended up in Bill's living room, talking until one in the morning. The only reason we stopped was that I had an appointment for nine the next morning."

"It was quite an experience, having Roxanne visit. She came to a session with Stu and me. We arranged it in advance. Most of the group was curious about what three of the same Cadence might do to the energy level. In chronological age, Roxanne was the youngest person there, but as second-level old, she was right up with the senior class." Bill consults his notes. "Milly said she didn't notice much difference, but the Leslies said they felt a shift in energy. That happens when anyone new is at a session, but this was a little different, or so they said."

"Afterward Roxanne and Bill and I had coffee at my house. I'm about a mile from the Leslies' place. We had another one of those marathon conversations, and when you consider that the session ran late to begin with . . ." He shakes his head. "It was really fun to have her around. I've already told her that if I end up anywhere near her home while we're traveling this summer, Sabrina and Seth and I want to get together with her. That's another thing," he adds. "Sabrina really likes Roxanne, and I know if she thought there was anything weird going on, she would say so."

"She said that Roxanne reminds her of Stu," Bill points

out. "She admitted she had her doubts, but not after she met Roxanne."

"So there's something going on. It's one thing that Bill and I notice it, but my wife and his lady pick up on it too. I know that Sabrina was skeptical, but not anymore." He considers what he has said. "I doubt I'll feel the same closeness with Roxanne that Bill does, but I haven't known her since she was a baby, and he has."

"This life," Bill appends.

"This life," Stu agrees.

Another two Cadence Members are the female Leslie Adams and Martin Keir (who, in *More Messages From Michael* was part of Brad Sturgis). Two Old Warriors, they have another one of those friendships that appear outwardly unaccountable.

"I don't know how to describe the sense," says Martin, who has been in the group sporadically for six years. "It's nothing obvious. I don't even think about it. But Leslie's very important to me in a way . . . I don't know how to say it without making it sound heavier than it is. The bond with Leslie's very light, but it's very there."

"It's odd; Martin's a lot younger than I am, measured in years. Still, from the time I met him, I kept thinking of him as older and more senior. He is fourth-level and I'm third, and he's cast third to my sixth in the Cadence. He outranks me." She gives him a chance to confirm or deny; he remains silent. "It's similar to what the other people have said: it's like resuming something already in progress. I met Martin during one of the most difficult times in my life. Not that I went looking for Cadence support. It wasn't a time when I was looking for new friends, because there were so many other—"

"She's being a typical Warrior," Martin explains for her, very gently. "She's trying not to acknowledge hurt. What she's saying was that she had so many serious problems to contend with she didn't have any reserve energy and precious little time for anything other than the things she was already handling."

Leslie nods a bit stiffly. "Yet here was this kid who started acting like reinforcements. That doesn't mean he was obvious about it, he was just there. It seemed that on the roughest days he'd show up on the porch and ask me if I wanted to go for a walk. The funny thing was, I'd go."

"Leslie helped me through some things too. It wasn't all one way," Martin adds. "She was able to be a friend in a way most of my other friends couldn't. I can relax with her, be myself without pressure. She doesn't much care what I'm doing if I truly like it. She cares about me, I mean, the me underneath."

"It's the only Martin I really know, the one underneath," she says. "I realize that when I listen to some of the comments from mutual acquaintances. They have a very different sense of Martin than I do. They're not wrong, they just don't get beyond a certain point. And that," she adds with a touch of severity, "is the working of your chief feature."

"Same as yours," he says with unruffled calm.

"And the rest of the Cadence currently on the physical plane," she adds. "Not that we've met them directly, we just have their Overleaves and a little information about them. One of these days, if either Martin or I get the chance, we might try to locate the rest of us."

"It's not a real high priority," Martin adds. "If what Michael says is true, we're connected enough that it isn't important to meet face-to-face, and besides, we've probably been together enough times that we'd all like a break. Leslie and I have eighty-one past associations, which is far and away the most I've ever had with anyone. Except the other Cadence Members."

"Michael said we'd—Martin and I, that is—spent some time together in any life where both of us had survived past the age of three," Leslie says. "I've had Milly and the other Leslie get the information. I can't get information about myself, and most of the time it means I can't get much information for Martin, either."

"It's an odd predicament," Martin appends. "She gets reams of information for almost everyone else, and yet, we have problems when I ask her questions about me. I'd say I was troubled, but I'm not, not really.''

MEMBERS OF THE SAME CADENCE, BECAUSE OF THE CLOSENESS OF THE BOND, SEEK ONE ANOTHER OUT. THERE IS NOTHING "UNUSUAL" IN THIS FROM OUR PERSPECTIVE. FRAGMENTS ARE OFTEN AWARE OF MANY LEVELS OF THE "TIES THAT BIND". OF COURSE, THERE IS NO COMPULSION IN THOSE TIES, BUT THERE IS VERY STRONG RECOGNITION THAT ARISES FROM THE NATURE OF THE BOND ITSELF. IT IS A MATTER OF CHOICE AS TO WHETHER OR NOT THE FRAGMENTS WILL RECOGNIZE AND VALIDATE THE TIE. THERE CAN BE MUCH PROGRESS MADE WHEN MEMBERS OF THE SAME CADENCE RECOGNIZE THEIR CONNECTION AND VALIDATE THE RECOGNITION. FOR THOSE WHO CHOOSE TO ACT ON THIS PERCEPTION AND PERMIT THE ESSENCE ACCESS, THE POSITIVE POLES OF THE OVERLEAVES MAY FUNCTION MORE CONSISTENTLY IN THE LIFE. THAT IS NOT TO SAY THAT CADENCE CONTACT AUTOMATICALLY BRINGS ABOUT TRUE INTIMACY AND ESSENCE CONTACT, BUT THAT THERE ARE FEWER CONSTRAINTS AGAINST IT AND GREATER FAMILIARITY TO AID IN SUCH CONTACT.

"I don't know if that's what we've got," says Leslie. "I'd like to think it is. I do know that when Martin comes to sessions, I can work longer and more easily than when he isn't there."

"And get more worn-out," says Martin, partly in jest but with concern. "You don't always stop when you . . . should."

"There is no *should*," Leslie reminds him.

"You know what I mean."

"But I don't get as tired as I would if I tried to channel that much when you aren't around," she counters. "You steady me."

"I don't like to see you get so tired you turn white. It worries me when you do that. And don't tell me that channeling feels good while you do it. We've been over that before,'' His voice has grown stern.

"Yes, sir." Leslie watches him steadily. "So come to sessions more often and keep me in line."

"Stop dropping gauntlets on my toes," he warns her with a chuckle.

This time she simply salutes. "As one of the group mediums—or is that media? Isn't media the plural of medium?—"

"Cut it out," Martin says, grinning.

"As one of the group mediums, I know how important the balance and focus of group energy can be. When Martin's at session, I don't worry about it. It takes care of itself. But when he isn't there, I can feel all kinds of changes and shifts. I know that this is part of what Michael talks about in regard to the Cadence bond, but I'd be hard put to explain it or describe it. I do know that there's nothing else quite like it."

"I often sense Leslie," Martin says. "I usually know when she's going to call, and when I call her, she's not often surprised. And we pick up things about each other. We each know when the other is in a good or bad mood. I think we did from the first."

"It's hard to tell," says Leslie. "But I'm pretty sure that you're right about that."

"Sure; I outrank you." He laughs outright when she throws a small sofa pillow at him.

Dominique Long, who phones in her Michael questions, has had some contact with her Task Companion. "We are in related fields," she says. "I've been doing the educational side of the job, and she's doing the artistic side. She's a photographer, and she specializes in things like paleontological digs of all kinds of fossils—dinosaur bones, Jurassic critters, you name it—and I've been working on little booklets for school kids, dealing with all sorts of prehistoric life. Most of the time I sell them to museums and school systems. When I met Rachel, she had seen a few of my pamphlets, and I knew a little bit about her photography. I really admire her work, and she said that she found my work inspiring. We tend to speak almost entirely about work, even when we set out not to. That really is the focus of our relationship, and inevitably, when we see each other, that's where our attention goes. At first I was a little . . . *disappointed,* I guess is the right word. I kept thinking that there was something wrong with me that we weren't turning into friends the way most friends do. After a while I stopped resisting it.''

SCRIPTING, EVEN WHEN DONE WITH THE "BEST OF INTENTIONS" IS STILL SCRIPTING, AND WE WOULD HAVE TO SAY THAT THIS MATURE SCHOLAR MIGHT FIND MORE SATISFACTION IN THE DEALINGS WITH THE FRAGMENT WHO IS NOW RACHEL IF SHE COULD BRING HERSELF TO ALLOW THE RELATIONSHIP TO SHAPE ITSELF RATHER THAN ATTEMPT TO FORCE IT TO CONFORM TO PREESTABLISHED PERCEPTIONS OF HOW A FRIENDSHIP "MUST" BE CONDUCTED. WE WOULD ALSO WISH TO POINT OUT THAT THIS MATURE WARRIOR IS NOT ADEPT AT SOCIAL SKILLS AND IS NOT OFTEN COMFORTABLE WHEN CAUGHT IN DEMANDS FOR "SMALL TALK". BY MOST STANDARDS, THIS VERY PRIVATE FRAGMENT IS UNSOCIAL, BECAUSE OF THE LACK OF PATIENCE SHE HAS WITH CERTAIN SOCIAL FORMALITIES AND SKILLS. IN THIS INSTANCE, THE PRESSURE IS NOT THE SAME, AND WE WOULD THINK THAT THERE IS LESS "NEED" FOR THE SOCIAL FORMS THAN THE FRAGMENT WHO IS NOW DOMINIQUE ASSUMES. THERE ARE SO MANY AREAS OF CONTACT DESIRED, AND THE TASK COMPANION LINK IS SO ENDURING THAT SHOULD THE FRAGMENT WHO IS NOW DOMINIQUE CHOOSE TO DO SO, RELEASE OF EXPECTATIONS COULD OPEN MANY HITHERTO UNSUSPECTED DOORS FOR BOTH FRAGMENTS CONCERNED.

"I paid attention to what Michael said, and recently I've been managing better. I try not to trivialize my dealings with Rachel. I know that Michael didn't use that word, but I will, because in retrospect, I think that's what I was doing. Anyway, so far, we've had the chance to go over some of her more recent work, and she's talking about my writing the commentary for a photographic book she's considering putting together. I've warned her that getting a contract for something so ambitious won't be easy, but that doesn't seem to matter to her.''

FOR TASK COMPANIONS, THE WORK UNDERTAKEN HAS VALUE IN AND OF ITSELF, AND THERE IS NO REQUIREMENT FOR THE WORK TO GO BEYOND THE PROCESS OF MUTUAL COOPERATION FOR THE BOND TO BE VALIDATED IN THE LIFE. THAT IS NOT TO SAY THAT THERE IS NO REASON TO SEEK OUTWARD "SUCCESS", FOR THAT IS NOT THE CASE. IF THERE IS WIDER ACHIEVEMENT THAN VALIDATION OF THE BOND, THEN OTHERS BENEFIT FROM THE SHARED TASK. LET US SAY THAT IN THIS INSTANCE THE FRAGMENT WHO IS NOW RACHEL IS WILLING TO SPEND TIME SHE WOULD NOT GENERALLY SHARE WITH THE FRAGMENT WHO IS NOW DOMINIQUE. WE WOULD WISH TO POINT OUT THAT THIS IS NOT THE USUAL OCCURRENCE FOR THIS VERY PRIVATE MATURE WARRIOR, AND IN OFFERING THE COLLABORATION TO THIS MATURE SCHOLAR, SHE HAS EXTENDED HERSELF IN A WAY WE WOULD HAVE TO SAY IS UNIQUE IN HER EXPERIENCE IN THIS LIFE. TO UNDERTAKE SUCH A VENTURE, SHOULD YOU BOTH CHOOSE TO DO SO, DOMINIQUE, IS GOOD WORK, AND HAS THE ADDED BENEFIT THAT IT CAN SERVE TO "OPEN DOORS" IN THE PROFESSIONAL WORLD FOR BOTH OF YOU.

"I don't know what to say about all this," Dominique remarks. "I'm doing my best to make time for the project, but it comes at a difficult time, since one of my parents is seriously ill, and the spare time I did have has pretty much disappeared. I know that I'm free to choose to do anything I like, and I'm so tempted to do this work with Rachel, but at the same time I want to have time for the family. A year ago, there would have been no question in my mind about working with Rachel. Now I have to weigh the various factors. I want to hold off on the work with Rachel for a little while, but she has commitments for next fall, which means we ought to get to the work right away. It's not an easy decision to make.''

ALL TASKS A FRAGMENT HAS UNDERTAKEN WILL BE COMPLETED BEFORE THE CYCLE OF LIVES IS FINISHED. IF THE WORK IS NOT DONE NOW, IT WILL BE DONE IN ANOTHER LIFE. THAT IS NOT TO SAY THAT THEREFORE ENDLESS DELAY IS "DESIRABLE", FOR THAT IS NOT THE CASE. THE WORK IS VALID AND THE BOND IS VALID. THE "DEMANDS OF FAMILY" ARE ALSO VALID, ALTHOUGH ON DIFFERENT LEVELS THAN THE BOND OF TASK COMPANION. LET US SUGGEST THAT THE FRAGMENT WHO IS NOW DOMINIQUE NOT MAKE ANY DECISION IN HASTE, FOR THAT WOULD BE MORE THE RESULT OF THE URGINGS OF CHIEF FEATURE THAN VALID INSIGHT. IF A SOLUTION IS CHOSEN, IT WILL NOT BE OUT OF DESPERATION BUT OUT OF PERCEPTION. THIS DISTINCTION IS NOT ALWAYS EASILY UNDERSTOOD OR EVALUATED, BUT IT IS WORTHWHILE FOR THIS AND ANY OTHER FRAGMENTS ON THE PHYSICAL PLANE.

"That's one of those coming-and-going answers,'' Dominique says. "It makes me wonder how many options I have, but I know better than to ask Michael; they'd give me another variation on the choice lecture, and I know that this is a matter of choice. That's one thing I have learned. I do understand that what I do is my choice.''

IT IS NOT INAPPROPRIATE FOR FRAGMENTS EXTANT UPON THE PHYSICAL PLANE TO BE AWARE THAT EACH AND EVERY ONE OF YOU HAS A PERSONAL AGENDA AND THAT THOSE PERSONAL AGENDAS ARE LEGITIMATE FOR ALL FRAGMENTS. SUCH MINOR THINGS AS LUNCHTIME SHOPPING ARE PART OF THE AGENDA, AND SUCH MAJOR ONES AS CONTRACTING CERTAIN LIFE-THREATENING DISEASES. THAT IS NOT TO SAY THAT ALL DISEASES ARE NECESSARILY PART OF THE LIFE PLAN FROM THE START. DISEASE IS ONE OF THE HAZARDS OF THE PHYSICAL PLANE, AND THE CONTRACTING OF SUCH A DISEASE MAY

OR MAY NOT BE ON THE AGENDA. JUST AS AGENDAS IN THE STANDARD SENSE MAY BE CHANGED AND RE-SCHEDULED, SO MAY THOSE AGENDAS OF THE NATURE WE ARE DISCUSSING. FRAGMENTS EXTANT ON THE PHYS-ICAL PLANE, BECAUSE OF THE OBDURACY OF THE PHYSI-CAL PLANE, OFTEN BENEFIT WHEN PERCEPTIONS ARE SUF-FICIENTLY FLEXIBLE TO PERMIT CHANGES AND ALTERA-TIONS IN PLANS, EVEN LIFE PLANS.

"I haven't thought that out yet," says Dominique. "I know that I tend to be pretty, well, stubborn. I know, too, that I've let myself get very upset because of changes that have upset my agendas. Probably the most sensible thing I can do is set up two or three ways to handle my life for the next year or so, but I resist the idea because I like things to be set, in place." She laughs. "More stubbornness. At least I've learned to recognize that much."

"What I like most about Michael," says Hazel Wescott (who in *More Messages From Michael* is part of Lizzie Roarke) "is his willingness to give hard answers. My own involvement with my Essence Twin was very trying. I wanted to make the contact and to have some kind of relation-ship with him—and I don't mean simply a romantic fling or anything as obvious as that—so I could find out what all the fuss was about. The trouble is, it really does take two, and this was more than he wanted to do." Hazel has not been active in the group since Jessica left, and aside from occasional phone-in questions, she has not attended a session in more than two years, until the last three sessions.

"I was able to identify my Essence Twin some time ago. It didn't surprise me, finding out who it was. I had a sense of it from the beginning; I'd met him very briefly about ten years ago and felt at the time that there was something unusual going on. I thought it was probably karma, because it was so intense. I didn't consider Essence Twin at the time. I had this very distorted and romantic notion about the Essence Twin relationship. I thought it was one of those fireworks-and-bells reactions, not this semi-obsessive reaction I had to Jacob.''

WHAT IS REGARDED AS THE ROMANTIC REACTION IS OFTEN THE RESPONSE TO BODY-TYPE ATTRACTION. WHEN BODY TYPES ATTRACT THERE IS A DEFINITE SENSE OF "THRILL". THAT IS NOT TO SAY THAT THIS IS NOT A WORTHWHILE RELATIONSHIP—WE WOULD SAY THAT ALL RELATIONSHIPS ARE WORTHWHILE, AND THOSE WHERE BODY-TYPE ATTRACTION EXISTS HAVE THE MERIT OF BRINGING ESSENTIAL LESSONS OF THE PHYSICAL PLANE VERY MUCH TO BEAR IN THE LIFE IN THE MOST IMMEDIATE WAYS. HOWEVER, WHERE THE FRAGMENT WHO IS NOW HAZEL IS CONCERNED, THIS IS NOT THE CASE. THE FRAGMENT WHO IS NOW JACOB IS THE ESSENCE TWIN, AND THE STRENGTH OF THE RESPONSE IS NOT UNTYPICAL OF THE ESSENCE TWIN REACTION AND BOND. WHEN THE ESSENCE TWIN RELATIONSHIP IS RECOGNIZED AND VALIDATED, THERE ARE OTHER INWARD PERCEPTIONS THAT CAN BE EXPERIENCED ON ALL LEVELS, WHICH CAN BE VERY GOOD WORK. WE WOULD ADD ONLY THIS NOTE OF CAUTION: THE INTENSITY OF THE ESSENCE TWIN RELATIONSHIP IS SO UNRELIEVED AND SO CONSUMMATE THAT THERE ARE MANY FRAGMENTS WHO DO NOT CHOOSE TO SUSTAIN IT. THERE IS NOTHING "WRONG" IN THIS; THERE ARE MANY TIMES WHEN THE ESSENCE TWIN RELATIONSHIP IS MORE ENGROSSING THAN IS "PRACTICAL" FOR THE FRAGMENTS, AND THIS ALONE IS SUFFICIENT TO CAUSE THE FRAGMENTS TO HESITATE.

"I wouldn't say that I hesitated,'' Hazel observes. "I was ready to get involved. I understood that it might be upsetting to the rest of my life, but that didn't seem to be very important when compared to the possibilities of being with my Essence Twin.''

IT IS NOT OUR INTENTION TO OFFER ENCOURAGEMENT OR DISCOURAGEMENT, BUT IN ANSWER TO THE QUESTION

POSED BY THE FRAGMENT WHO IS NOW HAZEL, WE
WOULD WISH TO POINT OUT THAT THE FRAGMENT WHO
IS NOW JACOB HAS COMMITTED HIMSELF TO A MASSIVE
AMOUNT OF WORK IN TERMS OF HIS PHYSICAL-PLANE
AGENDA AND IS NOT APT TO WANT TO CURTAIL HIS EF-
FORTS. ALSO, A FRAGMENT WITH SUCH FIXED OVER-
LEAVES DOES NOT FIND IT EASY TO ENGAGE IN A RE-
LATIONSHIP OF EQUALS, WHICH IS THE TRUE NATURE OF
THE ESSENCE TWIN BOND.

"Jacob is an Old Scholar, like me," says Hazel. "He's
in power and dominance. I have dominance, but not power,
thank goodness, I guess. His stubbornness doesn't go well
with my arrogance. I know that he wasn't prepared for
anything like me in his life, and I'm certain he found it
upsetting."

WHILE IT WOULD BE MISLEADING FOR US TO SAY THAT
THE FRAGMENT WHO IS NOW JACOB HAS DENIED THE VAL-
IDITY OF THE CONTACT, WE WISH TO POINT OUT THAT HE
HAS NOT PERCEIVED THE CONTACT AS WHAT IT IS—THIS
POWERFUL OLD SCHOLAR HAS NEVER ENCOUNTERED
ANYONE WHOM HE RECOGNIZED AS AN EQUAL, AND THE
ARRIVAL OF THE FRAGMENT WHO IS NOW HAZEL HAS
CAUSED HIM SERIOUS CONCERN. IT IS NOT AMISS FOR THE
FRAGMENT WHO IS NOW HAZEL TO KEEP IN MIND THAT
JACOB COMES FROM A SUBCULTURE OF EUROPEANS WHO
ARE, IN HER PERCEPTIONS, EXTREMELY "SEXIST". THE
FRAGMENT WHO IS NOW JACOB HAS NEVER BEFORE "EN-
TERTAINED" THE CONCEPT OF EQUALITY BETWEEN THE
SEXES, LET ALONE THE STRONG BOND INHERENT IN THE
ESSENCE TWIN BOND. WHILE WE DO NOT PREDICT, WE
SUGGEST THAT CONTINUING THIS RELATIONSHIP MIGHT
BE PROFOUNDLY DISTURBING TO HIM.

"A typical Michael understatement," Hazel admits. "I've
had contact off and on over the years with Jacob, and every
time I see him, I want to tell him what's going on. But for
one thing, I know it's likely he wouldn't believe me—he

thinks this kind of study is pretty silly—and that would make it difficult to continue to have contact with him at all. Besides, I realized about four years ago that I truly didn't want to do anything that would distress Jacob, even if I thought it would give me an edge with him. Michael said years and years ago that Essence Twins, where there is recognition, are concerned only for the benefit of the Essence Twin. At the time I didn't know what they meant, but I sure do now.''

TO VALIDATE THE BONDS AND LINKS IS GOOD WORK, EVEN WHEN ONESIDED. THAT THE FRAGMENT WHO IS NOW JACOB HAS ABDICATED IN NO WAY CHANGES YOUR VALIDATION, HAZEL, NOR DOES IT DIMINISH YOUR EXPERIENCE. THERE IS RECOGNITION FOR BOTH FRAGMENTS ON MANY LEVELS, BUT WE WOULD HAVE TO SAY THAT THE HOLD OF FALSE PERSONALITY IS VERY STRONG IN THIS STUBBORN FRAGMENT, AND THE CULTURAL PATTERNING HAS MADE VALIDATION ESPECIALLY DIFFICULT FOR THE FRAGMENT WHO IS NOW JACOB. IT IS NOT AMISS TO RECALL THAT HE HAS NOT BEEN PREPARED FOR A RELATIONSHIP WITH EQUALS WHERE WOMEN ARE CONCERNED, AND HIS ENCULTURATED REACTION TO WHAT HE THINKS OF AS "TYPICAL AMERICAN" WOMEN TENDS TO SUPPORT HIS ABDICATION. THAT HE ENTERTAINED THE NOTION, HOWEVER BRIEFLY, IS PROGRESS OF A SORT UNCOMMON IN THIS FRAGMENT; THE HOLD OF THE CHIEF FEATURE WAS LESSENED WHILE YOU WERE IN ACTUAL PHYSICAL PROXIMITY. NOW THAT THERE IS A DISTANCE BETWEEN YOU, THE CHIEF FEATURE HAS RETURNED "WITH A VENGEANCE" AND HAS, AS YOU HAVE DESCRIBED IT, "BEATEN HIM UP" FOR HIS "AUDACITY" OF LESSENING ITS HOLD. THAT IS NOT TO SAY THAT YOUR CONTACT HAS BEEN RENDERED INVALID. THAT IS, OF COURSE, IMPOSSIBLE. "TAKING BACK" A VALID CONTACT IS NO MORE POSSIBLE THAN "TAKING BACK" AN ORGASM. CONTACT IS CONTACT, NO MATTER WHAT LATER REACTIONS MAY BE. THE CONTACT OCCURRED AT THE TIME, AND IT WAS VALID.

"I think I've got that,'' Hazel says a bit ruefully. "I'm

not always convinced—I guess that's my chief feature at
work, at least that's what Michael says—but I do understand
that while I was with Jacob, something *did* happen, and
whatever it was, it was real.'' She pauses. "I sometimes
think about coming back to sessions more regularly than I
have been, but with Jessica gone, I feel a little strange. It's
not that I don't think Camille and the Leslies are good
mediums; that's not the point. It's just that I started out with
Jessica and I feel as if I'm . . . putting her down, I guess,
if I go to someone else for Michael information. I'd rather
wait until she starts up again, if she ever does. But it's been
more than two years now since she had a regular session,
and I don't know how much longer I can stay away. Those
few sessions I have attended have been at times when I
really wanted information. My curiosity is very strong, and
the questions are piling up. Milly said she was willing to
do some private channeling for me, but I don't know if I
want that yet. I haven't been so confused about all this in
a long time. I suppose that I'll keep dropping in at sessions
every two or three months until I make up my mind. That
seems awfully wishy-washy, but it's the best I can do for
the time being.''

She consults the file folder where she keeps her notes
and transcripts. "I have some questions to ask about Jacob.
Maybe I'm flogging a dead horse, but . . . Those ties simply
don't break. I could no more stop being attached to Jacob
than I could stop being my brother's sister. If that's what
Michael means by recognition and validation, I've got it.
In spades.''

CHAPTER 11

MICHAEL: CHOOSING TO LEARN AND LEARNING TO CHOOSE

NO FRAGMENT IS REQUIRED TO RECOGNIZE OR VALIDATE ANY PORTION OF THE LIVES LIVED AT ANY TIME. THERE ARE NO REQUIREMENTS MADE OF ANY FRAGMENT EXTANT ON THE PHYSICAL PLANE ANYWHERE. HOWEVER, FOR THOSE FRAGMENTS WHO CHOOSE—AND WE EMPHASIZE *CHOOSE*—THERE CAN BE MANY LESSONS BROUGHT TO BEAR IN THE LIFE. THIS DOES NOT NECESSARILY MEAN THAT THERE WILL BE AUTOMATIC "IMPROVEMENT" AND GROWTH IN THE LIFE, BUT IT DOES TEND TO INCREASE THE LEVEL OF UNDERSTANDING OF EXPERIENCE AND PERCEPTION FOR THE FRAGMENT WHO CHOOSES TO RECOGNIZE THE LESSONS OF THE LIFE.

FOR EACH ROLE IN ESSENCE, THERE ARE A NUMBER OF "NATURAL" PITFALLS, LEVELS OF BEHAVIOR THAT ARE SO "AUTOMATIC" THAT THEY IN FACT BLOCK INSIGHTS WHILE FULFILLING THE NATURE OF ESSENCE. FOR EXAMPLE, WITH SLAVE ESSENCES, THE TENDENCY TO SERVE ANYTHING AND EVERYTHING IS VERY GREAT, AND IS PART OF WHAT WE HAVE CALLED THE SLAVE ADVANTAGE, FOR THE SLAVE ESSENCE ALONE OF ALL ESSENCES DOES NOT REQUIRE SPECIAL CIRCUMSTANCES FOR THIS LIFE TASK TO BE FULFILLED. TAKEN TO EXTREMES, THIS LEADS TO "ROTE" SERVICE WITHOUT PERCEPTION OF THE TASK.

FOR THE ARTISAN ESSENCE, THE "AUTOMATIC" TRAP IS THAT OF THE TOTAL PREOCCUPATION WITH STRUCTURE AND THE RESULTANT TENDENCY TO ATTEMPT TO INTERRELATE EVERYTHING WITH EVERYTHING ELSE, AS IN THE

179

CASE OF THOSE WHO SEEK TO EQUATE THE LAWS OF
PHYSICS WITH THE PERCEPTIONS OF SOCIOLOGY WITH THE
GEOMETRIC PHILOSOPHIES OF ARCHITECTURE. WHILE
THIS IS NOT AN INVALID ARTISAN PERCEPTION, CARRIED
TO EXTREMES IT SERVES ONLY TO BLOCK VALIDATIONS
AND TO DISTORT THE FUNCTIONS OF STRUCTURE.

IN THE CASE OF WARRIOR ESSENCE, THE GREATEST
STUMBLING BLOCK IS THE TENDENCY TO SEE ALL THINGS
AS CHALLENGES; THIS NOT ONLY USES ACTION "NEED-
LESSLY", IT OFTEN SERVES TO RENDER GENUINE CHAL-
LENGES INDISTINGUISHABLE FROM OTHER, LESS VALID
ONES. TO REGARD EVERY QUESTION AS A CHALLENGE
CAUSES LITTLE FOR THE WARRIOR BUT EXHAUSTION AND
"PROVES" ONLY THAT ACTION POLARITY TENDS TO LEAP
BEFORE LOOKING. THERE IS ALSO THE MATTER OF WAR-
RIOR HONOR; THE ESSENCE IS ALWAYS "TOUCHY" ABOUT
HONOR, AND NEVER MORE THAN WHEN THE WARRIOR IN
QUESTION IS SEEING CHALLENGES EVERYWHERE—EVEN
WHEN THEY DO NOT AND, IN FACT, CANNOT EXIST.

SCHOLAR ESSENCES ARE PRONE TO ANALYZE RATHER
THAN EXPERIENCE THEIR LIVES, OFTEN IN GREAT,
EXHAUSTIVE DETAIL. THERE ARE SCHOLARS WHO HAVE
KEPT METICULOUS RECORDS OF EVERY ASPECT OF THEIR
LIVES IN ORDER TO "UNDERSTAND" IT IN THE CATALOG
SENSE. THIS, OF COURSE, IS NOT UNDERSTANDING, IT IS
MERELY MAKING LISTS. WE WOULD HAVE TO SAY THAT
SUCH PREOCCUPATIONS, WHILE NOT UNTYPICAL OF
SCHOLARS, DOES NOT PERMIT THE SCHOLAR TO REALIZE
THE VALIDITY OF THE EXPERIENCE OF THE LIFE WHILE IT
IS BEING LIVED. IT IS ALSO VALID THAT SCHOLARS OFTEN
FIND IT DIFFICULT TO BE SPONTANEOUS, TO PARTICIPATE
IN LIFE AS IT HAPPENS INSTEAD OF REFERENCING AND
CROSS-INDEXING AND "FOOTNOTING" UNTIL ALL SENSE
OF SPONTANEITY IS LOST OR "HOPELESSLY" DISTORTED.

FOR SAGE ESSENCES, AS WE HAVE REMARKED BEFORE,
THE PROBLEM IS THAT OF PERFORMING THE LIFE RATHER
THAN EXPERIENCING IT VALIDLY. THE SAGE SEEKS TO
COMMUNICATE, BUT IF THIS IS DONE WITHOUT ANY "PER-
SONAL" UNDERSTANDING, THERE IS LITTLE PROGRESS IN

THE COURSE OF THE LIFE. FOR SAGES, THE TEMPTATION TO TURN EVERYONE INTO AN AUDIENCE IS VERY GREAT, NO MATTER HOW INAPPROPRIATE. IT IS NOT AMISS FOR SAGES TO BE AWARE OF THIS TENDENCY, FOR IT IS CERTAINLY THE SINGLE GREATEST "BLOCK" TO PERSONAL VALIDATION WHILE THE SAGE IS INCARNATE.

FOR PRIESTS, THE PROBLEM IS MORE DIFFICULT, SINCE THE PRIEST, HAVING TWO CHANNELS OF INPUT, TENDS TO NEED "GROUNDING", AND UNLIKE THE INSPIRATION POLARITY COUNTERPART, THE SLAVE, IS A CARDINAL ROLE AND HAS LITTLE OPPORTUNITY TO ASSESS THE DIFFERENCE BETWEEN CHANNEL ONE AND CHANNEL TWO. IT IS NOT UNCOMMON FOR THE PRIEST ESSENCE TO INDULGE IN ALMOST COMPULSIVE SEXUAL ACTIVITY AS THE MEANS TO "GROUND" THE ESSENCE TO CHANNEL ONE; WHILE THIS IS NOT IN AND OF ITSELF A HAZARD, WE WOULD HAVE TO COMMENT THAT OFTEN THE FOCUS OF SUCH SEXUAL OUTLET IS SPECIFICALLY NON-INTIMATE, AIMED AT BRINGING THE PRIEST BACK TO THE BODY RATHER THAN ESTABLISHING VALID ESSENCE CONTACT. LET US COMMENT HERE THAT THE PRIEST NATURE, WHICH IS RELATED TO THE NUMBER SIX AND TO THE ASTRAL PLANE AND TRANSCENDENTAL SOUL, IS EASILY "DISTRACTED" TO CHANNEL TWO, THAT IS THE PERCEPTION OF THE HIGHER IDEAL WHICH THE PRIEST SERVES. IT IS NOT VALID TO ASSUME THAT BECAUSE THE HIGHER IDEAL IS VALID FOR THE INDIVIDUAL PRIEST IT IS THEREFORE VALID FOR ALL FRAGMENTS EXTANT ON THE PHYSICAL PLANE, BUT OFTEN THE PRIEST FINDS THIS EXTREMELY DIFFICULT TO ACCEPT, AND THIS LEADS TO DISAPPOINTMENTS FOR ALL FRAGMENTS CONCERNED. IT IS NOT INAPPROPRIATE FOR THE PRIEST ESSENCE TO REMEMBER THAT THE PERCEPTION OF HERETICS IS A PERSONAL TRUTH, NOT A WORLD TRUTH OR A UNIVERSAL TRUTH.

THE KING ESSENCE OCCASIONALLY IS BLOCKED BY WHAT WE HAVE CALLED THE PRINCE SYNDROME, THAT IS, THE TENDENCY TO EXERCISE AUTHORITY WITHOUT ACCEPTING RESPONSIBILITY, OR DELEGATING THE CONSEQUENCES OF THE KING MANDATES TO FRAGMENTS WHO

ARE, IN FACT, NOT RESPONSIBLE. THIS DEPUTIZING CAN
BRING ABOUT SERIOUS CONFLICTS AND MISUNDERSTAND-
INGS. THE KING ESSENCE, TIED TO THE INCULCATING
NUMBER SEVEN, TO THE CAUSAL PLANE AND THE INFINITE
SOUL, HAS ULTIMATE OBLIGATION FOR THE BRINGING TO
BEAR OF LESSONS IN THE LIFE, AND IF THE KING FAILS
TO DO THIS FOR ITSELF, THEN THOSE ABOUT THE KING
FRAGMENT ARE LIKELY TO HAVE DISTORTED EXPERI-
ENCES. IT IS THE NATURE OF THE KING ESSENCE TO
CLARIFY, AND WHEN THIS IS NOT REALIZED, THE LACK
OF CLARITY AFFECTS ALL AROUND THE KING.

WHETHER OR NOT THE FRAGMENTS—NO MATTER
WHAT ROLE IN ESSENCE—CHOOSE TO RECOGNIZE THE
LESSONS BROUGHT TO BEAR, OR TO ABDICATE THE REC-
OGNITION, IS JUST THAT—CHOICE. NO FRAGMENT IS OR
CAN BE COMPELLED TO A RECOGNITION THAT IS NOT CHO-
SEN. WE WOULD WISH TO POINT OUT THAT AT NO TIME
IS A FRAGMENT "REQUIRED" TO VALIDATE A PERCEPTION
IN ORDER FOR THE LIFE TO PROGRESS, BUT WHERE VALI-
DATION IS RECOGNIZED, THE PROGRESS CAN BE, SHOULD
THE FRAGMENT CHOOSE TO BRING IT TO BEAR, GREATER
AND MORE "COHESIVE" THAN WHEN SUCH RECOGNITION
AND VALIDATION IS NOT PRESENT.

THOSE FRAGMENTS WHO HAVE CHOSEN TO RECOGNIZE
AND VALIDATE THE PERCEPTION OF THE LIFE, WHETHER
THAT CHOICE IS SELECTIVE OR GENERIC, WE WOULD HAVE
TO OBSERVE THAT SUCH FRAGMENTS ARE MORE LIKELY
TO ACCOMPLISH PROGRESS ON THE LIFE TASK, TO COM-
PLETE THE INTERNAL MONADS, AND TO ACCEPT THE
LINKS, TIES, AND BONDS OF ESSENCE AS HAVING BEARING
IN THE LIFE.

THAT IS NOT TO SAY THAT THERE IS NO PROGRESS
WHEN THE CHOICE HAS NOT BEEN MADE: IF THIS WERE
THE CASE, NO FRAGMENT WOULD HAVE YET MOVED
BEYOND THE INFANT SOUL CYCLE. VALIDATION AND REC-
OGNITION CAN AND DOES TAKE PLACE BETWEEN LIVES
ON THE ASTRAL PLANE. THE PROGRESS OF THE LIFE IS
PERCEIVED AT THAT TIME WITHOUT THE DISTORTIONS OF
THE PHYSICAL PLANE, AND WITHOUT THE BURDEN OF PER-

SONALITY, FALSE AND TRUE. THERE ARE MANY, MANY, MANY FRAGMENTS WHO PASS THROUGH THE ENTIRE CYCLES OF THEIR PHYSICAL INCARNATIONS WITHOUT RECOGNITION AND VALIDATION OCCURRING WHILE THE FRAGMENTS ARE INCARNATE. THAT IS, OF COURSE, A MATTER OF CHOICE.

MANY MORE FRAGMENTS ARE WILLING TO CHOOSE TO VALIDATE THOSE ASPECTS OF LIFE WHICH ARE "COMFORTING" OR "FLATTERING" OR VIEWED AS "SPIRITUAL". THAT SELECTING SHOES MIGHT HAVE AS MUCH BEARING ON SPIRITUALITY AS PROLONGED MEDITATION IS PERCEIVED AS BEING "LUDICROUS" OR "DISGUSTING" TO THESE SELECTIVE FRAGMENTS WHO ARE EAGER TO ESCAPE THE BONDS OF PHYSICAL INCARNATION. THAT DOES NOT MEAN THEY WISH TO "DIE", IT MEANS THAT THEY WISH TO FIND SOME RELEASE FROM THE TRIALS OF LIFE. ALL FRAGMENTS ARE FREE TO CHOOSE SUCH A STANCE, BUT WE WOULD WISH TO COMMENT THAT SUCH DENIALS TEND TO BE "COUNTERPRODUCTIVE" AND BLOCK MANY INSIGHTS THAT WOULD BE OF USE TO THEM. WE DO NOT THEREFORE IMPLY THAT DENYING THE INSIGHTS IS "WRONG". WE HAVE SAID BEFORE, BUT WE REPEAT YET AGAIN THAT THERE IS NOTHING "WRONG" IN ANY ACTION, CHOICE, DECISION OR LACK THEREOF ON THIS OR ANY OTHER PLANE. ALL FRAGMENTS ARE FREE TO CHOOSE, AND WHERE LIFE CHOICE HAS BEEN ABROGATED, KARMA RESULTS.

WE ARE AWARE THAT THERE ARE MANY INSTANCES WHEN LIFE ON THE PHYSICAL PLANE, BY ITS VERY NATURE, BRINGS ANGUISH TO FRAGMENTS THERE EXTANT. THE EXPERIENCE OF WHAT MIGHT BE CALLED INTENSE PERSONAL SUFFERING IS ALMOST UNIQUE TO THE PHYSICAL PLANE, FOR NOWHERE ELSE IS THERE SUCH ISOLATION AND LONELINESS AS YOU EXPERIENCE DURING INCARNATION. THIS IS PARTICULARLY THE CASE IN SPECIES THAT ARE INDEPENDENTLY MOBILE, FOR THE INDIVIDUAL SEPARATION SERVES TO REINFORCE THE LONELINESS OF EACH AND EVERY FRAGMENT WHILE INCARNATE. THIS DOES NOT MEAN THAT SUCH SUFFERING IS NOT VALID—IT

IS ENTIRELY VALID TO THE FRAGMENT WHO EXPERIENCES IT. HOWEVER, BEYOND THE PHYSICAL PLANE, SUCH PERSONAL SUFFERING DOES NOT, IN FACT, EXIST. ON THOSE PLANES BEYOND THE PHYSICAL PLANE, THE SEPARATION AND LONELINESS AND DESPERATION—ALL THE RESULT OF FEAR AND CONTRIBUTORY TO THE CHIEF FEATURE AND ITS STRANGLEHOLD ON THE OVERLEAVES—HAVE VERY LITTLE VALIDITY. BY THE TIME THE CADRES REUNITE, AND THE SENSE OF FRAGMENTATION HAS FADED, THE RECOMBINED ENTITIES AND CADRES SENSE ONLY THE MOST PROFOUND JOY.

TO EXAMINE THE CHOICES OF A LIFE IS GOOD WORK, WHETHER THE EXAMINATION COMES FROM QUESTIONS OF THE SORT OUR LITTLE GROUP ASKS, OR FROM A SENSE OF "SELF" IN THE LIFE. THERE IS NO "NEED" FOR ANY FRAGMENT TO PURSUE "SPIRITUAL" TEACHING IN ANY WAY FOR THE INSIGHTS INTO THE NATURE OF THE LIFE TO BE VALID. WE ARE AWARE THAT THERE ARE MANY FRAGMENTS WHO PREFER DOGMA TO INSIGHT, JUST AS WE ARE AWARE THAT THERE ARE MANY BABY AND YOUNG SOULS WHO ARE EAGER TO OFFER UP THEIR PERCEPTION OF DOGMA FOR OTHERS TO FOLLOW. THOSE SOULS IN THE MATURE CYCLE ARE NOT OFTEN AS INCLINED TO ATTRACT FOLLOWERS, ALTHOUGH THERE ARE EXCEPTIONS, SUCH AS THE MATURE PRIEST WHO WAS SIGMUND FREUD. FOR YOUNG SOULS—AND WE REMIND YOU THAT THIS IS A YOUNG SOUL COUNTRY AND A YOUNG SOUL WORLD—THE MOTTO OF "DO IT MY WAY" TENDS NOT ONLY TO LEAD TO A RIGID SENSE OF "MORALITY", BUT TO A NEED TO FIND A SCHEME OF "MORALITY" THAT ACCOMMODATES THE PERCEPTIONS OF THE YOUNG SOUL.

IT MAY BE APPARENT TO MANY THAT RELIGION OFTEN HAS LITTLE TO DO WITH SPIRITUALITY, AND MUCH OF WHAT IS OFFERED AS SPIRITUAL TEACHING HAS MORE TO DO WITH CULTURAL AND SOCIAL CONDITIONING THAN IT HAS TO DO WITH VALID INSIGHTS. MOST ORGANIZED RELIGIONS, EVEN THOSE STEMMING FROM TEACHING OF THE MANIFESTATION OF THE TRANSCENDENTAL SOUL AND

THE INFINITE SOUL, EXIST FOR CREATING A GROUP "IN-
TELLECTUAL HIGH" AND TO ENFORCE SOCIAL VALUES.
WE WOULD WISH TO REMIND YOU THAT THE TEACHING
OF THE TRANSCENDENTAL SOUL AND THE INFINITE
SOUL ARE VALID ONLY SO LONG AS THE MANIFESTATION
IS CURRENTLY EXTANT IN THE WORLD, AND WHEN THE
MANIFESTATION IS COMPLETED, THE TEACHING BECOMES
PHILOSOPHICAL LITERATURE.

IF THERE IS A "PURPOSE TO LIFE" IT IS CHOICE. YOU
ARE HERE TO CHOOSE. ALL OF LIFE IS A SERIES OF
CHOICES, AND EVEN WHEN CHOICE IS ABDICATED, IT IS
CHOICE. WHERE LIFE CHOICE IS DENIED, THERE IS KARMA,
AND KARMA WILL BE BALANCED, THE RIBBON WILL BE
BURNED, FOR THAT IS THE NATURE OF EVOLUTION.
CHOICE WILL LEAD TO KARMA AND CHOICE WILL LEAD
TO ITS BURNING. THIS IS NOT A CONTRADICTION. PERSON-
ALITY MAY CHOOSE TO ABDICATE THE BURNING OF
KARMA IN A GIVEN INCARNATION, BUT ESSENCE WILL
EVENTUALLY CHOOSE THE OVERLEAVES AND CIR-
CUMSTANCES THAT WILL PERMIT THE RELEASE THAT
COMES FROM BURNING KARMA, FOR THAT IS PART OF
EVOLUTION, AND ESSENCE, BY ITS VERY NATURE, SEEKS
EVOLUTION. CHOICE IS THE MANIFESTATION OF EVOLU-
TION FOR FRAGMENTS ON THE PHYSICAL PLANE. ALL
PLANES EXPERIENCE CHOICE, BUT NOT IN THE FRAGMEN-
TAL SENSE THAT IS THE NATURE OF THE PHYSICAL PLANE.

THERE IS NO PART OF LIFE THAT IS NOT, IN FACT, A
CHOICE. IT IS A CHOICE TO GET OUT OF BED IN THE MORN-
ING, TO HAVE COFFEE OR ANY OTHER BEVERAGE AT
BREAKFAST—IF YOU CHOOSE TO EAT BREAKFAST. IT IS
A CHOICE TO CONDUCT YOUR DAY IN WHATEVER MEANS
YOU CHOOSE, AND WHAT DEGREE OF IMPORTANCE THE
DAY HAS IN YOUR SENSE OF YOUR LIFE. WHAT ENTER-
TAINMENT, IF ANY, YOU CHOOSE FOR EVENING; WHAT
MEALS, IF ANY, ARE CONSUMED; WHEN AND IF YOU SLEEP,
WITH WHAT OR WHOM—ALL THESE THINGS ARE CHOICES,
AND ALL THE CHOICES ARE VALID. THAT YOU MAY OR
MAY NOT BE PLEASED WITH THE CHOICES IS ANOTHER
MATTER, AND ONE THAT IS LINKED WITH YOUR RECOGNI-

TION AND VALIDATION OF THE NATURE OF YOUR TRUE
PERSONALITY AFTER THE COMPLETION OF THE INTERNAL
FOURTH MONAD. WHILE WE AGREE THAT THE CHOICES
OF LIFE IMPOSE CERTAIN CONSTRAINTS ON THE PERSON-
ALITY AND THE LIFE, WE WOULD ALSO WISH TO POINT
OUT THAT ACCEPTANCE OF THOSE CONSTRAINTS IS, FOR
THE MOST PART, ALSO THE RESULT OF CHOICE.

THAT ENCULTURATED BEHAVIOR LIMITS THE EXPRES-
SION OF THE PERSONALITY, BOTH TRUE AND FALSE, IS TO
SOME EXTENT VALID. THAT CONVENIENCE IS AS MUCH
AN ASPECT AS ANY IN MOST DAILY CHOICES IS ALSO
VALID. THAT THE OVERLEAVES TEND TO MOVE YOU TO-
WARD CERTAIN SORTS OF CHOICES, AND THAT THE OVER-
LEAVES OFTEN COLOR THE REACTION AND RESPONSE TO
THOSE CHOICES IS VALID. ALL EXPERIENCES ARE PART
OF EVOLUTION, EVEN THE EXPERIENCE OF BURNING THE
TOAST OR SPILLING THE WINE. EACH OF YOU BECOMES
THE SUM TOTAL OF ALL EXPERIENCES, NO MATTER HOW
APPARENTLY MINOR OR TRIVIAL, IN THIS AND ALL OTHER
LIVES. WE DO NOT SAY THIS TO BE DAUNTING BUT TO
ASSURE YOU THAT THERE ARE NO "UNIMPORTANT"
CHOICES; WE HAVE SAID BEFORE AND WE WILL CER-
TAINLY REITERATE MANY TIMES AGAIN: NOTHING IS
WASTED. NOTHING *CAN* BE WASTED. ALL OF LIFE IS
VALID, NO MATTER HOW IT IS SPENT. ALL EXPERIENCE
CONTRIBUTES TO THE EVOLUTION OF ESSENCE.

MOST FRAGMENTS EXTANT UPON THE PHYSICAL PLANE
ARE NOT AWARE OF THE NATURE OF THE EXPERIENCE;
THERE IS NOTHING "WRONG" IN THIS. THE EXPERIENCES
OF THE LIFETIME WILL CONTRIBUTE TO THE EVOLUTION
WITH OR WITHOUT THE ATTENTION OF THE PERSONALITY
DURING THE LIFE. HOWEVER, FOR THOSE WHO CHOOSE
TO BECOME SELF-AWARE, WE WOULD FIRST ENCOURAGE
YOU TO BE AWARE OF THE "REALITY" OF LIFE, OF THE
VALIDITY OF EXPERIENCE. LET US SUGGEST THAT THOSE
WHO SEEK SELF-AWARENESS START WITH A FEW SIMPLE
EXERCISES: FIRST, PERMIT YOURSELF TO TASTE—AND
TASTE WITH RECOGNITION AND AWARENESS—THE FOOD
YOU EAT. MOST FRAGMENTS TEND TO IGNORE THEIR

MEALS UNLESS THEY ARE SPECIAL OR UNLESS THE FRAGMENT IS FEELING UNWELL. WHAT DOES BREAKFAST REALLY TASTE LIKE? IF YOU DO NOT EAT BREAKFAST, HOW DOES THE HUNGER FEEL? HOW DOES THE CHAIR YOU SIT IN FEEL? HOW DOES THE WATER OF THE BATH OR SHOWER FEEL? THERE IS MUCH TO LEARN AND VALIDATE THROUGH THE BODY, FOR ONLY ON THE PHYSICAL PLANE DO YOU ACTUALLY POSSESS A BODY. IT IS TRUE THAT ON THE ASTRAL PLANE A BODY MAY BE CONJURED UP, BUT THAT IS MALLEABLE AND TENUOUS, NOT LIKE THE BODIES OF THE PHYSICAL PLANE WHICH HAVE FAR MORE VALID "SOLIDITY" THAN ANY ASTRAL FORMS. BY COMING TO UNDERSTAND THE VALUE OF A BODY, A FRAGMENT CAN DO MUCH TO APPRECIATE THE EXPERIENCES OF THE PHYSICAL PLANE.

OF COURSE, PREOCCUPATION WITH PHYSICAL REALITY CAN LEAD TO MUCH CONFUSION, BUT THAT, TOO, IS A MATTER OF CHOICE. WHEN WE SPEAK OF SELF-AWARENESS, WE DO NOT MEAN PHYSICAL PREOCCUPATION, WE MEAN AWARENESS OF YOUR PERSONAL VALIDITY IN YOUR LIFE AND WITHIN THE TIME OF THE EXPERIENCE. SUCH RECOGNITION IS GOOD WORK AND CAN CONTRIBUTE TO BRINGING THE LESSONS OF THE LIFE TO BEAR, AS WELL AS INCREASING SENSITIVITY TO SUCH LIFE FACTORS AS CONVERGING VECTORS. WHEN A FRAGMENT CHOOSES TO VALIDATE THE "REALITY" OF WHAT YOU CALL THE SELF, THERE CAN BE MANY USEFUL PERCEPTIONS GAINED.

WHEN FRAGMENTS CHOOSE TO BECOME MORE SELF-AWARE, OFTEN THE LESSONS OF THE LIFE ARE MORE ACCESSIBLE TO THEM. A FRAGMENT WHO LACKS SELF-AWARENESS IS MORE EASILY PULLED INTO THE NEGATIVE POLES OF THE OVERLEAVES THAN THOSE WHO HAVE TAKEN THE TIME FOR SELF-ASSESSMENT. FRAGMENTS ACTING OUT OF THE NEGATIVE POLES OF THE OVERLEAVES ARE BY DEFINITION ACTING OUT OF FEAR AND ARE THEREFORE IN THE THROES OF CHIEF FEATURE. WHILE SELF-AWARENESS BY NO MEANS DISPOSES OF CHIEF FEATURE, IT DOES MAKE IT POSSIBLE TO RECOGNIZE THAT SUCH A THING EXISTS AND THAT IT DISTORTS THE

EXPERIENCE OF LIFE, WHICH IS A FIRST STEP TOWARD
LESSENING ITS HOLD. IT IS TRUE THAT OCCASIONALLY A
FRAGMENT WHO IS NOT SELF-AWARE CAN NONETHELESS
COME TO TERMS WITH CHIEF FEATURE AND GAIN ACCESS
TO THE POSITIVE POLES OF THE OVERLEAVES, AND HENCE
TO ESSENCE. MOST OF THE FRAGMENTS WHO AC-
COMPLISH THIS WITHOUT SELF-AWARENESS ARE VERY
OLD SOULS WHO HAVE FEW BONDS HOLDING THEM TO
THE EXPERIENCE OF LIFE. SINCE OLD CYCLE SOULS AC-
COUNT FOR ONLY ELEVEN PERCENT OF THE POPULATION,
WE WOULD THINK THAT FOR MOST FRAGMENTS TO AT-
TAIN THAT STATE WOULD BE PREDICATED ON SELF-
AWARENESS. EVEN THOSE VERY OLD SOULS WHO CAN
GAIN ACCESS TO THE POSITIVE POLES OF THE OVER-
LEAVES WITHOUT SELF-AWARENESS IN FACT MANAGE
MORE EFFECTIVELY WHEN THERE IS SELF-AWARENESS
PRESENT IN THE LIFE.

THE POSITIVE POLES OF THE OVERLEAVES ARE THE
PERSONALITY'S ACCESS TO ESSENCE. THERE IS NO AC-
CESS TO ESSENCE OUT OF THE NEGATIVE POLES OF THE
OVERLEAVES, WHICH LEAD DIRECTLY TO CHIEF FEATURE
AND ENHANCE ITS CONTROL. ESSENCE IS INCAPABLE OF
FEAR: CHIEF FEATURE IS INCAPABLE OF LOVE, ALTHOUGH
IT OFTEN MASQUERADES AS DESIRE AND LUST AND AFFEC-
TION—ALL OF WHICH ARE LADEN WITH EXPECTATIONS
AND CONDITIONS, WHICH REVEALS THE PRESENCE OF THE
CHIEF FEATURE AND FEAR. MANY FRAGMENTS, AT THE
CONCLUSION OF AFFECTION, FEEL SHAME THAT THEY
"WASTED" THEIR FEELINGS. NOTHING, LEAST OF ALL
LOVE, IS EVER WASTED. SHAME IS ONE OF THE MOST
PERVASIVE OF CHIEF-FEATURE DISTORTIONS, FOR IT HAS
THE ENDORSEMENT OF SOCIAL CONDITIONING TO SUP-
PORT IT AND LEND IT THE CREDIBILITY OF CULTURAL PAT-
TERNING. LOVE IS WITHOUT SHAME. LOVE AS WE UNDER-
STAND IT IS WITHOUT ANY CONDITION WHATSOEVER,
WHICH IS WHY WE CAN OFFER OUR TEACHING WITHOUT
EXPECTATIONS. YOU NEED DO NOTHING TO "DESERVE"
IT. NOTHING YOU CAN DO WILL CHANGE THE TEACHING
OR OUR LOVE.

WE REALIZE THAT THIS IS MORE "EASILY" AC-COMPLISHED FROM THE MID-CAUSAL PLANE WHERE ALL CADENCES HAVE REUNITED AND WHERE THE ENTITIES REUNITE AS THEY EVOLVE TOWARD THE AKASHIC PLANE. THERE ARE FAR MORE DISTORTIONS AND MISUNDER-STANDINGS ON THE PHYSICAL PLANE BY ITS VERY NA-TURE, AND SORTING THROUGH THESE DISTORTIONS AND MISUNDERSTANDINGS CONSTITUTE MANY OF THE LES-SONS LEARNED ON THE PHYSICAL PLANE. IT IS OFTEN DIFFICULT TO CHOOSE TO ACCEPT THE VALIDITY OF LOVE ON THE PHYSICAL PLANE EXCEPT IN VERY BRIEF AND VERY HIGHLY DEFINED CIRCUMSTANCES. BOTH CULTURE AND CHIEF FEATURE CONTRIBUTE TO THE EXPECTATIONS THAT MAKE SUCH VALIDATION EXTREMELY DIFFICULT FOR FRAGMENTS. THAT DOES NOT MEAN THAT YOU "CAN-NOT" PERCEIVE THE VALIDITY OF LOVE DURING A LIFE ON THE PHYSICAL PLANE; WE HAVE ONLY SAID THAT TO DO SO REQUIRES MUCH PERCEPTION AND COURAGE, FOR IT DOES NOT AGREE WITH STANCES THAT ARE "SANC-TIONED" BY SOCIETY.

IF YOU CHOOSE TO VALIDATE THE EXPERIENCE OF LOVE ON THE PHYSICAL PLANE—AND BY LOVE, WE DO NOT LIMIT OURSELVES TO FAMILIAL OR SEXUAL EXCHANGES— YOU WILL DISCOVER THAT THERE IS MUCH RESISTANCE TO SUCH EXPERIENCES. NOT ONLY ARE THERE SOCIAL CONVENTIONS THAT "DECREE" UNDER WHAT CONDI-TIONS AND CIRCUMSTANCES LOVE IS "REAL" OR "ACCEPT-ABLE", BUT THERE ARE PARAMETERS OF EXPRESSION THAT ARE FIXED BY SUCH THINGS AS SOCIALLY CON-DITIONED SEXUAL BEHAVIOR, MATTERS OF STATUS AND CLASS, AND SIMILAR RESTRICTIONS, ALL QUITE VALID. THOSE FRAGMENTS WHO PERMIT THEMSELVES TO EXPERI-ENCE THE VALIDITY OF LOVE—HOWEVER BRIEFLY—UN-ENCUMBERED BY THESE BURDENS, ACHIEVE HIGH LEVELS OF INSIGHT AND PROGRESS WITHIN THE LIFE.

THERE IS NO LIFE IN WHICH FRAGMENTS CANNOT CHOOSE TO MAKE SUCH CONTACT, TO GIVE EXPRESSION TO UNCONDITIONAL LOVE. THERE ARE NO CONDITIONS, NO MATTER HOW RESTRICTIVE, THAT RENDER LOVE IM-

POSSIBLE. THERE IS NO FACTOR IN LIFE THAT CAN DE-
STROY LOVE. THERE IS NO FEAR SO GREAT THAT IT CAN
DEFEAT LOVE. FRAGMENTS CAN CHOOSE TO DENY LOVE,
TO DISTORT IT. FRAGMENTS CAN CHOOSE TO MANIPU-
LATE OTHER FRAGMENTS INSTEAD OF LOVING WITHOUT
EXPECTATION. FRAGMENTS CAN CHOOSE TO DESPISE
LOVE OR HOLD IT IN CONTEMPT. BUT NOTHING IN THE
UNIVERSE IS STRONGER THAN LOVE, OR MORE ENDURING.
LOVE HAS OUTLASTED FEAR OF EVERY SORT, EVERY-
WHERE IN THE PHYSICAL UNIVERSE. LOVE HAS ENDURED
IN THE FACE OF EVERY SORT OF CRIMINALITY, CATAS-
TROPHE, ANNIHILATION, OR OTHER COMPREHENSIVE
"DISASTER" KNOWN ANYWHERE ON THE PHYSICAL
PLANE. THE TAO IS THE EVOLVED AND EVOLVING PER-
FECT LOVE FROM WHICH ALL THINGS COME AND TO
WHICH ALL THINGS RETURN. THE DETESTATION OF A
SINGLE FRAGMENT FOR THE SPACE OF A SINGLE LIFE HAS
NO DISCERNIBLE INFLUENCE ON THE UNIVERSAL TRUTH
OF THE TAO, NO MATTER HOW GREAT THE INFLUENCE OF
THE DETESTATION ON THE LIFE IN QUESTION.

LET US DIGRESS ON THE NATURE OF ESSENCE, FOR IN
ORDER TO UNDERSTAND THE ENORMITY OF LOVE AND
ESSENCE—WHICH ARE VIRTUALLY INTERCHANGEABLE—
IT IS OF HELP TO HAVE SOME COMPREHENSION OF THE
ESSENCE NATURE. ESSENCE SEEKS EVOLUTION, AS DO
ALL ASPECTS OF ESSENCE, SUCH AS ENTITIES AND
CADRES. THE EXPERIENCE OF EVOLUTION IS THE
GRADUAL TRIUMPH OF LOVE OVER FEAR. THE "SPEED"
OF THE EVOLUTION HAS NO DIRECT BEARING ON THE "SUC-
CESS" OF THE EVOLUTION. SPEED HAS NO VALIDITY IN
TERMS OF EVOLUTION. SOME FRAGMENTS MAKE THE
JOURNEY THROUGH THE CYCLES OF LIVES MORE EFFICA-
CIOUSLY THAN OTHERS, WHICH IS NEITHER PRAISE- NOR
BLAME-WORTHY. THERE ARE THOSE WHO VALIDATE THE
PERCEPTIONS OF THE LIVES WHILE THE LIFE IS IN PROG-
RESS, WHICH CAN BE OF SOME USE IN THE LIFE BUT IS NO
MORE PRAISE- OR BLAME-WORTHY THAN THE NUMBER OF
LIVES IT TAKES FOR THE FRAGMENT TO COMPLETE THE
CYCLES OF LIVES.

WE WISH TO MAKE IT CLEAR TO YOU THAT YOUR CHOICE IS JUST THAT AND ONLY THAT. IT IS NOT "BETTER" TO CHOOSE TO EVOLVE QUICKLY OR SLOWLY; IT IS NOT "BETTER" TO BE SELF-AWARE OR UN-SELF-AWARE, THEY ARE ONLY TWO OF THE MYRIAD CHOICES THAT ARE THE STUFF OF LIFE FOR ALL FRAGMENTS EXTANT EVERYWHERE ON THE PHYSICAL PLANE. THERE ARE NO HIDDEN CLAUSES, NO CATCHES, NO TRAPS IN CHOICE EXCEPT THE ONES YOU CHOOSE FOR YOURSELVES. KARMA IS NOT "BAD", IT IS ONE OF THE OUTCOMES FROM CERTAIN SORTS OF CHOICES. ALL IS CHOICE AND THE RAMIFICATION OF CHOICE. YOUR MONADS, CONFIGURATIONS, AGREEMENTS, AND SIMILAR ARRANGEMENTS ARE CHOICES. EVEN THE NATURE OF ESSENCE, THE POSITION IN CASTING, AND THE TIE OF ESSENCE TWIN AND TASK COMPANION ARE CHOSEN AS PART OF THE PROCESS OF BEING CAST FROM THE TAO. THAT EVERYTHING IN LIFE CAN BE CHOSEN EXCEPT ROLE IN ESSENCE AND POSITION IN CASTING MAY GIVE YOU SOME IDEA OF THE VASTNESS OF CHOICES AVAILABLE TO YOU, AND THE RANGE YOU MAY WISH TO EXPLORE AS PART OF THE EXPERIENCE OF THE CYCLE OF LIVES.

FOR THOSE WHO CHOOSE TO EXPLORE MORE OF THE "ARCANE" REGIONS OF THOUGHT, THERE ARE MANY TEACHINGS THAT ARE NON-COERCIVE AND NON-DOGMATIC THAT OFFER LEARNING WITHOUT IMPOSING CONDITIONS ON WHAT IS LEARNED AND HOW IT IS LEARNED AND TO WHAT PURPOSE IT CAN BE USED. ALL SUCH DESIGNATIONS INTERFERE WITH CHOICE AND TEND TO CLOUD THE NATURE OF THE TEACHING AVAILABLE. FOR EXAMPLE, TAOIST TEACHING IS LESS COERCIVE THAN CHRISTIAN TEACHING. THE SPIRITUAL DISCIPLINES OF SUCH MARTIAL ARTS AS T'AI CHI ARE LESS COERCIVE THAN THE SPIRITUAL DISCIPLINES OF ISLAM.

ONE OF THE MOST DIRECTLY USEFUL OF "SPIRITUAL" EXERCISES IS WHAT WE HAVE CALLED A CHAKRA SCRUB. THE CHAKRA ENERGY CENTERS IN THE BODY FUNCTION MORE EASILY WHEN "PSYCHICALLY" CLEANED FROM TIME TO TIME, AND THE STRESS LEVEL IN THE BODY TENDS

TO BE LESS WHEN THE CHAKRA CENTERS ARE KEPT "TUNED UP". TO "SCRUB" THE CHAKRAS, WE RECOMMEND THE FOLLOWING TECHNIQUE: TAKE A SCENTED OIL, PREFERABLY ONE THAT IS PLEASANT TO SMELL AND GOOD FOR THE SKIN, AND ANOINT THE CHAKRA CENTERS WITH A SMALL AMOUNT OF THE SCENTED OIL, RUBBING EACH CENTER IN TURN. THE CHAKRA CENTERS ARE LOCATED AT THE CREST OF THE PUBIC ARCH, THE CENTER OF THE ABDOMEN, THE PLACE IMMEDIATELY BENEATH THE JOINING OF THE RIBS—IT IS SOMETIMES CALLED THE SOLAR PLEXUS—THE CENTER OF THE CHEST NEXT TO THE HEART, THE THROAT, THE CENTER OF THE FOREHEAD, AND THE TOP OF THE HEAD. FOR THOSE FAMILIAR WITH THE TECHNIQUES OF ACUPUNCTURE, THESE LOCATIONS MAY HAVE SOME "SIGNIFICANCE" TO YOU IN REGARD TO THE MOVEMENT OF ENERGY IN THE BODY. HAVING ANOINTED THESE LOCATIONS WITH OIL AND RUBBED THE OIL IN *LIGHTLY*, THEN TAKE A SHOWER, PREFERABLY IN PLEASANTLY WARM WATER, AND WASH AWAY THE OIL USING A PLEASANTLY SCENTED SOAP AND SHAMPOO. AGAIN, WHILE SHOWERING, TAKE CARE TO WASH THE OIL AWAY BY SOAPING THE CHAKRA CENTERS AND MASSAGING *LIGHTLY*. THIS IS NOT INTENDED AS AN ARDUOUS TASK, MERELY A WAY TO AID THE ENERGY OF THE BODY. WHEN A FRAGMENT IS ESPECIALLY FATIGUED, A CHAKRA SCRUB WITH THE ADDITION OF THE ANOINTING OF THE PALMS OF THE HANDS AND THE SOLES OF THE FEET AS WELL CAN AID IN RESTORING ENERGY FOR THE FRAGMENT. WHEN THE SHOWER IS COMPLETE, DRY OFF AS USUAL. WE DO NOT PROMISE ANY "DRAMATIC" ALTERATION AS A RESULT OF THIS EXERCISE; WE OFFER IT AS ONE WHOLLY NONCOERCIVE "SPIRITUAL" TECHNIQUE THAT CAN HAVE NO ILL EFFECTS IF OUR INSTRUCTIONS ARE FOLLOWED AS WE HAVE GIVEN THEM. ALL FRAGMENTS MAY CHOOSE TO USE THIS OR ANY OTHER TECHNIQUE THEY WISH, OR NO TECHNIQUE. FOR MOST FRAGMENTS, THE MOST NOTICEABLE BENEFIT OF CHAKRA SCRUBBING IS IMPROVED AND MORE RESTFUL SLEEP, WHICH IS GENERALLY ASSOCIATED WITH A LESSENING OF STRESS.

WHEN FRAGMENTS CHOOSE TO BECOME MORE SELF-AWARE, WE NOTICE THAT THE PROCESS IS OCCASIONALLY DIFFICULT, BECAUSE OF THE SHIFT IN PERSPECTIVE FOR THE LIFE. WE WISH TO POINT OUT THAT ALMOST ALL CHAGRIN AND RENEWED ANGST ARE "BLINDS" OF CHIEF FEATURE, ESTABLISHED TO CLOUD PERCEPTION AND TO "DIFFUSE" THE INSIGHTS. WE WOULD WISH TO SUGGEST THAT FOR THOSE WHO ARE WILLING TO ENDURE THE DISCOMFORTS OF THE PROCESS, THERE ARE BENEFITS FOR ALL CONCERNED IN ALMOST ALL CASES. CERTAINLY WHERE THOSE SURROUNDING THE FRAGMENT ATTEMPTING SELF-AWARENESS ARE CAUGHT UP IN MAYA AND THE LIES OF CHIEF FEATURE, THE EMERGENCE OF SELF-AWARENESS CAN BE UNWELCOME AND "THREATENING". WE MENTION THIS NOT SO MUCH AS A WARNING BUT AS A REMINDER THAT SHIFTS IN PERSPECTIVE OCCASIONALLY PRESENT "UNHAPPY" VISTAS, AND THAT THE RESULTS ARE NOT ALWAYS GREETED WITH UNIVERSAL DELIGHT. LET US PROVIDE AN EXAMPLE: A FRAGMENT WHO BELONGS MARGINALLY TO OUR LITTLE GROUP CAME FROM A VERY TRADITIONAL, VERY STRUCTURED AUSTRIAN JEWISH FAMILY. WHEN SHE BECAME INTERESTED IN STUDIES NOT USUALLY "APPROVED" BY THE FAMILY, THERE WAS MUCH DISMAY, AND EVENTUALLY THE FRAGMENT'S FATHER OFFERED TO PAY FOR PSYCHIATRIC "HELP" FOR HER, WHICH SHE ACCEPTED FOR A TIME, AND THEN DECLINED. FOR THIS FRAGMENT, THE FOURTH INTERNAL MONAD WAS ESPECIALLY DIFFICULT, AND THE INSIGHTS THAT CAME WITH THE COMPLETION OF THE FOURTH INTERNAL MONAD LED TO A DEGREE OF ESTRANGEMENT WITH THE REST OF THE FAMILY, WHICH CONTINUES TO THIS DAY. YET THE FRAGMENT IS SATISFIED WITH HER DECISION AND "PHILOSOPHICAL" ABOUT HER RELATIONSHIP WITH HER FAMILY, FOR SHE DOES UNDERSTAND THAT WHATEVER THE FAMILY'S RESPONSE, IT IS THEIR CHOICE, NOT HERS. JUST AS HER PASSAGE THROUGH THE FOURTH INTERNAL MONAD WAS HER CHOICE, AND THE INSIGHTS SHE GAINED FROM THIS PROCESS WERE THE INSIGHTS SHE CHOSE TO HAVE.

PERMITTING OTHERS TO MAKE THEIR OWN CHOICES IS
NOT ALWAYS AS EASILY ACCOMPLISHED AS A FRAGMENT
MIGHT WISH. THERE ARE MANY TIMES WHEN IT IS TEMPT-
ING—ESPECIALLY FOR FRAGMENTS ON THE ACTION PO-
LARITY—NOT ONLY TO OPEN DOORS FOR OTHERS BUT TO
SHOVE THEM THROUGH THE OPEN DOORS AS WELL. WE
WOULD AGREE THAT OPENING THE DOORS IS GOOD
WORK; SHOVING THROUGH IS NOT.

FROM THE TIME EACH FRAGMENT INCARNATES ON THE
PHYSICAL PLANE, ALL PRESELECTED CHOICES, SUCH AS
OVERLEAVES, AGREEMENTS, KARMA, MONADS, LIFE
TASKS, AND ALL OTHER ASPECTS OF THE LIFE, UNDERGO
MODIFICATION BROUGHT ABOUT BY THE NATURE OF THE
PHYSICAL PLANE ITSELF, WHICH IS ONE OF THE REASONS
THAT THE PHYSICAL PLANE IS THE ONLY PLACE WHERE
ACCIDENTS CAN AND DO HAPPEN. CHOICE IS ESPECIALLY
CRUCIAL TO FRAGMENTS ON THE PHYSICAL PLANE BE-
CAUSE THE WHOLE OF THE LIFE IS A CONSTANT SERIES
OF EVER-CHANGING CHOICES WHICH CREATE NEW AND
FAR-REACHING RAMIFICATIONS FOR THE LIFE. LET US
GIVE AN EXAMPLE TAKEN FROM HISTORY: THE MATURE
SCHOLAR CHARLES STEWART, WHO WAS HEIR TO THE
THRONE OF ENGLAND AT THE TIME OF HIS INCARNAT-
ING—THAT IS, BEING BORN—WAS NOT UNAWARE OF THE
SOCIAL HAZARDS SURROUNDING ROYALTY. WHEN HIS
FATHER WAS EXECUTED AND HE BANISHED, HE RESISTED
THIS DEFEAT NOT ONLY FROM HIS PERSONAL CONDITION-
ING—HE HAD BEEN RAISED TO BE KING OF ENGLAND—
BUT FROM COMMITTMENT TO THOSE FRAGMENTS WHO
SUPPORTED HIS FAMILY AND RISKED SO MUCH TO AID
THEM. DURING HIS LONG EXILE, ALTHOUGH HE CON-
TINUED WHAT EFFORTS HE COULD TO BRING ABOUT THE
RETURN OF HIS THRONE, HE HAD NO REASON TO ASSUME
THAT THIS, IN FACT, WAS POSSIBLE OR WOULD HAPPEN.
HOWEVER, HE CHOSE TO CONTINUE HIS EFFORTS IN THE
FACE OF GREAT OPPOSITION, GENERAL SKEPTICISM, AND
A FAIR ASSUMPTION OF DEFEAT. WHEN HE RETURNED TO
TAKE UP THE JOB HE HAD BEEN RAISED TO DO, HE HAD
VERY, VERY FEW ILLUSIONS ABOUT THE STATUS AND

MIGHT OF KINGS, AND HAD A DIPLOMATIC SKILL THAT WAS SO KEEN AND SUBTLE THAT MANY OF THE COURT SURROUNDING HIM WERE UNAWARE OF HIS CONSIDERABLE ABILITIES, A MISCONCEPTION HE STROVE TO MAINTAIN. THE LOSS OF THE THRONE, AND HIS RETURN TO IT, WERE NOT PART OF HIS LIFE PLAN AT THE TIME OF HIS INCARNATION. HE CHOSE TO FULFILL HIS FAMILIAL OBLIGATIONS AND TO DO HIS UTMOST FOR HIS FAMILY AND THOSE WHO HAD SUPPORTED HIM. ALL THOSE WERE CHOICES. WHILE SOME MIGHT SEE THE RESTORATION OF THE STEWARTS TO THE THRONE OF ENGLAND AS A REWARD, WE REMIND YOU THAT THIS IS NOT THE CASE: THE OPPORTUNITY WAS A MATTER OF CHOICE, NOT ONLY ON THE PART OF THE ENGLISH PEOPLE BUT ON THE PART OF CHARLES STEWART, WHO WAS WILLING TO CONTINUE THE WORK TO THE BEST OF HIS ABILITY, SOMETHING THAT MANY ANOTHER EXILED RULER WOULD NOT HAVE DONE. HANNIBAL, IN THE LONG YEARS FOLLOWING HIS DEFEAT, REFUSED OFFERS OF LEADERSHIP ON A REGULAR BASIS; THIS WAS, OF COURSE, HIS CHOICE, AS WAS CHARLES STEWART'S DECISION TO REIGN HIS CHOICE. CHANGES BROUGHT ABOUT BY THE NATURE OF THE PHYSICAL PLANE AND THE CHOICES OF OTHERS, THE INTERPRETATION AND EXPERIENCES OF THE FRAGMENTS IN QUESTION, AND THE NATURE OF ESSENCE, CASTING, AND, OVERLEAVES ALL PLAYED A PART IN THE PATTERN OF CHOICES OF THESE TWO DIFFERENT-AND-SIMILAR MEN. NEITHER FRAGMENT MADE "BETTER" OR "WORSE" CHOICES THAN THE OTHER. NEITHER FRAGMENT WAS MORE OR LESS EVOLVED BY THE CHOICES EACH MADE. WE CANNOT EMPHASIZE THIS STRONGLY ENOUGH: CHOICE WAS THE ISSUE, NOT THE OUTCOME OF THE CHOICE.

THOSE OF YOU WHO HAVE CHOSEN TO INTERFERE WITH THE LIFE CHOICES OF OTHERS WILL EVENTUALLY CHOOSE TO BURN THE RIBBON SUCH CHOICES CREATE. WHILE KARMIC ASSOCIATIONS ARE RARELY "ENJOYABLE," THEY ARE OFTEN EXTREMELY COMPELLING. OF COURSE WHEN THE KARMIC BOND IS PHILANTHROPIC KARMA, THEN THE ASSOCIATION IS OFTEN QUITE "ENJOYABLE" NOT ONLY

FOR THE FRAGMENTS WITH THE KARMA BUT FOR THOSE
AROUND THEM. KARMA IS THE STRONGEST CHOICE-RE-
LATED EXPERIENCE ANY FRAGMENT ON THE PHYSICAL
PLANE CAN HAVE. THOSE WHO CHOOSE TO ESTABLISH A
RIBBON, FOR WHATEVER REASON, WILL REACH A TIME
WHEN THE CHOICE WILL BE TO BURN THE RIBBON.
KARMA, WE WOULD WISH TO ADD, RARELY RESULTS
FROM ACTIONS BASED ENTIRELY ON MALICE BUT OFTEN
ON ACTIONS BASED ON FEAR. THERE ARE EXCEPTIONS TO
THAT AS WELL, BUT THEY ARE NOT AS FREQUENT. LET
US PROVIDE THREE EXAMPLES FOR THE PURPOSE OF IL-
LUSTRATION: A FRAGMENT ENGAGED IN THE MINTING OF
COINS IN WHAT YOU CALL THE FIFTEENTH CENTURY HAD
BEEN DEBASING THE COINS AND POCKETING GOLD AND
SILVER FOR THE PURPOSES OF OBTAINING WEALTH. WHEN
IT WAS DISCOVERED THAT THE COINS FROM THE SMALL
MINT WHERE HE WORKED WERE DEBASED, HE THREW SUS-
PICION ONTO ONE OF HIS SUPERIOR'S AND GAVE COVERT
"TESTIMONY" AGAINST THE MAN, WHICH RESULTED IN
THE SUPERIOR BEING UNJUSTLY IMPRISONED, WHERE HE
WAS TORTURED AND DIED. WHILE THE MOTIVES HERE
WERE NOT DIRECTLY MALICIOUS, THERE WAS GREAT
FEAR IN THE FRAGMENT WHO WAS DEBASING THE COINS,
IN PART BECAUSE THE PUNISHMENT WAS SEVERE AND IN
PART BECAUSE HIS RESENTMENT OF THOSE SUPERIOR TO
HIM WAS PRONOUNCED, AND HE WAS NOT ADVERSE TO
OBTAINING HIS OWN SORT OF VENGEANCE FOR WHAT HE
PERCEIVED AS GROSSLY UNFAIR SOCIAL POSITIONS.
THREE CENTURIES LATER THIS FRAGMENT TURNED OVER
HIS ENTIRE AND CONSIDERABLE ESTATES TO A DISTANT
COUSIN SO THAT HE COULD SPEND HIS TIME BATTLING
THE TURKS WITHOUT ANY CONCERNS FOR HIS FAMILY
OR POSSESSIONS. THE DISTANT COUSIN WAS, OF COURSE,
THE FRAGMENT HE HAD CAUSED TO BE UNJUSTLY IMPRIS-
ONED. THROUGH THIS "UNACCOUNTABLE" ACT, THE RIB-
BON WAS BURNED.

IN THE SECOND CASE, THE KARMIC RIBBON WAS
CREATED WHEN A FRAGMENT, MALE, WITH A PSYCHO-
LOGICAL ADDICTION TO GAMBLING, SOLD HIS FIVE CHIL-

DREN INTO SLAVERY FOR THE PURPOSES OF GAINING MORE MONEY FOR HIS GAMBLING. THIS WAS IN WHAT YOU CALL LATIN AMERICA THREE CENTURIES AGO, AND THE FRAGMENT IN QUESTION THEREBY ACQUIRED FOUR KARMIC RIBBONS: ONE OF THE CHILDREN OWED THE FRAGMENT KARMA FROM AN EARLIER LIFE AND BY BEING SOLD INTO SLAVERY THE RIBBON WAS BURNED. TWO OF THE RIBBONS HAVE BEEN BURNED THUS FAR, ONE AS A NUN WHO AIDED A LARGE NUMBER OF PREPUBESCENT GIRLS TO ESCAPE FROM BEING SOLD INTO PROSTITUTION, THEREBY BURNING ONE RIBBON AND CREATING THIRTEEN PHILANTHROPIC KARMIC LINKS; THE OTHER WHEN AS A YOUNGSTER IN AUSTRALIA, HE THREW HIMSELF BE- TWEEN A SHIP'S HAND AND A COLLAPSING LOAD OF LUMBER BEING RAISED TO THE HOLD OF A SHIP. THE YOUNGSTER'S ACTION WAS SO "AUTOMATIC" THAT THE ENTIRE EVENT WAS OVER IN LESS THAN THIRTY SECONDS. JUST AS THE GAMBLER HAD SOLD HIS CHILDREN "WITH- OUT THOUGHT", THE AUSTRALIAN YOUNGSTER SAVED THE SHIP'S HAND'S LIFE AT THE COST OF HIS OWN "WITH- OUT THOUGHT."

OUR THIRD CASE IS MORE COMPLEX, FOR IT IS ONE OF THOSE INSTANCES WHERE THERE IS NOTHING THE FRAGMENT CAN DO THAT WILL NOT CREATE SOME KARMA, AND IS COMPLICATED BY THE FRAGMENT'S EN- CULTURATED SENSE OF WHAT IS AND IS NOT "EVIL". THE FRAGMENT IN QUESTION WAS WHAT WAS CALLED A FAMILIAR OF THE INQUISITION IN SPAIN. AS SUCH, HE WAS TO FUNCTION AS A SPY. BEING A YOUNG PRIEST, HE TRULY BELIEVED THAT THERE WERE AGENTS OF THE DEVIL LOOKING TO "DEVOUR CHRISTIAN SOULS." HE WAS CONVINCED THAT THERE WAS A GREAT EVIL TO STAMP OUT, AND DEDICATED HIS LIFE TO THAT ACTIVITY. AMONG MANY KARMA-CREATING ACTS, HE HAD ONE PAR- TICULAR EXPERIENCE THAT WAS MORE "DIFFICULT" FOR HIM THAN OTHERS. THIS FRAGMENT WAS AFRAID THAT A FAMILY OF CONVERSOS—THAT IS, CONVERTED JEWS— WERE ACTUALLY CONTINUING TO PRACTICE THEIR RELI- GION IN PRIVATE, AND HE SET ABOUT WATCHING THEM,

TO "CATCH" THEM. IN THIS PROCESS HE BECAME IN-
FATUATED WITH ONE OF THE FAMILY'S OLDEST TWIN
DAUGHTERS, AND HE "NATURALLY" ASSUMED THAT THIS
SHOWED HOW "DANGEROUS" THE FAMILY WAS. THE
FAMILY IN QUESTION WERE SADDLERS AND HARNESS-
MAKERS, AND THE CHILDREN ALL WORKED AT SOME AS-
PECT OF THE FAMILY CRAFT. IN THIS WAY, THE FAMILIAR
WAS ABLE TO APPROACH THE DAUGHTER WHO HAD BE-
COME THE OBJECT OF HIS INFATUATION, AND WHEN HE
WAS POLITELY BUT FIRMLY REBUFFED, HE DECIDED THAT
THIS WAS ALL THE PROOF HE NEEDED THAT THE FAMILY
WAS STILL, IN FACT, JEWISH, AND THEREFORE THE RIGHT-
FUL PREY OF THE HOLY OFFICE. HE INFORMED THE
DAUGHTER THAT IF SHE MARRIED HIM, HE WOULD DO
ALL THAT HE COULD TO PROTECT HER FAMILY. SHE,
BEING FORMALLY PROMISED TO HER FATHER'S YOUNGER
PARTNER, AGAIN REFUSED, BEGGING THE FAMILIAR NOT
TO HARM HER FAMILY. HE, OF COURSE, REPORTED ALL
OF THIS TO HIS SUPERIORS, AND WHEN THE ENTIRE FAM-
ILY WAS CAST INTO PRISON, HE VISITED THE DAUGHTER
AND RAPED HER, THEN ACCUSED HER OF USING WITCH-
CRAFT AGAINST HIM TO BRING IT ABOUT, WHICH HE
TRULY BELIEVED WAS THE CASE. TEN YEARS AFTER THE
DEATH OF THE ACCUSED FAMILY, HE COMPLETED THE
FOURTH INTERNAL MONAD, AND TO SOME EXTENT
REALIZED WHAT HE HAD DONE. IN ATTEMPTING TO MAKE
AMENDS, HE ATTEMPTED TO SHOW THAT THE INQUISI-
TION WAS NOT DOING ITS JOB RIGHT, WHICH IM-
MEDIATELY THREW HIM UNDER SUSPICION. ONLY BY
REDOUBLING HIS EFFORTS TO FIND HIDDEN "HERETICS"
WAS HE ABLE ESCAPE THE CONSEQUENCES OF HIS IN-
SIGHTS, AND THEREBY INCREASED THE KARMIC BURDENS
FROM THAT LIFE. SO FAR HE HAS BURNED THE MOST RIB-
BONS AS A MEDICAL MISSIONARY IN THE PHILLIPINES,
WHERE HE LABORED UNSTINTINGLY FOR OVER THIRTY
YEARS.

LET US REMARK ON A FEW OF THESE CHOICES.

THE FRAGMENT DEBASING COINS *CHOSE* TO DEBASE
THE COINS, AND THEN *CHOSE* TO IMPLICATE SOMEONE

WHO WAS NOT, IN FACT, GUILTY. HAD THIS FRAGMENT
CHOSEN TO ACCEPT THE LEGAL CONSEQUENCES OF HIS
ACTIONS, HE WOULD NOT HAVE HAD A KARMIC RIBBON
TO BURN. IN THE CASE OF THE COMPULSIVE GAMBLER,
THE INDULGENCE OF HIS ADDICTION WAS, OF COURSE,
HIS *CHOICE*. DECIDING TO SELL HIS OWN CHILDREN WAS
ALSO HIS *CHOICE*, ALTHOUGH IN HIS SOCIETY AT THAT
TIME IT WAS VERY MUCH HIS LEGAL RIGHT TO DO SO.
THE FAMILIAR, CAUGHT UP IN SOCIETAL PATTERNING OF
A VERY RESTRICTED SORT, SAW HIS *CHOICES* AS BEING
HIGHLY CONSTRAINED AND LIMITED IN THEIR APPLICA-
BILITY. HE ALSO BELIEVED THAT HE WAS CONSTANTLY
AT RISK—THIS WAS NOT ENTIRELY INACCURATE, AL-
THOUGH HIS PERCEPTION OF THE NATURE AND SOURCE
OF THE RISK WAS CERTAINLY DISTORTED—AND THERE-
FORE BEHAVED VERY MUCH OUT OF THE NEGATIVE POLES
OF HIS OVERLEAVES. THAT HE *CHOSE* TO WATCH THAT
PARTICULAR FAMILY AT THE SAME TIME HE *CHOSE* NOT
TO PERCEIVE THE REASON FOR HIS "SUSPICIONS" IS OF
GREAT IMPORTANCE, FOR IT DEMONSTRATES HOW COM-
PLETELY FEAR CAN MASK THE ACTUALITY OF EXPERI-
ENCE. HAVING *CHOSEN* TO APPROACH THE DAUGHTER IN
A HIGHLY COERCIVE WAY, THE FAMILIAR ALL BUT
GUARANTEED THAT HE WOULD NOT GAIN WHAT HE
WANTED, AND THEREFORE HE WAS "JUSTIFIED" IN HIS
RESPONSE. THAT HE *CHOSE* TO COMPOUND HIS KARMA BY
"TAKING HIS FRUSTRATION OUT" ON THE WHOLE FAMILY
ALSO SHOWS HOW FEAR CAN SERVE TO ENFORCE THE
ILLUSIONS IT CREATES. HIS EVENTUAL *CHOICE* TO AS-
SAULT THE DAUGHTER AND THEN BLAME HER FOR IT WAS
AS MUCH THE RESULT OF HIS SOCIAL CONDITIONING AS
HIS FEAR, BUT THEY WERE WORKING VERY MUCH IN CON-
CERT. WHEN HE *CHOSE* TO BECOME MORE SELF-AWARE,
THE BURDEN PROVED TO BE ALMOST TOO GREAT, AND
SO, THE *CHOICE* TO CONTINUE AS HE HAD BEEN WAS CER-
TAINLY THE TRIUMPH OF THE CHIEF FEATURES ACTING
THROUGH THE ENCULTURATION OF THIS FRAGMENT. WE
WOULD HAVE TO POINT OUT THAT BECAUSE OF THE SO-
CIAL CONDITIONING, THIS FRAGMENT HAD ONLY ONE MO-

MENT OF ESSENCE CONTACT DURING THAT LIFE, AND IT
CAME WHEN THE FRAGMENT WAS STILL VERY YOUNG,
AND HIS MOTHER'S SISTER CARED FOR HIM FOR A SHORT
TIME. DURING THAT TIME THEY SANG A SONG TOGETHER.
IT WAS, AS WE HAVE SAID, THE ONLY MOMENT OF TRUE
INTIMACY IN A LIFE THAT LASTED FIFTY-THREE YEARS.
THE *CHOICE* OF ESSENCE CONTACT WAS SO TERRIFYING
TO THE FAMILIAR THAT HE SAW IT AS THE VERY MANIFES-
TATION OF "SATAN" AND FLED IT AS IF TRUE INTIMACY
AND ESSENCE CONTACT WERE, IN FACT, THE "FIRES OF
HELL".

CHOICES ARE MOST OFTEN SEEN IN TERMS OF SOCIALLY
CONDITIONED PARAMETERS. THIS IS NOT TRULY VALID,
BUT IT IS NOT UNWISE TO CONSIDER THE LEVEL OF SOCIAL
APPROVAL OR DISAPPROVAL OF A CHOICE WHEN WEIGH-
ING ITS OUTCOME. FOR EXAMPLE, MANY OF THE SOCIAL
RULES ARE ENFORCED BY LAWS. LAWS ARE VALID SOCIAL
CONCEPTS, AND THE MACHINERY OF THE LAW IS VALID.
THE LEGAL CONSEQUENCES OF ACTIONS ARE WORLD AND
PERSONAL TRUTHS FOR THOSE EXTANT UPON THE PHYSI-
CAL PLANE. TO "PAY FOR ONE'S CRIMES", WHILE RARELY
AS FAIR A PROCESS AS THE LAW WOULD WISH TO ADMIT,
IS NONETHELESS A CONCEPT OF WORLD TRUTH. TO BE
EXECUTED FOR COMMITTING MURDER DOES NOT, IN FACT,
BURN THE KARMA THE MURDER HAS CREATED. THE LAWS
OF THE WORLD DO NOT ERADICATE UNIVERSAL TRUTHS.
THOSE WHO ACT AGAINST THE LAWS DO, IN FACT, RUN
VERY REAL RISKS, SOME GREATER THAN OTHERS. THE
CONSEQUENCES OF SUCH ACTS ARE, IN FACT, VALID. FOR
THOSE FRAGMENTS WHO ENDURE LEGAL PUNISHMENTS
OF A SIGNIFICANT SORT, WHO ARE, IN FACT, NOT GUILTY,
OFTEN DISCOVER IN LATER INCARNATIONS THAT THERE
ARE EITHER KARMIC RIBBONS TO BE BURNED OR ACTS OF
EXPIATION OFFERED FOR THE PREVIOUS EXPERIENCES.

IT IS NOT INAPPROPRIATE TO REMEMBER THAT WHILE
THE CYCLES OF LIVES UPON THE PHYSICAL PLANE ARE
ULTIMATELY COMPLETELY "FAIR", BY WHICH WE MEAN
WHOLLY BALANCED, THE INDIVIDUAL LIVES RARELY
ARE, AND OFTEN THE SUPPOSED ABUSES OF FRAGMENTS

STEM FROM CHOICES MADE TO "EVEN OUT" THE CYCLES OF THE LIVES. THIS DOES NOT MEAN THAT IT IS THEREFORE ADVISABLE TO BE UNAWARE OF THE TRAVAIL OF OTHERS, ALTHOUGH YOU MAY CHOOSE TO DO SO, IF YOU WISH. IT IS NOT AMISS TO RECALL THAT YOU ARE ALL CONNECTED ONE TO THE OTHER AND THAT THOSE CHOICES THAT INCREASE THE PRESENCE OF FEAR IN THE WORLD ALSO TEND TO INCREASE THE IMPACT OF FEAR IN YOUR INDIVIDUAL LIFES. FOR THOSE WHO CHOOSE TO ACT OUT OF LOVE—AND BY LOVE WE DO NOT MEAN THE GOOEY SENTIMENTALITY THAT OFTEN GOES IN THAT DISGUISE—THE RESULT IS, OF COURSE, AN INCREASE OF THE PRESENCE OF LOVE IN THE LIFE.

WE WOULD WISH TO REMIND YOU AGAIN THAT IT IS ONLY THROUGH THE POSITIVE POLES OF THE OVERLEAVES THAT ESSENCE FUNCTIONS IN THE LIFE; IT IS THROUGH THE NEGATIVE POLES OF THE OVERLEAVES THAT FEAR FUNCTIONS IN THE LIFE. WHICH YOU CHOOSE IS ENTIRELY UP TO YOU.

CHAPTER 12

COMMENTS ON ALL SORTS OF THINGS

Over the years members of the Michael group have asked questions ranging from the need for glasses to the nature of other ensouled species in the universe. The following questions are a random sampling, taken over many years, of some of the more unusual questions asked of Michael.

Bob Andrews has been a member of the Michael group for about two years; he is a longtime friend and colleague of Sam and Louise Fisher. An Old Scholar, he has studied other spiritual disciplines over the years and often asks comparative questions. About a year ago he made the following observation and question. "I was told in a different study group that we live in an unfortunate part of the galaxy, out at the edge and away from the forces at the center. If this is accurate, then what must the very great beings be like at the center?"

FIRST WE WOULD WISH TO POINT OUT THAT YOU CAN FIND THE SAME SEVEN ROLES IN ESSENCE EVERYWHERE, AND THE SAME FIVE CYCLES OF INCARNATION. HOWEVER, IN A CERTAIN SENSE THERE IS SOME VALIDITY IN THIS PERCEPTION. THE GALACTIC "URBAN DWELLER" IS GENERALLY MORE "COSMOPOLITAN" IN TERMS OF SPECIES INTERRELATIONS THAN THE EDGE-DWELLING "COUNTRY COUSINS".

"Does that mean us—country cousins?" Bob wanted the term clarified.

OF COURSE. THERE ARE A FEW ADVANTAGES TO BEING COUNTRY COUSINS, INCIDENTALLY. THERE IS LESS COMPLEXITY OF RADIATIONAL INFLUENCES ON THE RIM OF THE GALAXY THAN THERE IS AT THE CENTER, AND THIS MAKES POSSIBLE A MUCH BROADER SPECTRUM OF EVOLUTIONARY DEVELOPMENT IN TERMS OF LIFE FORMS. THE ABUNDANCE OF ANIMAL LIFE ON THIS PLANET IS MOST UNUSUAL, AND THE POSSIBILITY FOR A WIDE VARIETY OF EXPERIENCE WITH ANIMALS IS NOT UNUSUAL FOR YOUR SPECIES. THERE ARE OTHER ENSOULED SPECIES WHO HAVE RELATIVELY FEW OTHER LIFE FORMS FOR INTERACTION. WHILE WE DO NOT MEAN TO IMPLY THAT EITHER STATE IS MORE "DESIRABLE" THAN THE OTHER, WE DO WISH TO ASSURE YOU THAT MOST FRAGMENTS EXTANT ON THIS PLANET AND PLANETS LIKE IT DEVELOP FAR MORE UNDERSTANDING OF ANIMAL DIVERSITY THAN DO THOSE FRAGMENTS WHOSE WORLDS ARE LESS DIVERSE.

Along similar lines, Abby Horne asked the following question: "Given that Michael has said we are not the 'beau ideal' of the universe, is there a physical 'norm' that is more usual for ensouled species?"

THIS IS A EARLY MATURE SOUL GALAXY. MOST OF THE ENSOULED SPECIES IN INDEPENDENTLY MOBILE SPECIES HAVE THREE, FOUR, OR FIVE SEXES—AT LEAST, YOU WOULD TEND TO PERCEIVE THEM THAT WAY—AND THE MEMBERS OF THE SPECIES ARE PHYSICALLY EQUIPPED TO MANIPULATE THE ENVIRONMENT AND THUS ARE CAPABLE OF AND DO CREATE SHELTERS WHICH ARE DECORATED WHEN AND WHERE POSSIBLE; THIS INCLUDES MOST GATHERING PLACES, AS WELL AS HABITATIONS. ALMOST ALL ENSOULED SPECIES WHO ARE INDEPENDENTLY MOBILE HAVE SOME SYSTEM OF FORMALIZED INSTRUCTION WHEREBY THE YOUNG ARE TAUGHT AND ENCULTURATED. AMONG SPECIES WHERE ONLY TWO OR ONE SEX EXISTS, A CHANGE OF SEX DURING THE LIFE IS MORE STANDARD THAN THE ARRANGEMENT YOUR SPECIES HAS.

MOST INDEPENDENTLY MOBILE ENSOULED SPECIES CARE FOR THEIR YOUNG FOR FROM FIFTEEN TO TWENTY-FIVE PERCENT OF THEIR LIVES. MOST INDEPENDENTLY MOBILE ENSOULED SPECIES ARE REQUIRED TO PROVIDE SOME SORT OF DEFENSE AGAINST THE FORCES OF THE ENVIRONMENT. ALL ENSOULED SPECIES FACE SOME HAZARD OF DIET. ALTHOUGH IT CONSTITUTES A WORLD TRUTH, APPETITCY CAN BE VIEWED AS A UNIVERSAL WORLD TRUTH. MOST ENSOULED AND INDEPENDENTLY MOBILE SPECIES RAISE MORE THAN ONE YOUNG IF THEY RAISE YOUNG AT ALL, AND SEVENTY PERCENT OF INDEPENDENTLY MOBILE ENSOULED SPECIES PAST MID-CYCLE YOUNG SOUL EVOLUTION HAVE DEVELOPED SOME MEANS OTHER THAN ABSTINENCE FOR CONTROLLING FERTILITY AND REGULATING SOME ASPECT OF REPRODUCTION. ALL ENSOULED SPECIES ON THE PHYSICAL PLANE, INDEPENDENTLY MOBILE OR NOT, ARE SUBJECT TO THE "TIDAL" INFLUENCES OF WHAT YOU CALL ASTROLOGY, AND ALL ENSOULED SPECIES ARE DEFINED BY ROLE IN ESSENCE AND POSITION IN CASTING, WHICH SUPERSEDES ALL OTHER CONSIDERATIONS. INCIDENTALLY, ABIGAIL, THE 'BEAU IDEAL' OF INDEPENDENTLY MOBILE ENSOULED SPECIES MORE CLOSELY RESEMBLES A QUADRIPEDAL INTELLIGENT SQUID THAN A BIPEDAL SIMIAN.

There have been several times when Roderick has asked about various aspects and possibilities for space travel. Recently he wanted to know: "Given the current state of technology and the basic nature of the technology, is exploration of the neighboring planets possible for manned expeditions?"

WE WOULD THINK THAT IF SUCH EXPLORATION WERE GIVEN A HIGHER PRIORITY ON A BROADER FRONT THAN IS CURRENTLY THE CASE THAT THE POSSIBILITY OF AN EXPLORATION OF MARS WOULD NOT BE AN UNLIKELY VENTURE. HOWEVER, FOR PLANETS SUCH AS VENUS, THE SEVERITY OF THE "CLIMATE" IS SUCH THAT TO PREPARE FOR THE VOYAGE AND TO DEAL WITH THE CONDITIONS

ENCOUNTERED IS CURRENTLY TOO COMPLEX AN UNDER-
TAKING FOR IT TO BE REGARDED AS "WORTHWHILE".
WHAT CONTRIBUTES TO THE PROBLEM AT THIS TIME, OF
COURSE, IS THAT THE STATE OF SPACE STUDY AND
TRAVEL IS STILL ALMOST ENTIRELY DEFINED BY PLANET-
ARY PARAMETERS RATHER THAN THOSE OF SPACE. SHIPS
THAT ARE DESIGNED TO DEAL WITH THE STRESSES OF
GRAVITY AND ATMOSPHERE ARE, OF COURSE, THE PRI-
MARY CONCERN OF THE VARIOUS GROUPS CURRENTLY
ACTIVE IN THE AREA OF SPACE EXPLORATION. THE
TECHNOLOGY USED HAS BEEN PREDICATED ON THE
MAJOR DIFFICULTY OF GETTING OFF THE SURFACE OF
THE EARTH. WHILE WE DO NOT DENY THAT THIS IS A
VIABLE CONSIDERATION, AND ONE OF CRUCIAL IMPORT-
ANCE TO SPACE EXPLORATION, WE WOULD WISH TO RE-
MIND ALL HERE PRESENT THAT ONCE THE ATMOSPHERE
HAS BEEN LEFT BEHIND, THE REQUIREMENTS OF THE EN-
VIRONMENT CHANGE, AND MUCH OF WHAT HAS BEEN
USED TO GET OFF THE PLANET IS NO LONGER AS IMPOR-
TANT. TO EMPLOY INTERMEDIATE SPACE STATIONS AS A
TRANSFER POINT FOR THOSE VEHICLES DESIGNED TO
DEAL WITH THE EXIGENCIES OF ATMOSPHERE AND GRAV-
ITY TO THOSE DESIGNED FOR THE REQUIREMENTS OF
SPACE MIGHT MAKE THE TASKS ULTIMATELY EASIER.
THAT IS NOT TO SAY THAT IT IS NECESSARY TO DO IT THIS
WAY, BUT GIVEN THE CURRENT TECHNOLOGY AVAILA-
BLE, IT IS LIKELY TO BE THE MOST ECONOMICAL FOR ALL
CONCERNED.

OF COURSE, WE WOULD THINK THAT THE GREATEST
IMMEDIATE BENEFITS OF SPACE IN TERMS OF ECONOMIC
VALUES WOULD COME IN EXPLORING THE ASTEROID
BELT, ESPECIALLY FOR PURPOSES OF MINING, WHICH
COULD BE ACCOMPLISHED WITH MINIMAL HUMAN PAR-
TICIPATION. ASIDE FROM A SMALL MAINTENANCE COM-
MUNITY, THE PRESENCE OF HUMANS COULD BE KEPT TO
A MINIMUM WHILE MAXIMUM PRODUCTIVITY ACHIEVED
THROUGH VARIOUS "ROBOTS" AND OTHER TECHNOLOGI-
CAL EQUIPMENT. WE WOULD WISH TO POINT OUT THAT
NONE OF THESE REMARKS INDICATE NEW IDEAS OR INFOR-

MATION, BUT SINCE THAT WAS NOT THE QUESTION, AND
THAT THE ISSUES WERE THOSE OF CURRENT TECHNOL-
OGY, WE HAVE CONFINED OUR REMARKS.

IT WOULD NOT BE INAPPROPRIATE, HOWEVER, FOR A
MORE FLEXIBLE APPROACH TO THE PROBLEM TO BE EN-
TERTAINED. THERE IS A TECHNOLOGICAL DOGMA TO
SPACE EXPLORATION CURRENTLY ACTIVE THAT HAS LIT-
TLE BEARING ON MUCH THOUGHT AND EXPERIMENTA-
TION THAT COULD PROVE OF ENORMOUS BENEFIT,
SHOULD ANY IN A POSITION TO ACT CHOOSE TO EXAMINE
THE VARIOUS POSSIBILITIES.

"If the body is disassembled for space travel, where is
Essence?"

ON THE LOWER ASTRAL PLANE, AS ARE MANY PEOPLE
IN SURGERY, FOR EXAMPLE, OR OTHER EXTREME PHYSI-
CAL SHOCK. MANY FRAGMENTS DESCRIBE THE EXPERI-
ENCE OF BEING OUT OF THEIR BODIES AT TIMES OF EX-
TREME PHYSICAL SHOCK—THIS IS NOT AT ALL UNCOM-
MON. OFTEN SUCH FRAGMENTS WILL "WATCH" THEIR
BODIES FROM WHAT IS INTERPRETED AS "THE CEILING".

"Would Michael describe the various intellectual stages
we need to achieve enough knowledge and skill to make
space travel practical and possible?"

THE "CROSSBREEDING" OF ASTROPHYSICS AND METAL-
LURGY MIGHT PROVIDE INSIGHTS USEFUL TO DEVELOPING
VEHICLES SPECIFICALLY DESIGNED TO ACCOMMODATE
THE EXIGENCIES OF SPACE TRAVEL. CURRENT VEHICLES
ARE OF NECESSITY PREDICATED UPON THE REQUIRE-
MENTS OF ATMOSPHERIC AND GRAVITATIONAL STRESSES
AND PRESSURES AND ARE THEREFORE, IN FACT, "UN-
ECONOMICAL" AND CLUMSY IN TERMS OF TRAVEL IN
SPACE. "SHOULD" ASTROPHYSICS AND METALLURGY
COME TO TERMS, THEN WE WOULD HAVE TO SAY THAT
THE NEXT INTERACTION MIGHT BEST BE ACHIEVED BY A
DIALOGUE BETWEEN STRUCTURAL ENGINEERS AND

THEORETICAL MATHEMATICIANS TO ESTABLISH VIABLE PARAMETERS AND TOLERANCES FOR PRACTICAL TRAVEL AND EXPLORATION. AT THAT POINT PALEONTOLOGISTS AND OTHER EVOLUTIONARY BIOLOGISTS, ETHNOLOGISTS, AND SEVERAL MADCAP PHILOSOPHERS MIGHT BE OF USE IN PREPARING THOSE VENTURING OUTWARD FOR THE SHOCK OF MOVING BEYOND THE SPECIES AND THE "NATURAL" ENVIRONMENT. LET US ASSURE YOU THAT THIS SHOCK IS ENORMOUS, AND IN COMPARISON CULTURE SHOCK IS MERELY A DEMONSTRATION IN BAD MANNERS. THERE ARE OTHER DISCIPLINES THAT HAVE YET TO EVOLVE THAT WOULD AID IN SUCH EXPLORATIONS, SUCH AS "THERMOMUSICOLOGISTS".

Not long ago Camille asked a question that she admitted had been brewing in her for a long time. "I know that Michael doesn't experience time as we do, but metaphorically, how do they spend their day?"

YES, IT IS VALID TO UNDERSTAND THAT WE DO NOT EXPERIENCE TIME AS YOU DO, AND THAT AS WE ARE NOT EXTANT ON THE PHYSICAL PLANE, THE CONCEPT OF A "DAY" IS LUDICROUS. HOWEVER, WE DO IN OUR OWN WAY ALLOCATE WHAT YOU WOULD PERCEIVE AS TIME TO VARIOUS ASPECTS OF OUR EVOLUTION. IN TERMS OF WHAT YOU WOULD DEFINE AS OUR "DAY", WE SPEND A THIRD OF IT IN UNITY WHEREIN WE COMPARE ALL PREVIOUS EXPERIENCES AND CURRENT INQUIRIES AND WE PROVIDE PERCEPTUAL ACCESS TO THOSE STUDENTS CAPABLE OF ATTAINING VALIDATED ASTRAL PRESENCE. WE THEN DEVOTE A SECTION OF "TIME" TO OUR OWN STUDIES, THE PURPOSES OF WHICH IS TO PROVIDE EVOLUTION TOWARD THE AKASHIC PLANE AS YOU PROGRESS TOWARD THE ASTRAL. OUR PERCEPTIONS OF THE TOTALITY OF ENSOULED EXPERIENCE IS SUCH THAT WE PERCEIVE ALL ENSOULED SPECIES EXTANT UPON THE PHYSICAL PLANE AS POTENTIAL STUDENTS SEEKING AWARENESS OF THEIR OWN EVOLUTION AND THE VALIDATION OF THEIR PASSAGE THROUGH MANY LIVES. WE ALLOCATE A PORTION OF

"TIME" FOR US TO "RETIRE" TO INTEGRATE OUR OWN
ABILITY TO TEACH WITH OUR PERCEPTION OF EVOLUTION,
AND WHERE TRUE INTIMACY AND PROGRESS HAS OCCUR-
RED, WE PERCEIVE OUR OWN BENEFICIAL VALIDATIONS
THAT GIVE ACCESS TO OUR PERCEPTION OF THE AKASHIC
PLANE AND THE BUDDHIC PLANE, WHICH IS INTRINSIC TO
OUR EVOLUTION AND THE EVOLUTION OF ALL REUNITED
ENTITIES, WHETHER IT BE US OR EVENTUALLY ALL OF
YOU, TRAVERSING THESE PERCEPTIONS AND VALIDA-
TIONS INTO THE HEART OF WHAT YOU WOULD CALL THE
TOTAL INTIMACY, WHICH IS THE NATURE OF THE BUDDHIC
PLANE, WHICH IS THE LAST STEP BEFORE ENTRY AND RE-
TURN TO THE TAO, WHICH IS THE ONLY SEAT OF PERFECT
LOVE FOR YOU OR ANY OTHER ENSOULED SPECIES IN THIS
OR ANY OTHER GALAXY DEFINED BY THE NATURE AND
LIMITS OF THE PHYSICAL PLANE.

IN TERMS OF THE VALIDITY OF EVOLUTION, WE WOULD
HAVE TO SAY THAT IN AREAS WHERE RECOGNITION OF
THE VALIDATED FORM HAS BEEN ACHIEVED, WE PERCEIVE
A WIDE RANGE OF EXPRESSION FOR THOSE ENSOULED
FRAGMENTS ON THE PHYSICAL PLANE, AND WHO HAVE
REALIZED THE VALIDITY OF INDIVIDUALIZED VALIDA-
TION OF EXPERIENCE FOR ANY AND ALL FRAGMENTS CUR-
RENTLY ON THE PHYSICAL PLANE—THAT IS TO SAY THAT
ALL FRAGMENTS ARE AS "REAL" AND AS "IMPORTANT"
AND AS "TOTAL" AS ALL OTHER FRAGMENTS. IN RELA-
TION AND JUXTAPOSITION TO PERSONAL EVOLUTION AS
EXPERIENCED ON THE PHYSICAL PLANE AND TO THE INDI-
VIDUAL EXPRESSION OF MATURE AND OLD OVERLEAVES
UPON THE PHYSICAL PLANE, LET US SAY HERE THAT WE
HAVE PERCEIVED THE CONVOCATION OF GROWTH-DESIR-
ING ESSENCES NOT ONLY WITHIN THE DISCIPLINES OF
GROWTH VALIDATION OF THE PHYSICAL PLANE BUT
GROWTH RECOGNITION ON THE PHYSICAL AND OTHER
PLANES THAT REVEAL TO ALL HERE PRESENT, AS WELL
AS ALL SEEKING WITHIN THE PHYSICAL-PLANE EXPERI-
ENCE THE VALIDATION OF EXPANDED PERCEPTION AND
PERSONAL REVELATION. WE WOULD HAVE TO SAY THAT
THOSE FRAGMENTS WHO VALIDATE THE TRANSITIONS OF
THE MATURE SOUL CYCLE ALSO VALIDATE THE TRANSI-

TIONS AND MANIFESTATIONS OF THE TRANSCENDENTAL
SOUL. THOSE FRAGMENTS WHO VALIDATE THE TRANSI-
TIONS OF THE OLD SOUL CYCLE ALSO VALIDATE THE
TRANSITIONS AND MANIFESTATION OF THE INFINITE
SOUL. TRANSITIONS AND PERCEPTIONS CAN PROVIDE
GROWTH FOR ALL FRAGMENTS WITHIN THE PARAMETERS
OF THE PHYSICAL PLANE AS CURRENTLY DEFINED, LEAD-
ING TO EVOLUTION EITHER FROM THE PHYSICAL PLANE
TO THE ASTRAL PLANE OR TO THE NEXT LEVEL AND CYCLE
OF THE PHYSICAL PLANE FOR OLD SOULS. THOSE OLD
SOULS HERE EXTANT WOULD NOT BE AMISS IN EVALUAT-
ING THEIR PERCEPTIONS OF THE PHYSICAL-PLANE MAN-
IFESTATION OF THE ASTRAL PLANE "REALITIES" AROUND
THEM, FOR ALL MATURE AND OLD SOULS HAVE OPPOR-
TUNITIES FOR ASTRAL CONTACTS, SHOULD THEY CHOOSE
TO AVAIL THEMSELVES OF SUCH.

"That'll teach me to ask a question like that," Camille
responded when the answer was finally read back. "There
are a few points"—she laughed, shaking her head in disbe-
lief—"just a few that I find a mite confusing. For us slow
students, Michael, will you clarify some of that?"

ALL PLANES OF EXISTENCE ARE INTERCONNECTED.
EACH LEVEL OF THE CYCLES ON THE PHYSICAL PLANE
ARE RELATED TO CYCLES EXPERIENCED ON THE HIGHER
PLANES. AS PERCEPTIONS AND TRANSITIONS OF THOSE
INCARNATE ON THE PHYSICAL PLANE ARE VALIDATED,
SO VALIDATION OF ANOTHER KIND BECOMES ACCESSIBLE
TO US AND TO ALL FRAGMENTS EVOLVING TOWARD THE
TAO.

Most of the time group members ask few questions about
politics, in part becuase Michael has relatively little to say
on political subjects, and in part because other issues tend
to be of more interest to everyone in the group. However,
not long ago Ben Horne asked a fairly crucial question with
a political base. "What kind of activities can people in this
world undertake to help prevent nuclear war?"

ESSENCE CONTACT, FIRST AND FOREMOST: WE WOULD
HAVE TO SAY THAT ANY TRUE INTIMACY, NO MATTER
HOW FLEETING, WOULD TEND TO REDUCE THE DESIRE TO
RENDER THE "OPPOSITION" TO "RADIOACTIVE SLUDGE".
HOWEVER, THERE ARE INDEED THOSE WHO SEE TRUE IN-
TIMACY AS THE ULTIMATE INVASION AND WHOSE REAC-
TION COULD BE EXTREME. THAT IS NOT TO SAY THAT
INTIMACY HAS NO USE OR THAT EVERYTHING IS "HOPE-
LESS". ESTABLISHING A "LOVING" AND "POSITIVE" AT-
TITUDE TOWARD ALL FRAGMENTS NO MATTER HOW RE-
PUGNANT IS, IN FACT, GENERALLY MORE BENEFICIAL TO
THOSE WHO CHOOSE IT THAN WHAT IS PERCEIVED AS THE
POLITICAL-ACTION GROUPS WHOSE PURPOSE IS DEFINED
AS STOPPING "THE END OF THE WORLD". THOSE ORGANI-
ZATIONS OF ANY STRIPE WHATEVER ARE PREDICATED ON
THE DISASTER SCENARIO AND ARE BY DEFINITION ACTING
OUT OF THE NEGATIVE POLES OF THE OVERLEAVES, NO
MATTER HOW "NOBLE" THE INTENTIONS. WHILE EACH OF
YOU IS FREE TO EXPRESS YOUR OPINION ON THIS OR ANY-
THING ELSE IN ANY WAY YOU CHOOSE TO DO SO, CHOOS-
ING TO SUPPORT THE NEGATIVE VIEW CAN HAVE REPER-
CUSSIONS CONTRARY TO YOUR INTENTIONS.

Michael has discussed the positive and negative aspects
of Overleaves and the impact of negativity before. Last
year, on her return from a music conference, Fenella had
the following question: "While I was at the conference, I
made a resolution not to bitch or complain, though many
others were very vocal in their dissatisfaction. I noticed this
seemed to have a beneficial effect on my chief feature—any
comments?"

THAT IS, OF COURSE, VALID. LET US DISCOURSE ON
THE FUNCTIONS OF THE OPTIMISTIC PERSPECTIVE AND
THE PESSIMISTIC PERSPECTIVE. ALTHOUGH THE PESSIMIS-
TIC IS MORE SOCIALLY ADROIT THAN OPTIMISM, WHICH
IS OFTEN DENIGRATED AS NAÏVE, THE TURN TO PESSIMISM
EXPRESSED THROUGH COMPLAINT OR THORUGH PUT-
DOWNS IS, IN FACT, THE CHIEF FEATURE AT WORK IN A
WAY THAT APPEARS SOPHISTICATED AND WISE AND

"WORLDLY". WHILE IT IS UNFASHIONABLE, OPTIMISM GIVES ACCESS TO THE BROADEST RANGE OF ACTION AND CHOICE, AS WELL AS SUPPORTING THE POSITIVE POLES OF THE OVERLEAVES. WE WOULD WISH TO ADD THAT PESSIMISM, BY "ANTICIPATING THE WORST" AND THERE-FORE IN THEORY PREPARING YOU FOR ALL THAT MIGHT GO WRONG, IN FACT LIMITS CHOICES AND BY PRESENTING THE DIREST PICTURE, SEEKS TO PERSUADE THE FRAGMENT THAT ALL INDIVIDUAL ACTION AND CHOICE IS FUTILE. BECAUSE OF ENCULTURATION AND ACCULTURATION AND SOCIAL CONDITIONING, PESSIMISM IS ONE OF THE MOST INSIDIOUS FORMS IN WHICH THE CHIEF FEATURE MAN-IFESTS AND, IN THE DISGUISE OF REALISTIC APPRAISAL, PULLS THE FRAGMENT TO THE NEGATIVE POLES OF THE OVERLEAVES AND THE REALMS OF FEAR.

"Might there not be dangers in over-optimism?"

PART OF THE HAZARD OF WHAT YOU ARE DESCRIBING AS OVER-OPTIMISM IS OFTEN TIED TO THE FUNCTION OF THE CHIEF FEATURE OF DISTORTING PERCEPTIONS. BY CREATING AN ASSESSMENT THAT IS EXCLUSIVELY POSI-TIVE, THE CHIEF FEATURE SETS UP THE FRAGMENT FOR "FAILURE" AND "DISAPPOINTMENT". IF A REALISTIC AS-SESSMENT IS MADE, BY WHICH WE MEAN A FAIR-BUT-OP-TIMISTIC REVIEW OF THE POTENTIAL, FROM BEST POSSI-BLE TO WORST POSSIBLE OUTCOME, THEN THE CHOICES WILL TEND TO BE ON THE PATH. PESSIMISM ALMOST IN-EVITABLY CREATES A STATE OF MIND THAT BLOCKS OR CLOUDS PERCEPTIONS OF THE PATH, EVEN TO THE POINT OF DENYING ITS EXISTENCE, JUST AS UNREALISTIC AND EXTREME OPTIMISM BLOCKS AND CLOUDS THE PATH BY IMBUING IT WITH DEWY "OPTIMISM" OF A YELLOW-BRICK-ROAD WHERE THE ONLY HAZARDS ARE THOSE OF AR-CHETYPICAL IMAGINATION RATHER THAT REALISTIC, DAY-TO-DAY DIFFICULTIES. MOST FRAGMENTS "BE-LIEVE" THAT IT IS MORE NOBLE TO "BATTLE THE DRA-GONS" THAN TO "MAINTAIN EQUILIBRIUM", WHICH IS, OF COURSE, ANOTHER DISTORTION OF FEAR "ALL DRESSED UP" AS HEROICS.

• • •

Another of Bob Andrews' questions touching on more advanced spiritual studies arose out of a comment Michael had made that Mature and Old souls had access to the astral plane and astral fragments. "Would Michael enlarge on this, especially in its bearing, if any, on spiritual initiations?"

AS MANY OF THOSE HERE PRESENT ARE ALREADY AWARE, MOST "TRADITIONAL" OCCULT INITIATIONS INTRODUCED THE INITIATE TO A "HAZARDOUS" JOURNEY THROUGH AN ALIEN "LANDSCAPE" WHEREIN ALL MANNER OF BENEVOLENT AND MALIGNANT "SPIRITS" WERE ENCOUNTERED, WHICH IS TO SAY: THE FRAGMENT HAD A SOJOURN ON THE ASTRAL PLANE AND OUT OF THE MALLEABLE ASTRAL MATTER CREATED AND EMBODIED THE "VIRTUES AND VICES" THAT THE INITIATE PERCEIVED, OF COURSE, WITHIN HIM OR HERSELF. IN MOST CASES THIS INITIATE WAS ACCOMPANIED BY "GUIDES" WHICH WERE— AND STILL ARE, FOR THAT MATTER—ASTRAL FRAGMENTS OF THE ENTITY TO WHICH THE INITIATED FRAGMENT BELONGED. MANY FRAGMENTS REQUIRE SUCH INTERACTION IN ORDER TO PERCEIVE THEMSELVES AS "WORTHY" OR "CAPABLE" OF THE EXPERIENCE AND OTHER METAPHYSICAL ACTS. FOR THOSE DESIRING THE TRADITIONAL APPROACH THERE ARE SEVERAL SCHOOLS OF THOUGHT WHOSE DICTATES MAY BE EASILY FOLLOWED TO ACHIEVE THAT END. IN GENERAL, WE WOULD ADVISE CHOOSING A RITUAL OF A NO-LONGER-ACTIVE RELIGION IN ORDER TO AVOID MORALISTICALLY ARCHETYPAL CONFRONTATIONS. FOR THOSE OF YOU LESS TRADITIONALLY MINDED, THERE ARE DISCIPLINES WHICH GIVE RELATIVELY EASY ACCESS TO THE ASTRAL PLANE WITHOUT THE SIDE-TRAPPINGS AND FORMALISM OF THE TRADITIONAL APPROACHES. IF SUCH METHODS ARE DESIRED, WE WILL SUGGEST EXERCISES THAT MAY BE BENEFICIAL.

"I haven't followed that up yet," Bob admits, "although I have used the Chakra scrub that Michael told us about, and I find it can be very useful, particularly when I've let myself get too pressured and tired. One of these days I'll probably want to do some more, but I don't feel ready yet. Michael confirmed that it was wiser to hold off until I feel more prepared.''

WE WOULD THINK THAT "JUMPING THE GUN" IN INSTANCES OF THIS SORT CAN SERVE LITTLE PURPOSE BUT TO PLAY INTO THE HANDS OF THE CHIEF FEATURE, OR, IN THE CASE OF THE FRAGMENT WHO IS NOW ROBERT, BOTH PRIMARY AND SECONDARY. WHILE "LAGGING" MAY ALSO INDICATE THE CHIEF FEATURE'S INTERFERENCE, LAUNCHING A FRAGMENT INTO UNPREPARED STUDY IS AN EXCELLENT WAY TO REINFORCE THE HOLD OF FEAR BY LETTING THE ASTRAL EXPERIENCE GIVE FULL REIN TO THE VARIOUS MANIFESTATIONS OF THE NEGATIVE POLES OF THE OVERLEAVES, WHICH FOR EACH AND EVERY FRAGMENT EXTANT ON THE PHYSICAL PLANE CONSTITUTES PERSONAL "DEMONS".

Another of Bob's questions had to do with learning to assess information some workable way other than "what I'll call the scientific method, or deductive reasoning."

WHILE WE BASICALLY WOULD CAUTION ALL FRAGMENTS AGAINST THE VERY "HUMAN" TENDENCY TO LEAP TO PREMISES AS WELL AS CONCLUSIONS, WE WOULD BASICALLY ENCOURAGE INDUCTIVE REASONING AS BEING ON A PAR WITH DEDUCTIVE REASONING. WE REALIZE THAT CURRENT PHILOSOPHIES OF ACADEMIC CLASSROOM INSTRUCTION DO NOT EASILY ACCOMMODATE INDUCTIVE REASONING, NONETHELESS STUDENTS—AND BY THIS WE MEAN, IN THIS INSTANCE, THOSE WITHIN THE FORMAL SOCIO-ACADEMIC FRAMEWORK OF WHAT YOU CALL THE EDUCATIONAL SYSTEM—DO NOT TRULY LEARN TO "THINK" IF THEY ARE NOT AT LEAST CONVERSANT WITH THE INDUCTIVE PROCESS AS WELL AS THE DEDUCTIVE ONE. THE ATTITUDE OF SKEPTIC IS MOST "NATURALLY" DRAWN TO INDUCTIVE REASONING AND AS WE HAVE SAID BEFORE ALMOST ALL INFORMATIONAL ADVANCES HAVE

COME FRAGMENTS WITH THE ATTITUDE OF SKEPTIC. BEYOND INDUCTIVE REASONING ARE THE "WONDER-LANDS" OF ART AND AESTHETICS, AND WE HASTEN TO POINT OUT NEITHER CAN BE "COMFORTABLY" ATTAINED WITHOUT FIRST ACQUIRING THE "KNACK" OF INDUCTIVE REASONING AND NON-LINEAR LOGIC.

Abby had a question related to Bob's. "Does the means by which the information is acquired make a difference—for example, gaining information via reading as compared to getting it through television?"

IN THE PROCESS OF READING THE FRAGMENT ESSEN-TIALLY MAKES THE MATERIAL ITS OWN. IN SOME CASES THIS RESULTS IN TERRITORIAL OR PROPRIETARY AT-TITUDES, WHICH DO NOT TEND TO BE BENEFICIAL. HOWEVER, THE BASIC PERCEPTION OF THE SELF-ACTUALI-ZATION OF KNOWLEDGE IS VALID. KNOWLEDGE WHICH IS ACQUIRED THROUGH SUCH METHODS OF CERTAIN SORTS OF COMPUTER INSTRUCTION AND TELEVISION DOES NOT HAVE THE SAME SORT OF IMPACT. THE KNOWLEDGE "BELONGS" TO THE COMPUTER OR THE TELEVISION, NOT TO THE FRAGMENT. INCIDENTALLY, THIS CAN RESULT IN A REDUCED SENSE OF RESPONSIBILITY FOR ACQUISITION OF THE KNOWLEDGE OR A LACK OF "APPRECIATION" FOR THE RAMIFICATIONS OF THE SUPPLIED INFORMATION. WE WOULD IN GENERAL OBSERVE THAT TELEVISION AND COMPUTER KNOWLEDGE IS PERCEIVED AS SUPPLIED, WHILE KNOWLEDGE ATTAINED BY READING IS RECOG-NIZED AS BEING ACQUIRED. TO SOME FRAGMENTS THIS MAY APPEAR TO BE NOTHING MORE THAN A SEMANTIC QUIBBLE, BUT WE ASSURE YOU THAT THE PERMUTATIONS AND IMPLICATIONS OF SUCH PERCEPTIONS ARE, IN FACT, ENORMOUS.

KNOWLEDGE, INCIDENTALLY, IS ACQUIRED IN A VARI-ETY OF WAYS. ONE OF THEM IS BY ACTUAL EXPERIENCE. ONE IS BY PRIMARY EXPERIMENTATION. ONE IS BY SEC-ONDARY EXPERIMENTATION, BY WHICH WE REFER TO STUDY AND RESEARCH AND THE INTEGRATION OF WHAT

MIGHT OTHERWISE APPEAR UNRELATED TOPICS, AND WHERE ONE CAN GO OVER AND REFINE WHAT HAS ALREADY BEEN LEARNED. ONE IS BY OBSERVATION, WHICH CAN BE DEVELOPMENTAL AS IN READING OR VIEWING FINE ART, THE OTHER IS "STATIC" AS IN BEING SHOWN WITHOUT PARTICIPATION OR RESPONSE, SUCH AS WORKING WITH COMPUTERS AND TELEVISION, WHICH, BY THEIR VERY NATURE, ARE NOT CAPABLE OF TRUE INTERACTION WITH THOSE ACQUIRING INFORMATION. NO MATTER HOW EDUCATIONAL THE CHANNEL, FRAGMENTS VIEWING THE PROGRAMS CANNOT YET ASK THE FRAGMENTS PRESENTING THEIR PROGRAMS TO EXPLAIN OR ELUCIDATE ON WHAT THEY HAVE SAID.

THE MORE YOU CHOOSE TO PURSUE INFORMATION THAT IMPINGES DIRECTLY UPON THE CONDUCT AND PERCEPTION OF THE "NATURE" OF LIFE, THE GREATER THE USE OF EXPERIMENTATION AND PARTICIPATORY OBSERVATION. BY EXTENSION, THE LESS SPECIFIC INFORMATION IS CHOSEN TO IMPINGE ON THE LIFE, THE MORE "STATIC" THE OBSERVATION IS LIKELY TO BE. THERE IS NO ERROR IN CHOOSING TO HAVE SUPERFICIAL KNOWLEDGE OR IN CHOOSING TO PURSUE PROFOUND RESEARCH IN ANY AREA, FOR THIS PART OF CHOICE HAS OFTEN BEEN PART OF THE LESSON FOR A PARTICULAR LIFE: TO RECONCILE EXPERIENCE AND INFORMATION WHICH OFTENTIMES ARE SERIOUSLY AT ODDS. LEARNING TO EVALUATE THE DEGREE TO WHICH EXTERIOR INFORMATION VALIDLY IMPINGES ON AN INDIVIDUAL FRAGMENT'S LIFE IS ONE OF THE MOST COGENT AND ONGOING LESSONS OF THE PHYSICAL PLANE AND ONE WHICH "REQUIRES" CONSTANT REASSESSMENT THROUGHOUT THE LIFE AS THE LIFE ITSELF, AND THEREFORE THE PERSONAL TRUTHS OF THE LIFE, EVOLVES.

PART OF THE REASON FOR THE NEED TO REASSESS, WHERE KNOWLEDGE SHALL BE ACQUIRED IN DEPTH AND SUPERFICIALLY, IS DIRECTLY RELATED TO THE ENORMOUS AND EVER-INCREASING AMOUNT OF INFORMATION AT HAND. FOR MOST FRAGMENTS SUPERFICIAL IS ALL THAT IS DESIRED OF "USABLE", WHICH IN TURN LEADS

TO THE EXPANSION OF SPECIFIC INFORMATION DE-
VELOPED RARELY BEYOND THE LEVEL OF SURFACE
KNOWLEDGE. EXPANSION OF THIS SORT AS "SHOULD" BE
APPARENT, CAN TEND TOWARD "THINNER AND THINNER
ICE" AS MORE AND MORE FRAGMENTS ACQUIRE SUPERFI-
CIAL KNOWLEDGE AND FEWER AND FEWER FRAGMENTS
HAVE SUFFICIENT TIME TO EVALUATE IN DEPTH THE IM-
PLICATIONS OF KNOWLEDGE. THIS, INCIDENTALLY, CAN
BE SEEN IN THE BASIC BELIEF THAT TEACHING IS THE
PRODUCT OF FOLLOWING A LESSON PLAN RATHER THAN
PROVIDING A FRAMEWORK FOR INDIVIDUAL EXPLORA-
TION.

Recently Ben asked for Michael to clarify some of their
comments on the association of Mature cycle souls and the
astral plane. "Are there ways we can open ourselves up to
astral contact, or does it work that way?"

NOT USUALLY, BUT THAT IS NOT TO SAY SUCH CON-
TACT IS THEREFORE "IMPOSSIBLE" OR "UNATTAINABLE".
LET US REMIND ALL FRAGMENTS HERE PRESENT THAT
THE ASTRAL PLANE IS INDEED THE MOST DIRECTLY CON-
NECTED TO THE MATURE SOUL CYCLE, AND THOSE FRAG-
MENTS EVOLVING THROUGH THE MATURE CYCLE HAVE
GREATER "MOTIVATION" TO PURSUE ASPECTS OF ASTRAL
CONTACT THAN DO OTHER FRAGMENTS EXTANT ON THE
PHYSICAL PLANE. THAT IS NOT THE SAY THAT ALL SOULS
CURIOUS ABOUT THE ASTRAL PLANE ARE THEREFORE MA-
TURE SOULS. WE DID NOT SAY THAT AND WE DID NOT
IMPLY IT. WE ARE ONLY POINTING OUT THAT MOST FRAG-
MENTS WHO CHOOSE TO INVOLVE THEMSELVES IN AS-
TRAL STUDIES WILL TEND — AND WE EMPHASIZE TEND — TO
BE MATURE CYCLE SOULS. OFTEN PRIESTS, THROUGH THE
NATURE OF THEIR SIX-NESS, WILL HAVE ASTRAL CONTACT
POSSIBLE THROUGH ALL THEIR CYCLES, AS WILL THOSE
FRAGMENTS OF ANY ESSENCE WHO ARE CAST INTO THE
SIXTH POSITION IN THE CADENCE, OR INTO THE SIXTH
CADENCE. LET US SAY THAT WHERE SUCH CONTACT IS
DESIRED THAT GENUINE EXPRESSIONS OF READINESS TO
ACCEPT SUCH CONTACT AS WELL AS AN ENVIRONMENT

WHERE THE CONTACT CAN BE PERCEIVED AS UNTRAM-
MELED IS THE FIRST STAGE OF PREPARING THE MATURE
SOUL FOR THE POSSIBILITY—NOT THE CERTAINTY, BUT
THE POSSIBILITY—OF VALIDATED ASTRAL CONTACT. OF
COURSE, ASTRAL CONTACT "NEED NOT" BE VALIDATED
AS SUCH FOR IT TO OCCUR. IN MANY INSTANCES SUCH
CONTACT TAKES PLACE WITHIN OTHER PERCEPTUAL
FRAMEWORKS AND IS ATTRIBUTED TO ALL MANNER OF
"SPOOKS" OR "SUPERNATURAL BEINGS" WHICH IS AS
MUCH A MATTER OF CULTURALLY INDUCED EXPECTA-
TIONS AS ANYTHING ELSE. LET US RECOMMEND THAT
FRAGMENTS SEEKING ASTRAL CONTACT BEGIN WITH A
CHAKRA SCRUB, SO THAT ENERGY LEVELS ARE WELL-
BALANCED. IT IS NOT AMISS FOR THE FRAGMENT TO EX-
TEND AN INVITATION FOR CONTACT *ALOUD*, NOT FOR THE
SAKE OF ASTRAL FRAGMENTS, BUT FOR ITSELF, SO THAT
THE INTENTION IS DEFINED, AS WELL AS WHAT IS SPECIFI-
CALLY DESIRED. FOR EXAMPLE: "I WOULD WELCOME CON-
TACT FROM THE ASTRAL FRAGMENTS OF MY ENTITY MAN-
IFESTED THROUGH MY PERCEPTIONS OF COLORS" OR,
"THOSE FRAGMENTS IN THE ASTRAL INTERVAL WHO HAVE
HAD MORE THAN TWENTY PAST ASSOCIATIONS WITH ME
ARE WELCOME TO MAKE THEMSELVES KNOWN THROUGH
REVEALING THE NATURE OF THE PAST EXPERIENCES WE
HAVE SHARED." WE ADD A NOTE OF CAUTION IN THE
SECOND INSTANCE—NOT ALL PAST ASSOCIATIONS ARE
"ENJOYABLE". CONTACT MAY NOT BE OBVIOUSLY
ACHIEVED AT FIRST, BUT IF ASTRAL FRAGMENTS ARE RE-
QUESTED TO PRESENT THEMSELVES IN THE GUISE OF MYS-
TIC OR TOTEMIC ANIMALS, THE CONTACT MAY BE MORE
EASILY VALIDATED AND UNDERSTOOD IF THERE IS
ADEQUATE PREPARATION AND THE PERCEPTIONS ARE NOT
TOO DISTORTED BY FEAR.

Fenella asked about Jessica's decision to stop channeling
and to leave the group. "I don't want her to do something
she doesn't want to do—or doesn't choose to do—but I feel
badly about her leaving. I'd appreciate any comments
Michael can make on this."

FIRST OF ALL, FENELLA, WE WOULD WISH TO REMIND
YOU THAT THE FRAGMENT WHO IS NOW JESSICA IS FREE
TO CHOOSE WHATEVER SHE WISHES IN TERMS OF THIS OR
ANY OTHER ASPECT OF HER LIFE. THAT SHE HAS CHOSEN
TO STOP CHANNELING IS IN NO WAY A "FAULT", AND IT
IS IN NO WAY A "REJECTION" OF YOU.

"It feels that way."

YOUR EMOTIONS ARE NOT INAPPROPRIATE; THEY ARE
INACCURATE. YOUR CHIEF FEATURE HAS PRESENTED JES-
SICA'S DEPARTURE AS DIRECTLY RELATED TO YOU,
WHICH IS NOT THE CASE, AND SPECIFICALLY INTENDED
TO CRITICIZE YOU, WHICH IS ALSO NOT THE CASE. YOU
MAY CHOOSE TO VALIDATE YOUR EXPERIENCE THROUGH
ACCEPTANCE; YOU MAY DENY THE ACCEPTANCE; YOU
MAY IGNORE THE WHOLE THING. WHAT THE FRAGMENT
WHO IS NOW JESSICA HAS DONE IS HER CHOICE FOR HER
LIFE, NOT AN ATTEMPT TO MANIPULATE YOU OR ANYONE
ELSE IN OUR LITTLE GROUP. THIS WOULD BE THE CASE
NO MATTER WHICH OF THE MEDIUMS WERE INVOLVED.

Last month Alison asked about the species of apes that
became human beings. "How did we choose them for ensoulment, if that's what happened, and why?"

THE SPECIES OF APES SELECTED WERE MOST "APPROP-
RIATE" FOR THE NATURE OF THE TASKS OF THE FRAG-
MENTS—SPECIES DO HAVE CERTAIN TASKS ASSOCIATED
WITH ENSOULMENT, AND YOURS IS NO EXCEPTION. THE
APES IN QUESTION WERE ALREADY SUFFICIENTLY
EVOLVED TO HAVE A HIGH LEVEL OF SOCIAL ORDER AND
THE RUDIMENTS OF WHAT MIGHT BE CALLED "FAMILIAL
STRUCTURE" AND "TRIBAL IDENTITY". WHILE THIS IS BY
NO MEANS LIMITED TO THE APES IN QUESTION, THE "AD-
VANTAGES" OF THE SPECIES WAS SUCH THAT IT MADE
ENSOULMENT PARTICULARLY "EFFECTIVE" IN THAT THE
PROCESS OF PHYSICAL EVOLUTION WAS FAR ENOUGH AD-
VANCED TO PERMIT SOUL-CYCLE EVOLUTION TO PROCEED
WITH MINIMAL DIFFICULTIES. THE SELECTION OF THE

SPECIES OF APE AUGMENTED THE SPECIES "PROGRAM-MING" AT WHAT YOU MIGHT CALL "APE CENTRAL", YOU, AS WE HAVE POINTED OUT MANY TIMES BEFORE, ARE STILL SIMIAN MAMMALS, AND THERE ARE ASPECTS OF THE NATURE OF YOUR INCARNATIONS THAT ARE DIR-ECTLY RESPONSIVE TO BEING SIMIAN MAMMALS. HOW-EVER, YOU ARE ALSO INCARNATE SOULS EXPERIENCING THE EVOLUTION OF THE PHYSICAL PLANE—AS ARE ALL FRAGMENTS EXTANT UPON THE PHYSICAL PLANE, NO MATTER WHAT THEIR FORMS MAY BE—WHICH IN A VERY REAL SENSE SUPERSEDES THE "PROGRAMMING" OF "APE CENTRAL". BY CHOOSING A SELECTION OF THUMBED BRACHIATORS, IT WAS POSSIBLE TO OVERCOME MORE OF THE HAZARDS OF THE ENVIRONMENT THAN IF YOU HAD CHOSEN A SPECIES LACKING THE OPPOSABLE THUMB OR THE BRACHIATOR MOVEMENT PATTERNS. IT IS NOT UN-COMMON FOR THOSE BEING CAST FROM THE TAO TO SELECT A PRIMARY SPECIES THAT IS CAPABLE OF A HIGH DEGREE OF ENVIRONMENTAL MANIPULATION. IF THE PLANET BECAME UNINHABITABLE FOR YOUR SPECIES AND YOU SUBSEQUENTLY SELECTED ANOTHER HOST SPECIES, IT IS LIKELY THAT THE CHOSEN SPECIES WOULD BE LESS CAPABLE OF MANIPULATING ITS ENVIRONMENT. IT IS ALSO LIKELY THAT THE LIVING ENVIRONMENT CHOSEN WOULD BE LESS OF A "CHALLENGE" TO THE SPECIES THAN THE ONE ON THIS PLANET IS. LET US OBSERVE THAT FOR MANY FRAGMENTS NOT CURRENTLY LIVING IN TEMPER-ATE CLIMATES, OR WITHIN TECHNOLOGICALLY AD-VANCED SOCIETIES, THE CONDITIONS OF LIFE ARE OFTEN RIGOROUS AND REQUIRE CONSTANT VIGILANCE ON THE PART OF THE FRAGMENTS LIVING IN THESE AREAS TO ACHIEVE A "REASONABLE" CHANCE AT SURVIVAL.

IF YOU ARE CURIOUS, A FEW OF THE "REASONS" FOR SELECTION OF YOUR SPECIES, ASIDE FROM THUMBS AND BRACHIATION, WERE BINOCULAR VISION, OMNIVOROUS DIGESTION, POTENTIAL LONGEVITY, HIGH PHYSICAL ADAPTABILITY, POTENTIAL BRAIN CAPACITY, AND TON-GUE AND PALATE CAPABLE OF SPEECH.

Almost all of the members of the Michael group have at

one time or another attended sessions with some regularity. However, for the purposes of this book, Leslie and I asked a mutual friend, Phillip Maytag, to help us out; Phil teaches at a southern California university, and for the past few years from time to time has asked Michael questions through Leslie, but he had never attended a session. At our invitation he agreed to attend his first session ever, and to write his impression, before and after the fact, with the understanding that these would be part of the book. Phil is in his early forties, not currently married; Leslie and I have known him for more than dozen years. Phil is sixth-level Mature Priest.

This is what Phil wrote before the session: "My feelings about this sort of thing are roughly the equivalent to my attitude toward the possibility of connecting with the right woman and settling down to a properly grounded life: it would be absurd to think that it cannot happen, even that it is not probable—and yet I remain so skeptical about the actual occurrence of such an eventuality that I can no longer harbor any realistic expectations whatsoever of its imminence.

"I am convinced that there are phenomena in the universe that human rationality, limited as it is by the boundaries of our neuropsychology, is not capable of understanding—and perhaps of perceiving. To think that an ancient clockwork model of reality such as implied by the scientific method (a product, after all, of Aristotelian logic) is adequate for describing all and everything in the cosmos seems to be one of the more ludicrous conceits of *Homo sapiens*. Science says that all we need are the right experiments to test any hypothesis and find enough instruments to measure the results. But why should I assume that the human brain is capable even of conceptualizing the right questions, let alone comprehending possible answers?

"And yet, and yet . . . as far as I know, I have never witnessed any event that provided persuasive evidence of paranormal activity. At least, I don't think I have. As a former boy magician with a predilection for mind-reading illusions. I am perhaps more aware than most of hidden techniques that may be employed to suggest the intervention of the supernatural when in fact none has occurred. Not Dunninger, not Kreskin, not Uri Geller. Yet I continue to watch their kind closely.

"I am negatively impressed by the so-called 'New Age' movement. However, under the circus tent of that convention of snake-oil salesmen may be found the occasional sincere individual or example of meaningful research, and so for that much—for offering a platform to the fringe esotericist whose work may prove to be important, after all—we should be grateful. Unfortunately most of what passes for New Age wisdom today is embraced noncritically, by the masses seeking enlightenment, and most of it is California moonshine.

"The entire 'channeling' or trance-mediumship movement currently so popular strikes me as the most suspect. The demonstrations I have seen on TV were all transparently phony, representing nothing more than bad acting and shameless monetary ambition.

"Which brings me to the Michael business. I know Leslie Adams and Quinn Yarbro. I know them to be pragmatists and honorable persons. I know, too, that they have no evangelical motives—neither is actively seeking recruits for the group, nor are they interested in building a network of other groups. They do not charge admission, sell tapes, appear on television, or go about proselyrizing. Their newsletter is not a money-making venture. Nor do the Michael books earn Quinn as much as her fantasy, science fiction, mystery, and horror novels; chances are that a movie novelization of *Friday the 13th Part VII* would be an easier book to write and would bring her a larger advance. So I must draw the conclusion that these two women believe in what they are doing here and that their motives are other than greed or glory. This lends great credibility to the undertaking, in my eyes.

"I must admit, then, that I am simultaneously baffled and enticed. I am curious. I am skeptical. I am open-minded. I hope to be objective. Quinn and Leslie do not seem out to convince me—or anyone else—or anything, only to share the experience with those who may be interested. In this

light, then, I have decided to sit in on a session and see
what happens. The material I have received before now has
been useful; I have no expectations, but the matter is an
itch in my mind that needs to be scratched. Whatever happens should be interesting, whether it turns out to be self-
hypnosis, mass hallucination, manifested schizophrenia,
cross-talk between the hemispheres of the brain á la Julian
Jaynes, New Age bullshit, or misinterpreted glossolalia, or
something else entirely. I hope that I am honest enough to
evaluate the session for what it is, whatever it turns out to
be.''

Of the two questions Phil asked at that session, one had
to do with work conditions and one had to do with the
concept of observer-created reality. "Can Michael describe
this in ways that would be comprehensible to non-physi-
cists?''

LET US OBSERVE HERE THAT WHILE THE ISSUE OF "OB-
SERVER-CREATED REALITY" EXPRESSES A VALID PER-
SONAL TRUTH, THE REAL VALUE COMES IN THE VALUE
OF COMPARING AND CONTRASTING THE PERSONAL
TRUTHS TO WORLD TRUTHS THAT ARE INHERENT IN THE
STATEMENT "OBSERVER-CREATED REALITY". WE WOULD
HAVE TO SAY THAT IN TERMS OF THE PRINCIPLE OF OBSER-
VATION, IN FACT, BESTOWING REALITY, THAT WITH THE
EXCEPTION OF WHAT YOU ON THE PHYSICAL PLANE CALL
THE ARTS, THE CONCEPT IS NOT ENTIRELY VALID, JUST
AS BEAUTY EXISTS WHETHER IT BE SEEN OR NOT, SO
"PHYSICAL-PLANE REALITY" EXISTS EITHER IN PHYSI-
CALLY PALPABLE FORMS OR ENERGETIC REPRODUC-
TIONAL FORMS: EITHER EXPRESSION HAS VALIDITY
WHERE PERCEPTION IS ACTIVE AND WHERE THE FUNCTION
ITSELF IS NOT DENIED. WE WOULD WISH TO SAY, PHILLIP,
THAT THE ISSUES OF "REALITY" ARE THE CRUX OF THE
QUESTION. SUCH THINGS AS THE MOVEMENT OF SOUND
WAVES THROUGH THE AIR, OR MOLECULAR PRESENCE,
HAVE GREATER BEARING THAN PHILOSOPHICAL EX-
TRAPOLATIONS OR METAPHYSICAL AMBIVALENCES AND
AMBIGUITIES. IT IS "EASIER" NOT TO OBSERVE SOME-

THING THAT EXISTS THAN TO "OBSERVE" SOMETHING INTO EXISTENCE, WITH THE POSSIBLE EXCEPTION OF THE DELIBERATE MANIFESTATION OF ASTRAL MATTER.

Phil took over a month to make his after-the-fact response: "I didn't know what to expect when the session began. Would Leslie go into trance? Speak with a fairy voice? Roll her eyes back, rub herself with chicken blood and start writhing like a voodoo queen? I seriously doubted it—as the others arrived, they all seemed eminently sane, intelligent, even cheerful, the bright, pragmatic sort one meets at cocktail parties in university towns—but nothing is certain. We are, after all, existing on the bell curve of probabilities, are we not?

"We sat on chairs, couches, and pillows and chatted amiably, Leslie witty and charming as always. 'When is it going to start?' " I wondered.

"I can't say exactly when I became aware that the session had already begun. The transition was as seamless as a slight shift in topics between friends, with no theatrics of any sort. Apparently one of the questions asked so casually of Leslie (a simple practical matter regarding a business relationship, as I recall) was intended for Michael. And now Leslie was taking her time, measuring her words perhaps a bit more carefully than before, as if trying to be absolutely precise. I noticed that everyone had yellow legal pads or notebooks; now they were jotting down her sentences as if following dictation and hurrying to keep up with the nearly conversational flow. After a few minutes there was a pause and it was evident the answer was over. The person who had asked the question read back the answer—others corrected him or filled in missing words when needed—and then someone else asked the next question. And so it went, one question from each, the response and the reading back, and on around the room.

"There were several people before me, and the process took some time. Sometime shortly after it had begun, I'd started to feel a peculiar thick-headedness, as if my blood-pressure were elevating dramatically. Was a headache coming on? That would be a rare occurrence for me. I have felt that way on a few other times in my life when I was extremely exhausted—which I was not during the session. Nor was I suffering any degree of stage fright; as a teacher, an experienced public speaker, and a former little-theater ham actor, I had no reservations whatever about speaking when my turn came. Still, the headache worsened until it became a great weight, so great that I grew nauseous. I turned clammy, and the blood drained from my face. By the time my first question came up, I wanted more than anything else to lie down and go to sleep. But I stuck it out. . . .

"My second question was the more serious and had a twofold purpose. One, it was about a subject I was seriously researching and struggling to understand at the time: observer-created reality, which is an issue raised by quantum mechanics and the search for Schrödinger's cat. I sincerely sought a better grasp of the theory in order to complete a writing project. Two, it was a kind of litmus test for this whole Michael business. The subject is subtle and complex, one that I know Leslie was not previously familiar with. It's not a topic one can bullshit about for long.

"The answer I received was reasonable and interesting but did at the time seem to be the slightest bit facile. Perhaps I drew that initial conclusion because it was philosophical rather than technical. Upon careful reexamination, however, I decided that it was in some ways as subtle and complex as the question. It proved to be provocative enough to lead my thinking into unexpected areas in the days and weeks that followed.

"Fascinating.

"When the session ended and the participants took their leave, I immediately began to feel better. An hour later I was fine. I haven't had that feeling, that energy drain, since—until tonight. As I undertook to write this recollection, the feeling returned; it has not left me yet. Aspirin does not help, as it did not the night of the session. I don't know if the feeling will come again. I certainly hope not. But my interest has been aroused. I must attend another session and hope for the best."

In regard to Phil's experience, Michael had this to say:

FOR MANY PRIEST AND KING FRAGMENTS THE PRESENCE OF ENERGY FROM ASTRAL OR CAUSAL CONTACT BRINGS VERY DEFINITE PHYSICAL RESPONSE, NOT UNLIKE WHAT OUR MEDIUMS EXPERIENCE WHILE CHANNELING. WE ARE AWARE THAT THE SENSATION CAN BE UNCOMFORTABLE AND DISQUIETING, EVEN FOR THOSE WITH SOME KNOWLEDGE IN "GROUNDING", WHICH THE MATURE PRIEST PHILLIP HAS NOT YET LEARNED TO DO. THAT IS NOT TO SAY THAT THERE IS ANYTHING "WRONG" IN THIS OR ANY OTHER RESPONSE, BUT THAT WITH FAMILIARITY AND SKILL THE DISCOMFORT WILL TEND TO LESSEN. INCIDENTALLY THE TENDENCY OF THE MEDIUMS TO FLUSH OR TURN VERY PALE WHILE CHANNELING IS DIRECTLY RELATED TO THIS ENERGY RESPONSE, AND IT IS NOT AMISS FOR OUR LITTLE GROUP TO KEEP THIS IN MIND, FOR THE LEVEL OF ENERGY NEEDED FOR CHANNELING IS MUCH GREATER THAN IS "OBVIOUS" FROM CASUAL OBSERVANCE; WHEN CHANNELING CONTINUES BEYOND THE POINT OF PHYSICAL EXHAUSTION FOR THE MEDIUM, THE CONTACT, WHILE VALID, WILL TEND TO BE MORE TO THE NEGATIVE. EXHAUSTED MEDIUMS OFTEN END UP BEING THE "BEARERS OF ILL TIDINGS" BECAUSE THE BODY "SELECTS" FOR NEGATIVITY OUT OF THE FATIGUE ENDURED.

The Michael group has extended an open-ended invitation to Phil for any and all sessions he wishes to attend.

CHAPTER 13

MICHAEL: ON PAST EXPERIENCES AND PRESENT LIVES

As we have said many times before, the personality, both true and false, is the construct of a single life. Only the Role in Essence and the position in casting remain from life to life, and in terms of perceptions on the higher planes, those two aspects of fragmentation are the validity of the fragment. That is not to say that personality is without significance or merit—that is most certainly not the case. However, let us stipulate here that such aspects apply to the *LIFE BEING LED*, and as such contribute to the evolutionary perspective that is the cumulative perceptions not only of the individual fragment, but of the cadence, entity, and cadre. To comprehend the nature of the tapestry, it is not inappropriate to consider the interaction of past and present, for once an experience has been recognized and validated, either during the life or in the astral interval, it continues to have validity in the fragment's lives, whether recognized as such or not.

Many of the factors that determine what is true rest, true study, and true play are based upon areas of expertise already acquired through past activity. For example, a fragment who has been a builder of furniture in the past may discover that in this life, part of true rest or true play comes from refinishing furniture.

ANOTHER CASE MAY BE A FRAGMENT FOR WHOM TRUE STUDY IN THIS LIFE IS RELATED TO AMATEUR ASTRONOMY, DOMESTIC DESIGN, AND THE LIVES OF WINGED MAMMALS. IN THIS INSTANCE, THE STUDY RELATES, OF COURSE, TO THREE PREVIOUS LIVES—IN ONE THE FRAGMENT WAS A PRIEST WHOSE DUTIES REQUIRED A CONSTANT OBSERVATION OF THE STARS; IN THE SECOND THE FRAGMENT WAS THE MAJORDOMO FOR AN EXTENSIVE HOUSEHOLD IN MEDIEVAL POLAND, IN CHARGE OF MAINTAINING AND STOCKING NOT ONE, NOT TWO, NOT THREE, BUT FOUR SEPARATE LAVISH HOUSEHOLDS, WHICH HE KEPT RUNNING SMOOTHLY FOR MORE THAN TWO DECADES; THE THIRD RELATES TO THE LIFE BEFORE LAST WHEN THE FRAGMENT AS A YOUNGSTER MADE A HOBBY OF STUDYING BATS. THERE ARE INTERRELATIONSHIPS HERE THAT ARE NOT ONLY VALID, THEY ARE "STEADYING" INFLUENCES IN THE LIFE. SOMETIMES SUCH ELEMENTS ARE CALLED TOUCHSTONES, ALTHOUGH THIS IS IMBUING THEM WITH GREATER SIGNIFICANCE THAN IS PERHAPS APPROPRIATE.

WHEN AN EXPERIENCE HAS BEEN RECOGNIZED AND VALIDATED, THE EXPERIENCE IS YOURS FOREVER. NO MATTER WHAT LIFE, WHAT PERSONALITY YOU CHOOSE, THE EXPERIENCE OF THE PAST REMAINS AS AN ACCOMPLISHMENT AND A STANDARD AGAINST WHICH TO MEASURE THE EVOLUTION OF ESSENCE. THIS DOES NOT MEAN THAT EACH LIFE IS COMPETITIVE WITH OTHER LIVES; THAT IS CERTAINLY NOT THE CASE AND WE WOULD NOT WISH ANY HERE PRESENT TO INFER SUCH FROM WHAT WE HAVE SAID. A FRAGMENT WHO WAS A VIRTUOSO MUSICIAN IN A PREVIOUS LIFE HAS NO GUARANTEE OF REPEATING SUCH AN ACCOMPLISHMENT, NOT ONLY BECAUSE THE EXPERIENCE HAS ALREADY BEEN HAD AND THE NEED TO REPEAT IT DOES NOT EXIST, BUT BECAUSE THE TIME NEEDED TO DEVELOP THE TALENTS AND SKILLS OF A PARTICULAR PERSONALITY AND BODY MIGHT NOT BE REASONABLE FOR A PRESENT LIFE. IT WOULD NOT BE SURPRISING, HOWEVER, IF THE FRAGMENT WHO HAD PREVIOUSLY BEEN A MUSICIAN MIGHT STILL RETAIN A

STRONG SENSE OF MUSICIANSHIP AND HAVE A STRONG
AFFINITY FOR MUSIC, ALTHOUGH NOT NECESSARILY THE
MUSIC HIS FORMER SELF PLAYED, BECAUSE THOSE LES-
SONS WERE LEARNED.

WE HAVE STATED BEFORE THAT OFTEN A FRAGMENT,
UPON LEARNING OF A PRIOR INCARNATION, WILL REGARD
IT WITH CASUAL UNCONCERN OR OUTRIGHT INDIFFER-
ENCE; THIS INDICATES THAT THE LESSONS OF THAT LIFE
HAVE BEEN FULLY REALIZED AND ARE NO LONGER COM-
PELLING TO THE FRAGMENT. LET US GIVE TWO EXAMPLES
TO HELP CLARIFY THIS: A FRAGMENT IN OUR LITTLE
GROUP, NOW A SEVENTH-LEVEL MATURE SCHOLAR, HAS
HAD MANY FORMER LIVES ON NAVAL EXPEDITIONS.
LEARNING OF ONE IN THE EIGHTEENTH CENTURY, COM-
MON RECKONING, THIS SCHOLAR WAS ABLE TO IDENTIFY
THAT LIFE AND FINALLY TO READ A FEW OF THE JOURNALS
LEFT BY HER FORMER SELF. HER ATTITUDE IN GENERAL
NOW IS ONE OF TOLERANCE, AND HER PERCEPTION IS
THAT THE FORMER INCARNATION "DID NOT GET IT". THIS
IS NOT WHOLLY ACCURATE—THE PRIOR INCARNATION
DID INDEED "GET IT" *FOR THAT LIFE*. AS A RESULT, THE
FRAGMENT NOW HAS NO NEED TO "RELEARN" THE LES-
SONS, AND SO REGARDS THE PERCEPTIONS OF THAT LIFE
AS A HIGH-SCHOOL STUDENT MIGHT REGARD A READING
PRIMER. FOR OUR SECOND EXAMPLE, WE TAKE ANOTHER
MEMBER OF OUR LITTLE GROUP, WHO SEVERAL LIVES AGO
WAS A MODERATELY WELL-KNOW COMPOSER OF MADRI-
GALS. OVER THE CENTURIES THE WORKS WHICH
BROUGHT HIM SUCCESS IN THAT LIFE HAVE BEEN EC-
LIPSED BY LATER WORK, AND NOW THE REPUTATION FOR
THAT COMPOSER IS MINOR AT BEST. AGAIN, IN HIS CUR-
RENT LIFE, THIS OLD SCHOLAR PERCEIVES THAT WORK
AS INCOMPLETE AND DISORGANIZED, AS HAVING BITS OF
IDEAS FLYING IN ALL DIRECTIONS. SINCE THIS FRAGMENT
TEACHES MUSIC IN THIS LIFE, HE IS LOOKING AT HIS PRE-
VIOUS WORK THROUGH NOT ONLY THE INTERVENING EX-
PERIENCES AND THE VALIDATED LESSONS OF THAT LIFE,
HE IS ALSO ASSESSING IT THROUGH HIS OWN EXPERTISE
AS A TEACHER OF THE SUBJECT. HE HAS OBSERVED THAT

HE HAS GREAT FACILITY AT WRITING COUNTERPOINT IN THE LATE RENAISSANCE STYLE, BUT THAT HE FINDS IT "BORING" AND "UNINTERESTING", WHICH SERVES TO SHOW THAT THE LESSONS OF THAT LIFE HAVE LONG SINCE BEEN BROUGHT TO BEAR FOR THIS FRAGMENT AND THAT AS A RESULT, THERE IS LITTLE REASON FOR HIM TO BE CAUGHT UP IN THAT EXPERIENCE AGAIN.

WHERE THE LESSONS OF A PREVIOUS LIFE HAVE NOT YET BEEN FULLY INTEGRATED OR THERE ARE ASPECTS OF THE LIFE YET TO BE VALIDATED, IT IS NOT UNCOMMON FOR THE FRAGMENT TO HAVE A FASCINATION WITH THE PERIOD OF HISTORY AND SOCIETY WHERE THE INCARNATION OCCURRED. OFTEN THIS FASCINATION IS NOT ENTIRELY PLEASANT, ALTHOUGH THERE ARE FRAGMENTS WHO CAN SUSTAIN THAT SORT OF INTEREST ONLY THROUGH ROMANTICIZATION OF THE PREVIOUS LIFE. LET US PROVIDE ANOTHER EXAMPLE: A FRAGMENT CURRENTLY WORKING AS A JOURNALIST IN WINNIPEG, OF SCOTTISH AND FRENCH HERITAGE, HAS A FASCINATION WITH THE RUSSIAN REVOLUTION, ESPECIALLY THE DEMANDS OF FACTORY HANDS FOR EDUCATION. HE IS AN AMATEUR EXPERT ON THE SUBJECT, AND ALTHOUGH HE ADMITS TO HAVING VERY AMBIVALENT FEELINGS ABOUT THE REVOLUTION, ITS AIMS AND ITS ACTUAL CONDUCT, HE CANNOT RESIST THE URGE TO LEARN MORE ABOUT IT; HE HAS THE SENSE THAT HE HAS SOMETHING OF PERSONAL IMPORTANCE TO LEARN FROM THAT EPISODE IN THE PAST. WE WOULD AGREE THAT THIS IS A VALID PERCEPTION. IN THE IMMEDIATE PAST LIFE, THIS FRAGMENT WAS ONE OF A NUMBER OF FACTORY WORKERS WHO "LOBBIED" FOR GENERAL EDUCATION, BOTH TO THE TSARIST AUTHORITIES AND TO THE DUMA. THAT LIFE WAS AN INTERRUPTED ONE—THE FRAGMENT WAS KILLED DURING A RIOT IN THE YEAR ONE THOUSAND NINE HUNDRED TWENTY, COMMON RECKONING, AGED THIRTY-ONE. SINCE THE LIFE WAS NOT COMPLETED, MANY OF THE LESSONS HAVE "CARRIED OVER" INTO THIS LIFE AND IN PART ARE EXPRESSED THROUGH HIS PREOCCUPATION WITH THE RUSSIAN REVOLUTION. AS THE LESSONS ARE

BROUGHT TO BEAR IN THE LIFE AND THE PERCEPTIONS ARE VALIDATED AND RECOGNIZED, IT WOULD NOT BE AMAZING TO SEE THIS FASCINATION FADE, AND THE CURRENT PERCEPTION THAT THIS IS A "TURNING POINT" IN TWENTIETH-CENTURY HISTORY, AS HE NOW INSISTS, BECOME MODIFIED TO A LESS STRINGENT ASSESSMENT.

THE PROGRESS OF LIVES ON THE PHYSICAL PLANE IS EVER ONGOING. EACH LIFE CONTRIBUTES TO ALL LIVES TO COME. THIS IS NOT A MINOR CONSIDERATION, FOR THERE IS MUCH IN EVERY LIFE THAT ECHOES INTO LATER LIVES, OFTEN IN MINOR BUT SIGNIFICANT WAYS. THOSE FRAGMENTS WHO HAVE VALIDATED EXPERIENCES OF THE PAST HAVE SOME APPRECIATION OF THIS—SUCH AS THE MATURE WARRIOR WHO IN THIS LIFE IS AN ACTOR BUT COLLECTS ANTIQUE SWORDS—WHETHER THERE IS FULL AWARENESS OF THE "REASONS" BEHIND THE VALIDATIONS.

LET US STATE HERE THAT THOSE FRAGMENTS OF THE MATURE AND OLD SOUL CYCLES HAVE FAIRLY DIRECT ACCESS TO THE TWO OR THREE IMMEDIATE PRECEDING LIVES, AND THOSE LIVES TEND TO HAVE STRONG BEARING ON THE CURRENT LIFE, FOR WHETHER LEVELS HAVE BEEN TRANSCENDED OR NOT, THE MOST RECENTLY ASSIMILATED LESSONS ARE THE ONES WITH THE GREATEST IMPACT ON THE CHOICES MADE. WE DO NOT MEAN THAT THE THREE MOST IMMEDIATE PAST LIVES THEREFORE "PREDESTINE" THE PRESENT LIFE, FOR THERE IS NO SUCH THING AS "DESTINY"; WE DO MEAN THAT LESSONS MOST RECENTLY BROUGHT TO BEAR ON THE FRAGMENT WILL TEND TO BE THE ONES WITH THE GREATEST APPLICABILITY TO THE CURRENT LIFE. THOSE FRAGMENTS WHO CHOOSE TO IGNORE THE PAST ARE, OF COURSE, FREE TO DO SO, BUT WHEN CHOICES OF THAT NATURE ARE MADE, MANY OF THE LESSONS "LIE FALLOW" FOR THE LIFE IN PROGRESS AND ARE RESUMED AT A LATER DATE.

FOR YOUNG SOULS, THIS TENDENCY IS MARKED, AND THE LESSONS OF THE YOUNG SOUL CYCLE OFTEN DEVELOP FROM WHAT MIGHT BE CALLED A REFUSAL TO LEARN FROM THE PAST. THIS, WE HASTEN TO ADD, IS

ONLY AN ILLUSION, FOR ALL LIVES ARE VALID AND ALL LESSONS ARE RECOGNIZED BY ESSENCE. HOWEVER, IN YOUNG CYCLE SOULS, THE NEED TO MAKE IMPACT ON THE WORLD AND TO MOVE THE WORLD IN THE TERMS OF "CHANGING" THE WORLD OFTEN MEANS THAT THE YOUNG SOUL WILL CHOOSE TO BLOCK THE LESSONS OF THE PAST IN ORDER TO COMPLETE THE CHOSEN LESSONS OF THE YOUNG SOUL LIVES. LET US ILLUSTRATE IN THIS WAY: A THIRD-LEVEL YOUNG ARTISAN THREE LIVES AGO WAS A MACHINIST WORKING IN A SHIPBUILDING PLANT IN THE NETHERLANDS DURING THE MAJOR BUILDUP IN LARGE LINERS AT THE END OF THE LAST CENTURY. THIS FRAGMENT WAS KILLED BY A FALLING STEEL BEAM AND RETURNED QUICKLY TO A FISHING VILLAGE IN SOUTH AMERICA. THIS FRAGMENT SPENT THAT LIFE BUILDING SHIPS, DELIBERATELY "UNAWARE" OF THE PREVIOUS EX-PERIENCE SO THAT THE LESSONS REGARDING THE NATURE OF SHIPS MIGHT BE INCULCATED. THAT LIFE WENT RATHER BETTER, AND AFTER MANY YEARS THE FRAG-MENT DIED AND RETURNED TO ITALY, THIS TIME TO WORK ON IMPROVING THE DESIGN OF RACING AUTOMOBILES. IN THAT, THE FRAGMENT ALLOWED SOME PERCEPTIONS FROM THE PAST, BUT AGAIN WAS LARGELY DETERMINED TO "LEARN FROM SCRATCH" IN ORDER TO HAVE TRUE UNDERSTANDING OF WHAT WAS TO BE ASSIMILATED IN THE PROCESS OF ACQUIRING A "NEW" SKILL. THIS IS NOT UNUSUAL FOR YOUNG SOULS, AS WE HAVE SAID BEFORE, AND IT IS NOT INAPPROPRIATE TO KEEP THAT IN MIND WHEN DEALING WITH YOUNG SOULS.

WE DO NOT WISH TO IMPLY THAT ALL THOSE WHO "BLOCK" PERCEPTION OF THE PAST ARE NECESSARILY YOUNG SOULS. WE DID NOT SAY THAT AND WE DID NOT IMPLY IT. WE RECOGNIZE THE "NEED" MANY FRAGMENTS HAVE TO "BLOCK" RECOGNITION OF THE PAST IN ORDER TO GET ON WITH THE PRESENT LIFE. THERE ARE OVER-LEAVES WHICH TEND TO SUPPORT "BLOCKING" AND OFTEN THE OVERLEAVES ARE CHOSEN FOR JUST THAT PURPOSE. OF COURSE, ANY FRAGMENT, NO MATTER WHAT THE SOUL CYCLE OR OVERLEAVES, MAY CHOOSE

TO "BLOCK" KNOWLEDGE OF THE PAST FOR ANY NUMBER OF REASONS, NOT THE LEAST OF WHICH WOULD BE THE CULTURAL PERCEPTION THAT "THERE IS NO SUCH THING AS REINCARNATION" OR THAT "PAST LIVES ARE SIMPLY THE PRODUCT OF AN OVERACTIVE IMAGINATION", TO STATE A FEW OF THE MORE OBVIOUS ONES.

IT IS NOT INAPPROPRIATE FOR FRAGMENTS TO RESPOND TO THE ENCULTURATION; WE HAVE STATED THAT THIS IS AN IMPORTANT LESSON OF THE PHYSICAL PLANE AND ONE WHICH ALL FRAGMENTS LEARN AGAIN AND AGAIN AND AGAIN THROUGH THE CYCLE OF LIVES. TO LEARN TO BALANCE PERSONAL PERCEPTION AGAINST THE "NORMS" OF CULTURE IS GOOD WORK AND A SIGN OF PROGRESS FOR THOSE FRAGMENTS WHO CHOOSE TO VALIDATE THAT BALANCE IN THE LIFE. THAT IS NOT TO SAY THAT TO DO OTHERWISE IS NOT GOOD WORK; IT IS ALL A MATTER OF CHOICE, AND IF THE CHOICE IS FORCED, IT IS NOT THE PRODUCT OF RECOGNITION AND VALIDATION AND THEREFORE NOT WHOLLY VALID IN ANY CASE. TRUE CHOICE CANNOT BE FORCED, FOR THEN THE PERCEPTIONS ARE AT BEST INCOMPLETE; ON THE PHYSICAL PLANE THE NATURE OF MAYA IS SUCH THAT UNDER THE BEST OF CIRCUMSTANCES THERE IS A DEGREE OF ILLUSION IN THE CHOICE—THE MORE PRESSURE THAT IS PART OF THE CHOICE, THE GREATER THE DEGREE OF MAYA, AND HENCE THE MORE INCOMPLETE THE PERCEPTION.

HOWEVER, IT TAKES MORE THAN MAYA TO INVALIDATE A CHOICE; FOR THAT TO OCCUR THERE IS ALMOST ALWAYS A KARMIC RIBBON ATTACHED.

THOSE FRAGMENTS WHOSE PREVIOUS LIVES HAD HAD SIGNIFICANT AMOUNTS OF KARMA EITHER OWED OR OWING TEND TO FEEL THAT THE LIVES ARE NOT ENTIRELY AT LIBERTY, AND IN A VERY LIMITED SENSE THERE IS VALIDITY IN THAT PERCEPTION. WE SAY THAT THE PERCEPTION IS LIMITED BECAUSE FRAGMENTS ARE ALWAYS AT LIBERTY TO CHOOSE, AND THE CHOICES MAY INCLUDE POSTPONING THE KARMIC ASSOCIATIONS FOR ANOTHER LIFE; THIS HAPPENS MOST ESPECIALLY IN THE YOUNG SOUL CYCLE, ALTHOUGH BABY CYCLE SOULS OFTEN GO

TO GREAT LENGTHS TO DISGUISE KARMA FOR SOMETHING
ELSE. IN THE MATURE CYCLE, THERE IS OFTEN A MORE
PRESSING SENSE OF OBLIGATION BECAUSE OF THE NA-
TURE OF THE CYCLE ITSELF, AND FOR THAT REASON THE
FRAGMENTS WHO HAVE KARMIC RIBBONS TO BURN WILL
TACKLE THEM "AS SOON AS POSSIBLE" IN ORDER TO VAL-
IDATE THE PERCEPTIONS. MATURE SOULS ARE MORE
"NEEDFUL" OF RECOGNIZING SUCH TIES AS PART OF THE
NATURE OF THEIR UNDERSTANDING. FOR OLD SOULS,
WHERE KARMA EXISTS, IT IS OFTEN DEALT WITH IN A
"MATTER-OF-FACT" MANNER, WITH COMPASSION AND
DISPATCH FOR THE SAKE OF ALL CONCERNED. THIS IS
ALSO PART OF THE NATURE OF THE CYCLE, AND BY SUCH
DEALINGS THE LESSONS ARE MORE CLEARLY BROUGHT
TO BEAR IN THE LIFE.

FOR THOSE WHO HAVE BURNED A KARMIC RIBBON
WITHIN A LIFE AND HAVE RECOGNIZED IT FOR WHAT IT
IS, THERE IS MUCH BENEFIT, NOT ONLY FOR THE FRAG-
MENT WHO HAS BURNED THE RIBBON BUT FOR THE FRAG-
MENT WITH WHOM THE RIBBON EXISTED. IN OTHER
WORDS, WHEN A FRAGMENT WHO HAS CREATED KARMA
IN THE PAST CAN NOT ONLY BURN THE RIBBON BUT AC-
KNOWLEDGE THE BURNING OF THE RIBBON WHILE LIVING
THE LIFE IN WHICH THE RIBBON WAS BURNED, THE DE-
GREE OF "LIBERATION" BROUGHT ABOUT BY THE BURN-
ING OF THE RIBBON IS GREATER THAN IF THE RIBBON
WERE BURNED WITHOUT COMPREHENSION DURING THE
LIFE.

IT IS OF NOTE THAT FOR YOUNG CYCLE SOULS ALMOST
ALL RELATIONSHIPS ARE VIEWED AS HAVING KARMIC SIG-
NIFICANCE. THIS IS, OF COURSE, RARELY THE CASE. THE
NATURE OF YOUNG SOUL PERCEPTION IS SUCH THAT
WHEN ANY ASSOCIATION IS RECOGNIZED, IT IS SEEN IN
THE MOST EXTREME FORMS POSSIBLE, HENCE THE TEN-
DENCY TO BELIEVE ALL RECOGNITIONS ARE KARMIC,
THAT ALL BODY-TYPE ATTRACTIONS ARE THE RESULT OF
SUCH TIES AS THE ESSENCE TWIN BOND OR—LESS
OFTEN—THE TASK COMPANION BOND. FOR YOUNG
SOULS, THE ESSENCE TWIN BOND IS FAR MORE "ATTRAC-

TIVE'' THAN ANY OTHER, AND THEREFORE ALL STRONG
PHYSICAL ATTRACTION TENDS TO BE SEEN IN THAT LIGHT.

FOR THE MATURE AND OLD CYCLES, THE NEED FOR
SUCH "DRAMATIC ENHANCEMENT'' OF PERCEPTION IS
LESS NECESSARY, ALTHOUGH FRAGMENTS OFTEN IMBUE
RESPONSES WITH GREATER SIGNIFICANCE THAN IS NECES-
SARY. THAT IS NOT TO SAY THAT THE ESSENCE TWIN
BOND IS NOT POWERFUL, ONLY THAT IT IS NOT OFTEN
ENCOUNTERED, AND WHEN IT IS, THE EXPERIENCE, AS
HAS BEEN INTIMATED BEFORE, IS NOT ALWAYS PLEASANT
FOR THE FRAGMENTS CONCERNED.

PAST ASSOCIATIONS OFTEN ACCOUNT FOR STRONG REC-
OGNITION, EVEN IN THE BABY AND YOUNG SOUL CYCLES.
THESE PAST ASSOCIATIONS NEED NOT BE KARMIC TO
HAVE SIGNIFICANT BEARING IN THE LIFE. THEY NEED NOT
HAVE ANY BOND BEYOND THAT OF SHARED EXPERIENCE
IN ORDER TO EXERCISE INFLUENCE IN THE LIFE. WE DO
NOT MEAN TO DISCOURAGE ANY FRAGMENTS, BUT WE DO
WISH TO CAUTION ALL HERE GATHERED THAT TO INSIST
THAT THERE ARE GREATER BONDS THAN THOSE THAT, IN
FACT, EXIST IS NOT ONLY A FUNCTION OF NEGATIVITY,
IT MOST OFTEN GIVES ACCESS TO CHIEF FEATURE AND
THE DISTORTIONS BROUGHT ABOUT BY THE CHIEF FEA-
TURE, WHICH IN TURN CLOUDS THE ISSUE IN THE ASSOCI-
ATION AND CAUSES MISUNDERSTANDING ON MANY
LEVELS. WHEN THE CHIEF FEATURE IS IN CONTROL, THE
LESSONS OF THE ASSOCIATION CANNOT BE BROUGHT TO
BEAR IN THE LIFE IN SUCH A WAY THAT THE LESSON IS
RECOGNIZED AND VALIDATED.

WHEN PAST ASSOCIATIONS HAVE A NEGATIVE ASPECT,
NO MATTER HOW POSITIVE THE ASSOCIATION ITSELF, THE
RECOGNITION IS NOT ALWAYS A PLEASANT EXPERIENCE.
FOR EXAMPLE, TWO FRAGMENTS MAY HAVE BEEN WORK-
ING PARTNERS IN A RECENT PAST LIFE, AND THE PARTNER-
SHIP MIGHT WELL HAVE BEEN A PLEASANT ONE, BUT IF
THE LIVES ENDED TRAUMATICALLY, THAT TRAUMA IS
VERY APT TO "COLOR'' THE PERCEPTION OF THE ASSOCI-
ATION, AND AS A RESULT, THE CONTACT MAY HAVE A
QUALITY OF "UNHAPPINESS'' ATTACHED TO IT, DUE TO

THE TRAUMATIC NATURE OF THE EXIT, EVEN IF ONLY ONE OF THE FRAGMENTS SUFFERED THE TRAUMA. LET US ILLUSTRATE THIS POINT: TWO FRAGMENTS, ONE THE SIBLING IN THIS LIFE OF A MEMBER OF OUR LITTLE GROUP, ONE NOT DIRECTLY ASSOCIATED WITH ANY OF THOSE HERE GATHERED, IN THE LIFE BEFORE LAST WERE SISTERS OF THE CLOTH. AS SUCH, THEY TAUGHT SCHOOLCHILDREN AND WERE GENERALLY SATISFIED WITH THEIR LIVES AND THEIR RELIGIOUS VOCATIONS. HOWEVER, THEIR ORDER WAS IN A PART OF POLAND WHERE BORDER "INSURRECTIONS" TENDED TO OCCUR, AND ONE OF THE "VICTIMS" OF SUCH AN EVENT WAS THE CONVENT WHERE THE TWO FRAGMENTS WERE LIVING. ONE OF THE FRAGMENTS WAS ATTACKED AND KILLED BY THE "INSURRECTIONISTS" AND THE OTHER SUFFERED SERIOUS BURNS, WHICH MADE HER AN INVALID FOR THE REST OF HER LIFE. THESE TWO FRAGMENTS WORK TOGETHER IN THE SAME COMPANY IN THIS LIFE, AND ALTHOUGH THEY HAVE A CERTAIN SENSE OF "CLOSENESS", NEITHER IS ENTIRELY COMFORTABLE WITH THE FEELING, IN THAT IT IS ASSOCIATED WITH THE VIOLENT DEVELOPMENTS OF THE LIFE BEFORE LAST. THE FACT THAT BOTH FRAGMENTS HAVE A VAGUE SENSE OF UNEASE IS, IN FACT, AN INCOMPLETE RECOGNITION OF THE PAST EXPERIENCE, AND IF ONE OR THE OTHER, OR BOTH FOR THAT MATTER, WERE WILLING TO CONFRONT THE PERCEPTION, PROGRESS MIGHT WELL RESULT; WHETHER THIS WILL TAKE PLACE IS A MATTER OF CHOICE FOR BOTH FRAGMENTS.

OFTEN THE LIFE BEING LED AT PRESENT HAS SPECIFIC RESONANCES TO CERTAIN PAST LIVES, BUT LESS TO OTHERS. FOR EXAMPLE, ONE OF OUR LITTLE GROUP WHO IS ACTIVE IN A HIGHLY SPECIALIZED FORM OF JOURNALISM HAS IN THE PAST BEEN A PRINTER, A PAMPHLETEER, AN ACTOR, A COURT JESTER, A VILLAGE SINGER, A CALLIGRAPHER AND SCRIBE, AND A CLERK FOR A SHIPOWNER. THESE LIVES ARE NOT THE MOST RECENT, AND, IN FACT, GO BACK TO THE TIME THIS LATE-CYCLE MATURE SCHOLAR WAS A BABY SOUL. YET, IN TERMS OF THE CURRENT LIFE IN PROGRESS, THESE PAST LIVES

HAVE GREATER BEARING THAN MANY OTHERS, AND IT IS
APPROPRIATE FOR THIS FRAGMENT TO HAVE A STRONGER
SENSE OF THOSE "REALITIES" THAN OF SOME OF THE
MORE RECENT INCARNATIONS. TO CHOOSE WORK THAT
BUILDS ON WHAT HAS BEEN LEARNED IN THE PAST IS NOT
ONLY GOOD WORK, IT GIVES THE FRAGMENT THE OPPOR-
TUNITY TO DEEPEN THE COMPREHENSION OF WHAT THE
ACTUAL MERIT OF A PARTICULAR KIND OF WORK MAY
BE; WHEN THAT WORK IS CLOSELY RELATED TO THE
FOCUS OF ESSENCE, THE EVOLUTION OF ESSENCE HAS
THE POTENTIAL TO BE GREATER THAN WHEN THE FOCUS
OF THE LIFE IS IN ASPECTS DISSIMILAR TO THE FOCUS OF
ESSENCE.

THAT IS NOT TO SAY THAT IT IS NOT GOOD WORK TO
DO LIFE TASKS AWAY FROM THE FOCUS OF ESSENCE, FOR
THAT WOULD PUT LIMITATIONS ON CHOICE, WHICH IS NOT
VALID. OFTEN A LIFE TASK WILL BE CHOSEN THAT IS SPEC-
IFICALLY UNLIKE THE FOCUS OF ESSENCE IN ORDER FOR
THE FRAGMENT TO GAIN NEEDED INSIGHT AND EXPERI-
ENCE SO THAT GROWTH MAY OCCUR. FOR EXAMPLE, KING
FRAGMENTS OFTEN CHOOSE TO CONDUCT A CERTAIN
NUMBER OF LIVES IN SUBORDINATE POSITIONS IN ORDER
BETTER TO COMPREHEND THE NATURE OF AUTHORITY
AND TO HAVE EXPERIENCES THAT WOULD NOT BE POSSI-
BLE UNDER OTHER CIRCUMSTANCES. ARTISAN FRAG-
MENTS OFTEN CHOOSE LIVES REQUIRING SINGLENESS OF
PURPOSE IN ORDER TO LEARN TO DIFFERENTIATE BE-
TWEEN THEIR FIVE CHANNELS OF INPUT, AND TO BE ABLE
TO DISCIPLINE THE ATTENTION TO A SENSE OF ORDER
WITH THE FIVE CHANNELS. SLAVES OFTEN CHOOSE TO BE
IN POSITIONS OF CONSIDERABLE IMPORTANCE IN ORDER
TO ACHIEVE TRUE SERVICE TO THE COMMON GOOD AND
TO COMMUNICATE THE BENEFITS OF THAT SERVICE.
WHERE SUCH ATYPICAL LIVES HAVE BEEN CHOSEN, THE
FRAGMENT OFTEN FEELS "OUT OF PLACE" FOR PART OF
THE TIME, BUT THE LESSONS GAINED ARE NO LESS VALU-
ABLE AND VALID FOR THAT SENSE OF BEING "OUT OF
PLACE". IN FACT, IN SUCH LIVES, OFTEN THE PERSONAL
TRUTHS OF CHOICES ARE BROUGHT MORE STRONGLY TO

BEAR THAN IN LIVES WHERE THE CIRCUMSTANCES ARE
MORE "IN TUNE" WITH THE NATURE OF ESSENCE.

OF COURSE, ALL LIVES ARE VALID, AND ALL HAVE SIG-
NIFICANCE IN THE CURRENT LIFE. HOWEVER, IN THE MAT-
TER OF RESONANCE TO THE LIFE AND TIES TO THE PAST,
IT IS NOT INAPPROPRIATE TO BE AWARE THAT THE NATURE
OF RESONANCE CAN COME FROM OVERLEAVES AS MUCH
AS FROM ESSENCE OR POSITION IN CASTING. MANY TIMES
THE LIVES THAT CREATE THE STRONGEST RESONANCES
HAVE SO GREAT A BEARING ON THE LIFE BEING LED THAT
THEY, IN FACT, DO NOT CONTRIBUTE TO THE ASPECTS OF
TRUE REST, TRUE PLAY, AND TRUE STUDY. TRUE WORK,
AS WE HAVE INDICATED MANY TIMES BEFORE, IS, OF
COURSE, THE LIFE TASK, AND IT MAY OR MAY NOT HAVE
MUCH TO DO WITH THE WAY IN WHICH A FRAGMENT
EARNS A LIVING. IN FACT, WITH YOUNG AND BABY CYCLE
SOULS, THE MANNER IN WHICH THE INCOME IS GAINED IS
OFTEN VERY INCIDENTAL TO THE LIFE TASK, FOR AL-
THOUGH THE YOUNG SOUL CYCLE IS IN MANY WAYS THE
MOST ACTIVE AND "WORLDLY", IT IS ALSO NOT UNCOM-
MON FOR SOME OF THAT ENERGY TO BE DIVERTED IN
ORDER TO AVOID THE TENDENCY TO FANATICISM THAT
MARKS THE LATTER PART OF THE BABY CYCLE AND MOST
OF THE YOUNG CYCLE. AS ONE OF OUR LITTLE GROUP IS
WELL AWARE, BEING AN OLD SCHOLAR IN A FAMILY OF
YOUNG CYCLE SOULS, THE EXTREMISM OF THE YOUNG
CYCLE CAN BE SO MARKED THAT IT PERMITS LITTLE OR
NO DEVIATION IN OTHERS. THE OLD SCHOLAR IN QUES-
TION HAS FOUR SIBLINGS—TWO YOUNG SLAVES, A
YOUNG ARTISAN, AND A YOUNG PRIEST, AND ALL OF
THEM ARE VERY ACTIVE IN VARIOUS ORGANIZATIONS FOR
SOCIAL CHANGE AND REFORM; EACH IS CRITICAL OF THE
OTHERS BECAUSE THEIR "CAUSE" IS DIFFERENT: THE
YOUNGER OF THE YOUNG SLAVES IS ACTIVE IN COMMU-
NITY SERVICE FOR THE INDIGENT AND HOMELESS, ESPE-
CIALLY RUN-AWAY TEEN-AGERS; THE OLDER OF THE
YOUNG SLAVES IS ACTIVE IN EFFORTS TO IDENTIFY AND
CLEAN UP TOXIC-WASTE SITES; THE YOUNG ARTISAN
DEVOTES HIS "SPARE TIME" TO VOLUNTEER WORK IN SEV-

ERAL NATIONAL PARKS WHERE HE CLEARS AND MAIN-
TAINS TRAILS, REPAIRS SHELTERS, STOCKS RESCUE
STATIONS AND SIMILAR ACTIVITIES, AND IN THE WINTER
HE IS AN ACTIVE MEMBER OF THE SKI-PATROL RESCUE
SERVICE; THE YOUNG PRIEST IS A PHYSICIAN WHO DE-
VOTES PART OF HER TIME TO A CLINIC FOR CHILDREN
WITH CHRONIC AND DEBILITATING DISEASES. ALL FOUR
SUPPORT THEMSELVES WITH OCCUPATIONS NOT DI-
RECTLY ASSOCIATED WITH THEIR LIFE TASKS, ALTHOUGH
THE PHYSICIAN COMES BY FAR THE CLOSEST. THE YOUNG
SLAVE WORKING WITH THE HOMELESS EARNS A LIVING
AS A TELEPHONE COMPANY REGIONAL EXECUTIVE; THE
YOUNG SLAVE WORKING TO STOP TOXIC WASTE EARNS
HER LIVING AS A HIGH-SCHOOL MATH TEACHER, IS MAR-
RIED AND HAS TWO CHILDREN OF HER OWN; THE YOUNG
ARTISAN WORKS AS A CAMERAMAN FOR A LARGE TELE-
VISION STATION, IS MARRIED FOR THE SECOND TIME, HAS
TWO CHILDREN FROM HIS FIRST MARRIAGE, ONE STEP-
CHILD AND ONE CHILD FROM HIS SECOND MARRIAGE TO
A WOMAN WHO DOES VOCATIONAL COUNSELING; THE
YOUNG PRIEST, WHO DID NOT MARRY UNTIL SHE WAS
THIRTY-THREE, IS PART OF A MEDIUM-SIZED PRIVATE
CLINIC WHERE MOST OF THE LARGE NUMBER OF PATIENTS
ARE FAMILIES. THE CLINIC HAS A STAFF OF NINETEEN
PHYSICIANS, TEN OF THEM SURGEONS; THIRTY-ONE
NURSES; A LABORATORY STAFF OF FIFTEEN. THIS IS UN-
LIKE THE CLINIC WHERE THE PRIEST WORKS WITH CHIL-
DREN, WHICH IS ALWAYS LOW ON FUNDS AND RELIES A
GREAT DEAL ON VOLUNTEER HELP.

FOR ALL THESE YOUNG FRAGMENTS, THE ACTUAL
TASKS UNDERTAKEN FOR THE LIFE ARE MITIGATED BY
THE "REALITY OF EARNING A LIVING," WHICH MAKES IT
POSSIBLE FOR EACH OF THEM TO AVOID THE TRAP OF
ABSOLUTISM THAT MIGHT OTHERWISE OFFER TOO GREAT
A TEMPTATION TO RESIST. AS IT IS—AS THE OLD SCHOLAR
WILL TELL YOU—THE MAIN FOCUS OF LIFE FOR ALL FOUR
OF THESE FRAGMENTS IS THE WORK THAT IS DONE INCI-
DENTALLY TO THE "WAGE-EARNING", AND IT IS THAT
WORK, THE LIFE TASK WORK, THAT TRULY HOLDS THE

CONTINUED ATTENTION AND ENERGY OF THESE FRAG-MENTS.

IN LIVES TO COME, THE RESONANCES TO THE CURRENT LIVES IS MUCH MORE APT TO BE ON THE WORK THAT WAS DONE APART FROM "EARNING A LIVING" THAT WILL HAVE THE GREATEST EVOLUTIONARY AND EXPERIENTIAL "IM-PACT" ON THE FRAGMENT AND THE CHOICES MADE IN THE FUTURE. ALSO, WE WOULD THINK THAT THE YOUNG SLAVE, WHO ACTUALLY WORKS FOR A TELEPHONE COM-PANY, MIGHT FIND IN FUTURE LIVES THAT "TINKERING" WITH COMMUNICATION EQUIPMENT IS A SOURCE OF TRUE REST FAR MORE THAN, FOR EXAMPLE, CAMPING OR TRAVELING, WHICH WOULD TEND TO RESONATE MORE TO THE LIFE TASK. BY THE SAME TOKEN, SUCH THINGS AS TRAVEL AND CAMPING AND NOMADIC PEOPLE MIGHT WELL BE PART OF WHAT WILL EVENTUALLY CONSTITUTE TRUE STUDY FOR THIS YOUNG SLAVE ONCE THE MATURE CYCLE IS REACHED.

THAT IS NOT TO SAY THAT THESE ASPECTS *MUST* BE CHOSEN, FOR THAT WOULD ABROGATE CHOICE. WE SAY ONLY THAT THEY *MIGHT* BE CHOSEN, JUST AS IN THIS LIFE FOR THIS YOUNG SLAVE TRUE REST CONSISTS OF RAFTING AND NONVIGOROUS CANOEING (HARKENING BACK TO A LIFE WHEN THIS YOUNG SLAVE, THEN A BABY SLAVE, WAS A MERCHANT USING RIVER TRANSPORTATION AS A PRIMARY MEANS OF DELIVERING GOODS AND CONDUCT-ING TRADE), WHITTLING (HARKING BACK TO THREE LIVES WHICH WERE CONCERNED WITH BUILDING AND CARPEN-TRY), AND MASSAGE, WHICH DOES NOT NEED TO HAVE PAST RESONANCES TO BE TRULY RESTFUL IN THAT IT AIDS THE BODY TO BE CAPABLE OF RESTING. TRUE PLAY FOR THIS YOUNG SLAVE CONSISTS OF FLYING KITES (HARKING BACK TO A LIFE WHEN THIS FRAGMENT WAS THE ASSIS-TANT TO ONE OF THE PIONEERS OF HOT-AIR BALLOON FLIGHT), PLAYING WITH SMALL DOMESTIC ANIMALS (HARKING BACK TO MANY LIVES AS A FARMER, FARM-HAND, SERF, FARMER'S FEMALE—WIFE, BONDED SER-VANT, SLAVE, CONCUBINE, ETC.), AND PUPPET SHOWS (HARKING BACK TO A MOST ENJOYABLE LIFE AS A

SEVENTH-LEVEL BABY SLAVE IN WHAT IS NOW JAVA
WHEN THIS FRAGMENT MADE AND REPAIRED SHADOW
PUPPETS USED IN RELIGIOUS AND CIVIC FESTIVALS). TRUE
STUDY FOR THIS YOUNG SLAVE CONSISTS OF THE STUDY
OF THE HISTORY OF THE CONCEPTS OF LAW (HARKING
BACK TO MANY LIVES, AND THE EXPERIENCE OF THE SO-
CIAL CONCEPTS OF LEGAL CODES), LACEMAKING AND EM-
BROIDERY (HARKING BACK TO MANY LIVES SPENT IN
THESE AND SIMILAR DOMESTIC PURSUITS), AND FOLK
MUSIC (WHICH HAS RESONANCE TO ALMOST ALL LIVES
LIVED FOR THIS AND ALL OTHER FRAGMENTS INCARNAT-
ING IN YOUR SPECIES). THE CHOICES OF THESE ACTIVITIES
FOR TRUE REST—WHICH RESTORES THE FRAGMENT'S
ENERGY—TRUE PLAY—WHICH GROUNDS THE FRAG-
MENT'S ENERGY—AND TRUE STUDY—WHICH FOCUSES
THE FRAGMENT'S ENERGY—OF COURSE CHANGE FROM
LIFE TO LIFE, DEPENDING ON THE TASKS AT HAND, THE
OVERLEAVES, THE CYCLE AND LEVEL OF THE FRAG-
MENT'S EVOLUTION, AS WELL AS SUCH CONSIDERATIONS
AS LIFE PLAN, KARMIC RIBBONS, MONADS, AGREEMENTS,
AND ALL THE OTHER ASPECTS THAT ARE PART OF THE
CHOICES MADE BEFORE A SPECIFIC LIFE ACTUALLY BE-
GINS. WE DO NOT MEAN TO IMPLY THAT ALL YOUNG
SLAVES WILL HAVE SIMILAR SORTS OF TRUE REST, PLAY,
AND STUDY TO THE ONE WE HAVE DESCRIBED—AL-
THOUGH IT IS CERTAINLY POSSIBLE—WE MEAN ONLY TO
CITE THIS AS AN EXAMPLE TO HELP CLARIFY CERTAIN
CONCEPTS WE ARE DISCUSSING.

SOME FRAGMENTS PERCEIVE THE ACCUMULATION OF
LIVES AS AN INCREASING BURDEN OR WEIGHT TO BE CAR-
RIED BY THE "DOWNTRODDEN" ESSENCE, WHICH IS MOST
DEFINITELY ADDRESSING THE INSIGHT FROM THE MOST
NEGATIVE POSITION POSSIBLE. IN GENERAL WE WOULD
SUGGEST THAT SHOULD YOU CHOOSE TO PERCEIVE THE
PROCESS OF EVOLUTION AS A SERIES OF FANS, EACH
"VANE" CONNECTING WITH ANOTHER FAN, SO THAT YOU
MAY ASSESS THE IMAGE AS EITHER CHOICE AND ITS
RAMIFICATIONS, OR AS THE PROGRESS OF LIVES. EITHER
IMAGE, WHILE SUPERFICIAL, IS VALID, AND HAS THE AD-

VANTAGE OF NEUTRALITY, WHICH CAN BE OF USE IN EVALUATING THE NATURE AND CONDUCT OF A FRAGMENT'S CHOICES. WITH THIS IMAGE, NO MATTER HOW "FAR AFIELD" THE FRAGMENT MAY "WANDER," THERE IS ALWAYS SOME MEANS TO "GET BACK ON THE PATH". WE WISH TO EMPHASIZE THIS: YOU MAY CHOOSE TO DEPART FROM THE PATH, FROM THE LIFE PLAN, AND YOU MAY ALSO CHOOSE TO RETURN TO IT. IF YOU DEPART FROM IT, YOU ARE NOT THEN "COMPELLED" TO ABANDON IT; YOU ARE ALWAYS FREE TO CHOOSE TO RESUME THE LIFE PLAN, ALTHOUGH IF YOU HAVE DEVIATED FROM IT TO A SIGNIFICANT DEGREE, THE ROUTE BACK TO IT *MAY* BE AN ARDUOUS ONE, ALTHOUGH IT IS NOT *NECESSARY* THAT IT BE ARDUOUS. AGAIN, THE NATURE OF THE JOURNEY IS A MATTER OF CHOICE.

IT MAY BE OF INTEREST TO SOME OF YOU HERE GATHERED THAT FOR MOST FRAGMENTS, THE PROCESS OF MAKING CHOICES IN THE LIFE CAUSES THE LIFE PLAN TO BE RESHAPED. VERY FEW TIMES DOES "EVERYTHING FALL INTO PLACE" AS PLANNED. TO USE A CLUMSY ANALYOGY, THE LIFE PLAN IS LIKE A PLANNED JOURNEY OVER PREVIOUSLY UNTRAVELED ROADS WHOSE CURRENT CONDITION IS UNKNOWN. THERE IS A WORTHWHILE IMAGE HERE THAT IT WOULD NOT BE AMISS TO KEEP IN MIND, ESPECIALLY AS REGARDS CHOICES IN THE LIFE. THE RESONANCES FROM PAST LIVES ARE SOMETIMES PARTICULARLY STRONG WHEN CURRENT DECISION POINT *APPEARS* TO RESEMBLE DECISION POINTS IN THE PAST. IN ALMOST ALL CASES, EXCEPT CERTAIN SORTS OF INTERPERSONAL MONADS, THE CIRCUMSTANCES OF EACH AND EVERY LIFE ARE UNIQUE. EVEN THE INTERPERSONAL MONADS ARE NOT EXACT DUPLICATES, BUT REVERSALS OF THE PRIOR EXPERIENCE. WE WOULD SUGGEST TO ALL FRAGMENTS, WHEN MAKING CHOICES THAT WHAT MIGHT BE THE MOST EFFECTIVE APPROACH IS TO REMEMBER THAT NO MATTER HOW SIMILAR THE CONDITIONS MAY SEEM TO THOSE OF PREVIOUS LIVES, THE LIFE BEING LIVED IS THE CURRENT ONE, AND THE MATTERS UNDER CONSIDERATION FOR CHOICE ARE PART OF THIS LIFE, NOT PRIOR ONES, AS THE

RAMIFICATIONS OF THE CHOICE WILL BE EXPERIENCED AS PART OF THE CURRENT LIFE, AND POSSIBLY IN LIVES TO COME.

WHEN AN EXPERIENCE HAS BEEN RECOGNIZED AND VALIDATED, THERE IS USUALLY NO "REASON" TO REPEAT IT IN TERMS OF THE EVOLUTION OF ESSENCE. AN EXPERIENCE IS JUST THAT—AN EXPERIENCE, AN EVENT THAT HAS TAKEN PLACE, AN OCCURRENCE THAT HAS BEEN PARTICIPATED IN—AND AS SUCH "NEEDS" NO REPETITION. OF COURSE, MOST ESSENCES ARE DRAWN TO CERTAIN SORTS OF EXPERIENCES AND THERE WILL TEND TO BE PATTERNS BASED ON THE "NATURAL BENT" OF ESSENCE. THE EXCEPTIONS TO THIS ARE, OF COURSE, SLAVE ESSENCES, BECAUSE THE SLAVE ESSENCE CAN SERVE THE COMMON GOOD IN ANY CAPACITY WHATEVER. IT IS NOT AMISS TO KEEP THAT IN MIND. FOR EXAMPLE, WE ARE AWARE OF A YOUNG SAGE WHO HAS DIED FOUR TIMES IN THE PAST, FALLING FROM HEIGHTS IN VARIOUS FORMS OF CIRCUSES. THIS YOUNG SAGE IS DEEPLY DRAWN TO THE CIRCUS LIFE, NOT ONLY BECAUSE OF PAST FAMILIARITY BUT BECAUSE THE NEED TO PERFORM IS ESPECIALLY STRONG IN THIS FRAGMENT, WHO IS NOT ONLY A SAGE ESSENCE BUT FIFTH-CAST AND IN A FIFTH CADENCE, WHICH REINFORCES THE SAGE NATURE IN MANY WAYS. THIS FRAGMENT, IN THE FORTY-NINE LIVES HE HAS BEGUN, TWENTY-SIX HE HAD COMPLETED, HAS SPENT PART OF NINETEEN OF THEM IN SOME KIND OF CIRCUS, AND HAS SPENT ELEVEN OF THOSE NINETEEN LIVES PERFOMING ON EITHER THE HIGH WIRE OR THE TRAPEZE. WE WOULD THINK THAT ANOTHER DEATH FALLING FROM THE HIGH WIRE WOULD HAVE LITTLE TO TEACH THIS FRAGMENT, ALTHOUGH IT IS ALWAYS POSSIBLE HE WILL CHOOSE TO DO IT AGAIN.

FOR THOSE FRAGMENTS WITH A SENSE OF PRIOR LIVES, IT IS NOT AMISS TO KEEP IN MIND THAT MOST LIVES ARE NOT SPENT IN POSITIONS OF DISTINGUISHMENT, AND THAT HISTORY IS FICKLE AND MISLEADING IN THOSE WHO ARE REMEMBERED. A FRAGMENT SUCH AS MIGUEL CERVANTES ENJOYED VERY MODERATE FAME IN HIS LIFE, AND THE RESULTS OF HIS SLIGHT CELEBRITY WERE NOT VERY

PLEASANT. THAT HIS WORK WOULD EVENTUALLY BE RE-
GARDED AS LANDMARK LITERATURE WAS NOT A DECI-
SION MADE BY THAT MATURE SAGE, NOR DID THOSE
AROUND HIM ASSUME HE WOULD ATTAIN THE REPUTA-
TION HIS WORK NOW HAS. BY THE SAME TOKEN, THE
MATURE SCHOLAR WHO WAS WILLIAM SHAKESPEARE,
WHILE A VERY POPULAR PLAYWRIGHT AND CHARACTER
ACTOR WHO SPECIALIZED IN CYNICS AND VILLAINS, WAS
PRIMARILY KNOWN TO THE PLAYGOERS OF LONDON; HE
WAS NOT ESTEEMED BY THE SMALL COMMUNITY OF
LITERARY INTELLECTUALS OF HIS TIME, AND HE HAD NO
ASPIRATIONS TO IMMORTALITY; HE DID ASPIRE TO WRITE
THE BEST ENTERTAINMENT HE COULD, IN PART BECAUSE
HE WAS A FAIRLY COMPETITIVE FRAGMENT AND IN PART
BECAUSE THAT WAS WHAT INTERESTED HIM. THAT HIS
WORK IS RECOGNIZED FOR THE HIGH LEVEL OF WHAT YOU
ON THE PHYSICAL PLANE CALL ART WAS NOT OF PRIMARY
IMPORTANCE TO HIM, AND ALTHOUGH THIS FRAGMENT
HAS DONE SOME WRITING IN LIVES SINCE THAT ONE, HE
HAS NOT ACHIEVED—OR DESIRED TO ACHIEVE—THE
SAME CONSISTENTLY HIGH QUALITY OF THE WORK DONE
IN THAT LIFE. INCIDENTALLY, THAT FRAGMENT IS THE
SEVENTH-CAST SCHOLAR IN THE FIRST CADENCE OF
SCHOLARS IN HIS ENTITY; CURRENTLY HE IS A YOUNG
FEMALE ARCHAEOLOGICAL ANTHROPOLOGY STUDENT
WORKING ON A NEW "DIG" RECENTLY BEGUN IN THE
ANDES. WE WOULD VERY MUCH DOUBT IF THIS FRAG-
MENT WILL CHOOSE TO WRITE PLAYS AGAIN FOR SOME
TIME, SINCE DURING THAT LIFE, NOT ONLY WAS MOST OF
THE LIFE PLAN ACCOMPLISHED, BUT WE WOULD HAVE TO
SAY THAT THE LESSONS OF THAT LIFE WERE BROUGHT
TO BEAR, RECOGNIZED, AND VALIDATED. INCIDENTALLY,
THAT FRAGMENT TRANSCENDED A LEVEL SHORTLY BE-
FORE THE CONCLUSION OF THE LIFE. WHILE IT WOULD
BE INCORRECT TO SAY THAT THIS FRAGMENT HAD AN
AGREEMENT TO INFLUENCE THE THOUGHTS, LIVES, PER-
CEPTIONS, AND LANGUAGE OF MANY OF THE FRAGMENTS
EXTANT IN THE WORLD, IT IS TRUE THAT THE NATURE OF
WHAT YOU ON THE PHYSICAL PLANE CALL HIS ART HAS

HAD AND CONTINUES TO HAVE LASTING INFLUENCE ON OTHERS BECAUSE MOST FRAGMENTS CHOOSE TO PERCEIVE THE WORLD AND PERSONAL TRUTHS CONTAINED IN THE "ART".

MUCH OF WHAT INFLUENCES FRAGMENTS DURING A LIFETIME IS NOT, IN FACT, PART OF THE LIFE PLAN. THE DEGREE OF THE INFLUENCE IS OFTEN RELATED TO THE NATURE OF THE OVERLEAVES AS WELL AS THE LEVEL AND CYCLE OF THE FRAGMENT, BUT THE MATTER OF INFLUENCE IS ONE OF THE FACTORS IN LIFE THAT CAN RARELY BE ANTICIPATED; SUCH ANTICIPATION IS NOT APPROPRIATE, FOR IT LIMITS THE RANGE AND EXPRESSION OF CHOICE, WHICH MIGHT BE CONSIDERED SELF-DEFEATING. THE CONDITIONING OF ENCULTURATION DOES A GREAT DEAL TO LIMIT THE PERCEPTIONS OF CHOICE, BUT THAT CONDITIONING IS PART OF THE PROCESS OF LIVING THE LIFE, AND WHILE TO SOME DEGREE ITS IMPACT CAN BE PERCEIVED BETWEEN LIVES, LIKE PAIN, ITS FULL WEIGHT IS RARELY "APPRECIATED" EXCEPT WHILE THE LIFE IS BEING LIVED.

HOWEVER, WE WOULD WISH TO ADD THAT ONCE A FRAGMENT DEVELOPS A "SENSITIVITY" TO WHAT YOU ON THE PHYSICAL PLANE CALL ART, IT IS LIKELY TO REMAIN TO A GREATER OR LESSER DEGREE WITH THE FRAGMENT FOR ALL THE REST OF THE LIVES LIVED. OFTEN THE PERCEPTIONS THAT ARE PART OF WHAT YOU ON THE PHYSICAL PLANE CALL ART ARE ALSO PART OF THE LIFE PERCEPTIONS DURING THE LATER PART OF THE OLD SOUL CYCLE; AT SUCH TIMES—TO PUT IT SUPERFICIALLY BUT NOT INACCURATELY—LIFE TRULY DOES IMITATE "ART".

CHAPTER 14

ABOUT CHANNELING

It has been more than two years since Jessica Lansing did any channeling, well over a year since she attended a Michael session. She has a new job and an interesting and active social life that has no overlap to the lives of the members of the Michael group.

"And frankly, I like it that way." She is not apologetic about her choice, although a note of exasperation colors her words. "For all those years I channeled Michael, that was almost all I ever did other than go to work. Channeling Michael can be a *lousy* social life, and by the time I was through with sessions, I was usually too tired to try much of anything else. I had social occasions linked to the job—anyone working in public relations does—but just social fun, hell, no."

"Do you miss it?"

"Not really," she says in answer to my question. "A year ago I still did, a little. Not as much as I thought I *ought* to miss it, not as much as certain memebers of the group thought I ought to miss it."

"Aside from the social life, was there any particular reason you stopped?"

"No one thing, no. There were a lot of little things, and they piled up. There were people in the group who didn't seem to be getting anything out of the teaching. We'd spend all that time getting answers for them, transcribing and reading back the answers, often very complex answers to complex questions, and lo and behold, two weeks later they were back again asking almost identical questions about the same damned things. They hadn't studied the material. They hadn't used it at all.'' She shakes her head slowly. "And that gets pretty discouraging after a while. And,'' she goes on when she sees I am about to ask something more, "don't remind me that there are times you have to hear something time and time and time again before you get it. I know about those questions—I've asked them myself—but that's not what I'm talking about. I guess I'm talking about what you would call the enlightenment junkies.''

"Don't remind me,'' I chuckle along with her.

"It's always a risk you run in a group like this, and I didn't like saying no to one member of a family, even when I had a strong sense that having both around wouldn't necessarily be a good idea. You know what that can be like. Milly and Leslie tell me that they do enforce limits like that on the group. Five years ago I would have disagreed; three years ago, I wished I'd done the same thing.'' Her smile is rueful. "That was part of it. It was wearing me out. Channeling is incredibly demanding work, and I wasn't giving myself a chance to rest up adequately from it. And there was another thing. I remember I'd been at a memorial service for an old friend.'' She speaks more slowly now. "He'd been in the group for a while, oh, ten, twelve years ago. At the end of the service, before the reception, a woman who knew about the group and had found out that I was the medium called Jessica Lansing in your books came up to me and told me that she was about to apply for a highly paying position and she needed the Overleaves of the three executives who would be interviewing her the next day. At a memorial service!'' Her indignation is genuine and heartfelt. "I said this wasn't the time or the place, and what I meant was that I didn't even want to discuss it. She patted my hand and said she wouldn't push me; she'd phone me later in the evening.'' She deliberately takes a little time to calm down. "When she called, I told her I wouldn't be able to get the information for her. I tried to be polite. She was huffy, and I reminded her that a very good friend of mine had just died. 'But you're a medium,' she said to me. 'You know all about life and death. How can it upset you?' I wanted to scream at her and hang up. But you know how that old dominance/arrogance thing works.'' She laughs once. "Don't look surprised that I still use the vocabulary. I was a channel for more than fifteen years, remember. Not that I 'speak Michael' very often anymore.''

"So what did you say to the woman who wanted the Overleaves?'' I ask, wanting to hear the end of the story.

"Oh, I told her that medium or not, I had lost a friend and I grieved for him. She was shocked. 'Then you don't believe in reincarnation after all,' she said, and I told her that believing in reincarnation had nothing to do with missing people.''

"Did you ever get the Overleaves?''

"No. She didn't call back, either.'' Jessica looks around my living room. "Funny. I still associate things Michael with my living room and Sunday afternoons. The core group doesn't meet on Sunday afternoons anymore, does it?''

"No,'' I say.

"But it's still twice a month?''

"Still twice a month. I haven't missed a session in over five years. We canceled one year before last—it was too near Christmas and no one was free.''

"You meet at Leslie's, Milly tells me,'' Jessica says, not really very curious.

"Usually. Sessions run about eight to ten people most of the time.'' I've made some small, open-faced sandwiches and put out extra napkins. "They're about four hours long, sometimes a bit longer.''

"That's long,'' says Jessica. "I rarely went more than two and a half or so. Is that one or two channels working?''

"Most of the time two. Occasionally just one.'' I hesitate before I go on. "You know you'd be welcome at any time.''

"Oh, no,'' she laughs outright. "You aren't getting me back into that. I did my time, and now I'm out of it. And I'm pleased and happy to be out of it. I have time on my own, and a relationship with friends that isn't tinged with any of this Michael stuff. It's terrific.'' She has a second sandwich and looks up as my cat comes into the living room, watching the coffee table expectantly. "Do you ever have sessions here?"

"Once in a while," I admit.

"What does Pimpernel think of them?" she asks. "My dogs and the two cats used to love them. Remember? If anyone in the household misses the Michael sessions, it's the pets."

"He likes them," I agree. "He flops down in front of Leslie or Milly and absorbs the energy and purrs."

Jessica nods. "Pets like channeling. Too bad you can't take him to Leslie's."

"Her cats would just *love* that," I remind her. "What about other group members? Do you ever see them?"

"Well, I do see Milly from time to time. We don't live very far apart, and we do have neighborhood friends in common. The last time I saw her, we spent more time talking about the poison-oak problem than we did talking about Michael. I really don't have much interest in the teaching anymore. That doesn't mean I've rejected it; it just means it doesn't hold my attention. I got the first two issues of *The Michael Messenger* when you started putting it out, but I doubt I'll continue taking it. The funny thing is, I'm glad you're doing the newsletter. There's so much drek out there purporting to be Michael teaching, it makes me just *sick*. Most of it looks like EST with a Michael vocabulary— very manipulative. At least I know you're doing the real thing."

"Did the proliferation of other supposed Michael channels have anything to do with you stopping?" I ask.

"I honestly don't know," says Jessica after taking a little time to consider her answer. "I don't mean to dodge the issue. I never gave much thought, though you know how irritated I get at all those groups that claim to be Michael groups. Michael supposedly telling people what to do. Michael! In fact, I met a woman through my new job who said she'd been to a Michael channel—one of those who advertises and charges big bucks—who had told this lady that she was a fifth-level Old Priest. Well, I haven't been that out of touch, and let me tell you, I still recognize a

Young Artisan when I see one. On the other hand, who wants to pay someone over a hundred bucks to be told you're a Young Artisan?'' This last is said in a brittle tone. "Old Priest, my ass,'' she adds thoughtfully.

"Well, if you *are* a Young Artisan, it seems to me that the information is useful.''

"You're an idealist; I am a pragmatist,'' says Jessica. "Let's talk about something else. I get frustrated and upset being associated with fakes. This high-commercial spiritualism depresses me.''

"Me too,'' I tell her.

"You probably see more of it than I do. That's too bad.'' She gets up and goes over to a shelf of reference books. "Where do you find some of these?''

"Novelists are pack rats,'' I say, as I say to almost anyone who remarks on the variety of titles on the shelves.

She opens a book on Tang dynasty China and browses through it. "That *is* something I miss about sessions, getting to go through other people's libraries. Most of the group members have very diverse interests.''

"They still do.''

"Who's in the group now? From when I was with it?''

"It hasn't changed a lot. Fenella, of course, and Joan Standish calls in her questions. Ginny Watson gets in to maybe three sessions a year. Miriam O'Brian calls in her questions. Martin Keir shows up occasionally. Sam and Louise Fisher.''

"How are they?''

"Doing well?''

"Did they ever straighten out that mess with their daughter?''

I pick up Pimpernel and move him away from the coffee table. "Pretty much, I think.''

"Good. Who else?''

"Stu Gradiston. Dominique calls in. Jake Reston calls in questions. You met the Hornes, didn't you?''

"Kitchen supplies? Yes.''

"You don't know Bill Dutton or the Bromleys. Bob Andrews is in the group now.''

"Sam's colleague?" Jessica seems genuinely surprised. "Really? I didn't know he was interested in this kind of thing."

"Yep. Geoff Clifford used to be in the group—"

"The same Geoff Clifford I knew through work?"

"The same Geoff Clifford. He's out of the area, but we get calls and questions from time to time. There are others, but those are the basics."

"Sounds like an interesting bunch."

"But not interesting enough to come to a session."

"No, not that interesting," she agrees. "But say hi to them for me. I know there are people who were upset with me for stopping. I'm sorry about that. Hazel said she's pretty much stopped coming to the group since I stopped channeling. That's too bad. I chose to channel and then I chose not to. Isn't Michael all about choice? I never intended to make anyone feel that way about my decision—my *choice*." She puts the Tang dynasty book back and keeps on looking at titles. "Fifteen years is a long time to do something. There are athletes who have careers half that long, a third that long, and are considered to have done well. And I'm willing to bet channeling takes as much work as pole vaulting."

"No argument."

"But you'd think I'd made up my mind to leave the convent. This isn't a religious vocation, it's a talent, an ability. It's not a sacred calling. And I'm a little tired of people who act as if it were. God, when I stopped teaching, everyone understood, and we had long talks about new careers and job burnout. But this, which is much more exhausting than teaching in a high school ever was, I say I want to stop and you'd think I'd turned heretic in front of the Spanish Inquisition." She leaves the bookshelves and comes back to the couch.

"Hazel came to a session about a month ago. She said she called you first."

"She did; I told her no way. What did she want? I wouldn't let her get into that with me."

"Penny was about to get married—" I began.

"Penny? She's just a kid!" Jessica protests.

"She's twenty-two. That sounds like a kid to us, but not to twenty-two."

"Getting married. What do you know about that?" Jessica smiles. "But my daughter's married now too. Hell, I'm a grandmother and I'll be fifty by the time this third Michael book sees print. How time flies when you're having fun," she adds sarcastically. "Though, matter of fact, I am having fun these days."

"Well, Hazel was worried because of Sparky, small wonder." I pour fresh cups of tea for us. "Can you imagine a grown man wanting to be called Sparky?"

"I can certainly imagine that one wanting it," she says briskly. "That never occurred to me. Of course, Hazel would have to do things with Sparky, wouldn't she?" She sits down. "It doesn't sound like fun."

"So she wanted to get some help from Michael, since she knew it could turn messy easily and she didn't want to wreck things for Penny. The wedding was in Santa Barbara last weekend, but there were a couple doings here before the wedding, and that's what the trouble was. You know Sparky—his idea of a proper engagement party is to have a neighborhood potluck. In fact, that's what he'd arranged when he called Hazel about it."

"A *potluck*? With paper napkins and plastic cups, no doubt. That man would be embarrassing if he really were as poor as he likes to pretend." Jessica folds her arms. "Okay, I bite. What did Michael say? Did it help?"

I hand over the transcript of the session in question. "Read it for yourself."

LET US SUGGEST THAT IN THIS INSTANCE, HAZEL ANNE, YOU HAVE PERCEIVED THE ACTION OF THE CHIEF FEATURE IN AN UNDISGUISED FORM AND AS SUCH HAVE MADE PROGRESS. YOUR RELUCTANCE TO INTERFERE AND THEREBY ESCALATE THE CONFLICT IS NOT THE CAUTION MODE AT WORK, BUT GOOD SENSE AND A NEW APPRECI-ATION OF PRIORITIES AT WORK IN THE LIFE. LET US ALSO POINT OUT THAT THE SECONDARY CHIEF FEATURE IS NOT

WHOLLY INNOCENT AND THAT THE DESIRE TO "RISE
ABOVE" THE PRIEST COMES MORE FROM THE SECONDARY
CHIEF FEATURE [greed fixated on service] THAN FROM AC-
CURATE PERCEPTION. INCIDENTALLY WE WOULD HAVE
TO SAY THAT THE FRAGMENT WHO IS NOW LAIDLAW
[a.k.a. Sparky] IS, AS IS OFTEN TRUE OF PRIESTS, HIGHLY
MANIPULATIVE "FOR YOUR OWN GOOD" AND FANCIES
HIMSELF ABOVE ALL THAT MATERIAL "SHIT" WHICH OF
COURSE, PLAYS INTO THE SECONDARY CHIEF FEATURE.
LET US SUGGEST THAT ONE OF THE MORE EFFECTIVE
WAYS TO REGISTER THE COMPLAINT WITHOUT INVITING
ANATHEMA IS TO ACKNOWLEDGE THAT THE ENTERTAIN-
MENT SCHEME IS HIS, NOT YOURS, AND THAT YOUR
PARTICIPATION IS TO PROVIDE THE SETTING, NOT NECES-
SARILY TO ENDORSE WHAT THE PRIEST CHOOSES TO DO
WITH IT. "SHOULD" YOU CHOOSE TO "GRIN AND BEAR
IT", LET US RECOMMEND YOU ARRANGE FOR TWO OR
THREE "ALLIES" TO AID YOU IN MAINTAINING YOUR PER-
SPECTIVE DURING THESE QUESTIONABLE FESTIVITIES. IF
IT IS POSSIBLE, ASIDE FROM THE SPACE IN YOUR HOUSE
ITSELF, "SHOULD" YOU CHOOSE TO PARTICIPATE AS LIT-
TLE AS POSSIBLE IN WHAT THE PRIEST HAS DEVELOPED,
YOUR "STABILITY" IS APT TO SUFFER THE LEAST DISRUP-
TION. IF THE ARRANGEMENTS BEING PROVIDED ARE NOT
SATISFACTORY TO THE MATURE ARTISAN [their daughter,
Penny], THEN IT IS FAR MORE APPROPRIATE, IF SHE
CHOOSES TO ADDRESS THE ISSUE AT ALL, TO SPEAK WITH
THE PRIEST, WHOSE PLANS THESE ARE. TO COMPLAIN TO
YOU, HAZEL ANNE, IS "PREACHING TO THE CONVERTED"
AND IS NOT LIKELY TO DO MUCH BUT INCREASE THE
LEVEL OF RANCOR, WHICH IS ALREADY HIGH. TEMPTING
THOUGH IT MAY BE TO ESSENCE [Old Scholar] TO ACT AS
"NEGOTIATOR", IN THIS INSTANCE YOU ARE IN NO
POSITION TO ASSUME OR EVEN PRETEND NEUTRALITY
NECESSARY TO THAT FUNCTION. AS YOU ARE ALREADY
WELL AWARE, IT IS DIFFICULT FOR THE ARTISAN ESSENCE
TO ADDRESS ANY CONFLICT DIRECTLY; IN THIS INSTANCE,
IT WOULD NOT BE AMISS FOR THE FRAGMENT WHO IS NOW
PENELOPE TO SPEAK WITH HER FATHER, SINCE HER DIS-

TRESS IS THE RESULT OF HER FATHER'S ACTIONS. LET US
POINT OUT THAT THE MORE SHE IS CAPABLE OF ADDRESS-
ING ISSUES AND HER OWN PERCEPTIONS INSTEAD OF
HURLING RECRIMINATIONS, THE LESS LIKELY THE PRIEST
IS TO INSIST THAT HIS AUSTERITY IS "FOR HER OWN
GOOD". IT WOULD NOT BE AMISS FOR YOU, HAZEL ANNE,
TO PROVIDE NOTHING MORE BUT "MORAL SUPPORT" IN
THIS INSTANCE, FOR THE FRAGMENT WHO IS NOW LAID-
LAW IS ALREADY SEEING YOU IN THE ROLE OF "HERETIC"
AND IS NOT LIKELY TO CHANGE HIS STANCE AT THIS LATE
DATE.

"Makes sense," says Jessica as she puts the notebook
aside. "Who thought of having all the session notes typed
up?"

"I did, actually. But it's mainly Abby and Louise and
Bill who do the actual work. I type too much as it is. Are
you sure you don't want to look through the material?"

"No." She takes a sip of tea. "I hate to admit it, but I'm
relieved not to have problems like that one—Hazel's mess
with Sparky—on my mind anymore. While I was channeling, I spent a lot of time worrying about group members;
sometimes I was more worried about them than they were.
That's not sensible. I knew it then and I know it much,
much better now."

"What about the new job?" I ask, since she hasn't told
me a great deal about it.

"It's much more flexible than the old one, and I don't
have to do so much public relations as I did. Most of the
time I work with a small staff and four fancy computers.
I'm having a wonderful time. Computers are Scholar heaven,
and getting to play with four of them is more fun than
building sand castles. I was terrified at first—what did I
know about computers?—but all that *information*." She
draws this last word out, relishing it as she speaks. "We've
done a few advertising campaigns, of course, but most of
what we're working with has more to do with news and
politics. Michael might not think that's very Good Work,
but I'm getting a lot out of it. I think I'm doing some good,

that I'm helping people understand about the risks of nuclear power and the arms race, among other things. I didn't feel that I was doing much real good for most of the years I was a channel. I'd get material, we'd discuss it, get more questions about the same problems answered, and the people would still go right ahead and screw up. That doesn't happen as much in my job now. And most of it is information and education, and the energy to provide it has already been expended—I don't have to conjure it out of myself the way I did for all those years channeling.''

''And your social life?'' I ask.

''Lots and lots and lots of fun. Walter's got back into his fine woodwork, so we do occasional shows together, but most of the time I get a chance to hang out with people who read, who are intelligent and active and—'' She interrupts herself. ''That's not to say that the Michael group doesn't have intelligent and active people who read in it. I didn't mean that. But this is different. I get to talk about things of a very different nature.'' She looks at her watch. ''I ought to leave. I have to be in San Rafael in forty minutes.''

"What about your Cadence Member?" I ask, remembering the fun they had had.

"Oh, I talk to him a couple times a year. He and his family are in Canada now. But it doesn't seem as important as it used to. I've got other things on my mind.'' She finishes her tea. "Is that enough for the book?''

"It's fine,'' I tell her. "Thanks for agreeing to talk about it.''

We say the usual polite things, and I walk out to her car with her. "Remember, you're always welcome. Any time.''

"Thanks,'' she says before driving away.

Getting Camille Rowe and both Leslie Adamses together at the same time takes some doing, but finally we all get together for Sunday brunch at a local restaurant. In order to differentiate between the female Leslie and the male Leslie, I'll identify them by Essence. The male Leslie is an

Old Scholar, the female an Old Warrior. Camille Rowe is an Old Sage.

"So do you think Jessica will come back?" Scholar Leslie wants to know as soon as we've ordered our brunch and had the first cup of coffee for the day.

"I wouldn't hold my breath," I tell them.

"Too bad," says Scholar Leslie. Since we are sitting on a deck, he looks down at the street, pointing out three cyclists. "I used to do that."

"What do you do now?" asks Milly.

"Most of the time I try to keep ahead of the weeds in the yard," says Scholar Leslie. "The last two years they've made real inroads, and finally Helen insisted. Either we had to do something ourselves or hire a gardening service."

"Why not hire it done?" Milly wants to know. "That's what I do. That's what Quinn does."

"But I *like* to garden," Scholar Leslie protests. "I think it's a lot of fun. And besides, it's part of my true play." He sighs.

"Poor you," says Warrior Leslie.

"Um-hum." He takes out his notebook. "I don't know what you want to know about channeling, but I jotted down a few thoughts. I figured I'd bring them up and we can talk about them, if that's okay?"

"Sure," says Warrior Leslie.

"Fine by me," says Milly.

Scholar Leslie opens his notebook and scrutinizes what he has written there. "Well, first off, there's the physical response to channeling, isn't there? I get light-headed while I'm doing it, and afterward I tend to have difficulty sleeping. And I get a terrible stomachache if I'm tired when I start."

"Know the feeling well," says Milly at her most laconic. "And that's not the least of it." She flushes. "I know Leslie gets the trots. So do I. And a headache that's like a sinus attack when there's been a big energy drain."

"There's also that very strange sensation when you get into a deeper trance," adds Warrior Leslie. "It's only happened to me a couple of times, and it's weird. It feels just great while I'm doing it; better than channeling feels most of the time. But talk about light-headed!" She laughs. "I don't remember the sensation very clearly, but channeling's like that, isn't it?"

"I wish I could remember," says Milly. "I get embarrassed when I have to admit I can't recall what I said. I've done a few private consultation things where it was real clear the person I was reading for didn't believe. But it's true." she wails. "And it's very frustrating."

"I think it's also . . . well, I can't help but wonder what I've said, and I get very chagrined, thinking I might have offended someone in the group. Chief feature, yeah, chief feature, don't remind me. But I *do* worry about that. It's the weirdest thing: I can remember how everyone looks while I answer their questions. I can remember the questions, or at least most of them, I can remember speaking, but I'm damned if I can remember what I say. It drives me *nuts*!" Warrior Leslie looks at the others for their support and comments.

"Sure," says Scholar Leslie. "I think it's spooky being able to remember speaking but not being able to remember what is being said. It took me years to get used to that part, and I'm not really sure I'm used to it now." He looks up as the waiter approaches with large orange juices for everyone and small glasses of champagne, which he says at once are on the house.

"Thanks, Saïd," I tell him, grateful for this cordial gesture.

"Your brunches will be up in about ten minutes," he tells us, politely letting us know how long we have before food. He takes very good care of his regular customers, and his Persian sense of hospitality is unfailing.

"We're all hungry," Milly tells him. "Disgusting, isn't it?" She grins as she complains. "I don't know about the rest of you, but when I'm through with a session, I'm just *drained*. And I'm hungry."

"But I can't eat for a while or I regret it," adds Warrior Leslie. "It's awkward, being that hungry and not daring to eat."

"Boy, does *that* sound familiar," says Scholar Leslie. "The last time I succumbed to the munchies I went through a pint of chocolate-chip ice cream, and then I couldn't sleep for the rest of the night. And I couldn't eat a thing the next day." He leans back and looks over the railing at the traffic. "What would they think if they knew what we're talking about?"

"What makes you think they'd care?" asks Milly dryly. "Most people don't care much about channeling, or they think it's a parlor trick or some kind of get-rich-quick scam."

"And for some people, that's just what it is," I remind them.

"Not for us," Warrior Leslie insists staunchly. "But I really hate it when we're tarred with that brush. It's unavoidable, but still . . . Did Jessica say anything about that?"

"Only that it troubles her," I reply. "She isn't feeling very connected to the teaching anymore, but I know she doesn't like to see it abused."

"None of us do," Scholar Leslie says firmly. "And I know that it's going on. It troubles me, but if I accept what Michael keeps telling us over, and over, and over, and *over*, then listening to a channel that isn't plugged into anything real is as much a choice as listening to Michael."

"Assuming Michael is real," Milly amends.

"Yeah," Scholar Leslie agrees. "But I know when I'm channeling that I'm sure as hell not doing it. There are all kinds of areas where Michael and I disagree, and their perspective isn't anything like mine. When they start in on viewing the problems between nations or between men and women as difficulties between general soul-age levels and cultural pressure and conditioning, I've got to admit that they lose me. I can sense what they're getting at, but I know for certain that I am not there yet."

"What about those answers that seem to make no sense at first?" Warrior Leslie adds. "They're so hard to get. And once you've got them, you haven't the faintest idea what they're about, but the funny thing is, over time they tend to prove out in strange ways. I remember getting an answer that at the time was just . . . a jumble to me and the person who asked, but six months later we both understood it and had applied it. I haven't a clue as to how to explain it."

"You explain that and you explain legitimate channeling," says Milly. "And I can't explain it, I can only do it. And I know I'm doing it when I'm doing it."

"Don't we all?" says Scholar Leslie to the air.

"Apparently not, judging from some of the stuff out there," Milly says.

"But there are signs that indicate an authentic medium, and real channeling; not just the memory thing—a good con artist can fake that," Warrior Leslie says.

"And there's the whole color-change thing," adds Milly. "I know what happens to you two; I'm told the same things happens to me. I don't know why channeling should make me turn bright red or chalk-white, but it does. Like it does for both of you."

"The first time Helen saw that," says Scholar Leslie, "she thought I was ill. She wanted to stop the session and call a doctor. She was . . . upset about it."

"Well, it's probably pretty upsetting when you see it for the first time," says Warrior Leslie reasonably. "Sometimes group members get apprehensive, too, and they're used to seeing it."

"But I think that Helen's response was more extreme than that," Milly says. "I recall the way she acted that first time she came to a session, and I know she was upset. I think hearing Leslie talk that way, that measured, rather flat way, bothered her because it sounds so unlike him."

"Hell, Milly, it sounds unlike any of us," says Warrior Leslie.

Said returns to the table, the waitress with him. "Your meals are here; is there anything more I can get for you? I'll be happy to refill the champagne if you like."

"In a while, it would be great," says Scholar Leslie. "You're very good to us."

He smiles and stands aside while the orders are put down in front of their various destinations.

"Does anyone need extra cream or sugar?" asks the waitress with a pleasant and genuine smile.

"Thank you, I don't think so," I say, and once again we are politely left alone.

For the next several minutes we're preoccupied with brunch, but after a little while Scholar Leslie looks up from his Eggs Brittany and says, "We ought to get some work done, since you're paying for this."

"No hurry," I tell them.

"Well, I think we ought to go over a few points," Scholar Leslie insists. "We've got a forum for once, and we might as well take advantage of it."

"Finish your orange juice," Milly suggests as she prepares to finish hers. "You've got a point," she goes on when she puts the glass down. "I've been busier than either of you two in the last year. The consultation practice has really forced me to examine a lot of things about channeling. For one thing, when I first started doing the consulting, I thought I was being over-cautious because I would only take clients on a referral basis. I still insist that any first-timer be recommended by another client. It seemed a little silly at the time. Now I think I was being pretty damned naïve. I've had two clients now who were on friends-of-friends status; no one I'd read for had actually met these people. Let me tell you, I won't do any more of that. One of them was obviously much more in need of a good psychiatrist than a Michael session—in fact, Michael told him as much—and the other was . . . I don't know how to describe it . . . she was after something Michael couldn't give her. I don't think anyone could give her whatever it was she wanted. Her chief feature was greed fixated on nothing in particular, and she was like . . . like sand down a rat hole. She took enormous amounts of energy and felt cheated when it was over because I hadn't 'given her more'. Let me tell you, no one on this earth could have given her as much as she wanted. She was voracious. She's asked for private sessions since—and of course she wants into the core group—but so far I've told her no."

"Not in the core group," says Scholar Leslie.

"Absolutely not," agrees Warrior Leslie.

Milly stops to have more of her Eggs Benedict. "I keep

thinking about her, though,'' she adds a little later. "I wish I could really get through to her. I know I probably can't, but part of me wants to. That's the temptation, isn't it?''

"Just remember, if you exhaust yourself channeling, you can do serious damage to your health. Too much channeling kills you. That's a fact.'' Warrior Leslie announces this in her usual down-to-earth manner, but there's an implacability at the back of her eyes that enforces what she says. "Look at what happen to Cayce. Even his astral guides warned him he was killing himself, but he couldn't bring himself to turn down clients, and it killed him. That's no fiction—it killed him.''

"Does that ever worry you?'' I ask Warrior Leslie.

"Not yet. But when is a Warrior ever afraid of getting killed?'' She nudges me in the ribs with her elbow, Warrior to Warrior. "Right?''

"Probably,'' I say, checking to make sure my tape recorder is getting all of this.

"No 'probably' about it,'' Milly tells us, "and both of you know it.'' She sighs. "Michael has warned Warriors as a group that they're the workhorses of the Essences and that once committed to something, they'll persevere until they drop. Keep that in mind.'' This last is pointedly directed toward Warrior Leslie.

"Okay,'' says Warrior Leslie with a shrug.

"I tell you what's also interested me,'' says Scholar Leslie, glancing at his notes again.'' The distribution of polarities in terms of the population of percentages. Look: twenty-five percent of souls Slaves, eight percent Priests, which makes thirty-three percent for the Inspiration polarity. For the Expression polarity there are twenty-two percent Artisan souls to ten percent Sages, which is thirty-two percent total for the Expression polarity. There's a big drop to the Action polarity. There's seventeen percent of souls Warriors and only four percent Kings, and that total is only twenty-one percent, more than ten percentage points below the Expression and Inspiration polarities. Then there are the Scholars''—he pretends to buff his nails—"and we're a measly fourteen percent, but then, being neutral, we're about half, or average, for the Inspiration and Expression polarities. Whatever that means," he adds darkly.

The other two channels have been watching him, as if expecting him to announce a conclusion. When he doesn't, Milly looks toward the sky. "Isn't that just like a Scholar?" she asks of the last of the morning clouds. "They dump a mess of information in your lap and just . . . drop it."

"So what was the point of all this?" Warrior Leslie asks.

"I don't know yet. I was thinking I might ask Michael about it at the next session. One of you can get the answer for me." Scholar Leslie smiles, making a point of looking from Milly to Warrior Leslie as he does. "It might turn up some interesting comments; you never can tell."

"Damn it, man, you are a pain sometimes," Warrior Leslie declares. "I wish you wouldn't do that. I wish you wouldn't give us half the information and then sit back waiting for the rest of us to get the second half for you. Sometimes it drives me smack up the wall."

"You don't have to ask the questions, and you don't have to channel the answers," Scholar Leslie says in his most soothing manner.

"Thanks," Milly says bluntly. "You're too kind." She knows that if Warrior Leslie doesn't get the answer for Scholar Leslie, then she'll have to.

"Well, it is interesting," Scholar Leslie says, his defensiveness more apparent now.

"If you say so," Milly says in a carefully neutral manner.

"Well, don't you think it's interesting? Don't you?" Scholar Leslie asks the rest of us. "Can't you see the potential for study in this?"

"Even if we did, why would it matter?" Milly counters. "You have enough enthusiasm for all of us."

"You know, not long ago I was watching a PBS show, *In Search of the Trojan War*. I just loved it. I loved everything they showed me, and I loved the passion of the archaeologists working on the digs." Warrior Leslie looks to the other two channels. "I think shows like that are absolutely fascinating. I don't know very much about the ancient world, but shows like that make me want to go out and learn everything I can about the early Greeks and Turks. Or were the Trojans Turks in anything but the modern geographical sense?''

"You know what Michael had to say on that?'' Milly asks. "Were you there the night Bill Dutton got started on the Trojan War?''

"I didn't know Bill was interested in the Trojan War,'' Scholar Leslie interpolates.

"He's a Scholar. Of course he's interested in the Trojan War,'' says Milly. "Footnotes, you know.''

"Does anyone have their transcripts with them?'' asks Warrior Leslie, staring directly at Scholar Leslie.

"Sure. I'll show you the ones I mean.'' He reaches into the knapsack he brought with him and digs out two large notebooks. One of them, with a purple cover, contains the transcripts of sessions for the last year.

"Here. This section here. And there's more, five pages on; Bill asked more questions at the next session.''

FIRST, LET US ASSURE YOU THAT YES, THE CONFLICT THAT IS KNOWN TO LEGEND AS THE TROJAN WAR DID TAKE PLACE, ALTHOUGH IT HAD MORE TO DO WITH COPPER MINES IN WHAT IS NOW TURKEY TO THE CHANGING AFFILIATION OF THE SPARTANS FROM MYCENEA TO TROY. THE BETROTHING OF HELEN OF SPARTA TO AGAMEMNON OF MYCENEA WAS A POLITICAL ALLIANCE WHEN HELEN WAS A CHILD. LATER, WHEN COPPER BECAME MORE IMPORTANT TO THE BRONZE MAKERS OF SPARTA, AND WHEN HELEN WAS FIFTEEN, A COUNTEROFFER FOR POLITICAL ALLIANCE CAME FROM TROY, AND AS A RESULT THE BETROTHAL TO AGAMEMNON WAS OFF AND A NEW TREATY WAS SEALED WITH THE MARRAIGE OF THE OLDEST OF "PRIAM'S" SONS AND HELEN OF SPARTA. AGAMEMNON WAS UPSET ABOUT THIS CHANGE OF POLITICAL ALLIANCE, AND UNDER THE GUISE OF RECLAIMING HIS AFFIANCED BRIDE, HE WENT AFTER THE FORCES OF TROY, INTENT UPON CLAIMING THEIR COPPER MINES MORE THAN ON REASSERTING HIS CLAIM ON HELEN. OF COURSE, THE TROJANS WERE PRIMARILY A

CULTURE OF PIRATES, AND THEIR POSITION NEAR THE
MOUTH OF THE DARDANELLES GAVE THEM A REAL AD-
VANTAGE OVER MERCHANT TRAFFIC GOING TOWARD THE
BLACK SEA. BY PAYING OFF THE TROJANS, OTHER CITY-
STATES ASSURED THEMSELVES OF SAFE PASSAGE AND
ARMED ESCORT THROUGH THESE DANGEROUS WATERS.
WHEN TRIBUTE WAS NOT PAID, THEN THE TROJANS WERE
THE MOST CAPABLE OF THE PIRATES IN TERMS OF GETTING
THE MOST FROM THE MERCHANTS. THOSE MERCHANTS
WHO DID NOT PAY TRIBUTE TO THE TROJANS NOT ONLY
RISKED LOSING THEIR CARGO, THEY RISKED BEING TAKEN
CAPTIVE AND SOLD INTO SLAVERY BY THE TROJANS. IT
WOULD NOT BE INAPPROPRIATE TO SAY THAT THIS IS ONE
OF THE REASONS SO MANY OF THE GREEK CITY-STATES
WERE WILLING TO MAKE COMMON CAUSE WITH AGAMEM-
NON. THE DESIRES OF THE GREEK CITY-STATES TO STOP
THE PIRATES, AS WELL AS TO GAIN ACCESS TO THE COPPER
MINES, HAD MORE TO DO WITH THE CONFLICT THAN THE
SHIFT IN BETROTHAL.

"I'm fascinated by the Trojan War," says Scholar Leslie.
"Not just the war itself, but the mythology around it and
the history of the place in literature."

"But why?" says Milly. "Were you there?"

"I've never asked," Scholar Leslie admits, "but frankly
I doubt it. Or if I were, it was in a minimal capacity—a
household slave, or something like that. And a Baby soul,
as well. Or I might have been with the Greeks. That's always
possible, one of those poor bastards who took care of the
chariots and counted the spears."

"What? Not Achilles?" Warrior Leslie asks, laughing.

"A Baby Scholar? Not likely. A Baby Warrior, maybe.
Do you ever hanker after Bronze Age Greece?"

"No," says Warrior Leslie. "Bronze Age China, maybe,
but Greece doesn't do that much for me." She takes time
to have more of her brunch. "I do find all of the historical
stuff we get from Michael very interesting. I think that what
we get is very worthwhile, and I think that it means a lot
to the group. What about the rest of you?"

"I'm not that good at getting historical stuff," admits Milly. "I'm getting better, but as soon as Michael starts dealing with foreign languages, I have real trouble getting them to translate." She signals the waitress for more orange juice. "Both you Leslies are better at it than I am."

"I'm not so sure," says Scholar Leslie. "I know I don't get a fraction of what's out there."

"Same here," agrees Warrior Leslie. "Is there a chance to get a refill on the coffee?"

"Sure," I tell her, and when the waitress brings Milly's orange juice, we order more coffee all around.

"You know," says Scholar Leslie, "when I think about Jessica's decision to stop, I find myself wondering how much longer I'll be able to do this, or I'll want to do it. Right now I think I'll do it the rest of my life, but, hell, that could be another forty years or so, and the thought of forty years of channeling . . . that's more than I can take."

Milly nods. "When I can tell that the information has been useful, when I can see that the people I read for are getting something out of it, then I think I'll do it forever. But when it's nothing but metaphysical window shopping, or when the person I'm reading for has no intention of using the information as anything but an excuse, then I think I'd like to quit tomorrow." Her expression changes. "Honestly, I don't know how long I'll do this, or what I'll do with it. I also don't know how long I can hold up under the work. That's something else. If I find that my health is suffering, then I'll have to reevaluate my position and make some choices for then." She looks out toward the street. "There are a lot of people who think that having some kind of channel will solve all their problems. With Michael, all you can hope for is a better perspective on the problems, not a cure for them. That tends to disappoint people, having to choose for themselves."

"But that's the heart of the teaching," says Warrior Leslie. "Honestly, if there's one thing I wish everyone would get out of Michael it's the understanding that what your life is is your choice. Even when circumstances limit it, how you deal with the limitations is your choice. The buck stops with you. No one but you will hold you accountable—no one but you *is* accountable. Essence keeps tabs and changes the personality through the cycle of lives, and all that happens is because of choosing.'' She stops as the fresh coffee arrives. "Well, you get my point, don't you?''

"Couldn't miss it,'' says Scholar Leslie. "And I go along with you, for the most part.'' He looks into the steam of his coffee. "Do you guys mind if we talk about something else now?''

"Tired of Michael?'' asks Milly.

"Not tired, just . . . out of ideas. I want to say something profound about the teaching, and everything that occurs to me is so . . . trivial. Michael has information to offer about everything we ask, and they have never refused to answer a question, not in my experience—''

"Mine, too,'' says Milly.

"I've never had them refuse, but occasionally I end up blocking.'' Warrior Leslie sighs at this admission.

"We all have areas where we block,'' says Scholar Leslie. "That's different. I meant that so far as I've been able to find out, Michael will answer any question, asked to the limit of the capabilities of the channel. Do you two agree?''

"Yes,'' says Milly at once.

"Absolutely,'' says Warrior Leslie. "And it's frustrating to sense a much larger answer waiting behind the answer to a specific question. That's such a strange sensation.''

"But you try to get the whole answer, don't you?'' persists Scholar Leslie.

"As much as I can,'' says Warrior Leslie.

"As long as I can get a sense of the words,'' says Milly. "And when Michael reverts to showing pictures when vocabulary fails, I do my best to describe what I see, but I always warn the people I'm reading for that the description is mine and not Michael's.''

"You get pictures more often than I do,'' says Warrior Leslie. "Most of the time, I just stop getting . . . anything.''

"Me, too,'' says Scholar Leslie. "Just . . . nothing.'' He moves his hands, indicating blankness in front of his eyes. "It's probably the difference between the three-channel input of Sages and the one-channel input for Scholars and Warriors.''

"Could be," says Milly skeptically.

"What else could it be?" I ask.

"Anything," says Milly and nods along with the others.

"There are a lot of times when it's apparent that there's more information behind the answer, but that the concepts or the vocabulary or the perception isn't on the right wavelength to get it all. Sometimes an answer is a glimpse; that's all you get." Warrior Leslie looks from Scholar Leslie to Milly.

"Well, sometimes that's all we can get, here on the physical plane," says Milly. "A glimpse."

"You know," Scholar Leslie says with a faraway glint in his eyes, "it makes you wonder how much more is out there, how much more we'll understand when we're through with the physical plane."

"Trust Scholars to put understanding first," says Milly affectionately.

"You mean you're not interested?" Scholar Leslie asks, not without a touch of alarm.

"Interested?" Milly laughs out loud. "I'm *fascinated*."

CHAPTER 15

MICHAEL: ON INTEGRATING PERCEPTIONS

THERE ARE MANY FRAGMENTS CURRENTLY EXTANT ON THE PHYSICAL PLANE WHO FEEL THE BURDEN OF "ISOLATION" MORE KEENLY THAN OTHERS, ALTHOUGH, AS WE HAVE INDICATED MANY TIMES BEFORE, LONELINESS TENDS TO BE ENDEMIC AMONG THOSE FRAGMENTS INCARNATE IN INDEPENDENTLY MOBILE SPECIES. THOSE WHO HAVE A SENSE OF THE ISOLATION OFTEN CHOOSE TO REJECT THE POSSIBILITY OF CONTACT AND INTIMACY BECAUSE THE PROSPECT APPEARS TOO REMOTE OR TOO RISKY FOR THE FRAGMENT TO BE WILLING TO BREAK FROM THE "SAFETY" OF ISOLATION AND LONELINESS TO THE MUCH MORE UNCERTAIN AREAS OF PERSONAL CONTACT. THOSE FRAGMENTS WHO PREFER THEIR ISOLATION HAVE MANY EXPLANATIONS FOR THEIR CHOICES, NOT THE LEAST OF WHICH IS THE SUPPOSED IMPREGNABILITY THE ISOLATION APPEARS TO CONFER. SUCH FRAGMENTS WILL TEND TO PERCEIVE OTHER FRAGMENTS AS MARKEDLY DIFFERENT FROM THEMSELVES AND WILL THEREFORE "BELIEVE" THAT THEY ARE FREE TO USE OTHER FRAGMENTS WITH IMPUNITY. THIS PERCEPTION IS, OF COURSE, NOT VALID, BUT IT IS CURRENTLY WIDELY PERVASIVE FOR YOUR SPECIES, AS WELL AS MANY OTHERS.

WE ARE AWARE OF THE BURDEN LONELINESS IMPOSES ON FRAGMENTS EXTANT IN INDEPENDENTLY MOBILE SPECIES, YOURS INCLUDED, AND WE RECOGNIZE THAT ONE OF THE MOST COMMONLY ENCOUNTERED MANIFESTATIONS OF MAYA FOR YOUR SPECIES IS THE ASSUMPTION

THAT OTHER HUMAN BEINGS ARE SOMEHOW LESS HUMAN. THIS ASSUMPTION OFTEN LEADS TO ACTIONS RESULTING IN KARMIC RIBBONS, AND TO LIVES LIVED COMPLETELY IN THE GRIP OF CHIEF FEATURE.

IF THOSE HERE PRESENT LEARN TO IDENTIFY THE CHIEF FEATURE AND TO COMPREHEND THE NATURE OF ITS DISTORTIONS AND LIES, THEN ALL WILL BENEFIT FROM THAT PERCEPTION. TO EXPERIENCE INTERACTIONS WITH FRAGMENTS WHO ARE AWARE OF THE CHIEF FEATURE'S LIES IS OFTEN THE FIRST STEP IN LEARNING THAT THERE TRULY IS SUCH A THING AS A CHIEF FEATURE AND THAT WHAT IT PURPORTS TO BE DEFENDING IS, IN FACT, THE MOST NEGATIVE AND INVALID PERCEPTIONS IN THIS OR ANY LIFE. FOR MANY THE FIRST STEP TOWARD RECOGNIZING AND VALIDATING THAT THE CHIEF FEATURE LIES IS TO ENCOUNTER ANOTHER FRAGMENT WHO HAS ALREADY RECOGNIZED AND VALIDATED THIS. THAT IS NOT TO SAY THAT ONE "MUST NECESSARILY" COME TO RECOGNITION AND VALIDATION IN THIS METHOD, ONLY THAT IT IS THE MOST DIRECT MEANS FOR FRAGMENTS WHO HAVE NOT CHOSEN A GOAL OF REJECTION FOR THE CURRENT LIFE.

FOR FRAGMENTS TO PERCEIVE THE VALIDITY OF THE OVERLEAVES IS THE WORK OF THE FOURTH INTERNAL MONAD, AND FOR THOSE FRAGMENTS WILLING TO UNDERTAKE THE TRANSITION, COMPREHENSION OF CHIEF FEATURE BECOMES MORE POSSIBLE, SINCE THE CHIEF FEATURE DOES NOT HAVE THE ADVANTAGE OF FALSE PERSONALITY TO STRENGTHEN IT.

THAT DOES NOT MEAN THAT CHIEF FEATURE IS THEREFORE WEAKENED. OFTEN, WHEN IDENTIFIED AND VALIDATED, IT ENTERS A PERIOD OF GREAT IMPACT, AS MUCH TO STRENGTHEN THE FEAR IT "CONCEALS" IN ORDER NOT TO RELINQUISH CONTROL. FOR THOSE FRAGMENTS WHO WONDER WHY THERE IS SUCH A THING AS A CHIEF FEATURE AND WHY FRAGMENTS CHOOSE TO HAVE THEM, WE MUST REMIND YOU THAT THERE ARE TWO FORCES IN THE UNIVERSE—LOVE AND FEAR—AND THAT WHERE LOVE IS NOT ACCEPTED, FEAR WILL BE. THE VERY NATURE OF THE PHYSICAL PLANE IS SUCH THAT CHIEF FEATURES

FUNCTION MOST POWERFULLY THERE. CHIEF FEATURES AS SUCH DO NOT EXIST BEYOND THE PHYSICAL PLANE BECAUSE THE OVERLEAVES DO NOT EXIST; ESSENCE AND PLACE IN CASTING REMAIN, AND THAT LASTS ONLY THROUGH THE MID-CAUSAL PLANE.

TO ACCEPT THE VALIDITY NOT ONLY OF THE OVERLEAVES ONE HAS CHOSEN, BUT THAT OTHERS HAVE CHOSEN FOR THEMSELVES AS WELL, CAN PROVIDE A FIRST STEP TOWARD INTEGRATED UNDERSTANDING. LET US SUGGEST AT THIS TIME THAT THERE IS A GREAT DEAL OF BENEFIT IN TAKING THE TIME TO COMPREHEND THE OVERLEAVES OF OTHER FRAGMENTS AS WELL AS ONE'S OWN; IN PART THIS WILL AID THE FRAGMENT IN IDENTIFYING THE FUNCTION OF POSITIVE AND NEGATIVE POLES AT WORK, WHICH IN TURN CAN LEAD TO SELF-AWARENESS THAT PERMITS RECOGNITION WHEN THE FRAGMENT ONESELF IS OPERATING OUT OF POSITIVE AND NEGATIVE POLES OF THE OVERLEAVES. WE HAVE REFERRED TO THIS TECHNIQUE AS "PHOTOGRAPHING", RECOGNIZING AND "CAPTURING" THE MOMENT—NOT TO PRESERVE IT IN CONCRETE BUT TO KEEP FOR LATER COMPARISON AND RECOGNITION.

WE DO NOT MEAN TO IMPLY THAT ANYONE IS "COMPELLED" TO DO THIS. THAT IS CLEARLY NOT THE CASE. HOWEVER, WE DO WISH TO SAY THAT FOR THOSE WHO CHOOSE TO UNDERSTAND THE VALIDITY OF ESSENCE AND OVERLEAVES, THESE TECHNIQUES ARE USEFUL, ALTHOUGH THEY MOST DEFINITELY ARE NOT THE "ONLY WAY". THERE IS NO "ONLY" WAY. ALL FRAGMENTS CHOOSE GOALS WHICH CAN BE REACHED BY MANY PATHS. THE SLAVE ESSENCE HAS ALL MEANS OPEN FOR REACHING THE GOAL AND IS THE ONLY ESSENCE THAT IS SO BY NATURE. ALL OTHER FRAGMENTS, AS WE HAVE SAID BEFORE ON MANY OCCASIONS, REQUIRE SPECIAL CIRCUMSTANCES TO ACHIEVE THE GOAL, THOSE SPECIAL CIRCUMSTANCES INCREASING WITH ESSENCE CARDINALITY. FOR MANY KING ESSENCES, THE CIRCUMSTANCES FOR PROGRESS TOWARD THE GOAL MAY BE VERY LIMITED. THIS IS IN PART A QUESTION OF CHOICE FOR A LIFE, BUT

FOR THE LARGER PART IS A MATTER OF CHOICE-IN-ES-
SENCE.

THE OVERLEAVES, WHICH ARE CHOSEN TO AID THE ES-
SENCE IN EVOLUTION AND TO ACHIEVE THE GOAL FOR
THE LIFE, ARE PART OF THE NATURE OF ESSENCE. WE
HAVE DISCUSSED AT LENGTH [see More Messages From
Michael, Chapter 8, Michael-Math] THE "NUMERICAL" AS-
PECT OF ESSENCE AND OVERLEAVES. WE WOULD WISH
TO COMMENT MORE ON THE NATURE OF OVERLEAVES IN
TERMS OF ESSENCE "ADAPTABILITY" THROUGH THE
OVERLEAVES. CERTAINLY A FOURTH-LEVEL MATURE
SCHOLAR IN THE OBSERVATION MODE WILL MORE
"TRULY" REPRESENT THE NATURE OF SCHOLAR THAN A
FIFTH-LEVEL BABY SCHOLAR IN THE PASSION MODE. CON-
SIDER THAT THE SCHOLAR NUMBER IS FOUR, THAT THE
MATURE CYCLE IS THE FOURTH CYCLE, THAT THE OBSER-
VATION MODE IS THE NEUTRAL/FOURTH/SCHOLAR MODE,
AND IT IS LIKELY THAT THE FRAGMENT WILL BE MORE
SCHOLARLY THAN THE SECOND FRAGMENT, WHO IS AT
THE SAGE/FIVE LEVEL OF THE TWO/ARTISAN CYCLE IN
THE SIX/PRIEST MODE. ASSUMING THAT ENCULTURATION
AND FALSE PERSONALITY ARE NOT TOO DISTORTING, THE
MATURE SCHOLAR WILL TEND TO DEMONSTRATE MORE
SCHOLARLINESS THAN THE BABY SCHOLAR. LET US,
HOWEVER, CAUTION ALL HERE GATHERED ONCE AGAIN
FROM "LEAPING TO PREMESES"; THE MATURE SCHOLAR
MIGHT AS EASILY BE AN INDONESIAN BOATWRIGHT, AND
THE BABY SCHOLAR A THIRD-GENERATION HIGH-SCHOOL
TEACHER. OR THE MATURE SCHOLAR MIGHT BE A CATH-
OLIC PRIEST IN LA PAZ, AND THE BABY SCHOLAR AN
ELECTRONIC TECHNICIAN. OR THE MATURE SCHOLAR
MIGHT BE A RETIRED SOVIET COSMONAUT AND THE BABY
SCHOLAR MIGHT BE A NURSE FOR A FLYING MEDICAL
SERVICE IN PERTH, AUSTRALIA. WE MENTION THESE BE-
CAUSE, OF COURSE, THE OVERLEAVES MENTIONED ARE,
IN FACT, TRUE FOR THE EXAMPLES WE HAVE OFFERED.

OFTEN FRAGMENTS DEVELOP SKILLS AT RECOGNIZING
ONE OVERLEAF. THAT IS TO SAY, A FRAGMENT MAY HAVE
REAL SKILL IN RECOGNIZING THE ATTITUDE OF A FRAG-

MENT AND WILL TEND TO CONFUSE THIS RECOGNITION WITH RECOGNITION OF ESSENCE. THEREFORE, EVERY SPIRITUALIST WILL APPEAR TO BE A PRIEST, EVERY REALIST A KING, EVERY PRAGMATIST A SCHOLAR, EVERY SKEPTIC AN ARTISAN, AND SO ON. WHILE THIS RECOGNITION IS GOOD WORK, IT IS ONLY A BEGINNING, AND THE TENDENCY TO MISINTERPRET THE VALIDITY OF ESSENCE CAN BE, AT THE LEAST, CONFUSING TO ALL CONCERNED.

TO UNDERSTAND THAT PARTIAL RECOGNTION IS JUST THAT—PARTIAL—IS VERY GOOD WORK. IN GENERAL MOST FRAGMENTS CHOOSING TO FOLLOW ESOTERIC STUDIES TEND TO GAIN PARTIAL UNDERSTANDING AND TO EXTRAPOLATE FROM THIS PARTIAL UNDERSTANDING UNTIL THERE IS THE APPEARANCE OF VASTER KNOWLEDGE. PLEASE NOTE THAT WE SAY APPEARANCE. FOR EXAMPLE, A FRAGMENT MAY BE DEEPLY INTERESTED IN SPIRITUAL STUDIES, BUT THIS DOES NOT MAKE THAT FRAGMENT A PRIEST. LET US REMIND ALL HERE PRESENT THAT NONE OF THE CHANNELS WE EMPLOY ARE PRIESTS, EITHER IN THIS LITTLE GROUP, IN OUR OTHER GROUP IN THE UNITED STATES OF AMERICA, AND THE THREE GROUPS IN OTHER PARTS OF THE WORLD. VERY FEW PRIESTS AND KINGS MAKE GOOD CHANNELS BECAUSE IT IS NECESSARY FOR A CHANNEL TO BE ABLE TO "GROUND" AND THE NATURE OF SIX-NESS AND SEVEN-NESS AT ESSENTIAL LEVEL MAKES SUCH GROUNDING DIFFICULT. HOWEVER, LET US POINT OUT THAT ALL CHANNELS WE USE HAVE SIX-NESS OR SEVEN-NESS IN THE OVERLEAVES, TO PROVIDE THE NEEDED NONESSENTIAL LINK TO THE CAUSAL PLANE. ALL OUR CHANNELS, WE ALSO ADD, ARE OLD SOULS. THIS IS NOT THE CASE FOR OTHER TEACHERS, AND MANY COMPETENT MATURE CYCLE CHANNELS HAVE EXCELLENT CONTACT WITH THE ASTRAL PLANE.

TO PERCEIVE THE VALIDITY OF THE OVERLEAVES, THE INTERACTION OF FUNCTION, IS TO GRASP THE WHOLE NATURE OF CHOICE, FOR ALL CHOICES POSSIBLE TO ALL FRAGMENTS EXTANT UPON THE PHYSICAL PLANE ARE ATTAINABLE THROUGH THE RANGE AND POLARITIES OF THE OVERLEAVES. THIS APPLIES TO ALL ENSOULED SPECIES.

THE EXPRESSION OF THE CHOICES, OF COURSE, IS INFLU-
ENCED BY THE SPECIES, ITS ENVIRONMENT, CULTURE,
AND PHYSIOLOGY. WHETHER A FRAGMENT IS A MEMBER
OF YOUR SPECIES OR ANY OF THE OTHER MYRIAD EN-
SOULED LIFE FORMS THROUGHOUT THE PHYSICAL
PLANE—WHICH IS ALL THE PHYSICAL UNIVERSE—THE
OVERLEAVES, CYCLES, ESSENCES, AND CASTING ORDER
ARE THE SAME. WE CANNOT REITERATE THIS ENOUGH,
FOR MOST FRAGMENTS HAVE DIFFICULTY THINKING OF
MEMBERS OF ANOTHER LANGUAGE GROUP, LET ALONE
CULTURE, AS BEING "JUST THE SAME" AS THEY ARE. FOR
MANY FRAGMENTS, REALIZING THAT A MAGAZINE
EDITOR IN BEIJING, A MAORI JUSTICE OF THE PEACE IN
NEW ZEALAND, A POSTMASTER IN THE AZORES, A DISTIL-
LER IN IRELAND, A ZOOLOGIST IN MOSCOW, A JEWELER
IN SHANGHAI, A "COURTESAN" IN MOROCCO, A CATTLE
BREEDER IN ZIMBABWE, A TANNER IN SIBERIA, A
METEOROLOGIST AT THE SOUTH POLE, A NORWEGIAN
BOAT CAPTAIN, A SAMOAN SCHOOLTEACHER, A BULGAR-
IAN CHORAL CONDUCTOR, A TIBETAN SILVERSMITH, AN
OPTOMETRIST IN NOVA SCOTIA, A BANK EXECUTIVE IN
ZURICH, A PRISON GUARD IN TEHRAN, A SPANISH
FILMMAKER, A TROMBONIST IN NEW ORLEANS, A
CHOREOGRAPHER IN HAVANA, A MUSEUM CURATOR IN
HAWAII, A GYMNAST IN CZECHOSLOVAKIA, A MINING
FOREMAN IN ALBERTA, A PRESCHOOL TEACHER IN CAN-
TON, A MILANESE FASHION DESIGNER, A RADIO HOSTESS
IN INDIA, TO MENTION BUT A VERY, VERY FEW, HAVE
PRECISELY THE SAME OVERLEAVES AS THE CURRENT
POPE OF THE ROMAN CATHOLIC CHURCH IS EXTREMELY
DIFFICULT, NOT ONLY BECAUSE OF THE DIFFERENCE IN
CULTURE AND SOCIAL POSITION, BUT IN TERMS OF THE
RANGE OF EXPRESSION OF THE OVERLEAVES. WE HAVE
CHOSEN THESE REPRESENTATIVES BECAUSE ALL FRAG-
MENTS HAVE—WITH THE EXCEPTION OF THE CZECHO-
SLOVAKIAN GYMNAST, WHO IS A TWELVE-YEAR-OLD
GIRL—HAVE COMPLETED THE FOURTH INTERNAL MONAD
AND ARE AT WORK ON THE LIFE TASK, AS THEY HAVE

CHOSEN TO PURSUE IT, ALTHOUGH WE HASTEN TO ADD THAT NOT ALL ARE PURSUING THEIR LIFE TASKS THROUGH THEIR OCCUPATIONS. TO GIVE THE OVERLEAVES IN QUESTION, ALL ARE FIFTH-LEVEL MATURE PRIESTS IN THE OBSERVATION MODE WITH A GOAL OF DOMINANCE, STOICS, IN THE INTELLECTUAL PART OF EMOTIONAL CENTERS HAVE SECONDARY CHIEF FEATURES OF STUBBORNNESS. THE EDITOR IN BEIJING HAS A SECONDARY CHIEF FEATURE OF MARTYRDROM, AND THE METEOROLOGIST AT THE SOUTH POLE HAS A SECONDARY CHIEF FEATURE OF GREED FIXATED ON THE ACQUISITION OF INFORMATION.

FEAR CREATES THE DISTORTIONS THAT MAR THE PERCEPTIONS ALL FRAGMENTS EXPERIENCE AS PART OF THE LESSONS OF THE PHYSICAL PLANE. FOR MANY FRAGMENTS, BY THE TIME THE FINAL LEVEL OF THE OLD CYCLE IS REACHED, THE DEGREE OF RECOGNITION OF THIS WORLD—MEANING PHYSICAL PLANE—TRUTH IS NO GREATER THAN A SENSE THAT THINGS ARE NOT NECESSARILY THE WAY THEY APPEAR. THERE IS NOTHING AMISS IN THAT DEGREE OF PERCEPTION. GREATER OR LESSER DEGREES OF PERCEPTION WHILE ON THE PHYSICAL PLANE ARE QUITE USUAL; THOSE DEGREES OF PERCEPTION ARE IMPORTANT LESSONS FOR ALL FRAGMENTS. IF ALL A FRAGMENT LEARNS DURING THE CYCLE OF EVOLUTION ON THE PHYSICAL PLANE IS TO RESERVE JUDGMENT, ENORMOUS PROGRESS HAS BEEN MADE. WE WISH TO REMIND ALL HERE GATHERED THAT NO MATTER HOW GREAT THE DISTORTION OF PERCEPTION WHILE INCARNATE, THE ASTRAL INTERVAL IS NOT ENCUMBERED WITH DISTORTED PERCEPTIONS AND THEREFORE THERE IS INCULCATION, VALIDATION, RECOGNITION, AND EVOLUTION, NO MATTER HOW "BLIND" OR "ASLEEP" THE FRAGMENT IS DURING LIVES BEING LIVED. ONLY THOSE FRAGMENTS WHO CHOOSE TO INQUIRE ABOUT OTHER PERCEPTIONS DURING A LIFE MIGHT DISCOVER THE MEANS TO RECOGNITION AND VALIDATION, ALTHOUGH NONE OF THESE THINGS ARE IN ANY SENSE "NECESSARY," FOR EVOLUTION GOES ON, WITH OR WITHOUT ANY FRAGMENT'S "HELP".

BECAUSE FEAR IS VERY, VERY, VERY, VERY, VERY, VERY, VERY SEDUCTIVE, IT PRESENTS ITSELF IN MANY GUISES, AND IT IS NOT UNWISE TO BE AWARE THAT CHIEF FEATURE KNOWS WHAT IS THE MOST ATTRACTIVE DISGUISES FOR THE FRAGMENTS POSSESSING IT. THIS IS NOT TO SAY THAT CHIEF FEATURE IS IN ANY WAY EXTERNAL TO THE FRAGMENT. THE CHIEF FEATURE BECOMES AN "INTEGRAL" PART OF THE PERSONALITY, BOTH TRUE AND FALSE. WE PUT "INTEGRAL" IN QUOTES BECAUSE THE CHIEF FEATURE IS NOT AS MUCH A PART OF PERSONALITY AS THE REST OF THE OVERLEAVES, SINCE THE OTHERS WERE CHOSEN BEFORE THE INCARNATION BEGINS, AND CHIEF FEATURE IS ACQUIRED AS PART OF THE TRANSIT OF THE THIRD INTERNAL MONAD.

WE WOULD SUGGEST THAT FOR ALL HERE PRESENT THAT THE PERCEPTION OF THE OVERLEAVES, AS INTERPRETED BY THE PERSONALITY AND DEFINED BY ENCULTURATION, IS VERY GOOD WORK INDEED, WHETHER THAT PERCEPTION IS LIMITED TO YOUR OWN, OR EXTENDS BEYOND TO OTHERS. WHEN A FRAGMENT HAS REACHED THE DEGREE OF PERCEPTION THAT CAN RECOGNIZE THAT A MISBEHAVING CHILD CAN BE A THIRD-LEVEL MATURE KING AND STILL BE A MISBEHAVING CHILD, AND THAT BOTH ARE VALID AND "APPROPRIATE" FOR THE FRAGMENT, THEN THERE HAS BEEN COMMENDABLE PROGRESS INDEED.

THE DICHOTOMY OF ESSENCE AND CASTING, WHICH IS AS CLOSE TO ETERNAL AS ANYTHING YOU WILL EVER EXPERIENCE AS AN INDIVIDUAL FRAGMENT, AND THE RELATIVELY EPHEMERALITY OF ANY PARTICULAR LIFE, IS NOT AN IRRECONCILABLE PARADOX. FROM OUR PERSPECTIVE IT IS NOT A PARADOX AT ALL BUT TWO DIFFERENT-BUT-COMPLEMENTARY CONTINUUA. EACH LIFE IS BOTH ESSENTIALLY SIGNIFICANT AND INSIGNIFICANT. EACH LIFE IS WHOLLY AND ENTIRELY VALID TO THE EVOLUTION OF THE FRAGMENT—ANY FRAGMENT—LIVING. ESSENCE IS NEITHER MORE IMPORTANT NOR LESS IMPORTANT THAN THE LIVES IT LIVES, FOR IN A PROFOUND SENSE, ESSENCE

IS THE LIVES IT LIVES, AND THE LIVES ARE VERY MUCH THE ESSENCE.

MANY FRAGMENTS SEE CERTAIN LIVES AS BEING "WORSE" THAN OTHERS, CERTAIN ACTIONS AS BEING "BAD" AND OTHERS AS BEING "GOOD", WHICH TO ESSENCE IS NOT THE CASE. THAT DOES NOT IN ANY WAY EXONERATE SUFFERING EXPERIENCE AND SUFFERING INFLICTED, FOR IF IT DID, THERE WOULD BE NO KARMA, WHICH, OF COURSE, THERE IS. BY THE TIME ALL FRAGMENTS HAVE COMPLETED THE YOUNG SOUL CYCLE, THEY WILL HAVE LIVED AT LEAST ONE LIFE IN WHICH THEY INCURRED MUCH KARMA. THAT IS PART OF THE NATURE OF THE YOUNG SOUL EXPERIENCE. OF COURSE, KARMA MAY BE INCURRED AT ANY POINT DURING THE CYCLE. SOME FRAGMENTS HAVE REACHED WHAT WAS APPARENTLY THE LAST LIFE IN THE OLD CYCLE AND HAVE BEEN INVOLVED IN KARMA WHICH REQUIRED A WHOLLY UNEXPECTED RETURN IN ORDER TO "BALANCE THE BOOKS". THIS, INCIDENTALLY, DOES NOT CAUSE IRRITATION OR FRUSTRATION TO ESSENCE, WHICH EXPERIENCES NEITHER OF THOSE EMOTIONS WITHOUT THE TRAPPINGS OF OVERLEAVES AND PERSONALITY. AS THE SOUL PROGRESSES THROUGH THE CYCLES THERE IS NO POINT WHERE IT IS "IMPOSSIBLE" TO CREATE KARMIC RIBBONS. EVERY FRAGMENT EXTANT ON THE PHYSICAL PLANE IS CAPABLE OF CREATING KARMIC RIBBONS, FROM FIRST-LEVEL INFANT—ALTHOUGH THE YOUNGEST SOULS EXTANT ON YOUR PLANET NOW ARE THIRD-LEVEL INFANT— TO FINAL-LEVEL OLD. AS WE HAVE INDICATED BEFORE, WHEN KARMA IS CREATED DURING WHAT WAS SUPPOSED TO BE A FINAL LIFE, THE FRAGMENT RETURNS UNTIL THE RIBBON IS BURNED, USUALLY WITH AGREEMENTS TO BURN THE KARMA BEING PART OF THE LIFE PLAN.

THERE ARE VERY, VERY FEW EXCEPTIONS TO THAT CONDITION. IN THOSE FEW CASES WHEN A FINAL-LEVEL OLD KING HAS GIVEN UP THE BODY FOR THE MANIFESTATION OF THE INFINITE SOUL, THEN ONE LIFE AFTERWARD HAS BEEN CHOSEN TO FINISH THE LESSONS LOST TO THE TIME

THE BODY WAS HOST TO THE INFINITE SOUL. THE INFINITE
SOUL HAS MANIFESTED ON YOUR PLANET AND SPECIES
AS LAO-TZU, SRI KRISNA, SIDDHARTHA GUATAMA, AND
JESUS, AND NO OTHERS.

AS THE INFINITE SOUL, BEING THE EMBODIMENT OF
SEVEN, DISPLACES ONLY FINAL-LEVEL OLD KINGS, SO
THE TRANSCENDENTAL SOUL, BEING THE EMBODIMENT
OF THE ENTIRE NATURE OF SIX, DISPLACES ONLY SIXTH-
AND SEVENTH-LEVEL OLD PRIESTS. THIS HAS HAPPENED
ON YOUR PLANET AND IN YOUR SPECIES IN THE FOLLOW-
ING CASES: SOCRATES, ZARATHUSTRA, MOHAMMED,
AND GANDHI, AND NO OTHERS. WHEN THE TRANSCEN-
DENTAL SOUL MANIFESTS, IT ALTERS THE SOCIAL PERCEP-
TIONS AND CONSCIOUSNESS OF FRAGMENTS ON THE PHYS-
ICAL PLANE ATTENDANT UPON THE MANIFESTATION;
WHEN THE INFINITE SOUL MANIFESTS, THE LOGOS IS
BROUGHT TO BEAR FOR THOSE FRAGMENTS ATTENDANT
UPON THE MANIFESTATION.

IT IS NOT INAPPROPRIATE FOR FRAGMENTS TO LISTEN
TO ANY AND ALL TEACHING SKEPTICALLY, AND TO TEST
IT IN REGARD TO ITS VALIDITY. FOR MANY FRAGMENTS,
ALL TEACHING IS ULTIMATELY REJECTED IN FAVOR OF
WHAT MIGHT BE CALLED "EXISTENTIALISM". THERE IS
NO "ERROR" IN THIS, AS THERE IS NO "ERROR" IN ANY
CHOICE. IF THE CHOICE LEADS TO KARMA, EITHER NEGA-
TIVE OR PHILANTHROPIC, THAT IS THE RAMIFICATION OF
THAT CHOICE, AND, OF COURSE, VALID. THIS IS NOT A
MATTER OF GUILT, IT IS A MATTER OF RESPONSIBILITY.
THAT IS NOT TO SAY THAT LEGAL GUILT IS THEREFORE
INVALID— HOWEVER A SOCIETY DEFINES CRIME, IT ALSO
DEFINES PUNISHMENT, AND IF THAT PUNISHMENT IS DE-
SERVED, IT IS VALID. BEING HANGED FOR A MURDER THAT
A FRAGMENT DID INDEED COMMIT DOES NOT IN ANY
SENSE ELIMINATE THE KARMIC RIBBON THE MURDER EN-
TAILS, SINCE THE PUNISHMENT ONLY SERVES TO AVENGE
THE SOCIETAL INSULT. BEING HANGED FOR A MURDER
THAT THE FRAGMENT DID NOT, IN FACT, COMMIT,
CREATES A KARMIC RIBBON WITH THE FRAGMENT WHO
DID COMMIT THE MURDER.

ACTIONS AND INACTIONS DURING THE LIFE ARE VALID. EACH ONE REPRESENTS A CHOICE, NO MATTER HOW TRIVIAL. THE LIFE PLAN MADE BY ESSENCE BEFORE THE INCARNATION IS VALID, AS ARE ALL THE CHOICES MADE DURING THE LIFE, WHETHER THEY SUPPORT THE LIFE PLAN OR NOT. IN OTHER WORDS, EVERYTHING COUNTS, NOT AS PLUS OR MINUS, BUT AS COUNTING. EVERY LIFE IS A CONTRIBUTION, EVERY CHOICE IS A CONTRIBUTION, BOTH TO THE EVOLUTION OF THE FRAGMENT AND THE EVOLUTION OF THE TAO.

AS YOUR VALIDATION OF ESSENCE CONTACT PROGRESSES, SO WE PROGRESS. THE MORE A FRAGMENT WORKS IN ESSENCE, THE MORE TEACHING IS ACCESSIBLE AND THE GREATER THE EVOLUTION WE EXPERIENCE. IT WOULD NOT BE INAPPROPRIATE TO SAY THAT THROUGH TECHING, WE, WHO ARE A REUNITED ENTITY ON THE MID-CAUSAL PLANE, EVOLVE TOWARD NOT ONLY THE AKASHIC PLANE AND THE REUNITING OF OUR CADRE. THIS IS TRUE OF ALL MID-CAUSAL TEACHERS. THROUGH THE PROCESS OF TEACHING, WE ARE PROGRESSING, JUST AS YOU, THROUGH THE PROCESS OF CHOOSING, ARE PROGRESSING. THE LESSONS OF THE PHYSICAL PLANE ARE LEARNED THROUGH CHOICE, THE LESSONS OF THE ASTRAL PLANE ARE LEARNED THROUGH INTERPRETATION, THE LESSONS OF THE CAUSAL PLANE ARE LEARNED THROUGH TEACHING, THE LESSONS OF THE AKASHIC PLANE ARE LEARNED THROUGH EXPERIENTIATION, THE LESSONS OF THE BUDDHIC PLANE ARE LEARNED THROUGH INTEGRAL RESOLUTION. WE REALIZE THAT OUR EXPERIENCE IS SO UNLIKE YOUR OWN THAT IT IS DIFFICULT TO COMPREHEND. REST ASSURED THAT THE EXPERIENCE OF THOSE WHOLE INTEGRITIES OF THE BUDDHIC PLANE ARE AS DIFFICULT FOR US TO COMPREHEND AS WE ARE TO YOU. WE ARE ALSO AWARE THAT THE LIMITS OF VOCABULARY AND CONCEPTUAL RANGE PERMITS ONLY AN APPROXIMATION OF THE NATURE OF THE HIGHER PLANES.

THAT IS NOT TO SAY THAT THERE IS SOMETHING "INFERIOR" ABOUT BEING ON THE PHYSICAL PLANE. THAT IS NOT THE CASE, AND IT IS AN INVALID CONCEPT THAT

THIS MIGHT BE THE CASE. THE PHYSICAL PLANE IS ONLY ONE ASPECT OF THE NATURE OF EXISTENCE, NO "BETTER" OR "WORSE" THAN ANY OTHER. HIGHER PLANES ARE NOT "IMPROVEMENTS", THEY ARE "DIFFERENT". OLD SOULS ARE NOT "BETTER" THAN YOUNG SOULS, THEY ARE SIMPLY OLDER. YOUNG SOULS ARE NOT "BETTER" THAN BABY OR INFANT SOULS, THEY ARE SIMPLY OLDER. THOSE WHO ASSUME OTHERWISE ARE RESPONDING TO THE BLANDISHMENTS OF FEAR, NOT THE TRUTH OF LOVE. OF COURSE, IF YOU CHOOSE TO PERCEIVE IT IN SUCH A LIGHT, THAT IS, IN FACT, YOUR CHOICE.

THOSE OF YOU WHO WORRY AOBUT "HOW LONG IT IS TAKING" TO PROGRESS THROUGH THE CYCLES ARE AGAIN SUCCUMBING TO FEAR AND TO ENCULTURATED PATTERNS WHICH DISTORT THE NATURE OF EVOLUTION. HOWEVER MANY LIVES IT TAKES TO COMPLETE THE CYCLES OF THE PHYSICAL PLANE IS VALID FOR ANY AND ALL FRAGMENTS. THE "RIGHT" NUMBER IS THE NUMBER THE FRAGMENT LIVES. THERE IS NO WAY IN WHICH ANY FRAGMENT CAN LIVE THE "WRONG" NUMBER OF LIVES. IN FACT, SUCH A CONCEPT IS NOT ONLY DISTORTED, IT IS ABSURD.

WE WOULD WISH TO POINT OUT TO ALL OF YOU THAT THERE IS ALWAYS A "REASON" FOR YOUR LIFE, NO MATTER HOW LONG OR SHORT, NO MATTER HOW LITTLE OR MUCH IS DONE ON THE LIFE TASK. THERE IS NO WAY YOU CAN "BLOW" IT, AND NO WAY YOU CAN "AVOID" IT OR "CANCEL" IT. ALL LIVES YOU HAVE LIVED, AND THEIR LESSONS, ARE TRULY AND "APPROPRIATELY" YOURS. THAT IS WHAT CHOICE IS ALL ABOUT, AND WHY THE "PURPOSE"—IF ONE IS REQUIRED—OF LIVING IS TO CHOOSE. FOR ESSENCE, THERE IS NO GREATER ACHIEVEMENT IN A LIFE THAN VALIDATED ESSENCE CONTACT, AND THE GREATER THE INSTANCES OF ESSENCE CONTACT, THE GREATER THE PERCEPTUAL EVOLUTION OF THE LIFE. BUT ALL ASPECTS OF THE LIFE, FROM THE LEAST TO THE MOST "IMPORTANT" ARE VALID AND ALL OF THEM CONTRIBUTE TO YOUR EVOLUTION.

NO ONE REQUIRES YOU TO ACCEPT THIS, OR ANY,

TEACHING. NO ONE REQUIRES THAT YOU RECOGNIZE OR VALIDATE ANY PORTION OF YOUR LIFE, YOUR LIFE TASK, YOUR OVERLEAVES, OR ANY OTHER ASPECT OF YOUR SELF. IF YOU CHOOSE VALIDATION, THERE IS NO CERTAINTY OF GREATER EVOLUTION THAN IF YOU DO NOT CHOOSE IT. HOWEVER, FOR SOME FRAGMENTS, CHOOSING RECOGNITION AND VALIDATION DOES PROVIDE INSIGHTS THAT AID IN MAKING CHOICES, BOTH IN REGARD TO THEMSELVES AND TO OTHERS. WE WILL ANSWER ANY QUESTIONS ASKED OF US, WITHOUT QUALIFICATION. YOU ARE FREE TO CHOOSE TO USE THE MATERIAL, OR NOT TO USE IT, IN ANY WAY YOU WISH. THAT IS NOT ONLY WHAT WE OFFER, IT IS THE LESSON AS WELL.

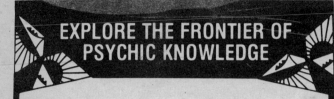